HACK:
THE COMPLETE GAME

D.J. Gelner

Orion's Comet

To Grant, Mom, Grandpa, (recently) Dad, and all of my baseball teammates and coaches through the years.

Your love for the game made these books possible.

First Inning

1

"So, what's the bad news, doc?" The old man sat in a "damned-fool" hospital gown at the foot of the exam table. Any sharpness to his voice had long since been eroded by a constant stream of whiskey and millions of puffs on cheap cigars.

The doctor cleared his throat, "You're sick, Mr. O'Callahan."

"Christ, that's a relief. 'Cause if I was shittin' and coughin' up blood and I was healthy as a horse, I guess I'd just be a fuckin' *weirdo*, wouldn't I? How much did you pay for your medical degree, son? What're ya, fifteen, sixteen years old like that kid doctor on TV?" O'Callahan punctuated his outburst with a coughing fit.

The doctor casually pulled two or three tissues from the box on the counter and threw them at the old man, "Very sick, actually. You have an advanced hepatocellular carcinoma—"

"Hepta-deca-whatnow?" O'Callahan asked.

"—Liver cancer. It's already starting to spread to other parts of your body, including a small tumor in your stomach, hence the rather disturbing symptoms you're experiencing."

O'Callahan's coughing finally subsided. He pulled the tissues away from his mouth only to find a dark, red spot the size of a half-dollar. He didn't even need to look; he'd been hit in the face hundreds of times by errant balls thrown or hit by his players, and probably a half dozen more by players who had aimed for his mug. He was familiar

1

with the metallic taste of his own blood as it pooled in his mouth and coated his tongue.

But Roger "Hack" O'Callahan also knew that something was off. This time there was an underlying sweetness to the blood, kind of a mixture of oranges and acetone, that stuck with him in the back of his throat even as he struggled to choke the blood back down.

"Cancer? Well...shit." Hack stared the young physician down for a moment, and not finding the sympathy he so craved, looked downward.

"Not *just* cancer, Mr. O'Callahan, but stage three liver cancer. It's one of the deadliest strains we know of, actually. Very rare. I'd recommend starting chemo—"

"How long?" Hack didn't bother looking up.

"Well, if you start chemotherapy tomorrow, as I was about to suggest, then maybe a year-and-a-half, maybe two years."

Hack shook his head, "I ain't gonna be some sad sack'a bones hooked up to a bag, waitin' for all my hair to fall out." The doctor raised an eyebrow, apparently not getting the joke even as Hack stroked his shiny head. "Without the chemo?"

The doctor's eyes were framed by his thick glasses and level, "Six months. *Maybe* a year."

Hack stroked his chin, "It's temptin' to make my detractors wait another few months ta' piss on my grave..." he paused for a laugh that the doctor never gave, "...but I'll pass on the chemo, Doc. Bet they wouldn't even let me sneak in any Ol' Reliable, would they?"

"Old Reliable?" The doctor's face scrunched up into a grimace.

"You know? Ol' Reli-ble?" He slurred the words enough that the doctor understood, "That cheap-ass paint thinner they try to pass off as whiskey. Kinda' an acquired taste."

"*Mister* O'Callahan, if you're suggesting that you can continue *drinking* with this cancer, as your physician I have to say that you simply—"

Hack extended a hand and patted the doctor on the head, "As my physician, son, all you have to do is shut yer' fuckin' *trap*—" he moved his hand to the doctor's face and gave him a couple of quick, semi-lighthearted raps on the cheek, "—and stay the fuck outta' my goddamned business. Okay?"

The color drained from the doctor's face as he took two steps back, hovered for a moment, and recovered from the two (Hack thought) innocuous slaps, that may as well have been haymakers.

"You don't want to listen to me? *Fine!*" The doctor thundered. His face reddened both with pain and anger. "Go ahead and die, you miserable old fart. Dr. Patel told me about you, and what a miserable, *awful* person you were."

"Really? I didn't think he could hear me through that turbin'a his."

The doctor scribbled a couple of notes in his file, then drew several vertical loops like he was trying to bore his way through the sheet. He then handed Hack a piece of paper with a prescription.

"What the hell is this?" Hack asked.

"A prescription for vicodin, for pain as it may arise. *Do not* take it with alcohol."

Yeah, right, Hack thought.

"As much as I may find you personally distasteful, I still took an oath that I would do no harm to others," Hack could tell the doctor was ready to explode, but the physician did well to contain his anger with a deep breath, "and so I shall try to respect your wishes and make you as comfortable as possible as you wait for your," he exhaled, "inevitable death."

"Thanks, Doc," Hack held out his right hand for the doctor to shake, and looked up to see the doctor's wide eyes. He looked down again and saw that his hand still clutched the bloody tissues from before.

"Shit, sorry," Hack placed the tissues on the counter a moment before his throat spasmed, and another coughing fit sprayed the air with blood. He grabbed the tissues and brought them to his mouth until the hacking subsided.

"Aw, god *damn* it!" Hack said, legitimately angry. Specks of blood dotted the doctor's white lab coat as the color of the physician's face struggled to match the dark red fluid now on his person. "Let me get that fer' ya..." Hack brought the bloody tissue to his tongue and moistened it before he rubbed the soiled kleenex on the blood spots on the doctor's garment.

"Mister O'Callahan, please—"

"I know—I'll get it out. Got any club soda? I think there's a soda machine down the hall somewhere—"

"*Mister O'Callahan!*" The doctor thundered. The elderly man in front of him didn't recoil as expected, but instead met his angry eyes with his own steely gaze.

"Listen, son," Hack's tone was even and level as he placed the hand containing the bloody tissue on the doctor's left shoulder, "I've been called every name in the book 'cept *Chi-nese*, and a few more that I reckon are just plain made up. Most of the time, it's some arrogant little shit, like yourself, come to think of it, who thinks he's got it all figured out. They come in and they tell you to fuck off, that they don't need to listen to some old timer bendin' their ears about throwin' a curveball, or where to position themselves with two on and nobody out in a close game.

"Every one of 'em who challenges me, who thinks that I don't know best—every one of 'em *to a man*," Hack exploded to within an inch of the doctor's face, almost as if arguing with an umpire back in his heyday, "who doesn't come around is sellin' insurance or askin' how some asshole wants his Jag waxed. And you know why?" He leaned in toward the doctor, who had finally lost his composure and was trembling uncontrollably.

"Because...I *do* know best!" he practically spat the words at the doctor, and added *uppity little shit* in his mind for good measure before he took a step back, stared the doctor down for a moment, and walked toward the door.

"Don't worry, Mr. O'Callahan," the doctor forced a smile.

Looks like someone suddenly developed a bedside manner, Hack thought.

"I'll get a new coat in the morning."

"Great seein' ya, doc," Hack didn't so much as glance at the doctor as he put on his overcoat and hat and walked out of the room.

"But…Mr. O'Callahan! Your clothes?!" The doctor yelled after him.

"Fuck it," Hack yelled back as he shuffled his bare feet down the hallway, with only the flimsy acrylic gown and tweed overcoat to cover him.

2

"Hey, 'evenin' Mr. O'C!" the large black man who guarded the press entrance to Jacobs Field beamed with recognition. They had changed the name of the stadium because some insurance company had cut a big check to the Indians a few years back, but to Hack, it'd always be the good old Jake.

"'Evenin' Jerry," Hack said gruffly, with a hint of a smile.

"How you think we're gonna do tonight?"

"Whattaya mean? Stevenson is pitching," Hack waddled into the waiting elevator and turned around just as the doors were about to close, "We're fucked."

"Have a goo—" Jerry's warm voice was cut off as the doors thudded shut. Hack hit the button marked "3," and the elevator stirred to life. He always relished these last few moments on the elevator before the doors opened to reveal the hoofing obnoxiousness of the "Press Animals," as Hack often referred to them. The subtle hum of the elevator still always brought a smile to the old man's face; given everything he'd been through, such grins were becoming increasingly rare.

The elevator jolted to a stop and the doors opened on the press box, already a hive of click-clacking drones who hammered away on their keyboards, even five minutes before game time. It wasn't nearly as busy as ten years ago, or even five, but there was still a healthy buzz around the room, which was just now beginning to show its age. A hint of stale pretzels and nacho cheese mixed with the remnants of the bleach-based antiseptic the Indians used to make the press box smell like the unhealthiest hospital one might ever come across.

Hack turned left out of the elevator and nodded at the various media-types; he was never overly-friendly with any of them, even (or perhaps especially) the ones who were close to his age, and who had thus battled words with Hack in the press room underneath old Municipal Stadium.

He stopped at the buffet and grabbed four or five packs of roasted, in-the-shell peanuts. Much to the consternation of the custodial crew, Hack had a bad habit of chewing the peanuts whole, shell and all, and spitting out the shells onto the floor, like he was Joe Fan in the stands. Unfortunately, the cleaning crew couldn't just hose the press box down like it was the bleachers, and thus were left to clean up Hack's mess through plenty of vacuuming and gallons of carpet spray.

Not that Hack cared. To him, baseball wasn't baseball without the salt-caked lips and intoxicating, slightly toasted aroma that the peanuts provided. It was especially true now that he couldn't really fully eliminate that sickly sweet, nail-polish remover taste out of the back of his throat.

He finally reached his seat on the far left side of the press box, next to the broadcast booth, which was partitioned off only by a layer of plexiglass. He'd never admit as much, but even the short walk from the elevator to the uncomfortable, threadbare fabric-over-plastic chair had winded him, though he had downed a whole bottle of Robitussin to drown any more of the bloody coughing fits before he headed to the stadium.

It was an arrangement that was probably best for both Hack and the Indians; Hack lived in Cleveland and loved watching baseball. Though the team couldn't very well deny access to the stadium of someone of Hack's stature, corralling him in the press box kept him away from the clubhouse, where but five years ago he nearly came to blows with a member of the coaching staff over the "dogshit hitting fundamentals" the coach preached.

Hack settled in, put on his reading glasses, and pulled out his scorecard and a chewed-up pencil as the Indians took the field. Soon enough, he had settled into his routine; he marked every pitch, every foul ball and ball put in play, through the first four innings.

By the fourth inning, though, it looked as if Hack was going to be proven correct once more. John Stevenson, the highly-touted Indians' starter, had given up six runs on eight doubles, and was laboring his way to another disappointing loss.

Arm like a cannon, head like a can of pea soup, Hack thought.

As if to punctuate Hack's thoughts, Stevenson fielded a ground ball down the first base line and launched the throw into the first base stands, well away from the first baseman, who threw his glove down in frustration.

Hack snorted and shook his head; it was almost too easy now. Even as the rest of him, his hearing, his vision, some would probably include his sanity (though many would question if he ever possessed the last) left, the thousands of baseball games he had managed through the years gave him a sense of the rhythm of the sport that beat surely as his heart inside of him.

That was the beauty of the game; even though the pace and tempo were more a part of him than the blood that coursed through his veins, and the result of whatever game he watched usually confirmed that expertise, there was always a chance for something out of the ordinary, an errant throw, a botched ground ball, a hung curve that could disrupt that even flow, throw the game into chaos, and make his brain pop with the delight of something new, something different.

He didn't particularly care who won the game; though he lived in Cleveland, the Indians had fired him over twenty-five years ago, and he still held a grudge against their opponents, the Baltimore Orioles, because their previous owner, Alfred Yossain, was "a cheap-ass, God-damned, camel-fucking Persian" in Hack's mind, in no small part because the two had a disagreement over a backup middle infielder that Hack had wanted to sign, and Yossain thought the Orioles could do without.

When Yossain held fast and the Orioles won the AL pennant that year, Hack attributed the team's success to his own remarkable managerial skills and was pleased he was able to win "in spite of" the generally calm, level-headed Orioles owner.

"And here's the pitch...SA-*WIIILNG* and a miss...STRIKE THREE!" The Indians' middle-aged radio play-by-play man, Johnny "Country" Engle, boomed through the plexiglass.

Hack rapped on the thin sheet of plastic several times with a disapproving grimace. When Engle turned to give him a mock thumbs up, Hack cupped his hands over his mouth against the plexiglass.

"Shut the fuck up!" he yelled through the plexiglass, "I'm tryin' to enjoy a ballgame heeya'!"

"There's our good friend, Hack O'Callahan," Engle said, sweet as pecan pie, into the microphone, "Hack, of course, is a venerable Cleveland institution. He has the four World Series titles managing four different teams, though none of those came during his short stint with the Indians in the eighties. He managed for a grand total of nine different Major League squads during his career. Maybe most importantly, he served his country in Korea *allllll* those years ago. And now he's enjoying his retirement at all of eighty-four years young, isn't that right, Hack?" Engle made the "jerk off" hand motion, which caused Hack to slam an outstretched middle finger up against the glass. "He doesn't act a day over eighteen, folks," Engle shook his head before he turned his attention back to the game.

"Okay, okay, settle down, Mr. O'Callahan," Josh Stein, the Indians' Director of Media Relations, rushed over to calm both parties.

"Can't you tell this prick to keep it down over here?" Hack's left hand waved dismissively at the radio booth several times.

Stein shook his head, which caused his loose-fitting glasses shake from side-to-side on his pale, narrow face, "Now, Mr. O'Callahan, you know that Johnny has a job to do, same as you used to."

"Yeah, but I wasn't a fuckin' idiot about doin' mine." Hack shot back. Engle looked over again while calling the action, and Hack "pulled" on a non-existent noose over his head to pretend as if he was hanging himself, before he pointed to Engle to complete the insult.

Without even pausing, Engle made the "throat-slit" gesture, and pointed back at Hack.

"Are you two children through?" Stein asked.

"Can't ya' move me somewhere else, Josh?" Hack asked.

Stein shook his head, "Consider it a spot of honor; closest to home plate, right next to the legendary Country Engle," this inspired a fresh disgust in Hack. "If I have to keep coming over here and breaking up these fights, we're going to have to restrict you to somewhere else in the stadium."

"Oh yeah?" Hack puffed out his chest and sat up in his chair, "Like where? You won't let me in the clubhouse anymore."

"How about with the grounds crew?"

Hack cocked his head and balled his fists. Though Stein's lip trembled a bit, he offered a curt smile and stood his ground.

"You know what?" Hack asked. "Fuck it. I know when I'm not wanted somewhere."

"Now, now, Mr. O'Callahan, nothing could be further from the—" Stein's delivery was somewhat less than half-hearted.

"No, no, no—fuck you, Stein. I'm goin'. You're not gonna have to worry about old Hack anymore."

"Oh...no...Mr. O'Callahan..." Stein could barely hide his grin.

"Fuck you AND your little chickenshit team. AL Central my ass— it should be either the *west* or the *east*. How're they gonna fuck this sport up next?" Hack shook his head for a moment before he turned to Stein, who raised his eyebrows at the man.

"Go fuck yourself, Stein."

This time, Stein beamed, "See you later, Mr. O'Callahan."

Hack stormed into the elevator and down to the parking lot, stopping only briefly to flip the bird at Jerry after the guard told him to "Have a good night" a little too cheerfully. He managed to carom his teal '67 Chevy the couple of miles home, mostly on his side of the road.

He pulled in front of his aging row house. Thankfully there was plenty of parking space available, as Hack barged onto the curb and left the car there.

Hack took a swig off the whiskey bottle he kept stashed under his seat and teetered out of the car and up the five or six steps to his front door. He jiggled the lock several times until the door gave.

The retired manager stumbled through the hallway that served as a museum to his numerous on-field accomplishments (despite the lack of any family pictures among the framed keepsakes). He made an abrupt right turn into the living room, and launched himself into his worn, green paisley chair that smelled of soaked-in gin and cigar smoke. The odor hung over the entire room like a thin fog, baked over the layer of mothball-and-joint cream "old person smell" which, of course, served as the base aroma of the dwelling.

The living room itself was befitting an elderly shut-in. Several bookcases lined the walls, filled with volumes and binders of all manner, though there was a decided bias toward both Korean War and baseball history, and a thorough lack of fiction.

In the corner opposite the chair sat a television, constantly on and permanently tuned to ESPN. The remote had been long lost, and Hack's sole interest in his off-hours was baseball, to the point that he suffered that "damn fool football" for half the year to get his scores and updates during the summer.

He grasped at any one of the three or four bottles that littered the floor on the right side of the chair, and eventually latched onto a mostly-empty container of Old Reliable. Hack greedily unscrewed the top, choked the harsh liquor down, and immediately began to cough again, this time a deep whooping with a force and vigor that nearly toppled him out of the chair.

Hack brought his flannel sleeve up to soak up whatever phlegmy mixture expectorated out of his mouth. During a lull in the fit, he slugged off the Old Reliable once more and drained it. This time, the belt had its intended effect, and calmed down the awful hacking tirade.

"Grandpa's ol' cough medicine, all right..." Hack muttered as he studied the empty bottle.

Unfortunately, at that moment, the talking heads on *Baseball Tonight* analyzed the Indians game.

"Another rough outing for John Stevenson tonight, guys," the host said.

"Yeah, you're right Karl, but you know what, this kid has all of the tools to get major league hitters out. You talk about a fastball—"

Unfortunately, the analyst didn't have a chance to make his case, at least in Hack's living room. Upon hearing Stevenson's name, Hack wound up with the whiskey bottle and hurled it toward the TV. He had only meant to shatter the bottle against the wall next to the TV, but as soon as it left his hand, he knew that it was a mistake, and that it was going to be a perfect strike, right down the middle.

The ancient cathode ray tube shattered in a glorious explosion of grey glass and sparks. A tiny column of smoke billowed from the cavity that had just been carved in the middle of the screen as the box teetered on the edge of the stand for several moments before it fell with a heavy "thud."

Hack didn't even flinch. He steeled himself for a full minute before the full gravity of what he had done washed over him. His eyes widened before he began to grind his teeth, always a tell for when he was legitimately angry with himself.

A large piece of the screen had come to rest at Hack's feet. He bent over, picked it up, and stared into it.

"Well that's great. Just god damned wonderful!" he chided himself. "What're ya' gonna' do now, ya' old, dumb bastard?"

Hack looked deeply into his reflection. He didn't mind the well-earned wrinkles, each one a reminder of the battles and blow ups of so many years ago when he still managed.

Nor did he particularly resent the slightly crooked nose or the scars that littered his face, which served as evidence of a life well-lived.

What he hated, though, were his eyes, sunken, complacent, and weak. They were the eyes of an old man, a creature at the end of the road, one struggling to survive another day, waiting for the inevitable.

And now, one without even a TV, or a welcome place in the Indians' press box to sate his hunger for, or rather addiction to, baseball. The game was the only thing that had brought Hack any joy, that had given him purpose to continue being such a miserable S.O.B., day in, and day out.

"What the fuck are you gonna do?" He looked past his reflection in the glass to a plaque in the hallway shrine behind him. Two players from the sixties joked around with each other while their shorter, sterner manager looked on disapprovingly.

And just like that, Hack had an idea...

3

Hoplite, Ohio served as a weigh station for both those embarking on the promising beginnings to their young careers and those winding down from mostly blue-collar lives to a quieter, less strenuous existence.

The former were served by Baucomb College, a small, liberal arts school that nonetheless dominated most of town with its spread out, modern campus, owed largely to a number of wealthy alumni who wished to raise the profile of both their alma mater and the relatively sleepy surrounding suburb.

Though many of the older residents of the town would claim if asked that they moved there to "be around young people," and "feed off their energy," the only sense in which this was even remotely correct is that they relished in enforcing every local ordinance, no matter how minor, against the town's younger denizens.

As a result, the town's population remained relatively steady, though there was always plenty of turnover as folks either moved on or died off.

There were six main streets in the city, which intersected one another in a four square block area known as "the hub," right off the edge of the Baucomb quad. There were all of the small mom & pop stores that one might expect to find in such a town, even some more obscure shopfronts like a tailor (Fred Knauss) and a cobbler (Marvin

Adams), who were the city's longest-tenured residents by over a decade.

That's not to say that the town wasn't modern; there was a nightclub that had sprung up five years before ("Club Trojan," playing off of both the town's Greek influences and the obvious sexual innuendo), several bars scattered about, and even an Old Navy and a Forever 21, the latter of which had been opened only several years before over the vocal opposition by the town's old guard.

It was the type of place where people and storefronts were in constant flux, yet nothing changed at all. By the time one cadre was ready to move on, another stepped in to take its place, and argued with their other-aged counterparts over the same problems as the town's previous residents.

Hoplite wasn't even a "Triple-A" town. The residents knew that, and that was fine; they were in the northwest corner of the state, well over a hundred miles from both Cincinnati and Cleveland, and only slightly closer to Columbus.

It was a "Double-A" town, through and through. Hoplite loved its Magpies, and that's the reason that the teal, '67 Chevy swerved and peeled down Exeter Street (one of the main drags) in halting starts and leaps toward the barely-visible silhouette of John Paul Murphy Field maybe a mile ahead.

"Goddamn wheel—turn, damn you!" Hack hit the wheel and unknowingly hit the horn, which startled the man in the crosswalk in front of him. The pedestrian's scornful look vanished, however, when it was clear Hack had no intention of paying heed to the "State Law Requires Cars to Stop for Pedestrians in Crosswalks" sign posted nearby; the passerby practically had to dive out of the way to prevent himself from being hit by the fiery old man behind the wheel.

"*I'm* bigger than *you!*" Hack yelled over his shoulder at the poor fellow on the ground as he unscrewed the top on a flask and took a pull off of it. The one comfort that absolutely helped both his cough and the awful taste in the back of his throat was Old Reliable; it was the only thing that could steady him, a familiar, grounded feeling in the storm of nausea that otherwise sent him reeling.

Damned pills, Hack thought. Fortunately, it was ten in the morning, and few people strayed away from the Hub, especially in the direction of the stadium which was known as the "shady" part of town. Hack was able to weave and stutter the sickly green monstrosity into first the parking lot, and then toward the spots reserved for the team's offices.

Hack turned off the ignition and removed the key before he took a deep breath, which caused a flurry of coughs. He reached for the handkerchief on the seat next to him, already stained with blood, and caught whatever material was expelled in the fit.

Once he had calmed down, he took another swig of whiskey, and, like any alcoholic worth his salt, grabbed a handful of peanuts from the open bag next to him, chewed them up to soak up any errant booze, opened the door, and spit out the shells on the asphalt. He then reached for a store brand bottle of mouthwash and took a swig. He nearly swallowed it out of habit before his eyes bulged and he expelled that, too on top of the pile of peanut debris on the ground next to the door.

He wiped his mouth with the sleeve of his plaid shirt and took one more deep breath. He looked in the mirror and found several hairs in his crown of male pattern baldness out of place. He grabbed a comb from his shirt pocket and dumped some mouthwash over it before he ran it through the remnants of his hair several times.

Finally satisfied, he grabbed the wrinkled sport coat on the seat beside him and heaved himself out of the driver's seat with difficulty. His knees screamed as he hit the pavement, but he smirked; at least that was one ailment that couldn't be attributed to the cancer that was slowly eating him away from the inside out.

As minor league facilities go, John Paul Murphy was fairly typical. Renovated maybe fifteen years ago, it still could've used a couple of fresh coats of paint and a good spray-down. Minor league affiliates were way down on big league parent teams' lists of priorities, though, and even if he would have never admitted as much, Hack was impressed by the job the Magpies had done on a shoestring budget.

Hack's breathing became heavier as he approached the glass doors stenciled with the team's logo, a rather severe-looking, bulked up, anthropomorphized magpie with an angry scowl and a bat thrown over its right shoulder.

He threw his weight on the door and expected it to yield, but it stood, resilient. Hack muttered a couple of curses and tugged the horizontal bar. The door swung open with a satisfying sucking noise, which made it seem like Hack was about to enter an airlock.

A pretty, corn-fed girl with a round face and long, brown hair sat at a plain, light-grey, enamel-coated desk. She clicked her mouse furiously, her eyes intently focused on the screen.

"Yes…YES…NO! *Stupid* zombies!" she said as she pushed the mouse away from her and off its pad. She sighed, resignedly, and cast skeptical eyes upward toward Hack.

"May I help you?" She asked without a smile.

Hack returned the favor, "Tell Keith Myrick that Hack O'Callahan is here to see him."

"I'm sorry, but Mr. Myrick only sees people with appointments, and he doesn't have any this morning. I'd be happy to make one for you for this afternoon if you'd like."

Hack's eyes shot to the ceiling before they leveled on the receptionist, "Look here, young lady, I managed Keith's father for twelve goddamned years in the majors. The sonofabitch followed me around like he was a puppy dog and my ass was made out of bacon. I got him his first job as a goddamned *bat boy*, and now he's too busy to see *me?*"

"No need to yell, sir." The receptionist mustered as much politeness as she could, "Mr. Myrick is un—"

Just then, the door swung inward. A lanky, fresh-faced, tanned man wearing expensive-looking sunglasses and slicked-back, brown hair walked in the lobby. He carried a set of golf clubs over his shoulder.

17

"I'll tell ya', Marcy, I don't even know why I play anymore," the man shook his head. "Had to quit after nine today 'cause I ran outta balls. Guess it's 'back to—" He started pulling his sunglasses off his head, but held them at the end of his nose when he saw the short, ornery old person standing at the desk.

"Hack? Hack O'Callahan? Wow, it's been forever. How the hell are ya?"

Hack reached out and grabbed the man's hand with a surprisingly firm grip.

"Little Keith Myrick. Grew a bit, have ya', son?"

"Gosh, I'd like to think so!" Myrick punctuated the thought with what Hack thought was a phony laugh. Hack couldn't even muster a grin. "To, uh, what do I owe the pleasure, Hack?"

"Why don't we go into your office?" Hack threw a wise-ass, "told-you-so" smile at the receptionist, who half stuck out her tongue and raised her eyebrows as her head bobbed side-to-side.

"Sure, sure. Just give me a minute to set these down."

Hack shook his head, "Always told your daddy that golf was a damned fool game for a baseball man. Goes against everything he's taught; score less, individual over the team. Also royally fucks up a good swing, gets a .300 hitter droppin' his fuckin' shoulder like he's Dave Kingman, makes him think he can hit the damn thing an Arkansas mile!"

Myrick laughed again, but one look at Hack's eyes let the man know that the old-timer was deadly serious. He set his golf clubs down next to the desk.

"Marcy, can you watch these while I catch up with Mr. O'Callahan here?"

"Sure, Mr. Myrick. Should I hold your calls?"

"Yeah. Yes, that would be fine. Hack?" Myrick extended an outstretched hand toward the short hallway that qualified as the Magpies' offices. Hack walked straight as an arrow; any hint of labor or pain covered through sheer force of determination.

At the end of the hallway, a cheap-looking, brass-colored plaque next to a white door read, "Keith Myrick, General Manager." Hack grabbed the knob and didn't even flinch when he was shocked by static electricity, built up as he had shuffled his feet along the shoddy, blue, indoor-outdoor carpet that lined the hallway.

Myrick's "office" was little more than a ten-by-ten room adorned with all manners of baseball memorabilia. Most prominently, in a case in the corner sat a trophy with the inscription, "High-A Carolina League Champions, Chesterfield Birddogs, 2007."

Perhaps a dozen or so pictures dotted the wall, nearly all of which contained both Keith and his father, John "Pug" Myrick. Of those, a couple featured a shorter figure in between the two men. Though his face was younger, and was framed by darker, thicker hair, Hack's stony, unsmiling visage was unmistakable.

Hack shook his head as he threw himself into one of the uncomfortable chairs opposite Myrick's comparatively plush, faux-leather chair, "Why do you keep those damned fool pictures around? I look like an asshole in 'em."

Myrick's eyes widened and his voice softened, "Hack...I don't know how to tell you this, but Dad's dead."

"What?"

Myrick nodded, "He died going on three years ago now. No offense, but I keep the pictures around more to remind myself of *him*, not really you."

"That's a damn shame about your daddy, Keith. Damn shame..." Hack tailed off.

"Thank you, Hack. He adored you; really would've done anything for you. Learned a lot from you."

"Well, I can't take all the credit. He was a fuckin' *moron* when I first met him, so I had a lot of work to do."

Both men took a few moments to process the statement.

Myrick looked up, took a deep breath, and forced a smile, "What can I do for you, Hack?"

"I ain't much one for beatin' around the bush or nothin', so I'm just gonna say it: I wanna' manage your ballclub."

Myrick laughed, "Glad to see you haven't lost your sense of humor, Hack! Dad always said you were a real card. What can I *really* do for you today?"

"I'm serious. I want to manage your ballclub."

Myrick started to laugh again, but Hack's unblinking stare tunneled through him from the other side of the table. He held out a hand to his side, "You're serious? Hack, we already have a very bright young manager, Willie Williams, really an up-and-comer——"

"He's a goddamned moron too," Hack interrupted. "And a fucking hot dog, to boot. Used to prance and preen after hitting a home run like goddamned King Fancypants. Once I told my pitchers to start nailin' him a few times a season, his trot sped up a bit."

"See, this is what I'm talking about—that old school, 'eye for an eye' bullshit may've worked in the old days, but the game has changed. The players have changed. You have players from a dozen different countries——"

"Now wait just a goddamned minute; one thing I've never been is a goddamned bigot." Myrick leaned a skeptical eye in at Hack. "I mean, takin' the piss outta guys and bustin' their balls is one thing. Shit, I'm as much of a Mick headcase as anyone else, and all'a my players lemme' know about it. But when it comes down to it, I don't have a problem with any of 'em. The nine best guys always play."

"Even the Japanese players?" Myrick asked.

Hack flinched before he caught his tongue and thought for a minute. "I think so. They aren't——"

"How about Koreans?"

Hack erupted into a flurry of coughs; it was the first time he was happy for one of the fits, since he didn't know what he would've said otherwise. He brought out a fresh handkerchief from his back pocket and covered his mouth. Fortunately, there wasn't too much blood, or at least too much for him to conceal with his hand as he placed the kerchief back in his pocket.

Hack forced a hint of a grin, "I'm over the war. If they can play, they can play."

He only mostly-lied.

"So you're asking me, a month into the season, to just throw Willie out on his ass, and hand you the keys to the team? Why in the *hell* should I do that?"

"Don't be an asshole!" Hack shot back. "I ain't a fool. Don't sit back and tell me that you aren't seein' dollar signs comin' outta' my mouth right now. A Hall of Fame manager? Taking on this, pardon my French, shithole team of yours? That'd put asses in the seats. For Chrissake, Keith, you're in last place right now!"

"With some of the Indians' most promising prospects in years coming up!" Myrick yelled.

"Could've fuckin' fooled me," Hack crossed his arms over his chest. "Seems like Willie Williams either isn't the manager you thought he was, or your players could use a dose of a different kind of managin', 'least for a while.

"Now, I'm not sayin' throw Willie out; that wouldn't be fair to him. Make him my assistant for a year, let him learn from a *real* manager what it's like to get the most out of these nitwits."

"Oh, is that all?" Myrick raised his hands out above his head and stood up, "So, we undermine everything Willie's built over the past month with these guys and bring you in, and *you* teach Willie how to be a 'real manager?'"

Hack stared Myrick down for a moment, "Yep. That about covers it."

Myrick shook his head, but Hack cut him off, "Look, you said it yourself, your pop said that playin' for me was the best thing that ever happened to him! All I wanna do is pass somma' that on before I croak. One last year, and hopefully some of that grit'll rub off on these panzie-ass players of yours."

"Are you dying?" Myrick asked, point blank.

Hack didn't flinch, "We all are. But if yer' askin' if I'm sick, well, hell, no more than any other damned fool my age," he lied.

Myrick turned to face the window, which was maybe a foot by a foot. Next to the tiny pane of glass was one of the pictures with his father and Hack. His dad's bright, beaming smile lit up the frame, the warm embrace of his old manager more than compensated for Hack's dour, focused puss.

Myrick shook his head, "You know, before dad died, he told me, he said, 'Son, I'm so damned proud of what you've done.' I'm paraphrasing a bit, of course, he said, 'what you've done in such a short period of time is nothin' short of amazing. You're on track to become a general manager in the big leagues by forty.'

"But you know what stood out to me most? He motioned for me to come closer, and so I did, and he said to me, 'Son, I just wish I could've talked to Hack O'Callahan one more time. The guy taught me more about baseball, life, whatever, than anyone else I've ever been around."

Hack smirked and nodded, "See? Told ya' your pop was a sharp one."

Myrick turned back to face Hack, "I can make you Willie's bench coach. That way he can—"

"Manager or I walk." Hack's lips went taut and humorless.

Myrick shrugged and shook his head, "I don't know how the hell I'm gonna explain this to the team. Let alone Willie..."

"Tell 'em you were sick of the losing and the Indians told you to do it."

"Shit, I have to run this by them, too..."

Hack pushed himself out of the chair and patted Myrick on his shoulder.

"You'll figure it out, Keith; you're a bright guy, ain'tchya?"

Myrick leveled his frown.

"*The first* inkling I have that the team is going in the tank, the first time I think Willie can do a better job, you'll be—"

"I'll be in the manager's office if you need me," Hack turned and walked to the door. "You may wanna' tell Willie to get his shit outta' my office whenever he rolls in." He reached for the knob and twisted.

"Oh yeah," Hack turned over his shoulder as he left, "Thanks fer' invitin' me to the funeral."

The door slammed shut, and beads of sweat pooled across Keith Myrick's usually easy-going, permanently-smiling face.

4

The Magpies' clubhouse wasn't half as glamorous as any of its major league counterparts. Even by Double-A standards, it was a bit of a pit. To the left as one walked in, the Magpie logo was stenciled on the concrete floor in between a couple of drains, installed for easy cleaning. A Spartan assortment of mesh metal lockers, many of them dented, rusting, or warped, lined the fringes of the room, which smelled mostly of grass and body odor, with enough of a twinge of antiseptic to fool any visitors into thinking that there was some consideration given to hygiene.

To the right of the main hallway, the concrete gave way to tile and a bathroom/shower area that looked like it belonged more in an underfunded high school than a professional baseball locker room; two stalls, four urinals, and maybe a few more than a dozen shower heads, all arranged with little heed to modesty.

Past the bathroom area was the training room, which had four trainers' tables, several cabinets for supplies, and an old brushed metal jacuzzi tub lined with calcium deposits.

Opposite the training room was the manager's office, a dingy little room with musty, red shag carpeting, as well as several bookcases filled with binders containing scouting reports, pitch charts, and other ancient information that had long since been digitized. The half-wall windows that previously looked out on the hallway had been frosted years before and barely let any light enter the dank little chamber.

A door in the manager's office led to the coaches' locker room, which smelled marginally better because it was currently only used by one man other than Willie Williams, assistant/pitching coach Pete Moray, and the only grime he tended to accumulate was due to an errant stream of spittle from the dip that he constantly packed. Attached to the coaches' locker room was a small toilet and shower area for the staff, which kept them away from whatever "grabass" was going on among the players in the general population.

Then there was the equipment room, which housed all of the helmets, shoes, balls, bats, and uniforms the team would need, along with the Magpies' laundry facilities.

And at the end of the hallway was the small press room, nicknamed "the dungeon," for the torture that both media and coaches endured alike inside its unfriendly confines, immediately before the right turn that led down the tunnel to the dugout.

It was a bare-bones complex, the kind of area that would drive lesser men to question whether it was worth it to spend most of their days in such a depressing environment, all in the hope of some day tasting the luxury that was the big leagues.

Hack couldn't help but smirk.

He finally felt at home.

He set his suitcase on the concrete floor and took in a large noseful of the musty air and breathed it out slowly so as to savor it. The utter lack of anything resembling comfort only increased his own contentment: one of his favorite sayings was, "The Spartans won the war, didn't they?" That the clubhouse had been unspoiled by the general trend toward mollycoddling and softening the nation's youth gave Hack the faintest glimmer of hope.

"Maybe we aren't gonna' be taken over by the Chinese, after all..." Hack said. The Magpies had a night game , so the entire complex was empty even at eleven a.m. Hack appreciated the solitude.

He portered his suitcase over to the manager's office and opened the door. Fortunately, Willie Williams was among those not yet at the stadium. Hack grinned at the realization that he finally had somewhere where he belonged once more, someplace to call his own, even if that place had a cheap, second-hand metal-and-wood paneling desk and matching green, foam-padded reclining rolling chair and sofa that all looked like they had been rescued from a particularly rowdy frat house.

Hack threw his suitcase on the horrid couch before he returned behind the desk and launched himself into the grungy green chair with gusto. The manager failed to gauge his size properly as the back gave and his momentum spun him around a couple of times before it petered out.

Hack grunted and pulled himself closer to the desk. On it was one of "those damned tablets" that Hack had seen bloggers use in the Indians' press box, though the seasoned manager saw no need for them when perfectly good pencil and paper were still more than abundant.

Unfortunately, none was readily available, so Hack began opening drawers, not caring that Willie hadn't had time to relocate his belongings.

"Where's the goddamn paper around here?" Hack asked. "How the hell is a guy supposed to make a lineup...?"

"Goddamn it!"

Hack turned in his chair to face the door, but only found a fortiesh black gentleman with stylish spectacles and prematurely grey temples standing in the entranceway.

"Charles," Hack said with a curt nod.

"I thought for sure Keith was just fuckin' with me when I came in and he said that Hack O'Callahan was taking over my team—"

"Great to see you, too, Charles."

Charles "Willie" Williams's eyes grew wide, "Don't start on me with that Charles shit. No one's called me that since I was in the minors myself."

"Where I come from, you have'ta earn your nickname. You sure as shit don't do that by preenin' after you hit a tater, and you *certainly* don't do it by being a dogshit manager of some piss-ass team in East Bumfuck, Ohio."

Willie clenched his fists, "I swear to *God*, I would hit you if I didn't think I'd kill you. Then we'd have a real fuckin' mess on our hands."

Hack's eyes narrowed as he pointed at the man whom he viewed as an interloper, "Let's get one thing straight: if yer' gonna' be my bench coach, you better start showin' me a little *fuckin'* respect."

Willie raised his hands in mock surprise, "Oh, lawdy, *lawdy*, massah Hack! Where*evah* did my manners go?" He balled up his fists again, "Racist old prick—if you think I'm gonna stay on as your bench coach, just so you can pull your minstrel routine with me, make me look the fool, then you've got—"

"Amazin' that no matter how much we shuffle, that race card always seems to find its way to the top of the deck for you brothers."

"You *brothers?*" Willie took a step forward. He puffed out his chest, cocked his head to the side and looked toward the ceiling in contemplation for a moment before he let out a deep breath and said through clenched teeth, "You're no brother of mine, ass."

Hack shook his head, "Forget it. Look, I don't give a shit if you're black or green, or purple...unless you're purple because you're dead, and despite what you think of me, that would be a fuckin' tragedy."

Willie grabbed the phone from the wall next to the door.

"What're you doin' now?" Hack asked.

"Callin' Keith. There's no way I'm stayin' on with some—"

"Where the fuck else are you gonna' go, Willie?" Hack adjusted his glasses. "Yer' team's loaded with good prospects, but yer' in last place. What other team's gonna' be interested in a manager who can't develop talented players or win with them? Huh!?

"Here's my guess, Willie; you'll probably head back to your hometown, catch on somewhere sellin' insurance or doin' something with money, since some old fool'll think a ballplayer like you'll be able to bring in some business, right? Shit, maybe you did that for a while after quittin' the game before, I don't know..."

Hack paused and looked at Willie for confirmation. Willie's silence was telling.

"…So you got sick of doin' that, and you figured, 'shit, I can manage. Any old asshole can manage, right?' And you got here, and you sat in this chair, and maybe it ain't so easy any more."

"So you're going to *make* it easy for me, right? White man come to rescue the poor black idiot in over his head?" Willie asked.

"Will you *quit* with the racial *bullshit*?" Hack's eyes narrowed. He let the silence hang over the room for a moment before he bobbed his head and continued.

"That's lesson one: it *never* gets easy. Yer' a pretty young guy, so you may *think* ya' can 'connect' with these players, or some bullshit like that. But each day, yer' gettin' older, and crankier, and as ya' lose ballgames, ya' start to lose hair, too. Until one day, they're callin' ya' 'out of touch.' Proud to say I never got that, not even now. And you know why?"

"Why?" Willie crossed his arms.

"'Cause I don't give half a shit what some little fuckhead ballplayer thinks about me!" Hack shouted. "I'm in this for one reason, and one reason only: I love the game. Deep down, I knew I could never love anything, any*one* else the way that I love this game. And *that* propels me through all of the other bullshit and awfulness that comes with this job.

"Now, I need a bench coach. You *were* a helluva ballplayer. I think you could make a helluva manager. But you were always so damned smart, you were *stupid* for it."

Willie raised a finger and opened his mouth, but stopped to frown and put his finger on his chin.

"I'll show you how ya' can get around that, how ya' can be great at something else for this season, and this season only. But I have to know, *right now*, if yer' passion for the game is 'same as mine. 'Cause if it's not," Hack shook his head, "I don't have room for ya' on my staff. Understand?"

Willie half-scowled at the old-timer. The recognition behind his eyes was visible. As the man's lip trembled, Hack knew he had struck a chord.

"Maybe this is one'a those 'so smart he's stupid moments,'" Willie ran his hand over his hair, "but I'm willing to stick around," Hack nodded and opened his mouth to speak, but Willie pre-empted him, "*If* you promise it's only this season, and that you won't make any of those awful 'black jokes' around the team."

"When have I ever made a 'black joke?'" Hack asked, far too offended and earnest.

"Literally one minute ago," Willie said.

"As I remember it, *you* were the one acting out the minstrel show. I just spoke my mind."

"You know what I mean, Hack. You and I came up in a different time. These guys now are more sensitive to that shit."

"I came up forty years before you did," Hack said, "If you ask me, the game could use a little of that grit from back then."

"Back then, you and I woulda' been dressin' in different locker rooms," Willie said. "Playing for different teams."

Hack nodded, "Did I ever tell you I played against Jackie Robinson?" Willie shook his head, "Helluva ballplayer. Fast as a jackrabbit, whip smart, could hit the shit outta the ball, just great. Our pitcher was a real country bumpkin, called Jackie every ugly name in the book, and even some that aren't used any more. For example, no one uses 'm—"

Willie raised an eyebrow and narrowed his lips.

Hack shook his head, "—Never mind. At any rate, tie game, bottom of the eighth, we're home, this hick is still pitching, Jackie comes up, and first pitch, *whoosh*—" Hack balled his fist and passed it right by his face, "buzzes him. This is before helmets, you know?"

"Jackie didn't so much as flinch—he could see the ball about as well as anyone I've known. He just stood there and glared at the pitcher, his eyes dared the sum'bitch to do it again."

"So what'd he do?" Willie leaned in.

"Next pitch—*pow!* Right on the shoulder. Jackie's lucky he stepped up in the box; otherwise he woulda' been down for the count. Now, I'm playin' second base, and I look over to Jackie, expectin' to see him charge the mound or yell at the pitcher or somethin' like that, but you know what Jackie did?"

Willie shook his head.

"He was laughin'. The sonofabitch was laughin' as he trotted to first. So I walk into the pitcher and read him the fuckin' riot act about what a dumb S.O.B. he was, and he stands there and takes it all in, and you know what he says to me? He says, 'he shouldn't even be on the same field with us. He should be packin' my bags in the clubhouse right now.'

"I wanted to hit'im right there. I would've too, but Bill Maloney was our manager, and he would've kicked me off the team for it, sure as shit. So I went back to second base, watched Jackie steal second, then steal third, and then he scored on a short sac fly, on three consecutive pitches. We lost the game. Funny thing is, old man Maloney cut that pitcher right after the game, and *he* packed his own bags on back to Shithole, Alabama."

Willie's jaw had dropped some time ago, and though he wanted to say *something*, he struggled to find the words.

"My point is, Jackie Robinson prob'ly had more grit and determination, more goddamned *courage* than anyone I've ever known, even in the service. He'd be pissed off at how these kids are coddled and 'developed' nowadays. So next time you're thinkin' or talkin' about 'black this' and 'racist that,' you better think long and hard before accusin' me of anything of the sort. Are we clear?"

Willie nodded.

"Are we *clear?*"

"Yes," Willie said.

"Good," Hack leaned back in the chair. "Besides, that's somethin' your people should be familiar with, isn't it, Charles? Long and hard? What with the—" Hack whistled twice as he looked down toward his crotch, "—long peckers and what not?"

Willie took two steps toward Hack and leveled his gaze at the old man for a couple of moments. Hack continued to lounge in his chair, either unaware of or untroubled by any potential problem.

Willie shot a finger in Hack's face, "You can joke about *that* shit *all* you want."

This even caused Hack to smile as Willie laughed for a moment before his expression turned serious once more.

"But I was serious about all the other shit," Willie said. Hack nodded in assent. "Well, then, I think we can co-exist for just a season."

Willie offered a reluctant hand toward Hack, and Hack reticently took it as the men cemented an uneasy truce.

Willie turned to leave, but just before he closed the door, Hack interrupted him, "Feel free to move yer' shit into the coaches' locker room whenever."

Willie thought about turning around and really letting Hack have it, but instead nodded.

"We have interns to do that kind of thing."

"Well, tell 'em that I wanna see 'em when they get in."

"Sure." Willie closed the door.

As soon as it had shut, Hack covered his mouth and stumbled over to the ugly sofa along the wall. He pulled out the handkerchief, laid it flat on a cushion, placed his face atop it to muffle the noise, and started coughing violently, expulsions giving way to more expulsions like fighter planes taking off from a carrier deck.

How long can I do this? Hack thought as the fit subsided enough that he could pull his head away to survey the large red spot overlaying the other faded red spots on the white handkerchief.

How long until someone finds out?

5

"KNOCK, KNOCK, KNOCK."

"Come in," Hack growled from the couch. He had been trying to nap for maybe an hour or more, but was only able to nod off for a few abbreviated stretches.

The door cracked open with sufficient temerity that Hack immediately knew it wasn't Willie coming back for "round two," nor was it Keith, who apparently fancied himself King Shit of Hoplite.

Instead, an attractive redhead peeked her head in the office. An awkward-looking, freckled boy with a mop of brown hair and long nose peered over her shoulder.

"Yeah?" Hack asked, already annoyed.

"Uh…Mr. O'Callahan? I'm Samantha Rappaport, one of the interns for the Magpies. This is Barry Wojciechowski," she turned to face the beanpole behind him, and he offered a timid wave.

"Are you the ones who're supposed'ta move Willie's stuff?" Hack asked.

"Yes…yes, we are," the look on Samantha's face indicated that they had already heard more than they ever wanted to know about Hack from the man who had recently been demoted to bench coach.

"I'm guessin' then that you can get some shit fer' me too?"

Samantha looked back at Barry, who shrugged.

"Sure. Sure, we can do that."

"Good. I'm gonna' need a pen and paper—how you people can run an organization without it is beyond me."

"Actually, our computer system has won several awards for user-interface and—" it was the first time Barry piped up. After the look Hack gave him in reply, he was sorry he had done so.

"I need a dozen black handkerchiefs. Or red, or blue—dark colors. I need all the Robitussin ya' can find. I need a hotplate and a supply of Campbell's Chicken Noodle; *not* that cheap imitation shit—it gives me the fuckin' runs. I need a case of Ol' Reliable, I need—"

"The fiber supplement?" Samantha asked.

"What? No—Christ! Actually, I need that too, but—" he waved a hand at them, "—the whiskey, the whiskey. Not the little bottles, either—the big sonsabitches."

"We're not twenty-one," Samantha shook her head.

"*Just*...get it." The two interns jumped as Hack raised his voice. "And I need a program."

"What OS do you use?" Barry jumped in.

"What? What kind of a dumb Pollack question is that? A program? You know, with all'a the players and their statistics and everything?"

"Oh..." Barry thought for a minute, "...I think we still have those."

"You better, 'cause if not, I need stat reports on all'a our hitters against the pitcher we're goin' against tonight, and pitch-by-pitch breakdowns on how our starter and our relievers do against all'a their guys."

"That's all in the database."

"The what-the-fuck now?"

Barry shook his head, "Forget it. I'll get you the relevant printouts."

Hack snorted, "How's that for a change? An enterprising Pollack..."

"What's that?" Barry asked.

"What?"

"A Po-lock?"

"Fer'get it," Hack waved the question away.

"Is that everything you need?" Samantha asked.

"For now, yeah."

"How're we supposed to pay for this stuff?" She asked.

"Tell Keith to take it outta my paycheck."

The interns stood and stared at Hack. He glared right back.

"Well? I'm waitin'. Get ta' gettin'!"

They quickly loaded Willie's modest belongings onto a pushcart and wheeled them away.

Not but an hour later, Hack heard another knock on the door.

"Yeah?" He had nodded off again.

Samantha and Barry appeared in the doorway.

"Well if it isn't Tweedledee," he looked at Samantha before he turned his scowl toward Barry, "and Tweedledumb. Need more instruction, do yas'? Old man didn't explain what—?"

"No, we have everything. Even the whiskey, just like you asked." Samantha said. Barry pushed the cart with the requested items piled atop it.

"No shit..." Hack said. He wobbled to his feet and grabbed a colorful, neon orange binder from the top of the pile. "What the fuck is this?"

"Those are the reports you requested," Barry said, confident for the first time in Hack's presence. "A team overview of stats, plus splits for all of Springfield's pitchers, and splits for our hitters against their hitters, indexed alphabetically."

"Christ, whattaya have, friends at NASA?" Hack thumbed through the printed out pages, "This'll be just fine...yeah...just fine..." he looked up at Barry without even a hint of a smile, "You keep this up and they'll be sure to give you a raise."

"Oh, we don't get paid," Barry said nonchalantly. "We're college students doing this for course credit."

"I knew it! I knew a Pollack couldn't possibly be this smart," Hack harumphed. "Why in the sam *hell* would ya' wanna work for a minor league team *for free?*"

Samantha shrugged, "Get in the industry. Work our way up."

Hack shook his head, "Look sweetie, I understand you're tryin' to bag yerself a husband," Samantha recoiled in horror, "but you, Pollack—this is dead end, son. There's no future in it. Stop wastin' your time."

Samantha scowled at Hack before she composed herself again.

"Will there be anything else, Mr. O'Callahan?"

"Naw, this should keep me busy for a while. Go on…" this time, he didn't have to say it twice; the interns couldn't hide their faces of displeasure as they left the office.

Hack sat at the desk and threw himself into the research for the next several hours. Two of the scouting reports in particular caught his eye: the catcher, Robert ("nickname: Truck," the scouting report read) Traynor, who, judging by the numbers, hit anything thrown at him like it had just insulted his mother: .344 average last season with 38 home runs and 138 RBIs.

The other one was the shortstop, Manny Poblado, who still started despite the following "glowing" review in his scouting report: "Can't hit, middling range, mediocre speed, decent arm."

"How the hell is this kid startin'?" Hack asked himself.

Within an hour, Hack had assembled his lineup for the evening. Players trickled in, but Hack kept himself busy by reading all of the binders the "Pollack kid, Woja-somethin'," had assembled. He wasn't the type to glad hand a bunch of minor leaguers, especially when they hadn't yet been fortunate enough to make his acquaintance, and *especially* when they were as sheltered and soft as this group looked to be from their pictures.

Game time was 7:05 that evening, and the Magpies were scheduled to take batting practice at 6:05. At 5:55, all of the players sat in the dingy folding chairs in front of their lockers. Some of them played video games on their phones, or, for the more serious gamers among them, their Sony or Nintendo portables.

Others congregated in the various cliques that had naturally formed, generally along racial lines, though there was a marked tension between the self-described "rednecks" and more suburban, affluent white players.

It didn't help that the clubhouse only featured one older, cathode ray TV, similar to the one Hack had smashed to bits in his home the previous evening. All of the various cliques fought over what channel it should be on.

"God damn it," a hulking man with sandy hair said in a Southern accent, "Who the fuck put it on *How I Met Your Mother*? No one likes that intellectual *bullshit*."

"Shut up, Mitch," a thinner brown-haired player with glasses shot back.

"Fuck you, Sid. I'm pitchin' tonight. If I do a shitty job, I blame it on this bullshit."

As if to make Mitch's point, Josh Radnor's character on the show launched into one of his insufferably self-important monologues.

"I don't think Larry the Cable Guy's on right now," Truck Traynor said with a grin.

"Nope. But *Duck Dynasty* sure as shit is, and that shit is funny as fuck," Mitch replied.

"Homesick, are we?" Sid asked.

Truck shook his head and laughed as he put on his shin guards.

"You little bitch—" Mitch took two giant-sized steps toward Sid, who's only defense consisted of a wise-ass grin.

All the while, the Latin players escalated an argument over an esoteric card game and the din of salsa music in their own corner of the locker area.

Hack had struggled into his uniform hours before, but was just now folding one of the crisp, dark handkerchiefs into his back pocket. He swigged down another gulp of Robitussin, and several deeper swallows off of the already half-full bottle of Old Reliable.

He heard a "crash" from the locker room and wiped his mouth on the sleeve of the turtleneck he wore under his uniform before he grunted and waddled to the door.

Hack shook his head at the scene that unfolded outside: Mitch Henry, that evening's starting pitcher, had Linus "Sid" Fynch in a headlock, as Truck Traynor tried to pull the hulking southerner off of the center fielder. Meanwhile, Manny Poblado and first baseman

Juan Patrón slapped each other as Spanish curse words resonated throughout the locker room.

"God damn it," Hack sighed as his eyes narrowed, the emotionless, sad orbs finally ignited in their sockets and began to dance.

"Hey! Stop it. *Stop it!*" Hack yelled as he stumbled toward the locker room. Even though he screamed over the din, the players were too engrossed in their various altercations to pay any heed.

Frustrated, Hack picked up a bat along the wall and swung it against the mesh metal siding of the locker next to him.

The ash connected with the mesh with a loud "BOOM," and dented the web of metal. The players looked up to see who or what had caused the commotion, and were surprised to see that it was a short, bald senior citizen.

And he was *pissed*.

"I don't know what the fuck kind'a country club operation Coach Williams was runnin' here, but the first rule of my locker room is that when I tell you all to *shut the fuck up*—" Hack screamed the words at the players and raised the bat toward them, all of whom took a half-step back, "—you god damn well do it! Are we clear?"

"Who the hell're you?" Mitch asked.

Hack galloped over toward Henry and shoved the bat in the towering pitcher's face, "I'm yer' worst fuckin' nightmare, son. No wonder our country's gonna be taken over by the goddamned *Chi*nese. Yer' a bunch of dumbass baseball players, and you don't even recognize greatness when it's swingin' a god damned *bat* around yer' locker room! My name is Hack O'Callahan. I'm yer' new manager."

Willie belatedly raced into the room to check in on the commotion.

A bespectacled black player in the far corner of the room gasped.

Everyone else looked blank.

"Hack *O'Callahan?*" The black player asked. "*The* Hack O'Callahan? Four World Series rings, greatest manager of *all-time* Hack O'Callahan?"

"I like this one already," Hack offered a half-grin. "This old ass of mine could use a good kissin'." The players half-laughed at the comment. "But on this team, make no mistake, you are to refer to me as Coach, or 'Coach O'Callahan.' If you earn my respect, maybe someday I'll let you call me 'Coach Hack.'"

"Is this true, Willie?" Truck Traynor asked.

Willie nodded, "In light of Coach O'Callahan's *remarkable* record, I've agreed to step aside for the season and become his bench coach. You all are to offer him the same respect that you would me."

"Bullshit, Charles," Hack shot back, "If you offer me the same respect that you offered him," Hack stuck a gnarled thumb at Willie, "You'll get the same shitty result. You *will* offer me *more* respect than any coach you've ever had. More than your shitty little high school coaches or..." he looked over at the stunned Latin players in the corner, "...whatever...y'all have down wherever you're from. For the Einsteins amongst'yas', more than yer' ivory tower, egghead college coaches.

"I command that respect, gentlemen, because I *am* better than those coaches. I have four of these," he balled his left hand into a fist and thrust it in front of him to showcase a glittering, ruby-and-diamond -studded monstrosity of a ring, "to prove it. So forgive me if I'll be damned if some little *pissant* comes in here and acts like he's King Shit. I've got news for you, buddy; yer' King shit, minus the 'king.' Are we clear?"

Maybe half of the players nodded. Others looked toward Mitch Henry or Truck Traynor for guidance.

"I'm not here to be yer' momma, and I sure as hell ain't here to be yer' buddy. In fact, I couldn't give a damn if you hate each others' guts, and can't wait to strangle each other. But men, those murders are gonna' have to wait until *after* the season."

A few chuckles went up from around the room.

"I know it can be tough for a lot of you, especially the Latin guys and the brothers—" Hack nodded in turn toward the Latin players in the far right corner of the room, and the bookish black player in the left corner of the room. "Where're the rest of you?" Hack asked the black player, unthinking.

"What do you mean? College men?" As if to underscore the point, he pushed the glasses up on the bridge of his nose.

"No, no—the brothers? You know…black guys?"

"Yeah, Eldrake—where the hell are they?" Henry asked.

"*El*drake?" Hack emphasized the first syllable.

"Eldrake Gamble," he stuck out his hand, "I'm honored to meet you, sir."

"Christ—what the hell is this, a box social? We're ballplayers, not bankers," Hack paused for laughs but received only quizzical glances. "You need a nickname. What'd the other kids in the hood call ya'?"

Willie smacked himself in the face, while Henry let out a low, ignorant laugh.

"Actually, I grew up in Buckhead, Georgia. Suburbs of Atlanta. Went to Georgia Tech, so I'm—"

"How about 'Flash?'"

"Excuse me?"

"Flash? Ya' know—like the comic book hero?"

Gamble snorted out a nerdy laugh, "Uh, I'm not exactly known for my speed, but—"

"Flash Gamble makes you sound dangerous, like you'd put a guy's head through a car window before he knows what's what."

"Uh…okay then…" Gamble tailed off, hand still outstretched

"No need to shake my hand, either. Like I said, I ain't here to be yer' buddy. I ain't here to discriminate on none'a'ya, either; I don't care if yer' white, black, brown, yella', or purple, 'cept if yer' purple 'cause yer' chokin' on somethin', and even then I only give a shit if you can hit or pitch a little."

This one elicited the desired chuckles, except from Willie, who rolled his eyes that the old codger was already repeating material.

"Everyone will get a shot, and we will win ballgames. The good ones of yous' might even make it to the show. But gentlemen, the next time I walk in and yer' fightin' each other like a bunch of goddamned *dogs* tearin' each other apart for a bone, I will take this bat, and shove it up somebody's ass!"

More chuckles followed, along with a couple of guffaws from Henry's corner. Even Manny Poblado smiled at the reference. Traynor winced and shook his head.

"The lineup for tonight is up on the manager's door. You got a problem with it? Tough shit. Show me somethin' in practice. Now get on out there and take some BP, will ya'?!"

Silence swallowed the room for a couple of seconds as everyone looked toward their various clique leaders as to how to respond.

Finally, Truck Taylor clapped and let out a sharp, "Yeah!"

Perhaps spurred on by Hack's casual racism, Mitch Henry soon followed suit, as did the Latin players, only some of whom had any idea what exactly had just happened, other than that a crotchety, elderly man barged into their locker room and hit a locker with a bat. Pete Moray, who still hadn't said a word to Hack, rushed over to try to interpret for those with clueless looks on their faces.

As the team took the field, Hack finally broke into a wide grin.

It's good to be home, he thought.

Second Inning

1

"BOOM!"

The door to the media room slammed against the wall. Hack's usual sneer was even darker and more dour than it had been only hours before the Magpies lost their first game under his management, 5-4.

It had been a while since Hack had confronted the media, save for some particularly nasty spats in the catering line in the Jake's press box back in Cleveland.

It was Hack's least favorite part of the job: explaining his decisions to the vile, pasty, overweight, obsessive lot who devoted their lives to covering the exploits of men who played a child's game.

That isn't to say that he didn't relish the occasional verbal sparring and repartee that accompanied press conferences, but by-and-large, Hack preferred to be in the safe cocoon of the clubhouse, away from the prying eyes of reporters eager to make names for themselves.

And yet, when Hack opened the door to the media room, he was shocked.

He had expected news of his arrival to have spread all over the state of Ohio, for reporters from Fox Sports and ESPN to travel to Hoplite to bother, or even beg him for a sound bite, a quote, a quip.

If that fellow who had caused him to smash his TV the previous evening showed up, all the better.

Instead, only four reporters and two cameramen sat in the rusty-looking squadron of perhaps a dozen folding chairs in front of the microphone, which sat atop a gerry-rigged podium. Behind the podium sat a professional-looking purple backdrop with the Magpies' logo interspersed with a string of letters and symbols that Hack didn't recognize as a web address.

The lack of attention angered Hack even more; he strutted to the podium and allowed his anger to take control.

When he was a couple of steps away, a young black man with close-cropped black hair and glasses stopped him with a handshake and a smile.

"Hey, Mr. O'Callahan! I'm Marc Blake, Magpie media relations. Nice to finally—" Blake whispered. A photographer's flash bulb illuminated the pair.

"Yeah, yeah, yer' the one that wrangles these animals."

Blake smiled perhaps a bit too broadly, "Something like that. Your introductory press conference is going to have to wait until after Friday's game, but we figured you could have a short meeting with the local media tonight so that—"

"Son, I've managed in this game for over forty years. I know what the hell I'm doin' when it comes to the goddamned press. Just stay outta my way, okay?"

Blake pursed his lips and shook his head, "This isn't Philly or even Cleveland, Coach. This is Hoplite; be gentle, okay?"

"Fuck off," Hack nearly pushed Blake aside as he stormed to the podium. Several more flashes.

"Turn that goddamned thing off," Hack hissed at the photographer. The stunned cameraman made a face and typed in several commands on his camera's touchscreen.

Hack stood as the assembled media sat at various levels of rapt attention, eager for the grizzled manager to make some sort of comment on the loss.

"Well…shoot," Hack commanded.

"Coach O'Callahan, Jim Taggert, *Hoplite Herald*," Taggert was a raspy old cuss of a newspaperman, cut from the cloth of the great beat reporters, to the point that his gray hair and complexion could be attributable to the newsprint that coursed through his veins. His voice was as deep and gravely as a potholed parking lot. "Tough one to take there in the bottom of the ninth. Your thoughts on the loss?"

"My thoughts? I thought it was pretty terrible, obviously. We were winnin', then we weren't winnin' anymore. Only so much I can do in six hours."

"So you pin most've the blame on the closer, Tommy Stearns, for the two home runs in the ninth?"

Hack knew a trap when he saw it, "Team sport, team loss."

"Coach O'Callahan, Liam Canard, Magpie Mayhem dot com," A short, thin kid with a bob-cut and thick, black plastic frames asked.

"What the fuck now?" Hack muttered with a cough. Fortunately, the bark didn't inspire a fit, and effectively masked his profanity.

"Magpie Mayhem? Only the premier site dedicated to all things Magpies?" Canard snorted with too much unearned superiority. "Did you think about pulling Stearns after the first homerun?"

"I'd have to be a damned fool not to," Hack said. "But fer' tonight, all I had to go on were scouting reports, turned in by scouts who may or may not be thick-headed shits who have no idea what the fuck they're talking about."

An attractive blonde female who wore a loud, pink business blazer winced and shook her head at the video cameraman next to her.

"So for now? *Right* now? Sure, Stearns is the closer. But he fell in love with his fastball too much tonight. Trusted 'the old way' of doin' things. Right now, everyone on this team should be on notice, no matter how good ya' are or what kind of a prospect the team thinks ya' are, if we don't start winnin', I'm gonna make some changes. Hell, I might make some changes fer' Friday, just fer' the hell of it."

"But his xFIP is off the—"

"His what now?" Hack asked.

"XFIP? You know, expected fielding independent pitching?"

Hack shook his head at Taggert, "And here I was thinking that Stearns had some kind of disease. Last time I checked, son, *nothing* a pitcher does is independent of his fielders."

"That may be true, but by using different metrics, it clearly was the right decision to——"

"It was clearly the *wrong* decision to give this kid a credential, Blake." Hack stared through Canard, who cowered in his seat.

Taggert raised his notebook, "Coach, talk a bit about that throw Manny Poblado made in the sixth."

Hack nodded curtly, "Hell of a throw. Rocket arm on that kid, ta' backhand it in the hole like that, and rifle it over to Patrón at first ta' get the guy, that's somethin' else."

Taggert could've sworn he saw the gears already turning in the salty manager's head.

"Coach O'Callahan, April Barker, Channel 7 News," the woman in the pink blazer said, "Why did you decide to make your return to Hoplite, and why right now?"

"Whoa, hey, sorry folks," Blake stepped forward, hands outstreched, "Coach is gonna answer questions about all'a that good stuff after Friday's game. This is a game night only session."

"Okay then," Barker said. "How was your first game in Hoplite? What'd you think of the fans?"

"The fans? You think I have time to think about the fans during a game, Missy? Let me tell you somethin', I didn't meet any of these players until an hour before game time," Hack paused to let the sentiment linger.

Hack didn't have to tell them that it was his choice not to.

"I was tryin' to get a feel for the club, figure out what's what."

"Did you?" Barker asked.

"What?"

"Did you get a feel for the club?"

Hack grimaced, "Gettin' there. I'd like to get a little better feel fer' 'em. So if you'll excuse me…" Disappointment washed over the faces of all those in the room, including Blake. Hack looked around for something to knock over and settled on the pitcher of ice water on the podium. He swatted the container with the force of a man half his age. Its contents spilled on the concrete floor below, fittingly close to one of the scattered drains as he waddled through the exit into the clubhouse.

He was met by Pete Moray's pleasant face, made deceptively pudgy by the large dip he packed.

"Pete, I wanna talk to ya' for a minute after I address the men."

Pete nodded sharply with a tight smile.

Hack shuffled into the locker room, which was abuzz with activity. Mitch Henry had an icepack on his left shoulder, but nonetheless held court with the other blue-collar players on the squad, including Kyle "Oiler" Derrick and Colin "Murph" Murphy, who was scheduled to be the starting pitcher on Friday after the Magpies' day off on Thursday.

Noticeably absent from the group was Tommy Stearns, who sat in front of his locker, hat brim pulled far over his head.

"Well, that was just fuckin' wonderful, gentlemen. Absolutely fantastic. Henry over here goes out and throws a gem, and how do ya' repay him? An error and a couple'a taters? And we lose the game."

Henry's glare over at Stearns pushed the nominal closer deeper into his chair.

"That was a dogshit game, men. A dogshit game by a dogshit group of players. Notice I ain't callin' ya' a team yet. That wouldn't be right. Because the way yer' all playin' right now, you're like a goddamned bunch of *girls*."

Hack spat the last word like it was the worst insult he could level at the players.

An errant chuckle echoed around the locker room, but whomever had released it collected himself before Hack could find the offender.

Hack slowly shook his head, "That may've been over the line a bit—I apologize. But mark my words, men: there *will* be changes. Tomorrow, we practice, 8:00 am."

Hack expected a collective groan that never materialized.

"That's all, gentlemen. Get plenty'a sleep tonight: this ain't Charles's practice yer' gonna be goin' through tomorrow."

Hack marched off toward the coaches locker room, opened the door, and slammed it behind him.

"Who the *fuck* is Charles?" Mitch Henry asked the still-silent room.

2

"How's it goin', Hack?" Pete Moray had spent the past twenty-five years of his life perfecting the art of talking with a dip packed firmly in his lower lip. The result was a booming baritone voice that seemed more fitting for a baptist minister than the hearty, but slim, assistant coach of the Magpies.

Especially since he still wore an old-fashioned chain connected to the temples of his out-of-style, gold glasses.

"Eh, we're all waitin' to die, ain't we?" Hack asked.

Moray chuckled, "Shit, the way you're goin', you won't have to worry about that for another fifteen years. I just assumed they'd dig a hole in the third base coach's box and throw you right in, wouldn't even stop the game."

Hack shook his head, "How the fuck did you get a copy of my will?" Hack sold the joke without so much as a smile, but Moray couldn't help but choke out a few hearty chuckles.

"Is that why you came back?" Moray had no way of knowing how accurate the jest was.

"Eh, just never shook the bug, Pete. You know how it is: through all of the ex-wives and season after season, we're baseball men, through-and-through."

"Ain't that the truth," Moray said. "What can I do ya' for?"

"Well Pete, I couldn't help but notice that we've got a lotta' Latin guys on the team."

Moray laughed.

"What the fuck's so funny?"

"Shit, we probably have the fewest Latin guys in the league, by far. We're so white, guys on other teams are always kiddin' with us that we should change our name to the Ghosts. Or at least the Seagulls. The game's changed, Hack. It's not like it was when we were in Oakland together for that year, all honkies and brothers."

"Well, I know we only have the one brother, but this is somethin' that was just startin' to pick up right as I was retirin'."

"You retired in 2006," Moray said.

"Yeah?" Hack replied.

Moray allowed time for Hack to make the connection before he shook his head, "Never mind."

"Anyway, I don't know how to speak Spanish. And I'll be damned if the Latin guys just sit in their own corner, playin' cards and listenin' to that shitty music of theirs."

"So whattaya want me to do about it?" Moray asked.

"You know Spanish from managin' down in winter ball, right?"

"Shit, I know it from a lot more than that. Playin' winter ball, Latin teammates, I'm not just some dumb farmboy from Nebraska, you know."

"Yeah, ya' always were one of the sharper ones, Pete," Hack walked over and put his arm on Moray's shoulder. "Which is why I want *you* to teach 'em all English."

Moray's eyes went wide and rolled, to the point that his head tilted backward momentarily, "What now?"

"Teach 'em English. Get 'em all up to speed."

"That's easier said than done, Hack. I haven't taught anyone English before, and—"

"You taught yourself Spanish, right?"

"Well…sure."

"How'd you do that?"

"I dunno…soap operas…cartoons…the odd hooker or two."

Hack nodded, "Well, there ya' go. Ya' have yer' blueprint."

Moray bobbed his head in with a smile that faded quickly.

"You're serious?"

"Shit *yes*, Pete! I'm too old and curmudgeonly to learn how to speak Spanish—"

"To be fair, I don't think you *ever* would've taken it up on your own," Moray offered a disarming smile.

Hack ignored it, "But the Latin guys seem to respect you. You need to get 'em over all of this culture clash, 'our way or the highway' bullshit and get 'em so I can understand what they're saying."

Moray shook his head, "It's not that."

"What?"

"It's not that they refuse to speak English. Most've 'em, at least— there's always gonna' be an asshole or two in any clubhouse, 'gardless of his nationality. Shit, look at Fynch and Henry; one'a 'em was born with a silver shovel in his mouth, the other poor-as-hell. Lotta' roads lead to 'asshole' in this profession.

"Most'a these Latin guys want to feel comfortable, and don't wanna come across as idiots. If you were thousands'a miles from home, you'd hang around with American guys and speak English, too."

Hack's eyes grew narrow and dark, "I *was* thousands of miles from home, in the god-damned jungles near the 38th parallel, bein' shot at by hundreds'a *Ko*-reans each day. So don't you lecture *me* about bein' thousands of miles from home."

Instead of inspiring the fear that Hack had hoped, Moray simply nodded and grinned.

"Sure, sure—I know, Hack. Didn't mean nothin' by it with regard to you. I'll work with 'em, but don't expect any overnight miracles, either."

Hack turned toward the door to the manager's office, "You have two months," Hack said.

"Or what?" Moray asked with a chuckle.

"Or God help us…" Hack muttered.

3

Hack hoped to be able to choke down a few more glasses of whiskey in the manager's office after he had unburdened himself with his various post game chores.

Instead, he looked to his right and found Keith Myrick sitting on a Magpies team sweatshirt carefully laid out over the dilapidated green sofa.

"Ah, Hack! Great to see you!" Myrick's smile was forced as ever.

"Why the fuck is everyone so goddamned happy around here? We lost tonight, didn't we?"

"Yes, well, you had it there until Stearns blew it for you in the ninth."

"Don't forget how Patrón 'Bucknered' that soft grounder down the line."

"Eh, Juan'll hit enough to make up for it," Myrick said.

"Will he?" Hack's eyes narrowed.

"Look, I'm not here to discuss the game—you did all you could. I got off the phone with the front office in Cleveland. They're saying that we just don't have the budget to bring you on."

Hack flinched at Myrick, but decided the better of belting the smarmy little shit. Hack attributed his restraint to "softening with age."

"What?"

"Your salary. Clearly you'll want something in the—"

"I don't give a shit about the money! You know, outside'a some incidentals and whatnot. I have plenty'a cash."

Myrick held his wrists together over his head, "Hey, my hands are tied here."

"I'm gonna call that guin—guy—" Hack caught himself, "—Tavatelli in Cleveland, and get this sorted out." Hack picked up the phone on the desk and hit the "0" key. "Yeah, operator? Cleveland Indians please...where the fuck do you think? Cleveland, Ohio...okay..." Hack glared at Myrick, who just sat across from the old-timer with an uneasy grin.

"Yeah, get me George Tavatelli...tell him it's Hack O'Callahan, the guy who won him his two World Series rings...yeah, Christ, I'll hold..." More waiting. Myrick checked his gaudy-looking gold watch.

"Yeah, George? Hack O'Callahan here...well, not so fuckin' great. I've got Keith Myrick in my office, and...sure, I'll put it on speakerphone."

Hack squinted at the rows of buttons on the phone console, but for the life of him couldn't find one marked speaker. Myrick was amused; he allowed the fiesty old man to fiddle for a good thirty seconds before he hopped up, reached across the table and hit the speaker phone button. Myrick reached out and grabbed the handset and put it down.

"God damn it, Keith! Why'd ya do that for? Now I gotta call again, and—"

"I hear you just fine, Hack. Keith, you there?"

"Yeah, I'm here, George."

"Great. Now, Hack, I just wanted to say that I'm honored and flattered that you'd choose to come back into the Indians organization for one last hurrah. I know things didn't necessarily go very smoothly during your years in Cleveland, but—"

"Cut the horseshit, George. I ain't askin' fer' money, other than a few incidentals, which I gather are less than what you'd pay a new goddamned batboy."

"Let's talk about those incidentals," George replied. "Having underaged interns get you a case of whiskey?"

"What?" Hack's face reddened with anger, his ears all but steamed with betrayal.

"That's what Keith told me. Isn't that right, Keith?"

"I uh..." Keith looked at Hack as the old man crouched in his chair, coiled and ready to spring, "I believe that's the case, yes."

Hack placed his left hand on his right elbow and brought up his right fist toward the greasy Magpie GM, who even curled into his chair in a thoroughly serpentine manner.

The old man wanted nothing more than to blow up at both of these assholes, to scream and shout and carry on to the point that he had a coughing fit. Then he'd personally kick Keith Myrick's ass in between full-body heaves and lurches until he had beaten the slimy bastard into submission. Hack allowed the fantasy to dominate his thoughts; he balled up his left fist and licked his lips.

Just as he was about to open his mouth, Hack had a better idea.

"Now, wait, I'm sure that Keith just misspoke. I didn't send no underaged kids to go get whiskey. Why in the sam *hell* would I do that? They wouldn't know the first thing about what they were doin'. Besides, Keith's their boss, and he'd *never* allow 'em to do such a thing. Would be downright negligent, and wouldn't look so good to a major league team iffin' he ever got the opportunity to interview with a big club, ain't that right, Keith?"

Myrick glared at Hack, and Hack responded in kind. The young Magpie GM scowled and shook his head; now it was his turn to appear ready to tackle the old coot and pound away on him until he sent him straight to hell, where, Keith thought, surely Satan already had a space at the V.I.P. Table reserved for the codger, right next to Hitler.

Instead, Myrick forced another bullshit smile.

"Oh, wait—you know what, George? Hack's right. I think the interns said something about 'we thought he was going to ask us to get whiskey,' probably just think ol' Hack here is a bit rough around he edges, but who the hell doesn't?"

There was a long pause on the other end of the line.

"Seriously?" George asked.

"I may be a dumbass sometimes, but I'm not *that* goddamned dumb," Hack said.

"Yeah, my fault, George. Must've just misspoke. I've been all outta sorts since my golf game got cut short this morning."

"I know how that goes," George responded. "Well, then there's the small matter of what Josh Stein tells me went on in the press box last night?"

Hack puffed his cheeks and pursed his lips, "Aw, hell, Georgie, it was just Engle and I givin' each other shit. Stein didn't have a dog in the fight 'til he created a big ruckus about it."

"That's not the way he tells it."

"Look, I know my language gets a bit…colorful sometimes. What does Stein want? An apology? Consider it done."

"Not just Stein; Country Engle wants one too."

Hack nearly pounded his fist on the cheap desk several times, but stopped just short of the chipped wood paneling surface.

"Fine—just fine," Hack said.

"Good. Now there's the matter of actually managing the team."

"God *damn* it, George, you of all people should know that I'm the fuckin' best in the biz!" This time, Hack's fist connected with the desk to accentuate "damn."

"You certainly were, and that's why I'm gonna' give you the opportunity to prove yourself. That was a tough one tonight, to be sure. But from a pure organizational perspective, we know we're rebuilding in Cleveland right now. A lot of those guys on the Magpies are legit prospects, some of the best we've had in years.

"I told Willie before the season started that we wanted them to come up through the system together, really forge 'em into not just one cohesive whole, but one that *wins*.

"Obviously, so far that hasn't been the case. I'm willing to give you a three game trial; win these next three games and we'll keep you on as manager. But lose one, and we give the team back to Willie."

Myrick looked toward Hack. He fully expected to see the geezer seeth at the mere suggestion that he have to prove himself.

Instead, the faintest hint of a grin washed over Hack's face as he nodded.

"Fine. Sure, I can do that."

"Win all three—no exceptions."

"God damn it, George, I'm old, not deaf. I'll sweep Palooka. No problem. But goddamn it, once I do, I expect to be left alone to manage the team as I see fit. No more meddlin' from Cleveland, and—" he looked at Keith, "—a short leash on Keith here, what with the 'misspeakin' and everythin'."

Myrick bristled at the suggestion, but didn't have a reply chambered and ready.

"Okay. Fair is fair. I think you've earned that, Hack. Win these three games and the team is yours for the rest of the year."

"Sounds good!" Myrick said, over-enthusiastically.

"Fine," Hack said. "Oh, and George? Yer' welcome fer' the attendance numbers we're gonna put up the next three games, too." He picked up the receiver and hammered it down again, but the red light on the phone remained illuminated. Hack began mashing buttons indiscriminately and grew flustered, "How the fuck do ya' turn this thing off?"

Myrick reached over casually and ended the call.

"Don't you *ever* extort me like that again, Hack! Are we—"

"Fuck yer'self," Hack replied. "I always knew you were a slippery little shit when you were runnin' around those clubhouses, blamin' your messes on the other kids. Maybe if you shut the fuck up and let me run this operation, you'll get outta this rinky-dink town and move up the ladder to somewhere you can fly to in somethin' other than a fuckin' crop-duster."

Myrick shook his head, "Let's just get one thing straight here, Hack; assuming you do win the next three games, make no mistake—*I'm* the one in charge here. Not you. Me."

"Whatever makes your dick look bigger in the mirror, Keith."

"You wanna' measure?"

"Give me a minute. The only thing that makes me hard anymore is these," Hack held his left fist, including the diamond and ruby-studded monstrosity of a ring out toward the GM.

"Men's jewelry?" Myrick asked.

"Rings, god *damn* it. Not that you'd know what one looked like. I got three more of 'em I can show ya."

"Any from this century?"

"Fuck off, Keith. You heard George—I win the next three, and it's my team."

"We'll see about that," Keith thrust himself out of the chair and marched toward the door.

"Just make sure that *when* I win these next three, you line someone up to get my provisions. Especially the Ol' Reliable."

Myrick didn't stop as the door slammed shut behind him.

Hack leaned back in his chair for a moment. He thought it odd that he hadn't had a coughing fit since right after his meeting with Willie earlier that day, but attributed it more to being able to enjoy copious amounts of Old Reliable unhindered than anything else.

Though Hack had brokered if not a peace treaty, then at least a cease fire among those involved, he was still sharp enough to realize that he'd need a backup plan in case the suits in Cleveland stuck their noses where they didn't belong.

As distasteful as the particulars of this plot were (the thought of what he was about to do chilled him to the core), Hack knew that he still had one trump card to play.

He forced himself out of the chair; the cartilage in his knees groaned and popped like rusty iron being cold-twisted. He stuttered out into the locker room, where Jim Taggert was wrapping up an exclusive interview with Truck Traynor.

"Thanks for the time, Truck."

"My pleasure, Mr. Taggert," Truck replied. "See you tomorrow, Coach."

"Traynor," Hack nodded. Truck walked strong and firm, like a bull comfortable on two legs, toward the clubhouse exit, and into the hallway that led to the parking lot.

"That's one helluva a ballplayer you got there, coach. Good kid, head's on straight. Solid upbringing."

"Yeah, well he's startin' from square one with me."

"He'll be at square twenty, soon enough," Taggert said.

"It's a ten square system, Jim," Hack said.

Taggert laughed.

Hack didn't.

"Anything I can do you for?" Taggert asked.

"Yeah. You got ten minutes?"

4

At exactly 7:55 the next morning, Hack stood in front of the assembled team on the field, using a bat as a makeshift cane.

"Lazy asses, the lot of 'em, Charles," Hack said.

"I think everyone's here, Coach. Right on time, too. I don't suffer tardiness well, either," Willie shook his head.

"Well...good then," Hack pulled his cap over his eyes. He took two steps forward to address the team, "Mornin' *la*-diesss..."

Hack expected some sort of reaction from the players, but was met by serious gazes.

He scowled and nodded once, curtly, "The way I run my practices is as follows: we start with a half hour of calisthenics, and a half hour of running..."

Still no reaction.

"...Then we split up into units: infield, outfield, and pitchers an' catchers go together. And we do *drills*, men. Fundamentals. Fielding, defense, throwing. Then, and only then, if I'm satisfied with what ya've done, then we hit.

"Unfortunately, you all hit like a bunch of candy-asses last night." This garnered a few chuckles from the pitchers, especially Mitch Henry. "So before we do anything else today, yer' gonna watch me take a few swings."

"Holy *shit*, this oughtta be good!" Henry whispered behind his glove at Murph Murphy.

"What was that, son?" Hack asked.

"What? I didn't say nothin'." Henry replied.

Hack narrowed his eyes at the Alabama farmboy, "You know what, Henry? I thought I'd like you. Thought we might be, how do ya' say, Charles? Kindred spirits?

"And, sure as shit, ya' pitched a hell of a game last night. Not your fault that babyface over here—" he pointed the bat at Stearns as he waddled over toward Henry, "—fucked things for ya'. But son, and please, take this in the best possible spirit it's intended, you have got a *fucking…attitude*…PROBLEM!"

It was all Henry could do to keep from laughing.

Hack butt-ended Henry with the bat, squarely in his gut.

Henry couldn't even howl; he doubled over in pain as the wind exploded from his lungs. Some of the suburbanites and Latinos guffawed with laughter as their erstwhile antagonizer writhed in pain.

"SHUT THE FUCK UP! I'll fuckin' do it again, swear to *God*!"

"To him?" Linus "Sid" Fynch asked. "'Cause if so, I'll laugh all fuckin'—"

"Don't you *dare* curse on my field!" Hack closed the fifteen feet between him and Fynch with surprising alacrity as he brought the bat down sharply on the centerfielder's left calf, which caused Fynch to drop to his knees before he grabbed back for his leg.

Most of the players immediately ceased, though Pete Moray ran over to the Latin players who didn't speak English to interpret.

"You're *psycho*, man!" Fynch yelled. "I'm gonna call my parents and have them *sue* you!"

"No yer' not!" Hack screamed back. "You know why? 'Cause what judge—most've 'em elderly, mind you—is gonna' believe that an eighty-four-year-old man hit a strappin' young man like yer'self with a bat? Worst comes to worst, I can just pretend like I don't know what the hell day it is—" Hack affected a disoriented, meek tone, "Oh, sorry yer' Honor, thought he was one'a the gnomes who's been stealin' my glasses. He'll understand!"

Most of the players' furrowed brows and tilted heads indicated that they most certainly did not.

Hack shook his head, "Never mind that. Pete—throw me a few, would ya'?"

Moray nodded and jogged toward the batting practice screen, which had seen better days. It was a tangled mess of dirty, knotted, replacement nylon that sagged into a paunch on the frame from taking too many comebackers.

"Now, we're gonna' win the next three games come hell or high water, or both. Even *God* his'self isn't gonna stop us from gettin' these." Hack's cheeks glowed red as he struggled to keep his words from slurring. "And you know *why*, men? Because I'm yer' goddamned manager, and I can still hit a home run at age eighty-four."

"Bull-*shit*" Henry whispered as Hack approached the batter's box.

"You wanna' 'nother?" Hack asked. He waved his bat at Henry.

Henry cringed and shook his head, his usually cocky, beaming face drained of its omnipresent smug, jocular smile.

"Awright then. Let'r rip, Pete!"

Hack raised the white ash stick above his right shoulder, which creaked with the strain of worn tendon on bone. He squinted at Pete, whose arm moved effortlessly through the crisp, spring Ohio morning.

Pete's hand released the dingy batting practice ball a half-beat past its apex in the fresh sky. Hack tracked the off-white orb (one of three, to his ancient, booze-addled eyes) as it appeared to dip and dance through the air and toward the plate.

Hack took a mighty cut, but connected only with the air as the force of his swing torqued him to one knee.

Mitch Henry couldn't help but muffle a snicker, along with several of his teammates.

Even Willie had to bring a hand to his face to cover the broad smile that developed.

"Goddamn it, Pete—no breaking balls!"

"I—" Moray ceased protesting as soon as Hack took a step toward the screen, even though the assistant coach tried to lob it in as straight and gently as he could.

"Sorry," instead he shook his head.

"Here we go—let's try that again. No making a damned fool'a me this time, Pete!"

Hack dug in once more. He was less than half as tall as the twelve foot batting cage, and his head barely topped the layer of vulcanized rubber that bore the brunt of most errant pitches and foul tips.

He kneaded the bat in his coarse, weathered hands as Moray lackadaisically started his smooth, abbreviated motion.

The ball flew out of Moray's hand in a slower arc, and though all three appeared to Hack once more, this time he singled out the one in the middle, put a swing on it, and connected with the bottom of the ball.

A loud "thump" resonated through the empty (if cozy, by professional standards) stadium as the foul tip hit the rubber backing of the cage.

Several of the players offered a smattering of mock applause, though some, including Truck Traynor, were legitimately impressed that the old coot had even made contact.

"Awright, damn it, one more. No monkey business, Pete. A little more heat now."

Moray widened his eyes and fixed them on his peculiar little new boss.

Hack stared back, unblinking.

Pete shrugged and grabbed another ball out of the five gallon paint bucket at his feet. He began his throwing motion, more deliberate this time as his tongue peeked through his lips and curled upward.

Hack steadied the bat. His mind went blank; even whatever drivel Mitch Henry spewed at the moment was lost as Hack found himself in the familiar sanctuary that was his mind on baseball.

This time, though the orb was blurry out of Pete's hand, there was only one of them. Hack's lips curled into a smile as his mind raced to calculate the trajectory of the ball. Pete had put a little mustard on it this time, and it sailed toward Hack in far less of an arc than the coach's previous offering.

Hack raised his left foot off the ground. He ignored the desperate pleas of the joint to be left at rest as he brought his weight back down upon it and pivoted his back foot, which threw both of his artificial hips toward the screen.

His hands chopped down at the ball as he rotated his right hand underneath the bat and leveled it at the sphere's flight path toward the plate.

"CRACK!"

Hack gritted his teeth and crumpled in pain, the muscles in his back alight with an awful, sharp searing like a branding iron cutting through flesh.

He collected himself and turned right toward the left field stands. The ball flew through the air, majestically defying gravity as it shot upward through the outfield. It hung for a brief moment, a small satellite over left field before it began its downward trajectory, over the fence, and into the second row of bleachers.

Pete Moray's jaw nearly came unhinged. He processed what had just happened for several moments before he broke into a broad grin.

Willie simply shook his head and smirked.

The rest of the team was dumbfounded. It was perhaps the first time in his twenty-one years that Mitch Henry was speechless.

"Dios mio," Manny Poblado remarked, the words awe-filled enough to be directed at Hack.

Truck Traynor let out a cheer.

Sid Fynch followed suit.

Soon, the entire team was hooting and hollering at what the old man had just done. Even the groundskeepers tending to the small bald patches in right field stood up and gave Hack an ovation.

By the time the screaming pain in his back had calmed to an acceptable level, Hack was the only one still on a knee.

He didn't so much as doff his cap at the outpouring of support; instead, he steadied himself with the bat and pushed himself up to his feet. Though the pain was still present, it was subsumed beneath his genuine wonder at what he had just accomplished.

Not that he hadn't expected to hit the home run, but rather that he was able to focus on the ball in doing so.

For the first time since he joined the Magpies, Hack limped visibly as he left the batters box, his back a twisted mess of knots and stiff muscles.

"*That's* why you should listen to me, gentlemen. Sheer willpower. I ain't sayin' that I could play second base tonight, but damn it, I can still will myself to hit a tater every now and then. It's beyond 'wanna' and 'gonna,' and well past 'shoulda.' No, men, it's gettin' shit *done*. Of doin' the improbable. Of convincin' everyone in this goddamned stadium of what I already know; that we can be a winnin' baseball team.

"So, men, I ask ya's: who's ready for practice?"

5

"Manny," Pete Moray pointed at the Magpies' starting shortstop.

"Qué?" Manny Poblado replied.

"Jefe quiere verte." Moray said. He nodded toward Hack, who was doing his best to conceal the horrible pain in his back by the batting cage.

Manny's eyes widened as he tapped his hand on his chest three times.

"Sí. Ahora." Pete deadpanned.

Manny looked at his double-play partner, the newly-christened "Flash" Gamble, who gritted his teeth and raised his eyebrows.

"Sí...sí..." Manny jogged over toward his ailing new manager, who fiddled with the top to a bottle of pills.

"Goddamned childproofing..." Hack cursed to no one in particular. He wrenched the cap off the track and sucked down a mouthful of pills before he turned to the shaking, wide-eyed shortstop.

"There ya' are, Manny. Hab-las English?" Hack asked.

"Sí, err...yes, señor—Coach."

Hack nodded, "Good. Very good." He struggled to remain composed as his back felt like it was being pulled in five different directions. "Now Manny, I noticed last night, how should I put this? Ya' swing like my second wife."

"Señor?" Manny asked.

"Yer' leanin' on yer' front foot too much, ya' barely pivot, and Christ, even if ya' *do* manage to make contact, your wrists flop over so that everything is a tailor-made double play ball to the left side of the infield. Second wife did the exact same thing."

Manny tilted his head; apparently the octogenarian's joke was lost on him.

"Regardless, yer' way too outta' sorts fer' me to fix what ya' got goin' on there with the herky-jerky *bull*shit. I may be a hell of a manager, but I can't work goddamned miracles, son. Understand?"

Manny nodded.

"Listen to me carefully: you will never make the majors as a shortstop. Yer' glove's okay, but not good enough to make up for that awful bat'a yours, awright?"

Manny hung his head.

"Now, lotta' coaches would have ya' on the first plane back to Mexico. But—"

"Santo Domingo," Manny whispered.

"I don't care what part'a Mexico yer' from, son. I'm sure Keith or someone in the front office would—"

"Santo Domingo. República Dominicana—the Dominican Republic."

"Christ almighty—do you wanna go back there?" Hack smacked Manny's lowered hat bill, "I'm tryin' to explain somethin' to ya', son, so let me finish. Now, like I said, ya' ain't gonna make the majors as a shortstop. But son, I've seen a lot of great arms in my day. I managed Steve Carlton with the Phillies and Tom Seaver with the Reds fer' a few years. But damn if you don't have a little more giddyup on yer' throws than even they did."

Manny adjusted the brim of his hat and cocked his head upward slightly.

"Pitch?" Manny asked.

Hack motioned toward the right field bullpen, "Traynor! Get over here!" he winced as his core muscles screamed.

Truck Traynor nodded and nearly sprinted toward the cage.

"Yes, Coach O'Callahan?" Traynor asked. He shot a glance and a nod at Manny, who smiled shyly in reply.

"Get behind the plate, and let's see what Manny here has from the mound, okay?"

"Yes, sir," Traynor said. He put on his hockey-style catcher's mask and crouched into his familiar squat behind the plate.

Hack held out a ball toward Manny, "Awright, just get up on that mound and let'er rip at Truck over there, okay?"

Manny looked at Truck, who already was smacking his mitt several times to form the pocket exactly as he preferred it.

"Okay, señor jefe," Manny grabbed the ball in Hack's hand.

"Coach." Hack didn't release it.

"Qué?"

"Coach jefe, Coach O'Callahan. Just Coach."

"Okay…Coach," Manny half-swallowed the words. Hack finally let go, and Manny took the ball to the mound.

"Hey Charles!" Hack yelled at Willie, who was instructing outfielders.

Willie pretended he couldn't hear him.

"Christ…" Hack looked toward the dugout. His eyes caught the shiny red brilliance of Sam Rappaport's short, but tasteful, hair. "You there—girly!"

Samantha dropped the binders she carried on the bench, took a deep breath, and narrowed her eyes toward Hack.

"Yes, Coach?" she affected an overbroad smile.

"Grab the radar gun in the equipment room and hold it for Manny here, wouldya?"

She took a step backward, "You want me…on the field?"

"God damn it, if you're gonna' start pullin' that women's lib shit on me, then I can get the Pollack to do it—"

"No, no—I'll be right there!" She scampered down the tunnel toward the clubhouse.

Hack leaned one arm on the batting cage. His other hand steadied himself on the bat that had been used to assault Mitch Henry, "Sid" Fynch, and the third baseball thrown his way earlier that morning.

Hack noticed that Traynor was still in a crouch.

"You gonna' stay like that all day, son?"

Truck shrugged, "I'm more comfortable crouchin' than I am standin', Coach."

Hack's gaze turned toward Manny, who paced on the mound, "Tell me if ya' feel the same way sixty-five years from now," he muttered through gritted teeth.

"Got it!" Samantha emerged from the tunnel with glee. She held a standard Jugs radar gun in her right hand.

"Awright, now you gotta' calibrate it with the—"

"Tuning fork?" Samantha completed Hack's sentence. "Already done—standard eighty-five on the dot."

"Well...uh...good! Good on ya', missy!" Hack removed his hat and rubbed a hand over his bald head, which caused him to recoil in pain.

Hack staggered sideways for several seconds before the talons of his claw-like hand gripped the netting of the cage and steadied him.

He looked at Samantha, on the far side of the cage, and Truck, who had both turned to see the source of the commotion.

Hack ignored them, "Okay, Manny, let's see what ya' got. Don't even bother with a windup er' nothin', just rock and fire, hit Truck's mitt, okay?"

Manny nodded. Several beads of sweat cascaded off of his face. He tugged on the brim of his cap, ball in hand, as he brought his hands together. He dropped his long, lithe arm toward the ground as his leg muscles contracted and formed an "L" shape underneath him.

He brought his arm straight over the top of his shoulder, a perfect, barely perceptible circle in the blur of easy movement.

Hack couldn't pinpoint where Manny released the ball, nor where it traveled. The only acknowledgement that the ball had found its target was the loud "THWACK" of leather-on-leather that ball-in-glove produced.

The corners of Hack's mouth raised imperceptibly. It was a pure sound, a noise he hadn't heard in years, one that signaled that his instincts hadn't failed him.

He looked at Samantha, who stared at the gun's readout, mouth agape. She shook her head and blinked, thinking that the numbers were a mistake, that they might somehow disappear since there was no way they could be real.

"102..." she gasped.

Truck removed his mitt and fanned his hand out, limp as he sucked in air.

Manny was locked in, his narrow eyes still fixed on Truck long after the catcher had stood up.

Both men broke into broad smiles.

Hack smirked, "Congratulations, Manny; startin' tonight, yer' our new closer."

Manny beamed and shrugged at Truck. The catcher pointed back toward his pitcher.

"I'm gonna need a thicker mitt..." Truck laughed.

Third Inning

1

"You're doing *what*?" Willie asked Hack as the men got undressed in the coaches' locker room.

"You heard me. Poblado's our new closer."

"The *fuck* he is!" Willie shouted loudly enough that he hoped the rest of the team could hear in the clubhouse.

"What does it matter to ya', Willie? You wanna' win games, ain't it?"

"What kind of a damned *fool* question is that?" Willie yelled.

"I couldn't tell based on yer' record's all…" Hack said.

Willie bit his lip.

"You wanna' waltz in here, take over my clubhouse for a year, teach me the 'ins and outs,' whatever the hell that means? That's fine.

"But when you make long-term positional changes of prospects who, by the way, are under Cleveland's control without consulting me or them, *that's* downright irresponsible! Who's gonna play shortstop now? Hadn't thought'a that one did—"

"I think we should shift Flash over to short."

"Who?"

"*El*-drake. Gamble. You know, poindexter in the corner. Friedmann can take over at second."

"Eldrake's too tall to play short!" Willie stood up and wrapped a towel around himself.

"If I had a nickel fer' every time I heard some bullshit scout's excuse like that…" Hack followed suit, though the towel nearly dragged along the ground.

"You're already a goddamned millionaire!" Willie grew agitated.

"My ex-wives are millionaires. I'm just some old codger who was eatin' canned vegetables and watchin' ESPN until I broke my goddamned TV set."

Willie shook his head, "Serves ya' right, you damned fool."

Hack gritted his teeth, "Look, one thing you gotta' understand, Charles, is that the scouts are full'a shit. I'm sure that comin' up, you were a young, strappin' athletic guy who had scouts' peckers harder than petrified oak when they came to see you.

"But I wasn't. And I understand that sometimes, all'a talent in the world ain't able to overcome a player's shit-fer'-brains. This Gamble kid can hit a bit more, and I think he can be just as good defensively as Manny was. Now, he doesn't have that same cannon, but if you and Pete work with him," Moray interjected a hearty spit of tobacco juice in assent, "I think you end up with a better shortstop for the Indians, *and* a damned good closer fer' 'em in a coupla' years, too."

Willie tilted his head in toward Hack, his slitted eyes focused on the old man.

"Besides, if I'm wrong, we'll lose one'a the next three and you'll have the team back anyway."

Another pause.

"I guess you're right…" Willie said.

"Christ! I *knew* it! I knew that snake-eyed fuck Myrick told you!"

"What now?" Willie asked.

"About the next three games. That sonofabitch would sell his own mother if he thought he'd get two bits fer' her!"

"What was the alternative?" Willie took a step toward Hack. "Let me hang in the breeze? Treat me like the help? 'Oh, Willie, turns out we need you to manage after all.' 'Sure thin', boss!'" Willie waved with a facetious smile for effect.

"Here we go again…" Hack said as he waddled away from his locker.

"I *told* him—" Hack stopped as Willie's tone grew instructive; the former manager looked around the room before he whispered, "—I told him that I don't plan on managing this season. 'Cause I think you're gonna *win* these three games, Hack. The players respond to you. And much as I hate it, I think they *get* you, in a way that I don't even understand yet."

Hack's lip quivered. For once, he didn't know what to say, so he simply remained silent and limped toward the door of the coaches' locker room that led to the clubhouse.

"Where're you going?" Willie asked.

"We gotta' trainin' staff, don't we? I'm gonna see if they can't rub me down before I get a soak. My back is killin' me."

Willie shook his head.

"And one more thing, Charles? Tell the sharp girl to meet me in my office afterward."

"The sharp girl?"

"Yeah, you know, the good-lookin' one with the red hair."

Hack struggled the twenty feet down the hallway and lurched himself into the training room. He inhaled deeply; the room smelled of Flex-all, Icy Hot, and a combination of other muscle rubs that came off as horrifically medicinal to most.

Hack found the odor to be utterly intoxicating and welcoming.

"Hi there," a muscular man with long, blond hair and a healthy beard welcomed Hack with a broad smile. "Come to see your grandson? I'll bet you're proud, maaaan!"

"Jesus Christ," Hack said, "we have a moron for a trainer."

The blond man shook his head, "Uh, I know a lot of fans like to say 'we' and 'us' all the time, but it's kinda disrespectful to the guys actually *on* the team like me, okay?"

Hack balled his fists and trembled, "I…am…your…manager…" He spoke loudly and slowly, so as to force the words into the dolt's head.

The blond man laughed, "You aren't Willie, maaan!"

Hack faked a calm, tight smile, "No, I'm certainly *not*. I'm Hack O'Callahan, the *new* manager. I'll be here for the rest of the season."

"Really? Like, seriously? Hang on a minute..." the blond man took several large steps into the hallway and toward the coaches' locker room.

"Hey Willie?" He ducked his head inside. "There's some...Hack...guy...says he's the manager now?"

Hack couldn't hear Willie's reply, but it sounded harsh and curt.

"Oh. Okay," he lumbered back toward the training room. "Sorry about that, uh, Hack, sir. I'm Randy Edwardson, the trainer."

"You don't say?"

"Yessir." Hack's sarcasm was lost somewhere behind the trainer's vacant blue eyes. "Sorry about that there, just, you know—"

"Stop yer' fuckin' *yammerin'*!" Hack brought his hand back as if to slap the hulking Scandinavian's face, but was met with a disarming grin.

"Right on," Edwardson chuckled. "So...what can I do ya' for?"

"I wrenched the hell outta' my back, and I was wonderin' if I could get a rub and a soak."

"Sure thing, bud," Edwardson patted the table next to him.

"And pills?" Hack asked. "You got any'a those pain pills? I'm fresh out."

"Sure, I'll give ya' all you want, but I can do ya' one better," Edwardson said. He opened a nearby drawer and removed a syringe filled with a clear liquid. The trainer removed the plastic tip and squirted a short stream of liquid out of the hypodermic needle. He smiled before something jarred and stiffened him.

"You're not...afraid of needles, are you?"

"No, no!" Hack bellowed at the trainer. "Just...get it over with already!"

Edwardson shrugged and plunged the needle into Hack's back. Hack muffled a yelp as warmth flooded and throbbed around the source of the pain. With each beat, the searing discomfort became a little bit less noticeable and more manageable.

"That's pretty nice there. Good work, Edwardson..." Hack sighed deeply; he didn't much know or care whether the trainer knew that it was about as powerful of a compliment as the coot ever paid.

Randy clapped his hands and rubbed them together, "My pleasure. Now, just relax a bit and let's see if we can't make things *all* better for ya, m'kay?"

Edwardson's powerful hands kneaded and pulled Hack's weary muscles. By any earthly measure, Hack should've been on edge on the eve of the most important series of the rest of his life.

But heavy lids fell over his bloodshot eyes as the tension in his back slowly eased its way out of the much-abused muscles, and he dozed peacefully off to sleep.

2

Hack toweled off after a long soak in the training room. Edwardson had long ago left, only after he made himself clear that Hack was to come in for treatment every day for the next month.

Hack would've normally protested the advice of anyone even tangentially connected with medicine or wellness, but he'd make an exception for Edwardson given that he could now towel off his back, a near-unimaginable feat mere minutes before.

Hack figured he was "clean enough," and shuffled down the empty hallway toward the manager's office. The damp towel drooped around his midsection.

He opened the door and found a curly-haired blonde girl with round, hungry eyes sitting in his chair, wearing little more than a teal halter top, a transparent scarf tied provocatively around her neck so as to accentuate her ample cleavage, and some beguilingly tiny cut-off shorts.

"Lemme guess…yer' the janitor?"

She laughed airily and leaned back in the chair.

"My, my, the rumors *are* true. *The* Hack O'Callahan, come all the way out to lil' ol' Hoplite to manage the Magpies."

"Equipment manager?" Hack asked.

Another lilting laugh.

"No, silly. I'm Meadow Dressel, Truck Traynor's girlfriend," she jumped out of the chair and caressed the old man's shoulder. "Though we do have a bit of an 'open relationship.'" Her cooing, slight southern accent would've driven more virile men wild.

"Girly, you're barkin' up the wrong tree. I think the only thing that'd get me hot n' bothered right about now would be a three game winning streak. Even then, you wouldn't have the first clue what ta' do with me."

"Oh, I know more than you think, Roger 'Hack' O'Callahan," she playfully picked up the scarf and wagged it in Hack's face before he waved it away. "Born April 1, 1930 in Springfield, Illinois. Bumped around in the minors for a while before you were called over to Korea to fight in—"

"Whattaya want?" Hack crossed his arms.

"My, my, somebody's grumpy. 'Course they always said you were a—how did it go again? 'Ornery old cuss who smiled about as regularly as he plum took off and flew,' which is to say rarely, unless a reporter asked you a sufficiently dumbass question."

Hack smirked briefly before his eyes burned on Meadow.

"So…?"

"So, I'm just an admirin' fan—" she batted her eyelashes at him, "—both of the Magpies and of *you*."

"I told ya' already, I got enough problems with my ex-wives, that I don't need—"

She laughed again, "I'm just messin' with ya', Coach! Even if you *would* be a nice lil'," she looked toward Hack's crotch, "notch for my belt. No, the reason I'm here is because I wanted to make sure that we were on the same page about Truck and his playin' time."

"What about it?" Hack asked. "Did he put you up to this? 'Cause if he did, I'll—"

She giggled, "No, silly! Truck would *shit* if he knew I was here. No, I have a bit'uva 'reputation' 'round these parts fer bein' the 'Annie Savoy' of the team."

Hack maintained his focused stare.

"Oh, don't tell me you of *all* people haven't seen *Bull Durham*."

"I' seen it," Hack said, jaw jutting out. "It was okay; too many mushy parts fer' my likin'.'"

"But the love story is *crucial*!"

"I ain't talkin' about the love story; I was talkin' about Crash gettin' all dewey-eyed at that big dumbshit pitcher. Known too many'a both."

Meadow smiled mischievously, "S'pose you could say the same'a me. I've been huntin' myself a husband for the past five years since I graduated from Baucomb empty-handed. If that means I have to spread these," she smacked herself loudly on the thigh and gasped, "a little more than other, nicer girls, so be it.

"Thing is, I think I finally found a keeper in Truck. Everyone knows he's got big leagues written all over him; he's gonna' be a star in Cleveland, then in New York once his rookie contract's up. Bein' a ballplayer's wife suits me well, and when I see you fuckin' around with the lineup, puttin' *Manny Poblado* in as a pitcher, well, I start to worry about Truck and my future."

"How the hell did you get into my—?"

"The groundskeeper, Lenny Sims. He and I had—" she grabbed one of her golden curls and twirled it around a finger, "—a bit of a thing. I watched it all from the outfield, just past the 'Hal's Steakhouse' sign in right."

Hack's relaxed back muscles tensed. His face reddened as he struggled to keep his anger at bay.

"You listen here, sweetheart, and you listen good. *I* don't tell *you* how to go around fuckin' half the town. So when it comes to managin' *my club*, you leave all'a that to me, got it?"

As Hack built up to his thundering crescendo, his back yelped for the first time since Edwardson had monkeyed it into shape. He reached toward the throbbing part of his lower back, but it only intensified the pain throughout the rest.

Meadow offered a spry chuckle as she leaned in toward Hack, "You listen to *me*, old man. I'm not some little girl who's gonna be scared by 'big, bad Hack.' I know how feeble you are, you old cuss, and if you ever, *ever* try to pull a stunt like that with my Truck, all'a your enemies an' I'll get ta' diggin' your grave and see that you make your way in there toot suite. Understand?"

She pulled a pair of oversized sunglasses from a rear pocket on the tiny shorts and snapped them to her face. She walked slowly, seductively; her hips swayed from side-to-side as she pushed the door to let herself into the hallway of the clubhouse.

"Was that a threat?" Hack asked. He staggered to the door, unable to keep up with Meadow. "'Cause if it was, get in fuckin' line! I've only ever hit two…" he looked upward in thought, "…three women before, and that was fer' hittin' me in barfights. I'll make it four, no sweat, especially if it's some whor——"

He didn't finish the word before a coughing fit set in. The towel dropped from around Hack's midsection to reveal him in all of his overweight, liver-spotted glory.

Meadow looked over her shoulder and laughed, a deep, cruel laugh at the pathetic man who trailed her. She gave a casual wave as she exited the clubhouse.

Hack fell to his knees, doubled over in pain. Each expulsion of air punished him with a sharp tearing in his back. The blood trickled from his mouth onto the concrete floor where it pooled for a moment before it flowed, a lazy river of suffering, into the drain.

Hack writhed on the floor until the fit stopped. He picked up the damp, musty towel and used it to clean up his mouth and chin. He rocked onto his side, and struggled to push himself upright.

Just when Hack was about ready to quit and sleep on the concrete floor for the evening, he felt a warm, fresh towel fall over his shoulders. The vaguely florid scent of dryer sheets covered up the dank odors of sweat-soaked garments baked into the concrete.

Hack looked up to find Samantha Rappaport, hand outstretched, a wan smile on her face.

He grimaced, "I don't need yer' help, missy. Just leave me——"

"What? Naked? On the floor? Come on, Mr. O'Callahan…" she grabbed his hand and hoisted him up. Hack's back bellowed with pain as the towel remained on his shoulders, but allowed most of his hideous body to remain uncovered.

Samantha took another towel, draped over her left forearm, and threw it at Hack. He instinctively caught it and wrapped it around his waist.

"What in the *hell* are you doin' still around here?" Hack asked.

Samantha grinned, "You're welcome, Mr. O'Callahan."

"Seriously. Pretty girl like you should have all kinds'a dates."

"On a Thursday night? I'm not that awful Meadow Dressel, if that's what you're trying to imply."

"Then why in the *hell* would you wanna work fer' a baseball team? A shitty one like this, ta' boot?"

Sam wrinkled her nose, "Did it ever occur to you that I might actually appreciate the game? That I might enjoy the wonderful, pastoral pace? The roar of the crowd whenever 'their guy' hits a bomb or steals third? Or maybe it's because it's the ultimate game of cat-and-mouse, making all of those strategic decisions based on mountains of data, sometimes cast aside by some surly old cuss's 'hunch.'"

She leveled her eyes at his as she finished the final sentence. She offered a kind grin and a chuckle.

Hack's eyes widened. The corners of his lips formed a slight, almost-imperceptible smile.

"Okay, so maybe yer' a fan'a the game. I'll give ya' that. But why help a 'surly old cuss' when he's on his back like a goddamn turtle, hackin' up half-a-lung?"

"Earlier today, when you let me out on the field with that radar gun," her eyes welled up, "that was the nicest thing anyone's ever done for me. Professionally, I mean. Most've the guys around here are just trying to humiliate me, or fuck me, or both."

Hack raised an eyebrow at the attractive redhead's curse.

She spasmed as the first tear ran down her cheek.

"But you...you let me out on the field. To do something scouting-related. To be involved with a decision that *you* made. It was...it was *awesome*. It felt so good for someone to cast aside their preconceived notions about what I might be or what I was looking for, for someone to let me—"

"Fer' Chrissake," Hack rolled his eyes, "All I needed was someone ta' hold the goddamned radar gun!"

Sam wiped the vaguely purple, barely mascara-tinged tear tracks from her eyes and took a deep breath.

"I know. I'm sorry, it's unprofessional. You're right." She nodded and offered a tight grin. "But thank you, Mr. O'Callahan. I can only hope to gain your trust to the point where you'll allow me to continue to expand my responsibilities."

Hack looked upward again, "You wanna' hold the radar gun during the game tomorrow?"

Sam's expression brightened, "Seriously? Would you let me?"

"Sure, sure. Maybe if yer' lucky, I'll let ya' collect all'a the balls after b.p., too."

"Oh, thank you! Thank you Mr. O'Callahan! This is…really a dream come true."

"If holdin' radar guns and pickin' old men up off'a locker room floors is yer' idea of a dream, I don't even wanna hear what yer' nightmares are like."

Sam laughed warmly.

Hack wiped a tear away from her cheek.

"Now go on—get on outta here. Folks're gonna start thinkin' you and I are an item 'er somethin'." He turned and shuffled toward the manager's office.

She laughed again, "Thank you, Mr. O'Callahan!"

He extended a hand back toward her without even looking.

"Don't mention it."

3

The Magpies enjoyed a 4-3 lead entering the bottom of the ninth inning against the Palooka Princehens in front of a packed-house crowd.

It had helped that Jim Taggert had run a piece in the Hoplite Herald that morning (headline: "Hack Finds a Home in Hoplite"), where Hack aggrandized his love for the small college town, and all of the residents ("'specially the fellow elderly folks," Hack had been quoted as saying) he had met thus far, even if he hadn't actually set foot outside of the stadium since he drunkenly blew into town two days before.

The article also hinted at a "heartwarming reunion" for the aging manager, with "more to come in Saturday's column."

Following his most vicious coughing fit to date, Hack had heavily self-medicated with a concoction he called a "Mean S.O.B.": Equal parts Old Reliable whiskey and Robitussin, chased with a couple of vicodin. He had been cooking up the things for weeks, but only now decided that they ceased to take on the heavy, medicinal taste of the Robitussin, and instead went down easily, almost like sodapop.

Hack struggled up the dugout steps and stuck out his right arm. He tapped his elbow three times, and Manny Poblado nodded as he reared back and fired his final warmup. The bullpen catcher yelped as the pellet rang his glove with a loud "THWACK."

If Manny was nervous, he didn't show as much. The familiar, care-free smile was plastered on his face. His eyes looked to be positively dancing with joy.

It was almost as if the converted shortstop relished the opportunity for a new challenge, something at which he could truly excel. He signed with the Indians out of their Dominican academy when he was sixteen, never imagining that he'd have the opportunity to make money playing baseball.

He hit a road block at Hoplite, where most of his teammates, true to the city, only made short stops on their way to washing out or making the majors. Manny had been on the Magpies for three years, and though he was a "capable" shortstop, he knew that unless he improved his glove or (especially) his bat, he was doomed to grind out a livable, if meager, existence until the organization let him go.

Now, with this oddest of old men's arrival in Hoplite, his career had new life. Manny wanted to prove his worth, that he had *value* in a sport that venerated skills and "God-given ability," whatever that meant.

He bounded to the mound and went through his warmups quickly. After each pitch, he bounced with energy, nervous and excited to face the first batter.

Murmurs tore through the packed-house crowd: why in the *hell* was the shortstop coming in to close the game? Where was Tommy Stearns? Aside from sulking in the bullpen, the deposed closer's narrowed eyes focused past Poblado into the dugout at the old man on the steps.

Hack shot daggers right back at him.

"Here ya' go now, Manny. Whattaya' say, kid? Whattaya' say now?" Hack clapped three times to punctuate his chatter.

Terry Simon stepped into the box. The hulking Palooka cleanup hitter shot a long line of dip juice onto the ground and made a point to grind the spittle into the thick layer of dirt as he steadied the bat over his back shoulder.

Manny bent over, glove on his left knee. He looked in for a sign. Truck shook his head and shrugged; Manny couldn't throw anything but a fastball. The star catcher put the obligatory one finger down.

Manny grinned and nodded. He came set in the stretch position and took a deep breath. He broke his hands over his knee and reached straight back, his arm a fulcrum exerting almost inhuman force on the ball.

His hand came over his shoulder and shot toward the plate.

"BOOM!"

The ball hit Truck's newly-reinforced mitt with authority.

"Stee-RIIIKE One!" The umpire bellowed.

Simon shot a glance back at Truck.

"This kid's for real, huh?"

"Aw, shit, I dunno, Terry," Truck settled into his crouch and looked toward the mound. "Sometimes I wonder myself."

Truck gave Manny his sign. The newly-minted pitcher nodded and came set before he delivered the ball again.

This time, Simon flailed wildly at the ball, and missed it by a good half-foot.

"Stee-RIIIKE Two!"

Truck chuckled; it even seemed like the umpire was getting juiced up by the fireballing righty; he added a *Naked Gun*-like flourish to his calls.

Hack looked over toward Samantha in the stands behind the plate. She held the radar gun in her left hand but flashed three numbers in succession on her fingers on the right.

"1...0...4..."

Hack allowed himself a grin.

"It'd help if I could see it," Terry snorted.

"Hey, at least you don't have to catch it."

"You better, son," the Umpire interjected. "I've got a family to think about."

The three exchanged half-assed chuckles as Truck readied himself for Manny's third offering. He noticed that Simon started his pronounced leg kick and "hitch" in his swing before Manny even released the ball.

It didn't matter.

Simon swung and fell to one knee as he failed to come close to connecting.

"Stee-RIIIKE Three!" The umpire pumped Simon out. Terry shook his head as he returned to the dugout.

"Buena suerte, Pedro," he said to the man striding toward the plate.

"Pedro" was Pedro Asención, the "five tool" second baseman for the Princehens, so-called because he possessed all five "tools" that scouts so covet in ballplayers: the ability to hit for batting average, hit for power, run lightning-fast around the bases, field his position well, and throw like a cannon shoots.

Truck removed his mask and stood up, his eyes wide. He held out both hands in front of him and pushed at the air in a "settle down" motion.

Manny's eyes narrowed, any previous joy drained from them. He nodded and took the mound.

Truck settled into his crouch. Before he replaced his mask, he hocked a generous loogy toward Asención's feet.

Pedro kicked it right back at him.

Truck put down the sign. Manny nodded solemnly, reared back, and fired.

The ball came in high and tight, around the chin. Asención spun away from the near-miss and glared at Poblado.

Manny stared right back.

Truck hit his mitt a couple of times and flashed his pointer finger again.

Manny nodded. He came set, started his motion, and delivered.

This time, Manny didn't miss. Asención yelped and crumpled in pain. The ball had hit him squarely on the left buttock.

The Princehens' manager bolted to the top of the steps and took two steps toward the Magpies' dugout.

"You fuckin' chickenshit, Hack! That's a piece of shit move, you fuckin' fossil!"

Hack grinned broadly and shrugged.

"Fuckin' wise ass. This ain't over…" the Princehens' manager offered ominously.

"Fuck you!" Hack shot back. "You take one'a ours? We'll hit three more'a yours!" He extended a middle finger to punctuate the sentiment.

Mitch Henry laughed softly at the far end of the dugout.

Asencíon picked himself up and glared toward Manny. Manny met his stare with a ferocious, icy look of his own. Pedro grabbed his bat halfway from the knob and carried it with him toward first, daring Manny to come at him.

Truck rushed out of his crouch and put himself between the two, who shouted Spanish curses at one another.

"Vete y chinga tu padre!" Pedro shouted.

Manny hit his chest three times and stuck his arms out wide.

"Dar por culo!" Manny yelled back.

"Get your ass to first!" Truck was resolute as he followed Asencíon down the line. "I'm sick of your shit!"

Pedro looked at the stocky, muscular catcher and decided the better of settling his feud with Manny at that moment.

Once Asencíon was safely at first, Truck asked for time and jogged out to the mound.

"Settle down," he said.

"I had to, Camión."

"I know. But that's done. Get outta' this mess. You don't wanna let Hack down, do you?"

Manny looked toward the dugout and saw Hack, grinning from ear-to-ear.

He shook his head.

"Good. Now maybe take a little bit off this next one. I have an idea."

Manny nodded and Truck jogged back behind the plate. The next batter, Ron "Scooter" Herman, his catching counterpart on the Princehens, already was settled into the lefty batter's box.

"How's it goin', Scoot?"

"Not so bad. Sorry they're gonna plunk ya' tomorrow, Truck."

"Ah, it's nothin' I can't handle. I'd be a lot more worried if I was you. This guy can bring it."

"I noticed," Herman turned his attention toward the mound.

"Well look out. The guy's gone nuts. Said he's gonna tear a fuckin' hole through my glove on this next one. Wants to get the crowd worked up—you know how it is, right? Nerves and everything?"

Herman looked back toward Truck.

"I know you aren't stealin' signs, since you know he's only got one. Here, I'll save you the trouble." Truck put his index finger in front of his chest protector for all to see. "You see? Everyone knows what's comin'. Let's see what you can do with it."

Manny came set. The sweat pooled on his forehead and dripped off the brim of his hat. He started his motion, reared back, and brought his arm forward.

This time, the torque on his arm was merely "ordinary," and the ball glided out of his arm, easy as a wiffleball.

Scooter tried to adjust, but he had already committed to swinging. He lunged feebly at the off-speed pitch and barely was able to get the bat on the top half of the ball.

He turned his wrists over and bounced an easy grounder to second. Nev Friedmann, the Magpies' new second baseman, collected the ball...

...and bobbled it.

A groan cascaded through the crowd.

Everyone exhaled as the shaky second baseman corralled the white leather sphere and flipped it to Flash Gamble, who was already waiting at second.

Asencíon slid hard, trying to take out Gamble's legs and break up the double play.

Gamble had turned thousands of double plays before, though; he expertly glided over Asencíon and rifled the ball across his body, toward Juan Patrón at first.

The throw beat Scooter by a good three steps.

"Out!" the ump covering second bellowed.

"He's ouuuuuttt!" The first base ump cried with an exaggerated fist-pump.

The crowd roared with approval as Manny pointed at Truck. Truck removed his mask and grinned; he rushed toward the new closer and put his arm around his shoulder.

Hack's eyes glistened with pride. More than anything, Manny's efficient ninth had reaffirmed his confidence in his hunches, and made him feel like he still belonged in the dugout. For a moment, all of the pain in his chest, his back, and his knees melted away.

He clapped his hands three times and scooted out to meet the rest of the team, gathered on the mound, exchanging handshakes with one another.

Like professionals.

4

"CALUNK!"

Despite the victory, Hack slammed the door to the media room against the wall.

The noise jolted Marc Blake out of his affected intimidation next to the podium, and sent him jogging toward the surly old manager.

"Coach O'Callahan! Great game, *great* game—" Blake moved to pat Hack on the shoulder.

Hack pulled away from him, indignant.

"Yeah, yeah, yeah, let's get this over with. Guess there's prob'ly a big fuss over—" Hack surveyed the gathered media. Other than one female reporter and cameraman decked out in "ESPN" signage, it was the same disappointing contingent from two nights before.

Hack was grateful for the slug of Old Reliable he had taken to dull the shooting pain in his gnarled back before he had ambled over to the press room. He covered up his limp as he marched to the podium.

He noticed Keith Myrick at the far side of the room. Keith affixed a phony smile to his face and waved to the manager.

Oddly, Hack passed the podium and gave Keith a hearty handshake.

Myrick almost had a heart attack.

After the most unusual gesture, Myrick followed Hack toward the podium.

"Whattayas got?" Hack started the question before he was even in front of the microphone.

"Uh, folks," Keith Myrick stepped in front of him. Hack could've sworn that as he did so, he shot a stern grimace at the fiesty old manager. "Thanks for coming here today. We'd like to thank our friends at www.myxnmatch.com for their generosity and continued support of the Magpies through the years."

Hack rolled his eyes.

"We're proud to announce that the Magpies have, pending a physical examination," a few chuckles filled the room. Myrick took a deep breath, "the Magpies are pleased to announce the hiring of the legendary Hack O'Callahan as manager on a provisional basis."

The assembled press gave the most cursory smattering of applause. Myrick stepped aside with a full, fake grin.

Hack responded in kind.

"Eat shit," Myrick said through gritted teeth.

"Fuck yer'self," Hack replied through his own fake smile.

Once the applause had ceased, the press waited in eager anticipation of Hack's introductory statement.

He never gave one.

"So...like I said. Shoot."

Jim Taggart from the *Herald* piped up first.

"So, Coach, what's gonna' happen with Willie for the rest of the season?"

"Well, Jim, Charles's agreed to stay on as my assistant, learn the ropes from me, best as I can teach 'em."

"And what does it mean, 'provisional basis?'" Taggert followed up.

"Like he said, Jim, pendin' a physical and whatnot. Can't be too careful with an ol' cuss like me. Right now though, I'd rather keep the focus on tonight's game."

Taggert raised an eyebrow and composed himself.

"Coach, obviously a great win for you guys. Anything to say about it?"

Hack glared at the veteran newspaperman. "Great win. Team effort. Work in progress, but we're gettin' there."

Taggert grinned, "But that was a big gamble you took there installing Manny Poblado as closer. What did you see in him that made you think that he could succeed in that role?"

"Are you fu—are you *blind*?" Hack caught his swear. "The kid throws one hundred miles an hour. He can't hit worth a lick. You'd have to be a moron to keep him at shortstop."

"But Coach," Liam Canard interjected in his nasally whine, "Poblado's defensive metrics were nearly league-average. Though Eldrake Gamble was—"

"Who?" Hack asked. "Oh, you mean Flash?"

"Uh…sure."

"Flash is a helluva athlete. Tall, rangy—he'll be a fine shortstop."

"Yes, but Nev Friedmann is a below-average second baseman. On whole, you're sacrificing almost two full points of range factor up the middle, and as we saw tonight," Canard allowed himself two raspy, awkward snorts, "Friedmann still is a little shaky as a fielder."

"Christ, everything is stats nowadays. Bullshit stat this, or horseshit stat that—" April Barker cringed and made a throat-slash motion to her cameraman. "Can't all of you stat nerds get in a room with all of the scouts, start a few cars, and kill yourselves?"

This inspired a husky laugh from Taggert and the cameramen. Blake's eyes went wide as he stepped up.

"One more question, guys—Coach needs to get his treatment."

The ESPN reporter raised her pen-clutching hand.

"Maria Carson, ESPN. Coach, I have to ask, after so much success in the majors, after four World Series championships, over a dozen division titles, and countless players you've coached, why come back to Hoplite now? Why manage the Magpies?"

April Barker leveled daggers at the woman for poaching her question from two nights ago.

Hack stared at the attractive young woman, not with hatred or disgust, but with amusement. It was the question that he had anticipated for three days now, and he relished the opportunity to answer it.

"Well there, young lady, I'm glad ya' asked that." Hack tried to smile, but his expression came across as a grimace. "Keith Myrick is the son of one'a my former players, Pug Myrick, and a dear, *dear* friend in his own right."

Hack looked over toward Myrick next to the podium. When he saw that Myrick was grinding his teeth, almost as if to make the bullshit coming from the microphone palatable to swallow, Hack couldn't help but smile.

"An' so I was there, in Cleveland, and I getta' call from Keith. 'Hey Hack, how's it goin'? I'm GMin' the Magpies over in Hoplite, and we ran inta' a bitta' trouble. We ain't doin' so well.'

"So I says, 'Oh? Really? Well, I'm enjoyin' retirement, keepin' busy an' all'a that, forty years in the big leagues, yada, yada, yada.'

"An' he comes back, 'Hack, before my daddy died, he made one final request. On his death bed, he said, 'Son, I'm proud'a ya. Yer' a great GM with great things in frontta' ya'. But if you ever find yerself with a bad, horrible team, an' you need someone to fix it, you give Hack O'Callahan a call, and he'll fix'er right up.'

"An' so I hem an' haw a little more, 'Gee Keith, I dunno,' just to mess with him a bit," Hack grinned at the GM as he said the words, a little inside joke between the two of them.

Though Keith gave every outward appearance of being so, he was most certainly not amused.

"An' he comes back over the top. Practically *beggin'* me. Actually, he *was* beggin' me, he says, 'Hack, I'm *beggin'* ya. Charles's got talent as a manager, but we need ya' to come in and fix the operation here. The whole town'a Hoplite needs ya'. We may be tryin' to develop the players down here, but damn it—' and please pardon my language, but this is what Keith says, he says, '—damn it, *I* care about winnin', too. I don't want these players ta' be so immersed, so *soaked* in losin' that they get ta' Cleveland and that's all they know. I'm a winner, and I want these guys ta' be winners, too.'"

Hack glanced at Myrick with a nod. Myrick's face grew red as the veins in his neck bulged to the surface. To his credit, he kept the forced grin on his face throughout Hack's story.

"An' I says back to him, I says, 'What about Cleveland?' An' he says, 'Forget about Cleveland. I'll deal with Cleveland.'

"An' so I figure if he's willin' to go to bat with the big club fer' me, I says to him, 'Keith, I'll do it. But only 'cause we're such good buddies, an' because yer' daddy was one'a the hardest-workin' players I ever knew.'

"An' he says, 'I know. An' God-willin' daddy's lookin' down from heaven—" Myrick stifled an eye-roll, "—an' sayin' 'ya' did good son...ya' did yer' very best.'"

Hack allowed the statement to wash over the room for several seconds as he luxuriated in the false gravity that sucked everyone, every*thing* in the room toward the podium.

He forced a false, wan smile, "An' so here I am."

Keith lunged at the podium. He ducked his head toward the microphone.

"That's not *exactly* how—"

"Mr. Myrick," April Barker wiped a tear out of her eye, "Is it true that you were so selfless, so professional that you could swallow your pride and make such a positive, emotionally-difficult decision to help *our* Magpies?"

Keith raised an eyebrow and took a step back.

"Well...I..."

Even Taggert's usual crusty temperment allowed a glistening, tear-slicked eye to shine as he cradled his notebook in the crook of his arm and clasped his hands together.

The reporters followed Taggert's lead and broke into a round of applause as a flummoxed Myrick wordlessly opened his mouth at the podium.

"Go ahead, Keith: take a bow!" Hack motioned to the press corps as they rose from their seats. Even the cameramen slapped their hands on their thighs as the gathering of eight thundered their approval at the podium.

Myrick shot a sideways glance toward Hack and shook his head almost imperceptibly. Hack arched a mischievous eyebrow at the GM before Myrick remembered the cameras on him, and lowered his torso into a stilted bow.

"One down, two to go, and then off ta' Featherstone!" Hack waved at the press and teetered into the clubhouse as Myrick followed close behind.

As soon as the door shut behind them, Myrick grabbed Hack on the shoulder.

"You manipulative, blackmailing, evil old sonofa *sonofa*bitch!"

"Yer' welcome Keith!" Hack shot back with a thin grin.

"Welcome? For what? That line of *bullshit* you just spun out there?"

"It's *all* bullshit, Keith! Every word said in that room——" he pointed at the dungeon, "—is as hot and steamin' as a fresh cowpie. But at least now they love ya', and hopefully they'll get off my back a bit."

"We'll see about that. Jim Taggert isn't easily fooled."

"Oh, I don't know about *that*…" Hack said as he turned and waddled toward the training room.

"Fuck!" Myrick hissed after the old man.

For the first time, the slick GM worried that he was being outmaneuvered.

5

The Magpies beat the Princehens handily in game two by a score of 11-3 in front of another capacity crowd.

This time, before the game Hack received a standing ovation from the somewhat blue-haired packed house, owing in no small part to the human interest story by Jim Taggert that had run in the *Hoplite Herald* that morning that detailed the fish story Hack had told in the press conference the previous evening, along with some quotes Hack had given him with the express instructions that they not run until after his introductory press conference.

Now, in game three of the series, with a 7-2 Magpie lead in the top of the ninth, all 5,642 in attendance were on the edges of their seats, hoping for the Magpies' first sweep of the season. They had no idea what the stakes were for Hack O'Callahan, and yet they watched as, after two strikeouts to start the inning, new closer Manny Poblado gave up two hits and a walk to load the bases, albeit with a five run lead.

Most troubling in Hack's mind was that Manny's arm-action wasn't the same flowing, elegant, circular motion of two days before. It was more angular, jerky and forced, almost as if Manny was reaching back for an extra five to ten miles per hour on top of the hundred he regularly brought.

Hack shook his head; if Manny needed to learn a lesson, better that he do it with a five run lead.

Even if it was in a game that could determine Hack's fate for the rest of the season.

"Whattaya say now, Manny, kid!?" Hack clapped three times.

The rest of the players in the dugout echoed Hack's chatter.

That didn't stop Hack from calling Pete Moray in the bullpen and telling him to get Tommy Stearns up and ready, just in case.

The next batter for the Princehens was Scooter Herman. He strode to the plate with purpose, eager to avenge his embarrassing, roll-over double play ball to end the first game.

"Hey Scoot. Want me to give you the signs again?" Traynor said with a grin.

"Fuck off, Truck." Herman shook his head.

"Okay, okay. Don't say I didn't warn you though…" Traynor lowered himself into his crouch and flashed Manny the fastball sign.

The sweat poured off of Manny's brow in torrents. He cradled the ball on the small of his back, right behind his belt. He nodded, and brought his hands together in front of him.

He checked the runner at second, then, as he began his motion, he looked over his shoulder toward first.

"BALK!" the first base umpire boomed.

"Qué?" Manny yelled out.

Truck only shook his head.

In his ill-advised look over to first, Manny had turned his front shoulder to the left, toward first base. It constituted a balk by the letter of the rule, albeit one that was rarely called even at Double-A, and allowed the runners to advance a base.

Hack muttered a string of incoherent curse words and felt obligated to give the umpire a piece of his mind, knowing full well that it was technically the right call.

"What the fuck was that?"

"Careful, Hack—I'll give you some leeway, but not much," the umpire shook his head. He was a younger man, maybe in his early thirties, with an athletic frame and a thick, bushy mustache that seemed to be an attempt to cultivate unearned authority.

"Come on, son. Ya' know well an' good that ya' don't make that call but once a year."

"Well, I guess that's my one time, then."

Hack scowled. His face reddened, "Smart ass."

"One more time, I dare ya!" The umpire bellowed. Though he wasn't particularly large, he still towered over Hack's comparatively tiny frame.

"I ain't gonna give some chickenshit little moron like you the satisfaction'a—"

"YOU'RE OUTTA HERE!" The umpire's finger shot skyward. He moved toward Hack for the deluge of abuse that was sure to ensue.

"ARE YOU *NUTS*!? Fuckin' pantywaist, I've been yelled at by Leo Durocher and John McGraw, you think some power-hungry asshole's gonna embarrass me in front'a all'a these fine folks who've come ta' see me tonight?!" Hack pointed to the stands.

The umpire folded his arms and yawned.

"Really! Really? That's all ya' got?" Hack removed his hat and stood on his toes to go "eye-to-nose" with the young umpire. "Lemme tell ya' somethin', son, Orson Holbrook was a no-good sonofabitch of an umpire. He yelled at me for God-knows-*what* kind of shittin' little things probably a hundred times, just because he liked ta' see us *squirm*. And you know what? Orson Holbrook had more umpirin' talent in his tiny *cock* than you do in your little peckerhead of a body!"

"Get outta here! Go on, git'!" The umpire laughed and waved Hack away, as if he was little more annoying than a housefly.

By this time, Willie and Pete Moray had rushed to Hack's side, and struggled to restrain him.

Perhaps the only thing that kept Hack from slugging the ump was a coughing fit, which caused Hack to double over long enough for his two coaches to corral him, and drag him off into the dugout as his lungs and back screamed their protest.

Throughout the entire spectacle, the crowd roared its approval of their new manager. By the end, even while Hack bent over in excruciating pain, the crowd chanted, "Hack! Hack! Hack!" John Paul Murphy Field hadn't been so jubilant and alive since the Magpies won their last Northern League title in 1998.

As Moray and Willie guided Hack into the tunnel, the players on the bench applauded and propped up their new manager.

"Atta' way, Coach O'Callahan, way to give 'em hell!"

"We got this one, Coach! We got it!"

Even Mitch Henry added a "Thatta' way, Coach!", despite the humiliation he had suffered at the old man's hands only days before.

Hack struggled to his own feet and forced himself to choke the blood-soaked spittle back down. This time, his head felt light and dizzy, and even when he was under his own power, he staggered semi-drunkenly toward the tunnel several steps before he turned to Willie.

"It's up to you, Charles," Hack said and shrugged, "Gotta do what ya' gotta do." He staggered into the tunnel and tucked himself just behind the dugout wall, enough to ensure that the pompous umpire wouldn't give him any further grief.

Willie nodded and turned his attention toward the field. He looked out toward the bullpen and saw that Stearns was already back into his warmups again.

What would he do? Keep Manny in and hope for the best? Hope that he could dial it up one more time to get the Magpies out of the inning?

Or would he keep Manny in for a more sinister reason? To try to rid the team of Hack, once and for all. He still thought Hack to be a horrid little man, a despicable racist and bigot who used and cajoled people into maneuvering himself into a position of power.

At the same time, though, Willie also knew that Hack had turned a listless, moribund team around in the space of four or five days. A new electricity surged throughout the stands and the clubhouse. And as underhanded as his tactics may have been at times, the players seemed to appreciate their new manager's direct, no-nonsense approach to managing the team.

Willie decided to split the baby.

"Time!" He yelled and jogged up the dugout steps. He walked lazily toward the mound, mostly to give Stearns more time to warm up in the pen. As Stearns reared back to fire warmup pitch after warmup pitch, he sucked in his lower lip and narrowed his eyes.

Willie couldn't tell if the deposed closer was pouting, or mad-as-hell, though the former closer's red hair gave the appearance of the latter.

Manny had his hands on his hips as the sweat continued to pour off of his face. He removed his cap and wiped his brow on the sleeve of his turtleneck.

Willie and Truck arrived at the mound simultaneously.

"How you doin', Manny?"

"Uno mas," he nodded.

"Whattaya think, Truck?"

"It's one more out, and Scooter looked pretty bad yesterday. We have some wiggle room, too; that insurance run is *big*."

"Yeah, yeah," Willie looked past Manny toward the bullpen for several moments. "Okay, kid—one more batter. I'm gonna trust you like Hack would, okay? Just relax, nice and easy, playin' catch with Truck here, okay?"

Manny nodded.

"And Truck, feel free to use a different signal for that changeup that made Scooter look like such an ass yesterday, okay?" He showed two fingers to both of them. "Changeup. At least until we can get you throwin' a breaking ball. Understand?"

Both men nodded.

"Good. Okay, it's all yours, Manny." Willie sauntered back toward the dugout, just as the home plate umpire was halfway to the mound to try to hurry the conference up.

Truck put an arm on Manny's shoulder.

"Lo tienes," he said. *You have this.*

Manny smiled and nodded. He grabbed for Truck's hand before he stopped himself, and stuck out a closed fist for Truck to "hammer." Truck jogged back behind the plate.

"Got two down, now! Play at one, infield!" Truck yelled. He held up two separated fingers on his right hand before he casually flipped his hockey-style catcher's mask over his eyes and kneeled behind the plate.

"Play ball!" The home plate ump pointed toward Manny as he settled over Truck's shoulder.

Manny looked in for his sign. Truck flashed two fingers, just like Willie had told him. Manny nodded. He came set; this time he learned his lesson and paid no heed to the runners.

His arm action was more whip-like, more elegant as he broke his hands over his knee, rocked, and fired the ball toward the plate.

"CRACK!"

Truck waited for the tell-tale, satisfying "BOOM" of the ball hitting his mitt, but never felt it. Scooter Herman had swung and hit the ball on the screws. It followed a long, high arc through the Hoplite night sky and landed a good fifty feet behind the right field bleachers. The first base umpire circled his finger in the air to signal what everyone already knew:

Scooter Herman hit a monster home run.

The Princehens' catcher gargled out laughs with glee as he lumbered around the bases. As he rounded third, he locked eyes with Manny and pointed at the mound.

Manny's downcast head bolted upright. The fire returned to his eyes as he pawed at the dirt with his foot.

Unfortunately for him, Willie was already making his way out to the mound.

Manny's night was over.

The steaming converted shortstop placed the ball in Willie's outstretched hand and jogged off the field to a smattering of applause. Even before Willie had touched his left arm to signal that it was now Tommy Stearns' ballgame to finish, Manny was into the tunnel, past Hack, and into the locker room.

Stearns similarly sprinted to the mound. Willie saw the fire in his eyes and thought the better of giving the former closer anything more than a "Go get 'em, kid," before he strode off the mound. Stearns sent Truck behind the plate wordlessly and tore through his warmups, each one nastier than the previous.

"I feel sorry for the poor S.O.B. who has to face him," Truck said to the umpire.

The burly home plate ump launched a healthy loogie into the dirt in reply.

Once Stearns had dispensed with all eight warmups, there was no preening, no superstitious routine on display. He toed the rubber with his left foot and looked in for the sign before the Princehens' shortstop, Ramón Perez, had dug in.

Truck had seen the movement on Stearns's fastball in warmups, and thought that a slider might suitably cross up the young Princehens' prospect.

He put down two fingers, and Stearns shook him off.

Truck caught himself from screaming at the pitcher. He took as much pride in his game-calling abilities as he did in his hitting, and wasn't used to being shaken off much.

Truck sighed and put down three fingers; at least a change-up might also catch the eager young hitter off-guard.

Another head shake by Stearns.

Truck had half a mind to call time and chew Stearns out in front of everyone. He had a "plus" fastball, but as Hack had noted after Stearns's final disastrous outing as closer, the fiery young lefthander often fell in love with the pitch, often overly so and to his detriment.

Instead, Truck gave in. Against every instinct in his body, he relented and put down one finger.

Stearns glared in and nodded. There was no way Perez hadn't caught on to the mini drama that was on-going in front of him. The slight shortstop dug in and raised his bat high in the air, far higher than most batters dared, and wrapped it around his head.

Stearns came set. His motion was more direct and compact than Manny's, like a middleweight boxer tossing body blows at his opponent.

His body was a spring uncoiled as he balanced only momentarily on one leg and shot his arm toward the plate.

The ball had heavy movement as it floated through the air. Truck was ready for it as it thundered downward toward the plate.

Unfortunately, so was Perez.

"CRACK!"

The lanky shortstop put everything he had into the swing and caught the ball flush.

Truck stood up immediately and flung his mask over toward the Magpies' dugout as he followed the long arc of the ball out toward center field.

He watched as Sid Fynch sprung into action; the centerfielder chopped through the outfield grass with short, staccato steps in pursuit of the ball. As the white sphere reached its apex, Fynch checked for the wall and calculated how much space he had left, all in less than half-a-second.

Maybe, his brain told him in not-so-many words.

Fynch raced back; it would certainly be close. He ignored his still-throbbing calf from the thrashing Hack had given him just days before as he reached back for the wall and felt the worn, splintery plywood of the "Ancinetti and Taylor, Attorney's at Law" Sign (complete with the misplaced possessive apostrophe) in left-center field.

The ball continued its downward flight toward the grass above the outfield fence. Fynch jumped up, one foot on the wall, glove outstretched over the top, hoping for a miracle.

A gust of wind brushed his unkempt hair on its way toward the plate.

It was enough.

The ball glided harmlessly into Fynch's glove, and secured itself in the well-crafted pocket.

The crowd leapt to its feet. Stearns let out a primal war-cry to go along with a fist-pump as Sid Fynch flopped off the wall and took off in a sprint, all the way toward the mound, holding his glove up like a recovered treasure all the while.

They mobbed Fynch and chanted "Sid! Sid! Sid!" loudly enough that the crowd joined in.

Fynch pulled his glove down and held the ball up for all to see, and the Sunday night packed house went wild with another round of cheers.

It was the first sweep of the season, and a well-earned victory, to be sure.

Still, Willie shook his head with a grin. These players and fans had no idea what rode on that play.

And yet, he thought, *their reaction is more than appropriate.*

6

Even though Hack cut his press conference short (he offered little more than a series of "no comments," more out of a perverse joy of watching the dumbfounded reporters try to figure out why than anything else), the clubhouse was nearly empty when he walked back in from the dungeon, owed in large part to the overnight bus ride that the team faced to get to Featherstone, Colorado. Players rushed through a quick shower and out into the parking lot to claim favored seats next to their friends.

Among them were Willie and Pete Moray, who had the unenviable distinction of keeping order on the bus as Hack attended to his various postgame duties.

Hack waddled over to the training room, but found that it was locked, with a simple note scrawled out in longhand attached with a piece of scotch tape:

"Coach O'C: Forgot to tell ya' that I don't work on Sundays. Bummer, man. Just take a couple extra pills until you get back. Maybe hit a spa on the road (*yeah, right,* Hack thought). C ya when ya get back! -Randy."

Hack pulled the note off the wall and crumpled it up. He muttered a few barely-audible curses that included, "fuckin' twelve hour bus ride" and "back'll be tighter than a priest's asshole" before he shrugged and trudged toward the coaches' locker room.

Just as he was about to open the door, he heard a muffled "crash" from inside his office.

Hack balled up his fist and hit the concrete wall.

"Goddamned in'nerlopers," he muttered. "Always thinkin' they can horn in on my office. Think a man ain't entitled to his own office, free'a this *shit*."

He decided to give Keith or that "Meadow" hussy, or whomever else it was causing the ruckus in his office a piece of his mind. Hack scowled as he marched over toward his office door.

Hack didn't knock as he gave the door a yank.

What he saw caused his jaw to drop to the floor.

Truck Traynor stood in front of the tragic green couch on the right side of the room, his pants down around his ankles.

Manny Poblado kneeled in front of him.

And fellated him.

Hack's face went red as the veins bulged from his temples all the way to the fringes of his exposed scalp.

Without missing a beat, he pointed at Manny and yelled.

"Well, you sucked *dick* on the mound tonight. Might as well do it in here, too!"

Manny stood as Truck fumbled to pull up his pants. The thoughts swirled in Hack's head as he took several steps backward through the door, closed it behind him, and faced the empty hallway.

Hack coughed out several gasping heaves as he struggled to process exactly what he had just seen. He embraced the fit as it developed; it was a shallow one, and he for once was thankful for the distraction, appreciative that something could take his mind off of what had just happened.

Unfortunately, it only lasted several seconds.

His lungs involuntarily sucked in a deep breath, eager for air, as Hack steadied himself against the door.

"This is a new one…" he mused to himself as he twisted the knob and pulled the door open again…

Fourth Inning

1

"What in the sam *fuck* are you two doin' in here?!" Hack thundered at Truck Traynor and Manny Poblado after he caught them in a compromising situation only moments before.

Truck hurriedly fastened his pants.

"Coach, it's not—"

"Don't tell me what I saw or didn't see. I know what I saw. You were...you were..." he turned toward Manny, "*blowin' him!*"

"Dios mio," Manny lowered and shook his head.

"English, god *damn* it!" Hack screamed.

"Okay!" Truck extended both arms out toward Hack, palms up. "Okay...you caught us. It was exactly what you saw."

Hack was taken aback by his catcher's honesty, "You think I'm gonna' let a couple'a underhanded, no good, despicable—" Truck and Manny braced for the slur, "—*trespassers* stay on my team?"

"Perdón?" Manny asked.

"What?" Truck followed.

"You heard me. Speak fer' yerselves, damn it!"

"Sorry, Coach, I just thought you were gonna say somethin' else there."

Hack took two steps toward the catcher and puffed himself up until Hack was as much in the catcher's face as he could be.

"What'd you think I was gonna say?" Hack hissed, almost a whisper.

"I dunno," Truck looked downward. "Fa…faggots?"

"FAGGOTS!?" Hack yelled and jolted both players. "Why in the *hell* would I care about that? Shit, my double play partner for four years was 'Fancy' Frank Falstaff, and he was as queer as a duck with toes!"

"So…you *don't* mind then?" Truck was incredulous.

"Did I say that?!" Hack's back seized up, but he used the pain as fuel for his anger, "What I don't like is yous two turnin' my office into a goddamned Greek bathhouse. Men…ladies…whatever…"

Truck and Manny exchanged narrowed glances.

"But Señor Hack, your back!" Manny protested.

"Damn right I'm back! I may be old, but I ain't dead yet!"

"No, your *back*," Manny reached behind himself and patted his shoulder blade. "Treatment. Medicina."

"What?"

Truck shook his head, "He's trying to say that we thought you'd be getting treatment on your back. It's not easy to find places in Hoplite where we can…uh…you know…"

Hack pointed toward the office's doors, "There's a god damned truck stop men's room on Highway 54. Use that fer' all I care! Listen, I don't care if yer' fuckin' sailors, two at a time, as they're steppin' off the pier, like Fancy Frank used to do in Boston."

Truck and Manny bit their lips and looked at one another.

"But I will be *damned* if you two's personal issues start to impact this team negatively. I'm not runnin' a datin' service here, queer or otherwise. When yer' in this clubhouse, you work fer' *me*. My time. It'd be the same fuckin' thing if you were givin' it to that hussy of a girlfriend'a yers', Truck."

"What?" Truck looked as if Hack had just cracked him across the face with his bat/cane.

"You heard me. She came in to visit with me the other day about Manny movin' to pitcher. Seems she thinks yer' a real keeper." Hack snorted. "Kinda…how do ya' say now? Ironic?"

"My God..." Truck took a step back. "I knew she was a climber, but jeez...she's messin' with my career."

"I guess you two ain't exactly steamin' the sheets in the bedroom, either?" Hack interjected with a wry grin, happy to be in control once more.

"If you must know, I'm *bi*," Truck held up his nose at Hack before he realized what he had said, "Wait, I mean, that's private—"

"*Exactly!*" Hack yelled. "Keep it that way." He turned toward Manny. "That goes fer' you, too. Can't have my closer becomin' some goddamned head case now, can I?"

Manny's eyes shocked open.

"Closer? Still? *Yo?*"

Hack rapped Manny quickly once on the forehead with his fingertips, "You think I'm gonna' trust that hothead Stearns to close games? He's more of a liability than you. Pete'll teach ya' a slider and a changeup, and sure as shit, you'll be on yer' way ta' all kinds'a wine, women, and—"

Manny lowered a skeptical eye at the manager.

"Ah, Christ, I ain't gonna change my expressions on account'a you two. Deal with it."

"Gracias, Señor Ha—"

"Go on, git' outta' here!" Hack waved the two toward the door.

"One more thing, Coach. We'd appreciate it if you kept this quiet. Don't need Henry or Murph or the guys finding out about this; *then* we'd have hell to pay."

"What? Actually Mitch Henry was gonna be the first one I told," Hack feigned innocence before he stuttered over to Truck and smacked him on the hat bill. "Whattid' I say about not wantin' distractions? Gentlemen, you have my word—I will never tell another soul," Hack looked past Truck into the opaque glass of the office. "Man's entitled to his secrets. I of all folks should know that."

Truck nodded. "Thanks, Coach."

"Get out to the bus! You guys'll make us late."

The two players vacated the office and left Hack to change quickly and fasten his shabby, teal, still mostly-unpacked suitcase.

Before he did so, Hack sighed as he opened the bottom drawer in his desk. The formerly empty compartment now housed two large bottles of Old Reliable whiskey, one full, the other about two-thirds full.

Hack replayed the scene that had just occurred in his office again in his head. Not that he fixated on the homosexual acts that had initially so jarred him; after all, he had been in baseball for over sixty years. Homoeroticism on many different levels was omnipresent, if not usually so brash.

He packed the full handle of Old Reliable in his suitcase, and unscrewed the lid of the partially-drunk one. He looked down the glass, rifled neck of the bottle, into the wonderful, vaguely vanilla-smelling sea that caressed the sides of the bottle below.

"Man's entitled to his secrets," Hack muttered to the empty room.

He brought the bottle to his lips, drained it in several gulps, latched his suitcase, picked it up, and wandered over to the bus.

2

Hack came to later than he was accustomed, around 6:15 the next morning. Though his elderly brain still felt like it floated upon a sea of cheap whiskey, as he looked over his shoulder and saw Truck Traynor's head buried in a magazine, the events of the previous evening came flooding back.

He rubbed the crust from his eyes and squinted at the seat opposite him. Willie's fingers already pinched and pulled and danced on a tablet as his eyes followed along, intent on whatever was upon the screen.

"Mornin'," Willie looked at Hack and gave a curt nod.

"Mornin' yer'self, Charles," Hack tried to steady his uneven tone. "How far out of Featherstone are we?"

"Oh, another two, three hours. You were out like a light there, Coach."

"Eh…used to sleepin' on these things, is all." Hack rubbed the crust from his eyes, "Though when I was in the minors, we didn't have fancy buses like this. Our catcher, Milt Ford, used to take up two rickety seats because his fat ass would've broke one. We gave him shit fer' it, but he got us back when he started tootin' the bus up, really nasty ones, too—"

"Coach, I—" Willie desperately interjected.

"—he *loved* seafood. Loved it. And I'll be goddamned if his fartin' didn't smell like dead shrimp. I would say that we got the last laugh the one time when he really felt a big one comin' on—and we knew it, too, 'cause he made a big production outta' it, 'okay boys, tube's loaded,' he'd say.

"And we'd all tell him, 'knock it off, Milt! Yer' gonna kill poor little Cap Harrow with his asthma.' Now, Cap was a little utility infielder, ya' see, nerdy little fella, and some'a the less 'forgivin'' guys would always grab 'im by the ankles and force his head right up next ta' Milt's asshole."

"Coach, come on now. I think I'm gonna be—"

"Well, this time, like I said, Milt was fixin' ta' make a big ol' deal outta' this one, really buildin' it up. He grabbed the sill of the winda' like he was about to have a fuckin' heart attack. He hunkered down, almost like he was crouchin' down, tryin' ta' throw a runner out at second or somethin'.

"Anyway, Milt lets out this really loud grunt, really loud, shakin' the windas' on the whole damned bus loud. Then, just when I thought he was about to drop a fuckin' kidney, he gets real quiet. And we don't hear nothin'. Even poor Cap was wonderin' what the hell was goin' on.

"Then, just when we thought Milt had died, Cap starts shoutin' and carryin' on. 'He shit! He fuckin' shit!'"

Willie turned to the side and cupped a hand over his mouth.

"The poor bastard had built up the goddamned fart fer' so long, he shit his pants. I would say the joke was on him, but we were the ones who had ta' sit on that bus with him the four hours 'til Altoona. Yep...those were the days..."

Hack trailed off whistfully. Truth be told, it was the first time he had ever finished the Milt Ford story without breaking into hysterical laughter. More than anything, Hack was happy to have replaced the disturbing mental image he had just seen with something familiar and enjoyable.

Willie collected himself and turned back to the old manager.

"Coach, I'm only gonna say this one time. That was the most disgusting, disturbing, wretched story I've ever heard..." his lip was resolute as he spat out each successive adjective.

Willie broke into a broad smile, "But god*damn* if it ain't some funny shit!"

Both men shared a laugh as Hack finally felt "normal" again, or at least as normal as he could without a few eye openers of Old Reliable to start the day.

"Look, Charles, about what ya' did after I was thrown out last night, I—"

"Don't mention it," Willie waved the thought away. "I thought I owed it to you to try my damnedest. Like I said, the guys really seem to be responding to you, and, if I'm bein' honest, I'm learning a thing or two along the way, too. So I—"

"It was a damned fool move to bring in Stearns!" Hack hissed. "Manny woulda' gotten us outta' it if you woulda' trusted him."

Willie's eyes widened before his brow furrowed, "*Excuse* me?"

"We got lucky that prick didn't tie the damned game! If it weren't fer' Fynch back there—" Hack shot a thumb toward the back of the mostly-sleeping bus, "—we woulda' gone ta' extras, and then, who the hell knows?"

Willie looked around to confirm that Stearns and Manny were still sleeping.

"It was the move that the percentages said to make," Willie whispered urgently.

"Fuck yer' percentages," Hack said. "You know why I look at all'a those stats so much, tryin' to figure out matchups and stuff? I ain't memorizin' percentages. If percentages were what made a manager, then I'll bet that Pollack kid or even the sharp girl intern could do just as good'uva job as I can."

Hack looked at the back of the bus, not out of any consideration for the other players, but in the way someone does before imparting a time-honored secret to someone else, so as to prevent it from conferring wisdom on anyone outside of the chosen few.

"The reason I stare at those damned stats, the reason I fill my head with 'em fer' a series and then throw 'em way deep in the back'a my forgetful old brain is so that when I make a decision, with my gut, like any manager worth 'is salt should, my gut makes an informed decision, how do ya' say? Concious er' not. I like to call it 'feedin' my gut.' Nice little doo-blay en-tender there, see what I did?"

Willie narrowed his eyes and spoke slowly and firmly, almost in a whisper.

"So you're telling me that all of that time you spend prepping for games, pouring over the binders and whatnot hours before game time, you're 'feeding your gut?' You don't *use* any of it?"

Hack made a movement as if he was going to knock the glasses off of Willie's face, but stopped short.

Willie didn't flinch.

"God *damn* it, I thought we was havin' a moment, or whatever," Hack said. "Didn't you hear what I just said? I like to think I'm a pretty sharp guy an' that—"

Thankfully, Willie's skull prevented his eyes from rocketing through the roof of the bus.

"—so sure, *some* atha' stats, they're right there fer' me durin' games. I ain't a *total* fool, you know." Hack leaned in closer to Willie and cupped a hand over his mouth.

"But mostly I remember who does well against a guy, who might be due, and feel the flow'a the game, get a sense of a situation, and let a guy work through it or replace him."

Willie nodded; he thought he understood what the old codger meant.

"Which is exactly why Tommy FUCKING Stearns—" Hack raised his voice only on the curse, "—shouldn't have been in there last night. He was too tight, too inside his own head, hopin' to prove that *he* should be the closer, and not Manny.

"I'll tell ya' what, though, in the few games I've seen Manny as a closer, he's tough. Damned tough, especially fer' a—" Willie leaned his head in, waiting for the inevitable Latino slur, "—converted infielder. He's a fuckin' *bull*dog, Charles—remember that next season."

Willie nodded his head as Hack leaned back in his seat. The horrendously rainbow-patterned seats were as uncomfortable as they were ugly, and reeked of a mixture of stale snack mix combined with whatever cleaner the bus company had used to try to eliminate said odor.

Hack winced as his back screamed.

"Back doin' okay?" Willie asked.

"Eh, fuck it. I think this itchy shit—" Hack rubbed the fabric of the seat, "—and thin paddin's just about as good fer' it as anything else. We could all use a little discomfort from time-to-time; toughens us up a bit, you know? That's why the Spartans won the war."

Hack found his gaze shifting toward the back of the bus, where Truck Traynor sat, still studying his magazine. He watched as Truck turned the page, and a beautiful bikini model came into view.

This inspired a coughing fit in Hack, who reached for his familiar handkerchief in his back pocket as if this one was of little more than an inconvenience.

"You okay?" Willie asked.

"Dry air," Hack stuttered out between coughs. "Must be gettin' close to the mountains."

Willie didn't know what it meant, but he was relieved when someone broke the silence.

Until he heard Mitch Henry's loud, Southern drawl fill the bus.

"Christ, I wanna hear more'a those shit yer' pants stories. 'Course no one on this team is man enough to hold Sid's face up to Truck's asshole as he's unleashin' the brown avalanche o'pain. Bunch'a fuckin' *faggots* on this bus."

"Qué?" Manny roused from his slumber.

"You heard me. Bunch of fuckin' *flamin'* cocksuckers on this team. Sid'd get his daddy to sue me, or some other gay shit like that. Before you know it, I'd be on some show with Richard Simmons or Oprah, tellin' me about my bidness."

"Bull-*shit* Oprah'd ever wanna talk to your hick ass," Truck said.

"Ellen then? Fuck I dunno. God-damned faggot commie conspiracy if you ask me."

Hack looked at the commotion over his shoulder and saw the mix of fear and anger in Truck's eyes as they narrowed wide, ready to fight for himself, but also afraid of what such a fight may bring.

He also noticed the oddly-shaped camouflage case on the seat next to Henry, on top of his crimson bag, which had "Don't Mess With Texas? Don't Fuck With 'Bama" stenciled on it.

Hack pushed himself up out of the seat and scowled as the pain shot through his back.

"Piss," he muttered to Willie.

"No one's askin'," Willie said, focused on his tablet.

Hack teetered toward the back of the bus and the developing scene. He grabbed the hand holds on top of the rows of seats along the way, determined to prevent Mitch Henry, of all people, from tearing his team apart.

"And another thing, Barack *Hussein* Obama, if that is his true, Kenyan name—" Henry bellowed toward Truck at the front of the bus.

"Nice case, Henry. You a bow hunter?" Hack interjected.

Henry bobbed his head backward an inch or so, taken aback by his manager's comment.

"As a matter of fact, I am, Coach."

"I'm sure it'll be *real*-ly useful when we're attacked by the vicious, wild deer of Featherstone, Colorado…" Sid Fynch said.

"I swear to *God*, Sid, I'm gonna put one through your heart like you're a fuckin' deer."

"Used to go every winter," Hack interrupted again. "My pal Mickey and I used to hunt in Oklahoma."

"Mickey? Like fuckin' Mickey Mantle and shit?" Mitch Henry asked.

"Hey! Lookie here—we got a sharp one!" Hack said sarcastically. "Yes, goddamned Mickey Mantle. If you think *I'm* a lush, then he—"

"Why would we think you're a lush?" Zeke Bailey asked, innocent as a nun's underwear.

Hack ignored him, "—he was sauced all the fuckin' time. Sometimes we'd use guns, but Ol' Mick...he had this old bow his daddy gave 'im when he wasn't beatin' the ever-livin' shit outta' him. Called it 'Clarabell.' Always thought it had a nice ring to it."

"He *named* his *bow*?" Fynch asked.

Henry simply nodded with pride.

"Whattid I say?" Hack smacked the brim of the centerfielder's hat. "His *daddy* gave it to him, so his *daddy* named it," Hack raised his eyes skyward, "I *fear* fer' our youth, I really do."

Hack looked at the players in the back of the bus, "Anyway, Mick an' I would go out, and we'd look fer' deers ta' hunt. Now, believe it er' not, I wasn't always the baddest little turd the devil ever shat out."

This inspired a number of laughs from the players, many of whom now sat rapt.

"First time I ever went huntin' with Mick was...I think Jan-U-ary of 1961. No, '60. No, wait, it was '61. Right before he and Maris hit all'a them taters. I had just been traded to the Yankees, had a cup'a coffee in the show in '60, and he wanted to welcome me with a good ol' time back in Oklahoma. Said it'd 'build character' or make me a man,' or some shit like that. Givin' his upbringin', I'm surprised 'makin' a man outta' me' didn't just consist'a takin' me down to Oklahoma ta' beat the shit outta' me with a strap.

"So I get to Oklahoma and he takes me out in this old, ugly, green Ford pickup, and we drive fer' hours. Maybe not quite as long as this bus ride, but a good damned while.

"We finally get to this clearin', and he tells me, he says, 'Roger, I know you ain't too keen on huntin', killin' things and the sort. But we're gonna' stay out here, without supplies, and we're not gonna' eat a goddamned *thing* until you kill us a deer to eat with Ol' Clarabell here.'

"Well, I was shocked. Damned straight I didn't wanna kill no deers. 'Specially with no damned fool crossbow like the fuckin' Sheriff of Nottingham huntin' Robin Hood!"

More laughs from the players.

"So I keep tellin' him, 'Mick, I ain't gonna' do it.' And he keeps sayin', 'The *fuck* you ain't.' We kept goin' back-and-forth like that fer' two whole *days*. We came across plenty of the damned things, and each time, it was, 'I ain't gonna do it.' 'The *fuck* you ain't.' All the while, Mick had that big ol' farmboy grin on his face, like he knew somethin' that I was only just fixin' to know.

"By the end'a that second day, I was starvin', boy, I would'a done anything for somethin' to eat. But, damned *fool* that I was, I held out as long as I could, outta' *spite* at that point. And Mick was just goofy ol' Mick, bidin' his time, waitin' for that deer to show his'self."

Hack stifled a hiccup.

"So finally, in the middle'a day three, I can't take it anymore, and I says ta' him, I says, 'Give me Ol' Clarabell. I'm gonna shoot one'a these fuckin' things. And he grins and tells me, 'Have at it, hoss.'

"So we wait...and wait...and wait...two days full'a deer, and then they disappear all afternoon.

"I'm goin' *crazy* with hunger at this point, just outta my mind. And Mick's just laughin' and foolin' me about how we're gonna starve out here, and how half'a New York's gonna curse my fuckin' name for eternity fer' killin' their Mick.

"So it's gettin' to be around sunset, and as I'm tellin' Mick what a horrible sonofabitch he is, he puts his finger to his lips, just like this," Hack raised his index finger to his lips. "And then points out to the field.

"Men, let me tell *you*, it was the biggest fuckin' buck I ever saw. Horns like the angriest bird's nest ever made, must'a been half-a-ton if it was a pound. Beady little eyes like coal in its brown, buck head.

"So this is it. I'm ready. I raise the crossbow up on a log. I steady it in my shakin' hands. I get the buck in my sights and take a deep breath..."

Hack held an invisible crossbow up to his eye and let a hush fall over the bus.

"RACAW!" Hack clapped his hands together. Most of the bus flinched reflexively. One player even shrieked. "A goddamned hawk screeched that shit out right as I pulled the trigger. That fuckin' buck took off right for us. Kickin' up dust, mean as shit, almost like he *knew* that I was fixin' to kill it just moments before.

"'Course, by now, Mick's screamin' at me, 'Give me the fuckin' crossbow! Yer' gonna kill us both, you dumb shit asshole!' But I just froze, as that buck kept chargin'…and chargin'…and chargin'…all kinds'a snotty and sore at me fer' tryin' to kill it.

"Finally, just as the thing gets, oh, I dunno, fifty yards away, somethin' clicks in my head. I give Mick a good shove and tell him, no *command* him, 'Mick, give me another arrow.' His eyes go real wide and he practically throws the damned thing at me.

"So I set it up, pull back the bow, all that good stuff, latch it into place, and without thinkin', I bring the thing back on the log, set it up, aim, and BANG! Fire!"

The players all jumped in their seats.

"I hit that sonofabitch right between the eyes. And I'll never forget it, the look on that damned deer's face—it was just as mean and nasty in death as it was when it was gonna' gore Mick and me.

"And I says, 'Say Mick, that didn't feel too bad, did it?' Cause I knew, sure as shit, that fuckin' deer would'a killed us otherwise.

"You know what Mick does? He nods once or twice, lights a cigarette, takes a pull, and says to me, 'Now, you're a man.'"

As Hack finished the nod to mimic Mantle's, everyone on the bus sat, awake and mouths agape, even the Latino players, who followed along with Hack's impassioned pantomimes.

After several moments, Sid Fynch broke the silence.

"So what's the point?"

"Goddamn it, Sid, don't you see?" It was Truck. "We could *all* use a moment like that," he turned toward Hack, "Outside of our comfort zone to truly show the courage that being a man requires."

Hack rapped Truck on the brim of the hat.

"*Fuck* no! It's that you never know when the fuck a mean ol' deer's gonna show up, even if you've been seeing nothin' but nice little lady deers for days."

He turned toward Henry.

"So goddamn right, you *bring* that crossbow with you, Mitch. Everywhere you go. Damned proud of ya', son; you're a red-blooded American."

Henry nodded, tentatively at first, but eventually forcefully as he mustered his usual bravado.

"Damn skippy! Unlike that fuckin' Presi—"

"*And* so it's your responsibility to teach that to some'a these other, softer guys," Hack locked eyes with Fynch. "They may be ballplayers, but any person offerin' to have his daddy do his fightin' for him, fists 'er otherwise, sure as *shit* ain't a man yet…"

Hack looked around the crowd that had leaned in, and which now included both Willie and Pete Moray. Even the bus driver was stealing glances toward the back as the charter continued down the highway.

"Now if you'll excuse me, I have to piss like Mick's horse after a two-day bender. But *that's* a story for another day…"

Hack casually pulled himself on seatbacks toward the small restroom at the back of the bus, fiddled with the door for several seconds before he could get it open, and practically threw himself inside.

Had he not been doing so, he would've seen Mitch Henry offer Sid Fynch a cap tip, followed by a most unusual sight indeed:

Henry sat back, quietly, and watched the scenery as it rolled by.

3

They arrived in Featherstone around eleven a.m.; it was only enough time to check into "Mike's Motor Inn," which was obviously (to Hack, at least) a converted, old Howard Johnson, and let the players try to get a couple of winks of sleep before the night's game.

For his part, Hack could only think about one thing as he practically kicked in the door to his room, flung his suitcase on the ancient, musty, floral bedspread, and greedily seized upon it.

"Come to PAPA!" he let out excitedly as the latch gave and the full bottle of Old Reliable sat, practically undisturbed.

"That was a close one, darlin'," Hack said. He guzzled half the bottle in one draught and wiped his mouth with his worn, vaguely fuzzy, plaid shirtsleeve.

No sooner had he lowered the bottle from his greedy lips than he heard a loud banging.

"KNOCK KNOCK KNOCK."

"Fer' cryin' out loud!" Hack yelled, hoping that whomever had interrupted his self-medication session would realize what a bother they were being. "Who is it?"

"It's Willie."

"Who?" Hack asked sarcastically.

"Wise ass old fuck. I need to talk to ya!"

Hack picked up the bottle in both hands and held it in front of his face.

"Sorry sweetheart. Daddy has some business to attend ta'." He swung the bottle under the bed.

"PING!"

"Fuck!" Hack yelled. Instead of the empty space he had hoped to find under the bed, the bottle hit the solid base flush and shattered, leaving a puddle of cheap whiskey and glass shards that only barely soaked into the heavily scotch-guarded muave carpet.

Hack dropped to his knees in the middle of the chaos; for the moment, he ignored the wrenching pain that he felt from the neck all the way down to his feet.

"Didn't even get to make my Mean S.O.B. yet!" He hissed at himself. He lunged for his suitcase and tore through its contents until he found the bottles of Robitussin and pills buried inside.

He unscrewed both tops and poured out a half-dozen pain pills before he chased them with the viscous cough medicine.

Hack grimaced; it was the first time in a good long while that he had choked down the medicinal-tasting liquid without following it with whiskey. Unfortunately, the sweet, familiar taste of Old Reliable to wash it down was no longer an option.

Or was it?

The pool of whiskey still fought to seep into the carpet. Glistening splinters of glass littered the quagmire like tiny, ominous icebergs that shone in the pale green fluorescent overhead light.

Hack felt the sweet acetone taste building from his throat. Before it could overtake him and induce another fit, he dropped to his knees in the middle of the mess and started lapping up the whiskey like a kitten.

Willie banged on the door again, but Hack was far too busy trying to soak up as much of the Old Reliable as he could to fight back another fit. The sweet taste was powerful and pungent; he knew the episode would be a doozy if he couldn't manage to fight it back.

"Coach? You in there?" Willie asked between hammering on the door.

"Just a—FUCK!" Hack recoiled in pain. While licking the whiskey off of the ground, he had inadvertently picked up a glass splinter, one which had lodged itself in his cheek with a sharp pinch.

He pursed his lips and spit the long, thin piece of glass out slowly. The jagged edges dragged across his cheek and tongue, and brought the coppery taste of blood from its former home in the back of his throat to the fore of his mouth.

The shard tumbled to the ground end-over-end like a bloody icicle from the roof of an arctic cave before it landed squarely in the pool of whiskey. It was followed by several more drops of Hack's blood that spread and diffused through the puddle, and gave it an eerie, almost tawny appearance.

Hack lowered his head once more, first to stare at the offending chip of glass, contemplating whether or not he could figure out a severe enough punishment for the fragment.

"Fuckin' little *shit* bastard!" Hack hissed at the thin splinter. He pursed his lips, half daring it to come back inside for a second round, half in reckless anticipation of sucking down some of the dwindling puddle of whiskey. Hack dug his fingers into the stiff carpet and tensed his arms, forcing himself not to give in, to let the carpet soak up its whiskey, to live to drink (maybe) one more day.

"What'd you call me?" Willie asked from beyond the door.

Hack turned toward the door. "I said, just a damned minute, Charles!"

"What?"

Hack looked back at the floor, only to find that the Old Reliable had sunk fully into the carpet, which left a dark, almost blood-colored stain on the ground. He grabbed the trashcan next to the dresser and tipped it over before he shoveled forearms full of glass into its too-tiny opening. Hack made a special effort to leave the lone splinter that had already caused him harm to be "dealt with properly" later.

Hack shook his head and and forced himself up. His back and knee protested, but Hack fought through the now-familiar sensations as he righted the trash can and haphazardly left it near its original resting place. Hack shook his head and sighed as a trickle of warmth dribbled over his head; at least in his mind, the "Mean S.O.B." was already having an effect.

He wobbled over to the door and yanked it. Willie appeared, ear still pressed up against the now-imaginary door, hand ready to knock again.

"Christ, you okay in there?" The faintest hint of concern tinged Willie's voice. "I thought I'd have to call the morgue, or a priest or somethin'."

"I think you'd need somethin' with a little more 'kick' than holy water to off me and get yer' job back, Charles," Hack said.

"Shit, I think that stuff would probably *dissolve* you if it got anywhere near ya'."

"Yeah, yer' prob'ly right." Hack met Willie's chuckle with a humorless stare.

Willie sized the little man up. Eventually, his eyes fixated on Hack's crotch.

"Everything okay in there?" Willie nodded toward he front of Hack's pants.

"Oh *sure*. I can still get as stiff as a teenager lookin' at a poster'a Jane Mansfield, you know, with the vig…vigara and whatnot."

Willie ignored the misspeak, "No, I mean—god damn it, look at your pants."

Hack did, and immediately saw the problem. Though Hack initially thought the carpet had absorbed most of the whiskey in the puddle, he now saw that when he moved to curse out the piece of glass that had torn up his mouth, the front of his pants sopped up the rest of the Old Reliable.

"Uh—" Hack was, for the second time in two days, caught completely off-guard. He thought quickly and shrugged. "Pissed myself."

Hack said it so matter-of-factly that Willie looked around to make sure that no one else was on the balcony of the motor lodge before he raised an eyebrow and leaned in toward the manager.

"Really?" Willie whispered.

Hack regained his confidence. "If you must know, then yes, Charles. Sometimes, us ol' timers can't exactly help it. I'm too old to give a damn, and too set in my ways to wear a diaper like a toddler."

"So, uh...hmm..." Willie made a fist and put it under his chin, in thought, before he whispered, "Does this, err, happen a, uh,"

"Fer' cryin' out loud, man! Stop stammerin' like Jack Kennedy and spit it out!"

Willie grimaced, "Does it happen, you know, *a lot* to guys your age?"

Hack barely curled his lips upward, "Yeah. Yeah it does. So along with the soft pecker and whatnot, you got *that* ta' look forward to, too. Though, in yer' case, that might leave a little more blood fer' yer' head, fer' thinkin' and whatnot, what with—"

Hack nodded at Willie's crotch.

Willie raised a finger and brought it right up into Hack's face. His eyes narrowed and his jaw tensed.

"I thought I told you—" Willie's scowl turned into a broad grin, "You can joke about that shit whenever you want."

Hack managed a curt smile. "Yer' comin' along just fine, Charles. Just fine..."

Willie's eyes went wide with concern.

"Your teeth! They're so *red*. Are you bleeding? Should I call a doctor?"

Hack waved the question away, already in full yarn-spinning mode.

"Naw, naw, you ever chew, Charles?"

"You mean, like *food?*" Willie said. He affected his earnest stare for several moments before he shook his head to let Hack know he was messing with him. "No, I never touched that shit. Not after playin' with Brett Butler my rookie year, seein' how awful that cancer can be. I ain't gonna lose my face over that."

"Might be an improvement..." Hack muttered as he stared off to the left.

"You lookin' in a mirror?" Willie asked.

Hack shook his head, "I love the shit. Red Man. Always Red Man."

"I've never seen you do that disgusting shit."

Hack paused, "It's an old road habit. Always have ta' have my Red Man after bein' on a bus or flyin' in a tin can fer' a few hours. Really helps me take off the edge…feel smooth, ya' know?"

Willie arched his eyebrow again, "So where is it?"

"Where's what?"

"The dip, or chew, or whatever—the Red Man?"

"Oh…" Hack turned to give Willie a better view of the puddle in the room, complete with the dark spot in the center. "I just spit it out."

"On the floor?"

"Yep."

"What about the maid? What about the cleaning crew?"

Hack leveled his steely gaze.

"Fuck 'em."

Willie frowned. "You're an animal. It's amazin' you're still alive."

Hack shrugged mischievously.

Willie shook his head. "Anyway, just came to tell you that Keith left a message in my room. Said he's gonna' call you after the game tonight. He actually sounded pretty pleased—almost like when he shoots under a hundred playin' golf."

"Reeeeallly?" Hack narrowed his eyes and tilted his head. "That can't be good."

Willie shook his head again, "No, it can't."

Both men chuckled for a moment at their if not mutual disdain (at least from Willie's perspective), then certainly recognition of their GM's peculiar work ethic.

"Is that it?" Hack said with a broad smile.

"Yeah, I guess. Oh, also—"

"Great!" Hack stepped back and slammed the door shut without waiting for Willie to get out of the way. He shuffled back toward the bed closest to the john.

Just as he bent his aching knee to cast himself onto the bed, Hack yelped as he felt a sharp pinch in his foot.

He landed on the bed and struggled with his leg, desperately pulling it up to see what had bitten him, even if he already knew.

Finally, after several such minutes, Hack reached for the spot, brought the tips of two stubby, gnarled fingers together, and produced the culprit:

It was the same splinter of glass he had nearly swallowed before.

Hack's jaw shut tight. He launched himself off the side of the bed and into the wall. After another swear or two, Hack marched over to the sink, muttering nonsense curse words all the while.

He turned on the faucet and picked up one of the flimsy, plastic cups on the sink. Without pausing to remove the plastic coating, he filled the cup with water, glared at the splinter in his fingers, popped it in his mouth and swallowed it with a glass of water.

He didn't even feel it go down.

As if the tiny piece of glass was a sleeping pill, satisfied and exhausted with how he had dispatched his nemesis, Hack staggered over to the bed and threw himself upon it.

Before his head touched the covers, he was out for a nap, in some ways happy both for the distraction of the piece of glass and the lies it had necessitated.

4

The visitor's clubhouse in Featherstone's "Sgt. Alvin P. Minor Memorial Stadium" still reeked of the fresh coat of paint and sawdust that indicated that it had been recently renovated.

Hack reviled the smell, if only because it was so damned *new*, so irregular, another aberration in a forty-eight hour span filled with them.

One occurrence that was becoming more regular was that the Magpies had won again that evening, 7-3, spurred on by homeruns by left fielder Ozzie Cabrera and (of course) Truck Traynor.

Though Willie and Pete Moray seemed to be enjoying the high ceilings, well-lit hallways, and generally clean surroundings offered by the coaches' locker room, Hack couldn't wait to leave.

Oddly enough, there was no entrance to the visiting manager's office directly from the coaches' locker room.

Hack grumbled at the oversight.

His disdain was balanced by the fact that earlier that afternoon, Hack discovered that Jim Taggert and the rest of the press corps wouldn't be following the team around on the road due to budget cuts at their respective employers.

On the one hand, Taggert had done Hack a huge favor by printing the two interviews that had helped endear him to the Hoplite faithful while the manager was in a precarious position.

On the other hand, fuck 'im, Hack thought.

He dressed in one of his three plaid flannel shirts and mothball-smelling pairs of blue slacks before he dared to enter the hallway through the clubhouse leading to the Manager's office.

As he approached the door and grabbed the knob, he paused. He looked first for Truck and Manny, who were still getting dressed in their respective corners.

Fearing any further surprises, Hack made an executive decision. He took a couple of steps toward the player closest to him to ensure that no one else got the jump on him in his office.

"Great game, Henry. Just a beaut'," Hack slapped the starting pitcher several times on the left shoulder.

"Thanks Skip. You made a pretty good decision yer'self, leavin' me in there and everything," Mitch Henry replied.

Hack forced a smile, "Damn fine work, son. Can I have a word with you in the office?"

"Sure. You got any more stories about huntin' with Mickey Mantle? Or maybe that one about the drunk horse you were fixin' to tell us?"

"Ah, another day, another day. Go on ahead inside and have a seat."

Henry casually turned the knob and opened the door. Hack approached the door from an angle and couldn't see what awaited his prized young starter, rough around the edges as he may be.

"What the FUCK?!"

Henry ducked and rolled away from the door before he bolted out of the crouch for his locker.

"What now?" Hack called after him. He teetered toward the door and peered inside.

He was a bit surprised to see Samantha Rappaport's meekly smiling face. She leaned against the desk facing the door, and offered a tremulous wave to the old manager.

"Oh, it's you." Hack couldn't conceal the eagerness from his voice. "What'd you do to Hen—?"

Before he finished asking, the chair beside her moved and turned slightly to face the door.

"Hello!" a smiling Asian face said with a head nod.

Hack barely had time to react. "Incoming!" he yelled and forced himself to the side of the room farthest away from the unusual visitor.

Mitch Henry sprinted toward the manager's office, camouflaged crossbow case in tow. Truck Traynor tore after the pitcher as the icepacks taped to his knees splashed gently against his joints.

"Goddamn zip—zipper!" Henry yelled as he struggled with the case. Just as Henry was about to slide the weapon from its sheath, Truck half-tackled the pitcher and forced him up against the wall.

"Easy, Mitch!"

"Goddamn it, Truck, we're bein' invaded here!" Henry replied.

"One oh four niner...one oh four niner...this is the U.S.S. Antietam...over..." Hack repeated in a trance.

Henry turned his head as best as he could toward the still-smiling man in the chair.

"Christ—look what you did. You sent him off his fuckin' rocker!"

The Asian man simply smiled and nodded.

"Hello!" he said cheerfully again.

Hack snapped back into reality, "He did not—" he eyed Truck for a moment before his suspicious gaze turned toward the polite Asian man next to the chair. Hack shook his head, "Forget it."

"Coach O'Callahan," Samantha was overbearingly earnest, "Keith—Mr. Myrick—sent me out here to meet up with our new second baseman—"

As soon as Sam mentioned Myrick, Hack picked up the phone and began dialing the Magpies' offices.

Or so he thought. He entered a string of meaningless numbers before the "call cannot be completed tone" blared through the receiver.

Hack slammed down the phone in anger.

"Charles!" he screamed. The purple veins ran hot and bulged through the manager's reddening neck.

Moments later, Willie appeared in the doorway.

"Yeah Coach?"

Hack picked up the receiver and held it out toward Willie casually, "Can you please dial KEITH...FUCKING...MYRICK'S CELL PHONE FOR ME!?"

Willie's eyes went wide as he took a step back. It was the first time he was legitimately afraid of the tiny codger, and even a little bit worried for his safety.

He wanted nothing more than to turn around and call in Pete Moray to make peace.

Instead, Willie calmly picked up the phone and dialed before he handed the set to Hack.

After three rings, a laughing Keith Myrick answered.

"Hello?"

"Do you wanna' tell me why there's a fuckin' CHINAM—" Hack looked at the smiling, unfazed Asian face in front of him. "—Chi-NESE in my office?"

Myrick laughed with glee, "First of all, he's not Chinese, he's Korean. His name is Sun Dae Woo, and—"

"Sunday WHO?" Hack screamed as he eyed the man in front of him suspiciously.

"Sun. Dae. Woo." Myrick separated out all three syllables.

"Hello!" The smiling player enthusiastically chimed in.

"Whatever!" Hack squinted at Woo, partially out of bald racism, but also to get a better look at his features, the deep creases that lined his forehead, and the—

"How old is this 'second baseman,' anyway?"

"He's a veteran of the Japanese league."

Hack smiled, eager to catch Myrick in a lie, "I thought you said he was Ko-rean."

"He is. He just played in the Japanese league for twelve years. Accomplished all he could over there, and the Rangers signed him this year and assigned him to their Double-A team. I just got him for a couple of Single-A washouts. Doesn't speak a lick of English."

"God DAMN IT!" Hack looked around the room and found that the only face that was still smiling was Woo's.

He lowered his voice, "God damn it, Keith, Friedmann's been doin' a fine job at second base. Just fine."

"Come on, Hack, you remember what you were telling me a few days ago about not having a problem with a Korean player, right?"

"This ain't about that," Hack lied habitually. "It's just…he's too damned *old*."

"Doesn't matter. I spoke to George Tavatelli already, and he seems to think it's a great move. Everyone's looking to get in the Japanese market these days, but Korea? No one's been in there since Chan Ho Park's heyday. The edict's from the big club this time, Hack—Woo plays. Every day. You're to try to get him major league-ready, and if you sit him, I'm authorized to replace you with Willie."

Hack instinctively looked up at his assistant. Willie leaned his head in, both resolute and eager to hear what the two were talking about.

Suddenly, Hack's expression brightened.

"Sure, Keith. I'll play Sunday here. It'd be my goddamn *pleasure*," He twisted his lips, now camouflaged by the redness of his face, into a forced smile.

"Now Hac—what? Really?"

"Yep. Like I said, the best nine'll play."

"That's…hmm…are you *sure* you can co-exist with Woo, Hack? I mean, with the post-traumatic stress and whatnot, I wouldn't want to force you into an early grave or anything like that. You're a war hero—this man's people tried to kill you and your—"

"It was a long time ago," Hack said without a hint of emotion. "I'm over it."

He slammed the receiver down without bothering to say goodbye. The manager glared at everyone in the room before he fixed on Woo. Hack brought his face within an inch of Woo's.

To his credit, the new second baseman didn't back down. Though his smile drooped, he was resolute as the manager sized him up.

Hack took a step back, "Everyone, this is Sunday. Sunday, everyone."

"Hello!" Woo said with a head nod.

"God damn it, doesn't he say anything else?" Mitch Henry asked.

"Fuck off, Henry," Truck said.

"Eat me, Truck. Eat me raw."

"Sunday here is our new second baseman," Hack interrupted the exchange.

Truck raised a hand that held down Henry and waved.

"Nice to meet you, Sun...day?"

"Sun *Dae*," Woo corrected him.

"Sun Dae." Truck turned his attention to Henry, "If I let you go to shake our new teammate's hand, can I trust you enough to not *shoot* him like a goddamned deer?"

Henry was silent.

"Well?" Truck asked.

"I'm thinkin'."

Willie approached the duo, "God damn it, Mitch, you act like you've never seen an Asian person before!"

"Well...truth be told, I haven't. Only time I've seen 'em is on the Military Channel, and they usually have bayonets attached to their fuckin' rifles, runnin' after good, hardworkin' Amur'can soldiers."

"You can't be serious," Sam interjected.

"Oh, sorry, Princess—not all'a us grew up in a goddamned multi-cultural college brochure kumbaya circle."

"Enough!" Willie interrupted. He turned his attention to Hack. "You sure you're cool with this?"

"No I most certainly am NOT," Hack replied. "I told Keith, I win three games, no bullshit from Cleveland. I get to run the team my way. Now they send in Sunday here just ta' get a rise outta' me. Well, I'm not about ta' let Keith Myrick, of all people, pull one over on me. Sunday's gonna' play, sure as shit, and we're gonna make him better. I won't let my..." Hack paused and brought his hand to his mouth in anticipation of a coughing fit that never came, "...history to get in the way."

Hack straightened his back and ignored the searing pain as it went taut, "But god *damn* it, it's gonna' be tough as well-done horsemeat to manage him if he can't speak English."

Hack turned to Woo, "DO...YOU...SPEAK...ENGLISH?"

Woo shook his head.

"Not a word?" Willie put a hand on the man's shoulder.

"Hello!" he responded with a wry grin.

Henry laughed at Woo.

Truck laughed at the joke.

"Hold on…" Willie raised a knowing finger. "Just hold on a damn minute…" he walked to the doorway of the manager's office, "Pete! Patrón! In Coach's office, now!" he called out.

"What is this, a fuckin' clown car?" Henry asked.

"With you in here it is," Truck said.

"God damn it—" Henry mocked a move to raise his crossbow, but Truck easily deflected it.

Willie made way for the gangly pitching coach and surly Latin first baseman.

"Whoa, guess the party's in here!" Pete exclaimed. It took several moments for the smile to dissolve from his face when he realized that no one else in the room shared his amusement.

"Cut the shit for a minute, Pete," Willie said. His eyes were fiery and intense, lit ablaze by the cauldron of shit the GM had dumped into the otherwise improving clubhouse. Willie nodded at Patrón. "Juan here had some visa problems when he first tried to sign up with our Dominican academy, right?"

Moray stroked his chin, "Well, shit, I don't rightly know…"

"ASK him then," Willie said. "En Español."

Pete shrugged and complied.

"Sí," Patrón replied. His expression was sour and bothered, a moody power-hitter if there ever was one.

"Didn't he have to play in Korea for a year-and-a-half or so?"

This time, Pete didn't wait to be told a second time.

Juan nodded.

Willie put his hand on Patrón's shoulder. The slugger narrowed his eyes, but Willie met them not with the confrontation leveled upon Pete Moray, but rather with understanding and compassion.

Hack's lips twisted up almost imperceptibly into a tiny smirk.

"Juan, did you pick up any Korean during your time there?"

Willie glanced at Moray, who translated.

Patrón's stare was level and even.

"Un poco."

"Bueno," Willie smiled, "Bueno." He walked over to Woo and pulled him toward the powerful Dominican. "Juan, Sunday. Sunday, Juan. You guys are gonna be road roommates for the rest of the year."

Pete dutifully translated.

"Hello!" Sun Dae nodded, his perpetual smile in stark contrast to his new roommate's scowl.

Patrón eyed the tiny, older Korean man skeptically before he turned to Pete and uttered several Spanish words in quick succession.

"What'd he say?" Willie asked.

"He wants to know 'what about Manny?'"

Truck stepped forward, "I'll take him in. Provided, you know, it's okay with Sid and everything."

Hack couldn't control sickly sweet, acetone taste in the back of his throat, that signal that, though lessened over the past several days, indicated another impending coughing fit. He grabbed the handkerchief from his back pocket and brought it swiftly to his mouth, covering the coppery spittle.

Sam Rappaport rummaged through the backpack on the ground next to the desk. She emerged with a bottle of water and unscrewed the cap before she brought the container to Hack's lips.

The old man gargled through the liquid before he was able to choke some of it down. It ran cool down his throat, a refreshing stream fighting against the hurricane of blood and phlegm struggling its way out of his diseased innards.

After several healthy gulps, the fit calmed and Hack wiped his mouth with the sleeve of his shirt. The faces around the room looked back with varying levels of concern, compassion, and amusement.

"We'll, uh…Coach Williams'll arrange the new road roommates. Truck, I may need a leader like you to help Sid out."

"Well, shit," Henry interrupted. "I'm a leader, I can take Sid under my wing."

"Goddamn it, Mitch, you're chasin' yer' own demons!" Hack yelled.

"What the fuck does that mean, Coach?" Henry was more surprised than anything.

Willie watched as the now-familiar glint in Hack's eyes told of a brewing plot by the cagey codger.

"Tell you what, Mitch, if you really wanna' be'a leader on this team, why don'tchya take ol' Manny in on the road? Teach'im the ropes of pitchin' and everythin'. Maybe even a lil' English here 'er there, or whatever's close ta' English 'y'all' have down in 'Bama."

Hack looked at Truck, "You need to keep Sid in line. 'Cause sure as I'm a cuss, if ya' give him any room right now, he'll be the same spoiled little *prick* fer' the rest'a his life. Make him a man, Truck—er, I—" Truck's eyes went wide as Hack recognized the error of his phrasing, "Make him not his daddy's boy anymore. I can't *stand* that type'a bullshit on my team. Are we clear?"

Hack looked around the room for dissent, but found none, save for the scowl affixed to Juan Patrón's face, even as Pete finished his translation and Juan nodded.

"Good. Now I need to have a word with sharp girl over here. As fer' the rest'a yas...git the fuck out!" Hack shoed the small cadre of players and coaches out of the visiting manager's office with little more than a wave, though none required any more of an invitation to leave.

As the door shut, Hack stumbled over to the wheeled chair behind the desk and heaved himself into it.

"I, uh, just wanted to properly thank ya' fer' earlier."

Sam smiled, "Oh, think nothing of it, Coach O'Callahan. I—"

"Please, Samantha, call me Hack."

Her bag sagged in her hand as she moved it to her chest.

"I...I don't know what to say. This is an honor, I—"

Hack nodded, "Damn straight it is. But you've saved me twice now—if anyone's earned it, you have. Seen me practically bare-assed, too."

Sam unconsciously averted her eyes out of bred modesty.

"Well, if I hadn't earned it before, maybe this'll seal it." She reached into her bag and lugged out a handle of Old Reliable.

Hack couldn't hide his pride, "Heyyyy, lookie there! Old Reliable." His face went pale as he sank back in his chair, "Ya' got no idea how much I needed this, Sam. Thank ya' from the bottom of my heart. How did ya'—?"

Sam laughed, "It's no problem. Sun Dae was more than happy to get it for me, though it involved some pointing and gesturing. I figured you might need it once you saw what Keith—Mr. Myrick— had in store."

"He'll be lucky if I don't bash the damn bottle over his head once I'm through with it!" He swiveled around toward Sam again, "Right now, I could adopt ya'." He popped out of the chair and rustled her hair. Red strands fell in Sam's face as she mock pouted.

"I hope you don't mind my asking, but did you have any children of your own?"

The happiness vanished from Hack's face.

"Tha—thanks for the whiskey, Sam. I'm tuckered out—still need to get back to the hotel. Keith fly ya' out for the night?"

Sam shook her head, "Taking the red-eye back to Cleveland, then a bus to Hoplite."

"A *bus*!" Hack nearly hit the ceiling. "Pretty young girl like you, on'a goddamn *bus* all by her lonesome?"

Sam smiled again, "I can handle myself, Hack. Besides, there'd be more degenerates pawing at me if I stuck around for the rest of the trip and took the bus back with you."

Hack couldn't help but smile, "Yeah, yer' prob'ly right. Well, have fun, and..." Hack looked past her for a moment, lost in thought. The nail polish remover smell was back, as was the taste of fresh blood at the back of his throat. Thoughts of the cancer slowly working its way from his liver to his gut and, probably eventually climbing his esophagus to God-knows-where else in his body started to flood his mind.

Soon...a voice from deep within bellowed. It jarred Hack in his seat; he felt his chest as it heaved with deep breaths, as the chair's arms seemed to come alive in his own mind and squeeze him until unable to breathe.

…but not yet…

More than anything, he wanted to kill that voice, to empty that sweet, inviting bottle of Old Reliable down his gullet until it drowned out that awful creature growing inside of him, until he was immortal in his own mind once more.

But he couldn't rightly do so until he was back in the relative safety of his own room, away from this wonderful girl, young enough to be his granddaughter, but still so bubbling with life and warmth that she was able to cut through his craggy surface and help the wounded soul within.

Hack snapped out of it and locked eyes with Sam once more, "Stay safe."

"I will. Goodbye Coach O'Ca—" she stopped and nodded once. "Goodbye, Hack." She opened the door to the office.

"Seeya in Hoplite, sharp girl."

Fifth Inning

1

The Magpies swept Featherstone in three straight, and followed that up with a 5-1 stretch over the next two series in Houston, Kansas and Henry Falls, South Dakota ("Named for my great granpappy," Mitch Henry had tried to convince everyone during their time in town).

It didn't hurt that Mitch Henry threw two gems and that the rest of the Hoplite pitching staff soon settled into their newly-defined roles with relative ease.

After the rocky start to his career on the mound, Manny Poblado anchored the bullpen with five saves over the stretch, and appeared to be gaining confidence with every outing.

Some of that confidence was owed to the efforts of Pete Moray, who used the necessity of teaching Manny a secondary pitch to play off of his heavy, lively fastball to try to get the shy converted shortstop to open up to the rest of the Latin players and become a leader in the clubhouse.

"Christ, Manny, you already speak better English than Henry over here," Moray entreated Manny on the way to Westfield, Indiana, the final stop on the road trip.

"Not in the motel room he don't," Henry said, confirming Moray's statement. "All this motherfucker does is listen to salsa music and read his fuckin' Spanish books on his Mexican Kindle. Doesn't say a goddamn thing."

Manny shook his head and smiled, simultaneously happy that Mitch Henry had finally noticed him and was treating him like one of the guys, but also terrified that since they were now roommates, it would be far easier for Mitch to discover his secret.

And if that happened, Manny wasn't so sure Mitch would take it so lightly.

"I'll bet you say enough for both of ya'," Truck tapped Mitch lightly on the left shoulder with his rolled-up men's magazine.

"What can I say? When I spit wisdom like a goddamned fountain, am I supposed'ta keep that shit to myself?"

"Fuck yes!" Sid Fynch echoed the thoughts of the rest of the bus.

"I swear to God, Sid, I'm gonna take you huntin' in the offseason, and then we'll see who's more of a man."

"Damn right we will," Sid mustered as much bravado as he could, though it was undermined by the tremulous crack in his voice.

Pete ignored the exchange, "My point is—" he looked around and found Juan Patrón passed out, sunglasses on, in his customary seat two rows from the back of the bus, "—Patrón's been hittin' fer' shit the past five games or so. I think it might help him if ya', you know, encourage him a bit. The big club's bankin' on him and Truck to be the middle of their lineup for the next ten years."

"I donno'," Manny shrugged. "Why would Juan listen a yo?"

"Because, I dunno' if you noticed, son, but you're startin' to catch the eye'a some'a the folks in Cleveland. You've got a legit shot of making the big club next year, provided that you can keep that fastball'a yours workin' off of that changeup I'm teachin' ya. Speakin' of which, take out that ball I gave ya' with the finger placements on it."

Manny produced what had become his prized possession as of late, a batting practice ball that Pete had painted "meticulously" (as far as Moray was concerned) to approximate the finger placement for a circle change-up.

140

"Now, why is it called a circle change again?" Moray had learned that by asking Manny more questions, he got the youngster into the spirit of talking more, and took his mind off of whatever far-off problems usually occupied it.

"Is circle change because—" Manny formed a circle with his thumb and index finger, as if giving the okay sign, "—these two fingers, they form a circle on the side'a the ball," he placed his middle and ring fingers on the seams, "and these fingers go on the stitches an' I throw it hard, but it come out slow."

"Good—very good!" Pete beamed. "You're becomin' a regular pitcher already."

Suddenly, Mitch Henry's booming voice interrupted the relative peace.

"God *damn* it, Sid, you faggot!" Henry boomed out. "Stop that gay-ass spitwad shit."

"Hey, wasn't me…" Fynch shrugged as he carelessly waved a straw around in his hand.

"I'm tryin' Pete, I really am," Henry turned to Moray, "But a fuckin' buttpirate like this makes it *real* tough on me…" Henry paused for effect. "Real tough…"

Truck bit his lip. Manny's eyes grew wide and fearful, not necessarily worried that Henry had found them out, but rather at what he might do if he did.

"Judge lest not ye be judged," Zeke Bailey said from beneath a Magpies hat pulled over his eyes.

"What the *fuck*, Zeke?" Henry asked.

"Matthew 7, verse one. Cool it with the slurs, Mitch."

"Well, well, lookie here. Looks like we've got the Jackie Robinson of faggots on this bus!"

"I ain't gay, Mitch," Zeke said. "But odds are someone on this bus is. They say it's ten percent worldwide. The Bible's very clear that our compassion for our fellow man comes before any other duty we owe one another. 'Let he who is without sin cast the first stone.' That one's from John 8, verse—"

"Shit, I don't need a fuckin' Bible lesson, Zeke; my granpappy was a preacher after they moved down to 'Bama from Henry Falls—"

"Again, with this Henry Falls shit?" Truck said, happy to try to change the subject.

"If a man lies with a fuckin' man like he has a woman, both of 'em have committed a God-damned abomination. That's from Leviticus," Henry said.

"I don't think 'G-D' is in the original text…" Zeke said.

"Shit, Zeke, you of all people, I thought with a proper Christian upbringing you'd—"

Zeke nodded, "I was lucky enough to *have* a 'proper Christian upbringin',' Mitch. One that focused on the compassion and forgiveness Christ showed to even the sinners and meek, those who can't defend themselves."

"It's fahkin' *sick*, is what it comes down'ta'," Murph Murphy interrupted in his thick Boston accent. "Guys fahkin' guys? Gives me tha' fahkin' *creeps*. It's retahded."

"Amen'ta' that, Murph," Mitch said.

"What the hell is *wrong* with you people?" Flash Gamble had pulled off his headphones and joined the discussion. "What the hell does it matter who's gay and who's not?"

"'Cause I don't want Sid back here tryin' to make out with me in the shower or blow me or nothin' like that," Henry said.

Truck locked eyes with Manny briefly, fearful that one might betray the other in a moment of anger.

Manny looked back, eyes wide, sweat starting to bead on his dark skin.

Truck broke his gaze and stared anxiously toward the front of the bus. He desperately wanted Hack to intervene again, to release the pressure valve with another charming story that would take all of their minds off of the unfortunate subject at hand.

Unbeknownst to Truck, though, Hack had "doubled down" on Mean S.O.B.s before he had left, and was blissfully passed out at the front of the bus, along with Willie, who was a fitting, conked-out front bookend to Patrón at the rear of their column of seats.

Truck was snapped out of his reverie as Henry slapped him on the shoulder.

"How 'bout you, Truck? Guy with a hot piece'a ass waitin' for him, educated, all that shit—whatta' *you* think about the gays?"

Truck took a deep breath, though he made an effort to disguise as much. He didn't have to pretend to think: was this the time? Could he do it right here, right now, yell with all of his might, "*The Emporer is Naked!*"

And totally gay? He thought.

…Or at least bi.

But when Truck opened his mouth, the fear deep in his gut took over and choked the words back down into his stomach. It seemed as if the dozens of eyeballs on him, the stares of his teammates wrapped around his neck and choked off the words even as they were coming up.

Truck shrugged, "To each his own, I s'pose," he nearly slurred the words he was so ashamed. A sharp pang of regret shot through Truck's torso and caused him to shiver.

Henry shook his head and took two steps toward the back of the bus.

"Shit, I'll bet ol' Sunday here is a flamer," Henry said, patting the new second baseman on the head.

Sun Dae waited several beats before he smiled and nodded.

"Hello!"

This caused an eruption of laughter among everyone on the bus. Even Juan Patrón's lips curled into an imperceptible smile as he listened to his roommate's antics.

"Shit, that's what I love about this fuckin' Chinaman—"

"Korean," Truck corrected Henry.

"—Whatever. Can't speak a lick'a English, but has the comedic timin' of fuckin' Don Rickles."

The rest of the bus went silent.

"Aw, come on, don't tell me none'ya ever heard of Don Rickles!" Henry seemed personally offended.

"How the hell are we supposed to know about Don Rickles?" Sid asked.

"The man's only a fuckin' comedic *genius*, that's all. Not afraid to go racial, sexist, whatever."

"It's part of his act," Truck said. "He gives it to everyone equally, and no one's offended."

"Just like me," Henry nodded proudly.

"Shit, you pitch about as well as Don Rickles could," Truck said. He forced a disarming grin.

Henry merely smiled and nodded, "That's 'cause you call a game like his fuckin' *wife*."

Truck laughed and shook his head as the familiar shame that came with the lump still in his throat tore at his conscience. He had tried so many times before, to tell so many people, his parents, his brothers, even some of his teachers and friends.

But whenever he tried to just say it, to put his sexuality out there in the world, to relieve himself of that suffocating burden that gnawed at him, and told him somehow he was inferior, he couldn't do it, in large part due to all of the "Mitch Henry"s that had haunted him through his amazing ascent to the brink of the majors, and now threatened to ruin that final step.

Not that he thought that Mitch was necessarily an evil person, but he was certainly ignorant, and ignorance can be worse than evil, especially when that ignorance allows those with truly evil motives to spit their nonsense to the masses and multiply their numbers tenfold.

While Truck sat near the back of the bus, contemplating all of these thoughts, his manager sat at the front of the bus, stirred out of his codeine-opiate-booze-induced stupor several miles back by a bump in the road.

And as he sat there, ballcap over his eyes, Hack's lips twisted into an unmistakable grin.

Good kid, Hack thought.

But the thoughts of what his catcher must be going through soon turned to his own personal hell, the one thing that he had been dreading about this final stop on the road trip. It would take him

144

dangerously close to Indianapolis, which meant that he would likely have to suck it up and have a meeting he had been dreading for the past twenty years.

Good kid, Hack thought again and fell back into his chair, cheek against the cool glass of the window.

Good kid…

2

Hack looked at his watch, a gold Rolex that the Marlins had given him when he finally retired those fifteen or so years before.

When he had first received it, Hack was honestly shocked. "Probably turn my wrist green," he mumbled to the owner, a little too close to the microphone by home plate during his retirement ceremony.

Perhaps because of his frugality, the Marlins' owner at the time, Phillip Voss, did nothing but smile and pat Hack on the back.

"We aren't gonna miss ya," he said.

"Fuck off," Hack replied.

What Voss didn't tell Hack was that he bought eight dozen of the watches from a wholesaler known for ripping off shipments of hot goods, laundering them through Southeast Asia, and selling them for pennies on the dollar.

Hack was amazed that the face read "11:35."

A red-and-white Crown Vic turned onto the access road for the clean, modern Holiday Inn Express. As the car drew nearer, Hack squinted and saw a younger East Indian fellow behind the wheel.

Oh goody... he thought.

That he didn't speak the sentiment could only be labeled a sign of "progress."

"Hello sir!" the cabbie said in moderately-accented English as he threw the car into park and opened the driver's side door.

"Yer' late," Hack replied.

"Yes, so very sorry. Traffic, very busy traffic right now, you know. I thought you might enjoy the beautiful day we were having."

The driver smiled at Hack. Immediately, several birds chirped out their songs and a gentle breeze wafted hints of the nearby patches of fragrant flowers through the uncharacteristically mild June day.

"Hadn't noticed," Hack remained stony and cold.

The driver skitted around to the rear passenger-side door and made a move toward the handle.

"Don't worry," Hack waited until the last moment. "I've got it."

Correctly intuiting that Hack was the type to use such a maneuver to get out of paying a passable tip, the driver did his best to grin and nod before he turned and scowled all the way back to the driver's seat.

Hack lurched into the car; though the Mean S.O.B. he had downed in the room had yet to take effect, his throat hadn't felt quite so clear in quite some time.

"Where to?" the cabbie asked.

"Uh…" Hack surveyed a crumpled piece of paper, "…4562 Henrietta Lane."

"Very well."

The driver pulled away from the hotel and into traffic.

"First time in Westfield?" The cabbie asked.

"Mmmnno," Hack mumbled, clearly not wanting to talk.

"How long has it been since you last visited us?"

This set Hack off, "I sure as shit didn't visit you, *pal*, since yer' accent's so goddamn thick and it's goin' on twenny' *years* now since I been here."

The cabbie smiled, unfazed, "I'll bet the town's changed quite a bit in those twenty years or so, hasn't it?"

"Yeah, you could say the 'complexion' of the town's sure changed a bit…" Hack rolled his eyes.

"Indeed. It's a beautiful town now. The mayor has done a great job with it, just wonderful, all of the flowers and everything, it is *gorgeous*. I think a magazine even named it one of the hundred best places to live in this wonderful country."

"Ya' don't say…" Hack reflexively locked his door.

"Oh yes. I think it all started once the Reds decided to bring their Double-A team here. The Mice have been a big boon to the economy—if they could take the wind out of those god damned Magpies and—"

"Yer' a baseball fan are ya'?" Hack perked up.

"Oh, yeeeessss, *huge* fan of the Mice. Huuuuge!" The cabbie banged on the worn vinyl coating on the Crown Vic's glovebox, which caused the compartment to drop, and revealed a collection of red-and-grey Westfield Mice gear.

The driver lunged over the center console and dove into the pile, momentarily taking his eyes off the road in the process.

"Watch the damned road, will ya'!?" Hack yelled.

"Sorry, sorry." The man grabbed a small card and held it into the back of the vehicle.

"What the hell is this?" Hack asked as he surveyed the card.

"See? V.I.P. *Mouse*! It is for *all* season ticket holders who have had their tickets for five or more years. V.I.P.! Me! What a country!"

"Yeah, it's pretty fuckin' fantastic," Hack deadpanned.

"So tell me, good sir, are you a baseball fan too?"

Somethin' like that… Hack wanted to say.

But he couldn't resist, "Actually, ya' know those Magpies you think yer' gonna' beat tonight?"

"Yeah?" The cabbie said with a broad smile.

"Well I manage 'em."

"Nooo!" The cabbie smacked his mouth with an open palm before he narrowed his eyes at the rear-view mirror. "It can't be—but it *is* you, isn't it? Oh my God! Hack O'Callahan!"

Hack blew out a mouthful of air in a fake sigh, as if bothered that this happened all the time, "Yep, it's me."

"Oh my goodness! I cannot *believe* it's you! Not in my wildest dreams did I ever think that you'd be sitting in my cab. Sir, I have to say, I appreciate everything you did for Cincinnati during your time there. Though I am a proud V.I.P. Mouse first and foremost, I follow all of my favorite players all the way to Cincinnati, and *you* were instrumental in their World Series victory those twenty-five years ago or so."

"Yeah, that was one hell of a club…" Hack looked out the window wistfully.

"Damn right!" The cabbie swerved to avoid a stalled car at the last minute, sending Hack reeling in the back seat. "But they needed you to be the skipper that guided the ship, no?"

"They needed a boot in their asses, is what they needed!" Hack said with a chuckle.

The cabbie thought this was hilarious, and launched into his own high-pitched squeal.

"And you were the one to boot their asses, yes?"

"Damn right!" Hack chuckled again. "I like you, kid. What's yer' name?"

"Sandy," he extended a hand to the backseat.

"Sandy?" Hack took it.

"Actually, it's Sanjay, but everyone here calls me Sandy."

"Well, San-JAY, very nice to meetchya. Yer' well ahead of all'a yer' buddies around these parts."

"What do you mean?" Sandy's eyes narrowed. "We have a very warm and vibrant community of East Indian immigrants who—"

"Christ, *again* with the race thing. Do I seem like a racist? Do I have 'racist' written all over my face or somethin'?"

Sandy shook his head. He didn't have the heart to give the man an honest answer.

"No, what *I'm* talkin' about is younger folks, folks yer' age."

"I am thirty-seven," Sandy said.

Hack nodded, "Yeah, young, like I said."

Both men paused.

Hack broke the silence, "None'a these young kids nowadays wanna' play baseball. It's all 'football, football, football.' And the inner-city brothers just wanna' play basketball."

"It is the same in my country—no one appreciates the game. All I hear about is cricket and soccer, cricket and soccer—it is so *boring.*"

"It's all a bunch'a *bullshit,* is what it is. These damned parents all think that with the right teachin' or instructin' or whatever, their little snowflake is gonna' become the next Mickey Mantle or Johnny Bench.

"What they don't realize is that both'a those guys coulda' been in Africa fer' twenty years, never heard a word about baseball, been dropped on a Major League team, and by the end'a the year, they would'a been serviceable players. Not the stars they were, but damn fine, just damn fine.

"It's so unfashionable ta' talk about things like 'God-given talent' and 'natural ability' nowadays. All anyone wants ta' talk about is how hard ya' haveta' work if ya' want somethin'. And that can be true. Johnny Bench worked his goddamn *ass* off from sunup to sundown on becoming a better catcher, and fer' my money, he was the best there ever was."

"Damn right!" Sandy looked in the rearview mirror and nodded with pride.

"But I swear to God, Johnny Bench also had the damned biggest hands you've ever seen. He could'a torn apart phonebooks or popped melons like grapes in the circus if he wasn't a ballplayer. So even then, there was somethin' generic about him—"

"Generic?" Sandy interrupted.

"Yeah, you know? 'Generic?' Like with the DNA and whatnot?"

"Genetic," Sandy corrected him.

"Goddamn it! Whatever!" Hack scowled at the driver. "I was on a roll, and goddamned if you don't stop me in my tracks like—"

"You were saying that even Johnny Bench, hardest working catcher ever, had to have some kind of natural, God-given ability."

"Right...thanks..." Hack mumbled. "My point is, Mick had even *more* God-given talent, and took care of himself about as well as a ten cent hooker. But look what Mick did with'it—hit over 500 homeruns, three-time MVP. And the thing that should scare the *shit* outta' everyone is that Mick could've done *better*. For all'a the awards and trophies and records he set, he could've done *better*."

"I feel the same way about my brother-in-law back in India, Nikhil. He was a real bastard guy, a sonofabitch who…"

Hack sat back in his chair and looked out the window. For whatever reason, those last two phrases seemed particularly relevant given his destination, and jarred him almost as much as the moment of sober clarity with his cancer days before.

As Sandy buzzed on about what an abhorrent crook and thief his brother-in-law was, Hack thought of all the ways he would have been served to take his own, now seemingly sage, advice through the years.

I could've done better…

3

From a distance, 4562 Henrietta Lane in Westfield, Indiana was just like any of its neighbors: a perfectly fine, wood-sided, cottage-style ranch house that appeared to be the perfect slice of suburbia with its white exterior and periwinkle blue shutters.

But upon closer inspection, the white paint had dulled and was beginning to chip. The well-manicured lawn contained large swaths of crab grass, and the driveway was uneven, cracked, and in need of repair.

Despite all of its faults, the house stood proudly along Henrietta Lane like a veteran soldier in a row of newbies, guarding its side of the sidewalk from whatever evils might turn their attention its way.

Unfortunately for the entire neighborhood, on this otherwise idyllic afternoon, Hack O'Callahan rolled up in Sandy's cab, with a dark and troubling secret on his mind.

"And he *still* had the nerve to return the blender I gave him for his birthday, that bastard guy!" Sandy still was engrossed in the one-way conversation about his brother-in-law.

"How much do I owe ya'?" Hack asked.

"Oh…let's see…" Sandy looked at the "$17.10" on the meter with a confused scowl. He shook his head and grinned, "Tell you what—" he slammed the glovebox again to open it, and produced two worn cardboard boxes containing "Official Major League Baseballs," sad not only because he had them in the glove box for just such an occasion, but also because it was obvious by the wrinkled tissue paper surrounding each ball that he had been snubbed multiple times previously.

A Sharpie was tucked into one of the boxes as Sandy passed them both back to his passenger.

"I'll stay here, and keep her running, but in exchange I just ask that you sign both of these baseballs."

"Sure," Hack grabbed them both greedily, without even the pretensions of mock protest; if there was one thing that overrode Hack's general misanthropy, it was his frugality.

"Oh, thank you, Mister Hack! My boy will be so proud!"

"Your *boy*? You have a son?"

"Oh, yes. I meant to mention it, but then you got me started on Nikhil and I could not control my temper. He *loves* baseball, and to bring him a ball signed by a gen-u-ine Hall of Famer…he will be very, *very* pleased. And nothing makes me more happy than the smile on his face at the end of a long day of work."

Hack half-smiled and grunted at the irony of the situation.

"Let's see…one for you, Sandy…" Hack handed one of the balls back. "And your son's name?"

"Ralph."

Hack grimaced.

"Ralph?"

"Yes. I am a big fan of *The Honeymooners*, as well. It was one of the few programs we got growing up in Mumbai. 'Wham! Pow! To the moon!'" Sandy punctuated his thought with a smile.

Hack shrugged, disinterested, "Okay then. To Ralph—" Hack took a minute to think about what to write. "Listen to your Old Man. He's a good one. -Hack."

"Oh, thank you so much, Mister—"

Sandy reached for the ball, but Hack waved his hand away as he shoved the ball into his front shirt pocket.

"I keep it until we're back at the motel. Don't need ya' runnin' off ta' get another fare!"

Sandy narrowed his eyes at the peculiar little man before he forced a smile and nodded.

"Very good, sir. I understand. I'll be waiting right here."

Hack opened the rear passenger's side door, "Damn right. See ya' in a bit, Sandy."

"Indeed you wi—"

Hack shut the back door before the driver could complete the sentiment.

He took a half-second to admire the house.

*What a fuckin' shithole...*he thought, overly harshly.

He waddled up the concrete path to the door and paused for a moment in front of the weathered, red door.

I have'ta...I have'ta tell someone, Hack thought.

But can I tell her?

Hack ignored the doorbell and instead slammed on the door several times with a heavy fist before he sighed. He shoved his hands in his pockets and waited five seconds...then ten...then fifteen...each increment chewed up by several thunderous beats of his heart as blood raged through his temples and into his ears.

Just as he was about to turn away, the latch clicked and the door flew open to reveal a fortiesh woman with strawberry blonde hair wrapped hastily into a ragged bun atop her head. Kind, gentle brown eyes sat atop deep, baggy lids and belied a prettiness that fell short of striking, but still conveyed a muted sexiness.

The kind eyes looked into the front yard before they started moving downward, toward the little old man who stood on the woman's stoop.

"Hi sweetheart!" Hack offered with a broad smile, the first one he had mustered in days.

"Christ, seriously?" The woman said, as her eyes went grey and cold.

"I know, I know, it's been a while—"

"A while, Hack?"

"I told ya' a thousand times, call me—"

"I'm not gonna' call you 'Dad.' You said it yourself, nicknames are for those who earn them."

"I don't think I said it quite so fancy-like, but—"

"Just cut the horseshit and tell me why you showed up on my doorstep. Whattaya want, Hack? Get bored in Cleveland again, so you thought it was a great idea to get loaded and drive your big ol' boat of a car down to see the daughter you never had time for growing up—wait, *scratch* that, never *have* time for, *ever*?!"

"Aw, come on, Lisa—gimme a break here. I come all this way to try an' tell ya' somethin' important, and you give me the same ol' sad-sack 'daddy wasn't there' routine?"

"You *weren't* there," Lisa shot back. "Mom and I always had to make do without you because of that *stupid* game of yours."

"She didn't seem'ta complain too much about the bags full'a money it brought you all come divorce time."

Lisa smiled incredulously, "You think that bought you a reprieve? My God, what were you when Mom had me? Forty-seven? Forty-eight?"

"Yer' mother was my second wife!"

"You didn't have the decency to even tell her you were still married before you slipped the ring on her finger."

"Whattaya talkin' about? I was divorced fer' damn near twenny'-five years before I—"

"It was an expression, Hack—married to *baseball*," she spat the word out like venom. "Is that why you still go to those horrible games in Cleveland and have never once asked about how your granddaughter is doing?"

"Huh? I…uh…keep up with her on the computer, the face-thingy. Seems like—"

"She's five, Hack."

He shrugged, "You know…kids these days—"

Lisa jabbed a finger in his chest, "I *do* know my kid these days, precisely so that she doesn't have to endure the same horse*shit* I had to put up with."

"I gave ya' everythin' a little girl could want! Box seats, clubhouse access, shit all kinds'a other kids would'a *killed* ta' have."

"Things little *boys* would've killed to have, Hack. Not me, and especially not Mom."

"Keep it down, the neighbors're gonna' hear!" Hack hissed.

"Let 'em hear! Let 'em hear what a gem Lisa's da—father is!"

"Ya' almost said 'dad' there, sweetheart…" Hack grinned.

Lisa locked eyes with him, all of the hope and kindness replaced by bloodshot streaks of anger and resentment, aching to lash out at this phantom from her past.

"I *have* no…no…" she struggled to complete the phrase through puffy cheeks and strained vocal chords. She puffed out several heaving breaths before she covered her face with her forearm and gave in, tears finally streaming down her face in torrents.

It was just the opening Hack was looking for.

"There, there," he said. He moved to his daughter's side and got on his tip-toes to put his arm around her shoulder. "I screwed up. I was a shitty dad, sure as hell, but it's gonna' be okay…"

"It's *not* going to be okay, though!" She shrugged off his arm as she raised her own to the sky. "It's *not*. No one's hiring lawyers anymore, least of all women in their thirties who decided to go back to law school to do something better, make a difference."

Hack shook his head, "I wish yer' mother hadn't been such a drunk, blown all'a that cash I gave her."

He delivered the phrase without a hint of irony.

"Damn it, it wasn't *her* fault. Even if you still had money, I wouldn't want it."

"That's crazy talk!" Hack exclaimed.

"I wouldn't! It's dirty money, bilked from all of those yayhoos who can't get enough of watching grown men chasin' after a *ball* before they all go out drinkin' and whorin'."

Hack trembled, a cauldron of emotion before he narrowed his eyes, "Is that *all* you think I did? Drinkin' and *whorin'*? I never once, *not once*, strayed from yer' mother. As much as it may pain yer' delicate lil' ears ta' hear, *she's* the one who was fuckin' around on *me!*"

"Because you were never home!"

"She knew that'd be the case when I took the job!"

"She didn't know you'd rather sleep in your office after home games than come home and be with her! She didn't know that you'd be such a horse's ass that you'd get fired ten separate times by nine different teams, movin' around the country from place to place! She didn't know that she'd have to raise a daughter on her own without any support from a man *whatsoever!*"

"That's not true!" Hack shot back with a scowl before he brightened, "She knew I was a horse's ass."

Lisa remained stone-faced. "Look, if you came here to say something, you should say your peace and be gone. My day was going rough enough already trying to raise that sick little girl inside," she pointed at the clear storm door, "without you barging in and thinking you were gonna' be hailed as father of the century."

Hack's eyes followed Lisa's outstretched arm to the front door of the house. Behind the glass storm door stood a young girl, her hair tied up similarly to her mother's though a brighter, truer strawberry blonde. As she clutched a stuffed, brown and white dog with big, floppy brown ears, he couldn't help but notice the similarities between her and a younger Samantha Rappaport.

The girl chewed on a marker as she leaned to one side.

"Damn it—Amy, stop it!" Lisa marched over to the door. "Get that marker out of your mouth! You don't want it to explode and make your tongue purple, do you?"

"But I *like* purple. I wanna' es'plode and make my tongue purple!" Amy announced.

Hack couldn't help but chuckle as he stifled a cough.

"Give me that," Lisa was firm, but couldn't help but grin as she took the marker from her daughter and placed it in her jeans pocket. "Now run along and put on some TV."

"Mommy, who's that?" Amy pointed at the short old man in the front yard.

Hack's eyes lit up as he waved back.

"Don't worry about him—he's just a stranger. Now go watch TV."

Hack bit his lip to keep his whole face from dropping.

Amy scurried into another room. Lisa lingered at the door for several seconds before she turned, sighed, and walked back over to Hack.

"She's…she's *sick*?" Hack asked.

Lisa shook her head, "Oh, it's nothing serious. Just been hackin' up a storm the past few days. Doctor said it's just whoopin' cough, but she can't go to art class or soccer until she's not contagious."

"Art *and* soccer?" Hack smiled broadly. "How 'bout that? Ain't that somethin'?"

"You know, *I* used to enjoy doing stuff outside of school, too!"

"Yeah, but *soccer*," Hack ignored Lisa and stroked his chin. "Back in my day, we *called* all the guys who played soccer 'girls,' but we never thought they'd let girls actually *play* it."

Lisa shivered with revulsion at Hack's genuine wonder. She put her hands on her hips.

"Are we through yet?"

Hack's smile faded. "No, no, actually I have somethin' serious ta' tell ya'."

"What?"

Her bluntness was off-putting. Hack hadn't told anyone else his secret, and for how long now? Surely someone must've noticed along the way, an overeager reporter or even one of his fellow coaches, or even one of the kids he was managing—surely some of them would be sharp enough to put two and two together, and figure out what was slowly eating him away from inside.

He took a deep breath and opened his mouth, ready to finally spill the truth of his situation to someone, anyone who would listen.

And then he heard it: the long, languid evil tones of the cancer inside his head. That same voice that had grabbed Hack and shaken him so deeply those weeks ago.

Tell her… it hissed. *Tell her evvvverrythinggg….*

Hack reflexively swatted at his head.

"What?" Lisa asked.

I won't release you until you tell her evvverrythinggg…

Hack tried desperately to summon the words, to spill his secret right there, in his daughter's front yard.

His throat seized up. He felt the sudden blast of coppery liquid in the back of his mouth that signaled a coughing fit and braced for its unrelenting onslaught.

His neck tightened and bucked, as if squeezing the words back into his stomach.

Nothing happened.

Instead, Hack shuddered, "I just came ta' tell ya' that I'm real sorry about everything I put ya' through, and I wanna' be a better dad ta'ya' and lil', uh, Amy over there as long as I'm still walkin' this earth."

Lisa folded her arms across her chest.

"*Really?*" Her eyes narrowed with skepticism.

"Yeah. I'm sorry from the bottom'a my heart. I'm, uh, managin' again—"

Lisa grimaced in disgust.

"—Not in the majors or anythin' fancy like that. Minor league team. The…uh…some kind'a Magpies…Greek-soundin' name…"

Hack winced. He had always been sharp as a tack. Was it just old age? Or was it—

"Hoplite!" he snapped his fingers as Lisa nearly jumped out of her shoes. "The Hoplite Magpies. We're in town fer' the next three days, playin' Westfield. I'm gonna' set aside two tickets, front row, all'a the ice cream Amy can eat, free'a charge. Or, I s'pose, courtesy of Westfield…Either way, they'll be there fer' all three games. I'd love it if you guys'd come on down and see me afterward, clubhouse access an' everythin'. Big series fer' us—Westfield's in first, ya' know. We sweep 'em, and we got'a a real shot at the playoffs."

Lisa tilted her head, mulling the old man's offer. She was more like him than she wanted to admit, and yet, did she want to have him as a part of her life? Of her daughter's life?

"I'll think about it," Lisa said. "No promises, though. Amy's still pretty sick."

"Sure, sure," Hack's eyes went wide. "No pressure 'er nothin'. I just thought you an' she might like to see ol' Hack while he's still around, let me try to make amends."

Lisa smiled thinly and nodded.

"Well, okay then," Hack turned toward Sandy, who sat in the still-running cab, "Guess I'll be on my way."

"Hack?" Lisa asked.

He looked over his shoulder, "Yeah?"

"Anything else you wanted to say?"

He threw her a tight smile, "Just that I'm sorry, sweetheart. Just that I'm sorry." He pointed at the storm door, "Now you get back in there an' get that lil' girl well enough ta' come down to the ballpark tonight!"

The thin smile still drew Lisa's face wide as she raised her eyebrows.

Hack turned and limped his way back to the cab, hoping against hope that he'd get to meet his granddaughter once before he died, and silently cursing himself for his cowardice.

4

It was the third game of the series against Westfield. After winning the first two games, the Magpies trailed 4-3 in the top of the ninth with Eldrake Gamble on first and nobody out.

Westfield was a powerhouse; they led the Magpies by 7 1/2 games in the Northern League's Eastern Division. As the new AA affiliate of the Cincinnati Reds, one of the top farm systems in all of baseball, the Mice were widely regarded to have a preponderance of near-major league-ready talent at every position.

Though it would be of little immediate effect in the standings, all of the Magpie players desperately wanted to sweep the Mice, if only to show that these Magpies were different; no longer pushovers, these Magpies *mattered*.

Truck Traynor dug in. At the end of yet another fantastic series (4 for 11 with a homerun), Truck was ready to deliver the deathblow to the Mice.

"Come on now, Truck." Hack's words were empty, almost rueful as he looked past the batter's box to the two seats to the right of the Mice's radar gun pit, which sat empty for the third consecutive evening.

"Don't get any ideas, Truck." It was the Mice's catcher, Shane Marcos, a stocky, tan kid with a California surfer intonation that seemed wildly out-of-place. "Let's just end it here and get you guys on the bus back home, no prob. 'Kay?"

"That's the plan," Truck said through gritted teeth without looking back. He ground the bat with his hands hard, without batting gloves, to the point where one would expect to see sawdust trickling through his fingers.

The shame of the bus ride to Westfield still sent his stomach churning with anger even three days after the fact; he hated this town and everything about it, from the perfect little suburban row houses to the flowers and fresh, early summer air.

These people took their normal, uneventful lives for granted, the antithesis to Truck's ever-present fear, wanting so badly to release the pain and anguish he carried about who he was into the world, and yet utterly terrified of what his teammates might think, let alone his family and the rest of the world.

He squeezed the bat tighter and harder as Westfield's closer, Tony Mancini, nodded, came set, and delivered.

A foot out of Mancini's hand, Truck already recognized the spin.

Fastball.

Another foot and Truck's mind raced, unconsciously calculating its trajectory and speed.

High. And out over the plate.

Two more feet to make the decision on whether or not to swing.

Yes.

He picked up his front foot, pivoted on his back foot, and threw the barrel of the bat at the ball like a woodsman felling a hundred-year oak.

"CRACK!"

Instinctively, Truck pronated his top wrist underneath the bat through contact and connected with the white-and-red orb a foot in front of the plate.

The bat flew right through its target, the dominant party in this violent collision.

It was Truck's favorite feeling in the world; better than sex. For those few moments, those split-seconds while the bat was on the ball and rang true, all of his anger, all of his hatred, all of his shame and despair was focused on that perfect off-white sphere, that singular target of every emotion he struggled to keep from bubbling up.

The ball rocketed off the bat to left-center field.

"Fuck," Mancini yelled with more awe than anger.

Truck had gotten all of it, but as he broke into his homerun trot out of habit, he recognized that the ball's trajectory was lower, closer to the ground than usual. It only reached maybe twenty feet high at its apex before it descended like a howitzer shell into the heavily-padded outfield wall with a "BOOM."

"God DAMN it, run, Flash!" Hack screamed at his shortstop, who had paused to watch the ball as it flew past.

Gamble took off. He hit third just as the center fielder reached the ball as it caromed off the wall in front of the warning track. Willie waved him home; he knew Grulich had a hell of an arm out in center for the Mice, but something told Willie that Eldrake could make it.

Eldrake hit third and pumped his outside arm. As he had told Hack when the ornery old manager had christened him "Flash," Eldrake wasn't the fastest middle infielder to ever play the game. Instead, he usually relied on his smarts and instincts on the bases to keep himself out of trouble on the basepaths.

As he straightened out into the third baseline, Eldrake's glasses flew off of his head.

Shit, he thought.

Shit, Willie thought.

"Fuck!" Hack screamed.

Grulich didn't even bother gloving the ball. He barehanded it and in a single motion crow-hopped and lofted the ball back toward home plate, not even bothering to look for the cutoff man.

The ball shot back toward the infield on about the same trajectory as Truck had sent it out. It burrowed through the night sky with a purpose, directly on line with the catcher's mitt.

Even a machine couldn't have made a more perfect throw.

Eldrake's eyes were wide and useless. He could barely make out the partially-covered plate, let alone whether or not the catcher had received the ball, which may as well have been the size of a tic tac.

He stuck his tongue out of the side of his mouth.

Five more steps.

No movement by Marcos.

Four more.

Uh-oh. Marcos took a drop step.

Three.

Eldrake heard a loud "THWACK" as the catcher turned to face him.

Two.

Eldrake let out a scream, he covered his face with his forearm and tensed his leg muscles, the collision now imminent.

One.

"BOOM!"

Flash's forearm connected with the squat catcher, nearly half-a-foot shorter than the man who bore down on him.

Marcos let out a loud grunt, willing the ball to stay lodged safely in his glove.

Eldrake completed his forearm shiver and launched himself through his target. Bone connected squarely with bone as he powered his way into Marcos, then tumbled on the ground next to the plate.

Marcos flew through the air, and landed flat on his back, sprawled, glove facing the sky.

Eldrake looked toward the umpire, who had yet to make a signal. The shortstop narrowed his eyes before they went wide with shock as he looked for the blurry white mass of the plate and crawled for it on his hands and knees.

He smiled when he saw a smaller, out of focus white object maybe a foot past his target.

The ball, he thought.

The grin faded when he saw an olive-skinned hand reach down for it.

Eldrake stuck out his hand, extending with every inch of his long, gangly arms to swat that plate, and get the all-important tying run.

"SLAP"

"THWACK"

It was a bang-bang play. The umpire hovered over the plate, immobile, brow furrowed. As the dust first swirled around the scene, then fell around them, he let the silence hover along with it until both players couldn't take it any longer.

The umpire balled both hands into fists and held them in front of his chest.

Then he extended them out to his sides, palms flat.

"SAAAAFE!" he bellowed.

Eldrake may as well have won the lottery. He jumped for joy, arms extended over his head before he did an awkward, nerdy, wild fist pump.

Marcos and Mancini immediately ganged up on the umpire and got in his face.

The mustached young umpire was resolute; he waved his hands horizontally with every entreaty, even after Westfield's manager stormed out of the dugout and kicked dirt over the plate to the point of ejection.

The Magpies' bench went crazy. Juan Patrón was on deck, and even he smirked as he smacked Flash's helmet with glee on his way to the batter's box.

The guy after Patrón, Ozzie Cabrera, wanted to storm the field, but was held back by Pete Moray, who was more concerned about acting professionally than any potential forfeiture for prematurely celebrating.

As Eldrake finally reached the dugout, dozens of hands reached out to smack him on the helmet and the behind, affectionate signs of a job well done, with one notable exception.

"Flash."

Eldrake's smile faded as his dour-faced manager leaned on his bat-cane in front of Mitch Henry.

"Yes, sir, Coach?"

"What kind of a damned *fool* wears glasses to play baseball?"

Eldrake swallowed and walked over to his manager, "I, uh, well Coach, I—"

Hack let him stew for several moments before he got on his tip-toes and smacked the shortstop's helmet.

"The luckiest sonofabitch in the world, that's who!" Hack said, his grimace finally erased for the evening. He stuck out his hand for the shortstop to take, and Eldrake reflexively launched into a low-five with a fist.

Hack grabbed his hand and pulled him close.

"But get some goddamned contacts or Rec Specs before the next game, would ya'? I managed Chris Sabo twice. He mighta' looked like an asshole with those things on, but he was playin' baseball, not winnin' beauty pageants, and damned fine at it, too."

"What's that, coach?" Flash stood, serious. "Sabo was damned fine at beauty pageants?"

Mitch Henry's booming southern laugh filled the dugout.

"Holy shit, Coach, I didn't know Flash had it in him."

Hack even had to smirk at this, "I knew there was a reason I called ya' 'Flash.'"

Flash took off his helmet and headed off to return it to the rack. Hack gave him a hearty smack on the rear end.

As his gaze turned to the empty seats past home plate once more, Hack looked around the dugout and saw Henry gathered with the Latin guys (and Woo, who curiously had become a part of their clique), talking about Flash, the former outcast's, zinger, and laughing with glee, it was all he could do to chuckle...

...if only to keep from crying.

5

Gamble's run only tied the game. The game-winning run was represented by Truck Traynor, who stood, still in disbelief at what his bookish teammate had just done, on second base. Footspeed was one of the few athletic gifts that Truck didn't possess at all, as his knees already were starting to knot and gnarl from years of catching.

Juan Patrón strode to the plate, his right hand wrapped around the bat at its midpoint. He glared at Mancini, who glared right back.

Not many of Patrón's teammates knew what he was thinking, other than that some variation on "Kill ball. Hit it far," repeated in his head like a mantra.

Not that he was dumb; far from it. It's just the way that Juan preferred things. Even if he rarely spoke English, he understood practically every word his teammates said, and a lot more Korean than he had let on, which quickly cemented his friendship with Sun Dae, or "Luz de Sol" ("Sunlight") for short.

The prolonged slump was starting to wear on the slugger, who was already miffed from being passed over for promotion to Cleveland (and the major league salary such a jump promised) in the interest of keeping the team together in Hoplite, and getting the organization's top prospects ready to graduate together.

"Paciencia, paciencia," his agent had told him numerous times, even when he hit .317 with 34 homeruns the season before.

Now, the slump had dipped his average to .256, and with his power also suffering, Juan was starting to press.

For very different reasons than Truck, Patrón dug into the batters box with gritted teeth.

Marcos didn't even bother making conversation with the surly man as he ground the dirt with his spikes.

Patrón cleared his mind, focused only on the ball leaving Mancini's hand. As the pitcher came set and pitched, Juan's recognition system was similar to Truck's as the ball flew through the air.

Only when he decided to swing, his aim was off, and he missed by a good three inches.

"Steee-RIIIKE!" The umpire yelled.

Juan hit himself on the forehead.

"Enfocaté!" He hissed. Juan adjusted his helmet and put the bat back on his shoulder.

But Patrón couldn't even take his own advice. Thoughts of the slump raced around his head, of money lost that he might not ever recover, of his widowed mother barely making ends meet with the money he sent back to the Dominican Republic each month.

Juan barely noticed when the pitcher rocked and fired a nasty slider at the knees.

"Steee-RIIIKE!" The umpire yelled again.

Patrón glared at the umpire, who met the slugger's stare with a scowl.

The first baseman slid his spike across the rear chalk line of the batter's box, hoping to gain that extra split second to read and react.

Much like Truck, Patrón didn't care for batting gloves; he preferred to feel the rough grain of the wood burn across his calloused hands whenever he unleashed the club on the ball.

Mancini nodded and came set. Juan focused on the ball in the pitcher's hand, but something was still *off*.

When Mancini started his motion, Patrón knew exactly what was amiss:

He could hear everything.

Normally, when hitting, his mind went blank, locked in and focused on nothing but the pitcher's arm and the ball.

But now, every cheer, every boo, every whistle and clap of the hostile crowd thundered down upon him. He broke focus and considered calling "time" ever so briefly, but Mancini had already released the ball.

This time, there was no chance to pick up the spin. The ball was upon Patrón before he could do anything but offer a feeble check swing.

"Did he go?" the home plate umpire thundered as he pointed at the first base umpire.

The first base ump raised a fist to signal that indeed he had.

"Steeee-RIIIKE three! Huuaaah!" The umpire punched him out forcefully.

"Chingárlo!" Patrón yelled as he whacked himself on the helmet with his bat. He kicked up a cloud of dust as he shuffled back to the dugout, shoulders slumped before he threw the bat down the tunnel, then knocked over the water cooler near the helmet rack.

"God *damn* it, Patrón, cut it out!" Hack got in the first baseman's face. "Yer' a ballplayer, not a goddamned toddler. Act that way! I didn't watch my buddies die in the goddamned muck in *Ko-rea* ta' come here and watch you toss yer' shit down the fuckin' tunnel! You wanna' get paid? Then act like a fuckin' adult!"

Hack conveniently neglected to mention his own childish tantrum at his first Magpie press conference.

Juan stared his manager down for a brief moment; Pete Moray normally would've played peacemaker, but the erstwhile envoy was coaching first base, and could only watch from afar.

Hack stared right back at the angry first baseman, still burning from Lisa's hurtful snub. He pointed down the tunnel, "Now pick up yer' shit and put it away!" Hack slammed his own bat against the dusty, concrete floor of the dugout, loud enough so that it startled several nearby fans.

Patrón's eyes narrowed as he contemplated whether to put this fiery old gringo in his place.

On the far end of the bench, Manny's eyes went wide. He had been pulling off his jacket to head down to the bullpen when Patrón started throwing his hissy fit. Now the enormous first baseman threatened the manager who had done so much for the converted shortstop, both on the field and off.

Not only that, but Manny thought about what Pete Moray said on the bus ride in about stepping up, and taking more of a leadership role among the Latin players.

As he saw Patrón's sneer twist into a snort, like a bull seeing red, Manny was compelled to act. He leapt to his feet and navigated the dip-and-sunflower seed shells that coated the dugout floor with the same long, smooth strides that had allowed him to make it as high as Double-A as a professional shortstop.

Patrón's head bobbed back, ready to unleash a string of Spanish expletives, or worse, his hand upon Hack's head when Manny sidestepped Hack's bat and put his hand on Juan's shoulder.

"Cálmate, cálmate!" Manny turned the slugger's attention toward him.

"Qué es esto? Este jefe loco me llamó un niñata!" *What is this? This crazy chief called me a baby!*

"Sí?" Manny responded matter-of-factly. "No es verdad?" *It's not true?*

"Es vergonzoso!" *It's embarrassing!*

"Te avergüenzas!" *You embarrass yourself!* "Recoge tus cosas." *Collect your stuff.*

Now Patrón fixed his stare on Manny, unblinking and fierce.

"No solo porque tengas problemas de bateo, significa que debas aventar tu bate, o tu casco." *Just because you're having problems hitting, you shouldn't take it out on your bat or helmet.* Manny smiled, "Sí fuera el caso, no hubiera tenido no más bates ni cascos cuando terminé de jugar el parador en corto!" *If that was the case, I wouldn't have had any more bats or helmets when I stopped playing shortstop!*

Patrón glared at Manny for several seconds in silence. The two had a bit of a rocky history when it came to cards, but Manny met the large first baseman's gaze, though he softened and widened his eyes to break through the tension.

Finally, Juan's face broke. He couldn't hold back the grin and chuckle at Manny's joke.

"Es la verdad!" *It's the truth!* He patted Manny on the shoulder, "Eras un bateador terrible." *You were a terrible hitter.*

Both men laughed.

"Y tus cosas?" Manny pointed down the tunnel to the clubhouse, where the discarded equipment still lay.

"Sí, sí…" Patrón shuffled off to collect first the helmet, then the bat, and placed both in their respective places on the equipment rack.

"Bueno," Manny said with a hearty smile. He darted his eyes over to Hack, who still leaned on the bat, astonished at what he had just seen.

Patrón sighed, "Lo siento. Sorry."

Hack nodded, but didn't say a word.

The manager then turned his attention to Manny, who shrugged. Hack offered him a tight-lipped smile and a nod before he wound up and gave Manny a smack on the behind.

"Now get yer' ass out to the bullpen and start warmin' up—we might need ya' yet."

Manny nodded and jogged out to the bullpen next to the right field stands.

As the drama in the dugout dissipated, Hack focused first on the empty seats in the front row, then on the action in the field. As expected, with one out, the Mice elected to intentionally walk Ozzie Cabrera to set up a potential double play, even with the relatively fleet-footed Sid Fynch on deck.

Mancini lobbed ball four to Marcos, and Cabrera trotted down to first base.

Sid sauntered into the first base side of the batter's box. He looked at Willie in the third base coach's box, but Willie signaled back nonsense—he was on his own.

Sid's mind went blank. Mancini was tough, to be sure, but he had a good track record against the pitcher, and thought he would try to exploit Sid's weakness for chasing breaking balls early in the count.

Mancini looked in. He shook his head twice before he nodded and came set.

Breaking ball, for sure, Sid thought. He put extra weight on his left leg, willing himself to stay back and unload on Mancini's offering.

As Mancini's arm came through the pitching window at three-quarters height, Sid knew he had guessed correctly. He unconsciously licked his lips as he wiggled his bat back-and-forth almost imperceptibly. Mancini let the ball go, a big, looping curveball, a mistake pitch, out over the plate.

Sid waited…and waited…and waited some more for the ball to continue its long, loping arc toward him. Finally, at the last moment, he shot his hands down and in, directly to the ball like a bolt of lightning.

"CRACK!"

Sid hit it absolutely on the screws. He bolted toward first and grinned as the ball lasered toward the gap between first and second.

Westfield had it played perfectly. The second baseman, Ramón Perez, dove and gloved the ball in one spectacular motion. As he tumbled to the ground, with no shot to get Cabrera at second, he rifled the ball toward first.

The stadium echoed with the "THUD" of the ball hitting the first baseman's mitt. Sid had arrived at the base only moments before, a bang-bang play if there ever was one.

"He's OUT!" The umpire pumped his fist authoritatively.

"Fuck!" Sid yelled at no one in particular.

"Yeeeerrrr outta HERE!" The umpire pointed at him and then at the dugout.

"God damn it, Sid!" Hack yelled in the dugout as he banged his bat on the ground again. Everyone on the field, in the dugout, in the entire stadium looked toward the Magpies' dugout, expecting to see their cantankerous old manager waddling out, waving the bat above his head before launching into another one of his tirades.

Instead, Hack folded his arms.

This would be one battle Sid Fynch would have to fight for himself.

"I wasn't cussing at you!" Sid pleaded with the ump.

"I know what I heard. Get outta' here, kid."

"That's ridiculous! Do you know who..." *my father is?* Sid didn't even complete the sentiment before he felt an invisible tug from the dugout, and the ghostly "THWACK" of Hack's bat on his calves.

"Who *what?*" the umpire folded his arms.

Sid shook his head, "Sorry, sir. Won't happen again."

"'Preciate that, son." The umpire smiled. "Now get the fuck outta' here."

Oh, come on! Sid thought. He wanted nothing more than to get back in the umpire's face, to throttle the arrogant S.O.B. for so flagrantly flaunting his authority over him.

He unclenched his jaw and fists, nodded, and trotted back to the dugout. He passed Hack without a word as he walked through the tunnel and into the clubhouse.

Fortunately, Truck and Ozzie both had the wherewithal to advance on the play.

Hack furrowed his brow. More troubling than Fynch's ejection was he fact that the manager couldn't remember who was scheduled to bat seventh for the Magpies.

Sid? No, Sid just hit. Maybe it's Derrick? Hmm...

He cursed his deteriorating mind as he turned his eyes toward the batters box, and then had to keep himself from covering them.

Sun Dae Woo strode confidently to the plate.

Hack's rage began to rise. He looked around for a drink of whiskey, Robitussin, pretty much anything to take his mind off of what the older Korean fellow represented to him, all of the pain and anguish through the years fighting ghosts.

"Come on now, Sunday," Hack clapped twice.

Woo immediately called time and hurried down the third base line toward Willie in the coach's box.

What in the sam fuck is he doin'? Hack thought.

Sun Dae motioned for Truck to join the huddle. Truck shrugged and complied.

Once all three men were gathered around one another, Sun Dae went through an elaborate ritual of signs that he had just learned weeks before, with the pained assistance of Pete Moray and Juan Patrón.

It was all Willie and Truck could do to keep up with the sharp second baseman as he put on various signs and wiped them off with the "kill" sign.

Fortunately, Willie and Truck represented two of the keener intellects on the team, and when Woo was through, they looked at each other in astonishment.

Willie turned his attention back toward Sun Dae and nodded.

Truck tried his damnedest to hide a rapidly-forming mischievous grin as he gave Sun Dae's helmet a sharp "RAP" of encouragement and trotted to the base to touch up.

Woo nearly sprinted back to the batter's box. A switch hitter, he decided to dig into the left handed side of the box against Mancini, the right hander.

Fortunately, the Mice decided to keep their young closer in. The six-foot-six Mice pitcher stood atop the mound and glared down at the diminutive Korean who dug in.

Sun Dae trembled, ever so slightly. He tentatively raised his bat to his shoulder, as his eyes went wide with fear.

Mancini ginned menacingly. He didn't even bother shaking Marcos off; he nodded once and waved his glove at the plate once as he came set, as if to say, *go ahead, try and hit it.*

Woo twisted into his knot-like stance, still shaking as the righthander began his motion.

As Mancini reached back, the most curious thing happened: Woo's eyes glinted with recognition. He broke his scared façade as Mancini, caught unaware, couldn't stop his motion.

Woo slid the bat up in his hands and caught the barrel midway up with his thumb and index finger, offering a bunt.

Truck took off, and the Westfield third baseman followed suit, both men breaking toward home to prevent that precious final run from scoring.

As Mancini brought his arm over his shoulder, he was stunned again.

Woo pulled the bat back but choked up, leaving nearly four full inches of the handle exposed. He raised the bat back up, and, as Mancini released the ball, Woo brought the bat down in a chopping motion.

It's a daring maneuver called a "slash," feigning a bunt before pulling the bat back and trying to shoot the ball through the moving infield.

Woo executed it perfectly.

The ball barely made a sound as it connected with his bat.

"Fuck!" The third baseman yelled out as the ball sailed ten feet over his head and sliced toward the line before it landed two full feet fair, and skitted toward the tarp along the third base line.

Truck raised a fist as he jogged home easily. Woo didn't dare show any emotion as he sprinted down the first base line full speed despite the fact that no one for Westfield was even near the ball. Cabrera stood on second and smiled, unwilling to risk being thrown out at third with the ball rattling around the wall not but twenty feet away from the base.

As Sun Dae reached first base, he jumped on the bag with both feet and bowed toward the Magpie dugout.

They went nuts.

Arms pumped the air as an impromptu chant of "Sun-DAE, Sun-DAE, Sun-DAE!" echoed through the otherwise silent Westfield stadium.

Cy Reynolds, the slick-fielding, light-hitting third baseman was up next, but he swung at the first pitch, dribbled a grounder softly to first, and the inning was over.

Manny trotted out to the mound from the bullpen, just a half-notch above "ice cold" since he got in maybe a dozen warm-ups before Sun Dae's heroics in the top of the ninth.

That didn't stop him from firing hundred-mile-an-hour darts to Truck even in warmups, with the same smooth, easy arm action that Hack had identified early in his tenure.

More than that, though, Manny now brought an undeniable swagger with him to the mound. Off the field, he was a shy, demure, unquestionably *nice* person.

But when he took the mound, his kind eyes became fiery and fierce. The sweat beaded on his skin as he soaked in the pressure of the moment and laughed it away with an intensity to rival the great closers Hack had ever seen.

He dispatched the first two hitters with ease; it took him eight pitches only because the Mice's first baseman, Connor Teeves, had fouled a couple back to the screen.

Their cleanup hitter was their right fielder, Geraldo Obregón, who had more than enough home run pop to tie the game and send it to extras.

It was power against power as the left-handed Obregón dug in. Truck's head was far too deep into the game at this point to make simple chit-chat, not that it was even an option with Obregón, who only made noise when he bothered to launch a dip-spit.

Truck put down a single finger.

Fastball.

Manny shook him off.

Truck wanted to scream. It was exactly the opposite problem that Tommy Stearns had: Manny was far too trusting of a pitch he had been fooling around with in his spare time. Truck would rather challenge Obregón with Manny's best, even if the imposing right fielder knew what was coming.

Truck bit his tongue as he put down one finger again.

Manny stared in for another long moment.

This time, he nodded.

Manny worked out of the stretch, even though no one was on. He broke his hands over his knee and swung the ball back in a smooth arc until he brought it over his shoulder and toward the plate.

"CRACK!"

Truck heard the ball come off the bat square. He looked up to see how far out of the park it would be.

But he couldn't find it.

Instead, he caught the tumbling form of Sun Dae Woo at second base.

Like Truck the previous inning, Obregón had crushed a low line drive toward the gap.

Unlike the ball Truck had hit, though, this rope had to contend with the wily Magpie second baseman. Seemingly before the ball came off the bat, Woo took two steps, positioning himself to account for where he thought Obregón might take it.

He moved before he even heard the crack of the bat, stealthily, like a cat, toward the ball, operating on pure instincts and reaction, no time to think.

Sun Dae launched himself in the air. He stabbed at the ball with his glove as he tucked his head down under his center of gravity and landed on his back in the immaculately-kept outfield grass.

Holding the ball.

Half of the team was already rushing to mob the evening's hero.

Hack wasn't among them, not out of animus, but because his knee had locked up, and he was having trouble navigating the steps. He felt two powerful hands on his hips, and before the manager could turn to berate whomever had lifted him up, he was safely on the warning track of the field.

Hack glanced over his shoulder and saw Truck, who had jogged all the way over from his spot behind the plate to put the cantankerous old coot on the field. Hack forced a weak smile and tipped his hat at his star catcher as Truck rushed to join the celebration.

The team gathered around Woo, jumping and shouting as Hack limped over with the aid of his bat. Pete Moray was in the thick of it all; Hack didn't want to think about how much dip spit the coach had already swallowed in his exuberance.

Willie, too, had rushed over, as had Truck; both the catcher and Juan Patrón hoisted Woo up on their shoulders. They carried him toward the dugout until they reached their dour manager halfway down the first base line.

"Okaaaay, okaaaay," Hack said, humorlessly. "We didn't win *shit* yet, fellas." He eyed his new second baseman, "You devious, sneaky little Korean devil…" Hack's eyes narrowed as Sun Dae cringed at the man's body language.

The manager reached down deep; he focused on the empty seats behind him, trying to muster some kind of anger to draw upon to lash out at this curious little Korean for all of the hurt he had been put through through the years.

Hack found nothing.

Caught up in the moment, the manager grinned mischievously, "I haven't seen a slash done that well since I did it back in my playin' days!" He punctuated the sentiment by reaching up with his bat and rapping the Korean's helmet twice. "An' I guess yer' catch was okay, too."

Upon seeing the smile, Woo nodded vigorously, happy to be accepted as the hero, for at least an evening.

But as the rest of the team hurried into the tunnel to get ready quickly and claim a seat on the bus for getaway day, Hack agonizingly made his way back toward the dugout.

Even as the stadium emptied, his gaze naturally turned toward those two lonely seats, left empty throughout all three games of the series.

And the usually stone-faced manager, that bottle of volatile emotions, allowed himself a single tear.

Sixth Inning

1

A month passed since that fateful night when the Magpies had swept the Westfield Mice to go over five hundred for the first time all year, and announced to the entire Northern League that they were officially in the playoff race.

Nonetheless, as Hack continued to self-medicate underneath the warm blanket of pills, whiskey, and over-the-counter cough medicine, the coughing fits that had so plagued him when he was in Cleveland, to the point of causing the great Hack O'Callahan to admit defeat and finally visit that doctor (pissant *doctor*, Hack reminded himself), finally began to subside.

Hack credited his rather unusual regiment of Mean S.O.B.s that he chugged down four times a day.

But there was certainly more to it than that. The cliques that formerly bound the players to their own little corners of the clubhouse were beginning to show the first signs of decay, leaving Hack with a too-long-dormant sense of accomplishment.

Nowhere was this more apparent than with the Latin players, who were eager to show off the progress they were making in their English with Pete Moray, and happily struck up conversations with the other players in the clubhouse.

It didn't hurt Sun Dae Woo immediately became a bit of a folk hero in Hoplite for his heroics in Westfield, as well as his penchant for dazzling defense at second base and timely hitting out of the seventh spot in the lineup.

More surprising than anything, Woo and Juan Patrón were inseparable. Within several weeks of his arrival, Woo was already beginning to pick up Spanish and have long, animated discussions with not only Patrón, but the other Latin players.

Every so often, the exchanges would be punctuated by sharp laughter from their corner of the clubhouse, often at something Woo had said or done.

Patrón beamed around "Luz de Sol," or "Mi Amigo Pequeño" ("My Little Buddy"), despite the man's advancing age.

Not all new roommate arrangements were going quite so smoothly, as Hack found out one day when he walked into his office before a game to find Mitch Henry's hulking frame somewhat humorously draped into one of the undersized chairs opposite his desk.

"Have a seat, Mitch," Hack offered sarcastically. "Make yer'self at home. You need me ta' getchya' anything? Goddamn foot rub, or a massage, er' a—"

"Massage'd be great. Shit, you've had me goin' eight innings every time out there."

"I didn't hear ya' complainin'," Hack shot back.

"Fuck, wait, I mean—shit! No, I—"

"Forget it, Mitch," Hack waved him away. "I ain't gonna' smack ya' again. What can I do ya' for?" Hack sunk into his rolling chair.

"It's my road roommate. It's Manny, Coach."

Hack coughed for the first time in two weeks as he fumbled with his back pocket for his handkerchief. He brought the black fabric up to his mouth to soak up the spittle and blood.

Fortunately, the fit only lasted a dozen or so seconds.

"Shit, you okay?" Henry asked.

"I'm fine, I'm fine—" Hack raised an eyebrow, "What about Manny? He been sayin' anything weird ta' ya'?"

"Naw, shit, in that regard he's the best. He don't ever say *nothin'*. Leaves me to my business, even lets me watch whatever I want on the tube. He just...like...*reads* all the time."

"So what's the fuckin' problem then?" Hack stifled his sigh of relief.

"It's a hygiene thing. Now, I've never had a Latin roommate before——"

"Shockin'," Hack interrupted.

Henry ignored him, "——so I don't know if all'a them do this or what."

Hack felt beads of sweat work their way toward the surface of his skin.

"But in the bathroom——"

The sweat began to pool around Hack's collar; if he had undone it, he could've unwrinkled a raisin.

"——when he takes a shit——"

Hack cocked his head sideways.

"——he wipes, and instead'a flushin' the paper, he puts it in the trash can next'ta the toilet."

Hack wiped his face, though he tried to remain nonchalant.

Then, he thought about what Henry had said, and furrowed his brow.

"What?"

"He puts shitty toilet paper in the goddamned trash can, coach. And I don't know what the fuck *he's* been eatin', but it is some rank-ass shit."

"So why don't ya' just flush it down for 'im?" Hack asked.

"And get up to my elbows in his shit? I don't think so," Henry shuddered. "Not to mention that I'd just be reinforcin' his dumbshit behavior. I'd be an enabler."

"Well, have you talked with Manny?" Hack asked through gritted teeth, annoyed that Mitch Henry, of all people, had found this reason enough to barge into his office while he wasn't there.

*It's okay...*Hack thought. *With it bein' about Manny, it could'a been worse...*

"'Course I did. I tried all the usuals; bustin' his balls, all-out shamin', bein' firm, and he always says he's gonna' do somethin' about it, but he never does."

"Shit," Hack said, then thought for a moment, "literally, this time, I s'pose. Let's get through this. Open the door fer' me, will'ya'?"

Henry pushed the door out into the hallway.

"Manny! Pete! Get yer' asses in here."

Pete Moray was first to amble through the doorway with an enormous dip packed in his lip and few other cares in the world.

"Yeah, Skip'?" he asked.

"Wait fer' Manny," Hack said.

After several awkward moments, the lanky closer walked through the doorway.

"Sí, jefe?" Manny asked.

"Henry here says you've been," he paused and made a grimace, "puttin' shit-tickets in the trash?"

"Shit tickets?" Manny asked.

"I told ya', Manny, you gotta' stop puttin' your used shit-paper in the trash. Flush it down the toilet."

"Ah, shit *paper!*" Manny beamed.

Hack scratched his chin.

Manny turned serious, "I sorry, Mitch, but it's a habit we are taught in the Dominican from very early. The...how do you say? Alcantarilla?"

He looked at Pete for confirmation.

"The sewer," Pete punctuated the statement by hitting a trash can six feet away with a wad of spit.

"Sí, the sewer, it is not so developed there. The paper clogs the tanks."

"That's all well and good down on yer' island, Manny, but here in America, we have workin' sewers. All ya' need ta' do is wipe and drop it in the bowl."

Manny looked at a still-scowling Mitch Henry.

"I will do better, Mitch. Sorry. I promise."

"Damn *straight* you will," Henry eyed Manny suspiciously out of the corner of his eye. "I gotta' get ready to pitch—Pete, talk to him about this shit 'er somethin'."

Pete opened his mouth to speak, but was cut off by Hack.

"Actually, Manny, I'll have a chat with ya' 'bout it. Don't worry, fellas. That'll be all, Mitch. Pete."

Moray shrugged and left the room as breezily as he had entered, with Henry lumbering close behind.

"Oh, and Mitch? Shut the door, will'ya?"

Before Hack had even finished, Henry had sent the door flying shut. It closed with a satisfying "CA-LUNK."

"Please tell me you wanna' talk about somethin' other than what yer' doin' with yer' *shit*," Hack said.

"Yes…well… sort of—" Manny whispered.

"Not *that* either—" Hack yelled.

"No, but, uh—" Manny removed his hat and scratched his head, "First of all, Camión and I are very, very grateful for keeping our secret…"

"Secret?" Hack completed the thought.

"Sí. Gracias."

Hack shrugged, "I don't really have a choice, do I?"

"But you help on the bus when you first get here with the story about hunting with señor Mickey, an—"

Hack grinned, "It is a good one, isn't it?"

"Oh, sí. Very entertaining."

"But I mean, Henry and those guys would beat the shit right outta' ya' if they knew about, you know…"

"An' that's my point. Mitch is a good roommate, fer' now. Bit of a pendejo, but he generally leaves me alone, and I do the same for him."

"So why the hell do you fuck around with the toilet paper then?" Hack asked.

"Because, I'm so worried he's gonna' find out, I jus' freece' up. I guess I wan' to give him somethin' else to complain about so that he doesn't get suspicious about me an' Camión."

Hack's eyes narrowed. He reflexively looked around the room before he leaned in to Manny and whispered, "That's not still goin' on between you two, is it?"

Manny looked down at his feet.

"Christ on Christmas! If you think ya' got a shitstorm now, pardon the pun, wait 'til somethin' happens, goddamn it."

"We are in love!" Manny hissed.

Hack raised his hands in the air and looked at the ceiling, "Fuck it all, fuck it all!" He leveled his gaze on Manny, "Now I'm gonna' tell ya' this once, and one time only, so you listen good, okay?"

Manny nodded.

"Normally I'd call Pete in to translate, but I assume ya' don't want me doin' any such sort thing, now do ya'?"

Manny shook his head.

"Okay. And I ain't gonna' call Truck in here, neither, lest we arouse anyone's suspicions."

Manny nodded again.

Hack took a deep breath, "Now, son, yer' what? Twenny'? Twenny'-one years old?"

"Twenty-one," Manny smiled with pride.

"And Truck is what? Twenny'-two? He's a college guy, right?"

"Sí. So what?"

"So my point is, and I can't *believe* I'm even sayin' this about two'a my players," Hack shook his head for effect, "But ya' both are so goddamned *young*. Kids yer' age shouldn't be runnin' around, gettin' married. I did a damned fool thing like that before I joined the service, and ya' know what it got me when I came back?"

"A lifetime of happiness?" Manny deadpanned.

Hack remained unamused.

"Is a joke…" Manny offered.

"She became the goddamned town tilt-a-whirl: everybody got to go up and down and around once."

Manny squinted, failing to get the reference.

"She was foolin' around with other guys. Even some'a my buddies from high school. An' let's just say I wasn't exactly husband'a the year material, either. Over in Asia, there was all sorts'a stuff ta' keep a young sailor occupied.

"We were too young. We should'a never got married. An' even when I got married a second time, when I was a lot older, I wasn't ready then, either. Ya' need a certain level'a maturity to make any relationship work, and I don't know if you guys should be together."

Hack pointed at the door, "*Especially* when guys like Mitch Henry and Murph are out there just waitin' to hold a goddamn lynchin' fer' the first queer they see."

Manny puffed out his chest, "Is different for Camión and me, jefe. We get each other. We're *made* for each other."

"He's not even bein' faithful to ya'!" Hack hissed. "He's runnin' around, havin' a good time with that *awful* hussy'a his most'a the time."

"She means *nothin'* to him!" Manny fought away the tears.

"Oh yeah? Tell that ta' *her*. She's got his whole future mapped out fer' them."

Manny tried to choke the tears down, but they bubbled to the surface anyway. He turned to leave the room, a blubbering mess.

"Ah, see, this is *exactly* the kind'a shit I was tryin' to avoid. Fuck it—yer' due fer' a day off anyway. I've been pushin' ya' too hard. Go ahead an' go home—I'll just let Stearns mop up tonight if we get a lead."

Manny stopped in his tracks.

"Stearns?" he asked over his shoulder.

"Damned right, Stearns. He may be a hothead, but he's not gonna' become a sissy little mess when I push him a bit about his girlfriend."

"Who you callin' a sissy, jefe?" Manny turned to face the manager.

"Well, you *were* the one…" Hack tilted his head downward and lowered his eyes toward his feet.

"That doesn't mean *anything*!"

"Fer' Chrissakes! It was a fuckin' *joke*! Tasteless and sick as it may've been, that's the only flavor'a jokes I got!"

Manny shook his head.

"Besides, I couldn't let ya' go out there cryin' like a baby. You would'a never heard the end'a it from Henry."

Manny's eyes looked upward in contemplation.

"You make a point," he said. "But I'm playing tonight. I'm ready to pitch."

Hack took a baseball out of his pocket and flung it at the closer.

"Good. That's more like it!" Hack pointed to the empty shelves in the far corner of the room, "Now go ahead and throw that there."

"Qué? The ball?"

"Yep. Then storm outta' the room like I just chewed ya' out real good."

A knowing smile crept over Manny's lips. Without any further prompting, he launched the ball into the metal cabinets full force. A loud "BOOM!" resonated around the dingy walls of the well-lived-in manager's office as Manny pushed out the door, determined scowl on his face.

"You can kiss my ass, Poblado! Fuck RIGHT OFF!" Hack yelled behind him as the door shut.

Henry was talking with Murph Murphy and Zeke Bailey near their lockers, maybe ten feet from the entrance to the manager's office. They saw the dried tears on Manny's face and winced.

"Holy fahhk!" Murph said. "He musta' really reamed the *fahk* outta' you!"

Manny glared at the group as he passed by on the way to his locker.

"Good," Mitch Henry said.

Manny's heart skipped a beat. How much had he heard?

"Maybe he'll think twice before he puts shitty toilet paper in the trash again…"

2

A couple of hours later, the Magpies' clubhouse had settled down into its now-familiar rhythm, even if that rhythm would've been unrecognizable only months before.

As a testament to this newfound camaraderie, the Latin players invited Sid Fynch and Eldrake Gamble to play in their card game in order to practice their steadily-developing English skills. Pete Moray leaned against one of the rusty, old metal-caged lockers and observed.

"Wait a minute, so I just take one from the discard pile or the deck?" Sid asked.

"Sí," Ozzie Cabrera said. "I mean, yes, that's correct."

"And we're trying to make—?"

Sid was preempted by middle reliever Chucho Torres, "three or more of the same number, or three or more of the same...uh..."

"Don't get frustrated, Chucho—it's okay," Pete Moray offered before he raised a styrofoam cup to his mouth and spit in it.

"The same...like, with the diamonds and corazónes, and—"

"The same suit?" Flash asked.

"Yes!" Torres clapped, proud to have conveyed the thought. "The same suit—in a row, like four, five, six—"

"So it's basically gin rummy?" Flash followed up.

Cabrera held up both hands in a "keep away" motion. "I, uh, no liquor for me before a game."

"No, no, that's the name of the game," Gamble said. "Gin rummy." He patted his chest with both hands, "We have this game too. It's very popular here in America."

"Oh?" Cabrera asked as he drew a card and placed one on the discard pile. "So how do you say, when you win?"

"That's easy," Sid said with a hint of condescension. "Gin."

"Oh. Okay then," Cabrera laid his cards face up on the folding card table, "*Hin*."

Sid and Flash looked at the cards lined up on the table.

"Sonofa*bitch*!" Sid said with genuine wonder.

"We do play a lot..." Torres said.

"Chingarsé!" Juan Patrón's deep voice bellowed from the hallway next to the manager's office.

"What the hell?" Gamble asked. The table emptied to see what possibly could've driven Patrón to the emotional outburst.

When they reached the bulletin board outside of the manager's office, they were shocked.

The lineup card for that night's game was normal through the third spot, which Truck comfortably occupied.

Penciled in Patrón's customary fourth spot, though, was "4. Cabrera, LF"

It jumped to "5. Finch, CF"

Then "6. Woo, 2B"

And finally, "7. Morris, 1B"

"Peyton's playing today?" Truck asked.

Peyton Morris was a tall, lanky lefthander, all elbows and angles. Only twenty years old, he was a polite enough kid from Tennessee, but he had yet to grow into his 6'4" frame, and had only accrued a dozen at bats over the course of the season, all in pinch-hitting work.

That he was an outfielder by trade made the move all the more surprising.

But sure enough, Hack had done what Willie and nearly every other manager throughout Patrón's adult life had never dared do:

He took Juan out of the lineup.

He benched him.

Patrón's already dark complexion glowed with anger. His jaw jutted out and locked as his eyes narrowed.

"I, uh, I have to take a shit," Morris said. His voice cracked on the last word as he nearly sprinted to a vacant stall on the other side of the hallway. "A long one," he yelled over his shoulder moments before the lock on the door clicked loudly into place.

No one else knew what to say to the jilted slugger. His breaths deepened as he heaved each lungful in, contemplating whether or not to bother knocking on this interloper's door, or if he should just punch through the paint-coated glass.

Manny shook his head. Mitch Henry didn't even dare muster a chuckle, let alone a smart-ass remark. Even Sun Dae, who would've normally been able to say or do *something* to make his friend feel better, decided that saying nothing was the best course of action.

After ten full seconds of silence, Truck cleared his throat.

"I'll take care of it. You guys…go watch TV or something."

The crowd lingered.

"Now!" Truck yelled forcefully.

The group scattered back to whatever they had been doing previously.

"Holy shit, this oughtta' be good!" Mitch Henry covered his mouth with his glove as he spoke to Murph Murphy.

"You comin' with me?" Truck asked Patrón.

Patrón stared at Truck.

"Guess that's a 'no,' then…" Truck rapped sharply on the door three times.

"Yeah," Hack yelled out.

"It's Truck."

Truck couldn't make out the unintelligible stream of curse words that Hack uttered.

"Come in, come in."

Truck pulled the door open and found Hack chugging down the contents of his coffee mug.

"Christ, I have'ta deal with one'a yas before, and the other one now?"

"Whattaya mean 'one of *you*?'" Truck asked.

Hack waved the question away, "Fer'*get* it. I s'pose you wanna talk about what Manny an' I talked about earlier?"

"What? No…no, I'm here to talk about Juan."

"Oh," Hack almost chewed the word. He brought the mug to his lips again, only to find it empty. He eyed Truck suspiciously before he shrugged, opened the bottom drawer of his desk, and pulled out a fresh bottle of Old Reliable.

"What—you're *drinking*? Before a game? Does Willie or Keith know about this?"

Hack unscrewed the cap and poured a healthy slug into the cup before he tilted his head, "Yeah? What're ya' gonna' *do*? *Tell* on me? You tell on *me*, I tell on *you*!" Hack took another belt.

Truck shook his head. He had half a mind to have it out with the manager right then and there, but he had come into the office for a reason, and first thing was first.

"Coach, I just came in to tell you that I—we, the team, think that what you're doing to Juan tonight is pretty shitty."

Hack shrugged, "I think he's hittin' pretty shitty."

"It's not right, though," Truck said. "Even if he's only hitting .243 or whatever, Juan Patrón still gives us the best chance to win."

Hack shook his head, "Pitchers have figured out he can't hit off-speed stuff. Doesn't swing at 'em. If they can get 'em over, he's like a deer in headlights."

"So work with him! Have Pete throw him extra BP—plenty'a changeups."

Hack raised an eyebrow, "Now, that wouldn't be very fair, would it?"

Truck shook his head, "Who cares? Everyone knows that Juan and I are the best hitters on the team."

"Pretty high opinion'a yer'self there," Hack said.

"Come on, Coach. You know it's true. I'm seein' the ball well right now, and Juan isn't. That's all there is to it. He's crushed change-ups in the past, I've seen him do it. He'll come around. Just give him a few more games."

"I dunno," Hack said slyly. "Maybe we should see what Morris can do. I'll bet he's just itchin' ta' get out there, just rarin' ta'—"

"He's pretending to take a shit so that Juan doesn't beat the hell out of him."

"Good," Hack said. "Maybe he'll also pretend to run faster."

Truck ignored him, "Look, I know you're the manager. I know you've been managing longer than I've been alive, and you're pretty damned good at it. We've all seen the changes you've made, what they've done to the club, how you've made everyone on this team, even Willie, better for it.

"But to bench a guy without any warning at all, when that guy is as important to this lineup as Juan is, that's just *wrong*. Just because I respect your experience and defer to your wisdom in this matter does *not* mean I or anyone else out there has to agree with it."

Truck turned to leave the office. As he reached for the doorknob, Hack stopped him.

"Good," Hack said. "I've been waitin' fer' you to say that all season, Truck."

Truck tilted his head as he wheeled on his heels.

"Excuse me?"

"That—right there. *That's* leadership," Hack's voice was even and steady, unchanged from whatever whiskey he had swallowed down. "Ta' walk in here, tell an ornery ol' cuss like me that he's flat-out *wrong? That* takes some courage."

"You're not *drunk*?" Truck asked.

"Son, when ya' drink as much as I've drank...drunk? Whatever. When ya've had enough booze over a lifetime, you can handle a couple'a belts pretty easily."

"So...you admit you were wrong though?"

"Damn right," Hack nodded. "Not about the benchin'. That's my right as a manager. If I wanna' watch Peyton Morris piss all over himself whenever a power-hittin' lefty comes up fer' the rest'a the season, then by God that's my fuckin' right. Just like it was my right ta' make Manny a closer earlier in the year. It was what was best fer' the team, whether er' not you all appreciated it.

"But me not tellin' Juan about it—*that's* what's wrong. Christ, you think I'm scared'a Juan Patrón? When I was in Oakland, I had'ta tell Mark McGwire and José Canseco they were sittin' the bench occasionally, ya' know, and those guys make Patrón look like, well, Peyton Morris.

"I knew puttin' that lineup card out there would pull a couple'a his asshairs out, get him nice and mad an' seein' red. And I hoped that someone would have the balls ta' call me on it. Hoped it would be you, but really anyone would'a done.

"I needed ta' see that there's a leader on this team, fer' when I'm not here—" Hack looked to the side, "—uh, next year."

"I won't be here, either, I hope," Truck said. "I would think I'm gonna' be in at least Triple-A, maybe even—"

Hack swatted Truck on the hat brim.

"That's what I mean, ya' damned idiot! *In Cleveland*. Where *this team*'ll be next year. Hopefully they'll ditch that ditzy fuck Stevenson, but that's another matter entirely."

"So Juan *is* going to play tonight then."

"Shit yeah he is! Maybe he'll even hit a little bit now, too. This old fool *does* still have a couple'a tricks up his sleeve yet, y'know. Funny thing is, even though you all got yer' fancy phones and computers, I used that ol' saw fer' the first time when I was with the Pirates in '71. Willie Stargell just about killed me," Hack shook his head and stared whistfully into the obscured glass.

Truck allowed the old man to savor the moment for several sips of whiskey before he cleared his throat.

"What did you think I was in here to discuss?"

"What? Oh, well Mitch's been givin' Manny some shit lately about—"

"I'll fucking kill him," Truck said, jaw clenched.

Hack rolled his eyes, "—About puttin' his used T.P. in the trash."

"Oh…" Truck relaxed.

"And at the end, Manny came in and was talkin' about how ga-ga you two are about one another."

Hack looked at Truck for any hint or sign of emotion, but Truck willed his face blank.

"Yeah?" Truck asked, his tone calm and even.

"Oh yeah. Look, I'm gonna' tell ya' what I told him, what you two do ain't none'a my business. But what happens in here sure as shit is. And if one'a you fucks around on the other, or otherwise makes it so that there's unnecessary tension in my locker room, yer' gonna' *beg* for somethin' as innocent as what I just did ta' poor Juan Patrón out there. Am I clear?"

Truck narrowed his eyes and frowned slightly, almost imperceptibly, before he nodded.

"I'm serious, Truck—that poor kid thinks the world'a ya. Don't fuck 'im up."

"I got it!" Truck said, a bit too defensively.

"Good," Hack said as he folded his arms across his chest. "I'll tell Patrón he's in the lineup."

"Thank you, Coach," Truck said.

"Shit, yer' not done yet," Hack said.

"What?"

"You don't wanna lose that locker room, you show 'em a little piss 'n vinegar as yer' leavin'. Tell ya' what, how 'bout you pick up that chair and throw it?"

"Are you serious?" Truck asked.

"Yeah, pick it up and give it a good toss."

"You're sure about this?"

"Christ, if ya' take any longer, I'm not gonna' have ta' act pissed off. Now pick up that fuckin' chair and give it a throw, God damn it!"

Truck stood up and shrugged. He grabbed the bottom of the seventies-era chair and pulled.

It barely moved.

"Shit, this is a little heavier than it looks," Truck said.

"Come on now! Maybe I should put ol' Morris in fer' *you!*" Hack chuckled.

Truck was not amused at the suggestion. Instead of trying to lift the chair, he squatted under it, pushed, and extended his arms, launching the piece of furniture at the wall like a blocking sled.

"BOOM!"

The projectile connected with the cinderblock wall and took a healthy chip out of the façade.

Hack and Truck looked at each other in shock and amazement for several moments before each affected a scowl. Truck strode purposefully through the door into the clubhouse.

"Is that so, Traynor? Well, then in that case, you can suck my wrinkly—"

"CA-CHUNK!"

The door to the manager's office closed behind Truck. Juan Patrón stood across the hallway in the doorway to the training room.

Truck locked eyes with the first baseman and gave him a confident smile and a nod before he returned to his locker.

Several seconds later, Hack's office door swung open. He glared at Patrón across the hallway before he teetered to the bulletin board and replaced the lineup card with a new one.

"Sorry, Juan, looks like I mixed up tomorrow's lineup with today's," Hack said. His eyes narrowed on the scowling first baseman. "Consider yer'self on notice, though. Sure as shit, if ya' don't hit tonight, you'll be ridin' the bench and Morris'll get a few turns in there at first. Am I clear?"

The murder slowly drained from Patrón's eyes. His English had come a long way over the past several months, but he still didn't completely understand what his manager was saying.

"For fuck's sake," Hack raised his hands to the sky before he pointed at Juan, "You—play. Tonight. If no hit," Hack took an abbreviated swing with his bat before he slammed the butt end into the layered plywood wall of the manager's office, "No play. Understand?"

Patrón nodded. He wasn't used to being challenged, not like this. Though he still wanted nothing more than to pick up the old man and launch him into a trashcan somewhere in the clubhouse, something told him that if he tried to do so, he'd be on the receiving end of that bat, much like Mitch Henry and Sid Fynch had before him.

"Good! Now what time is it?" Hack looked at the Rolex from the Marlins, "Shit. Okay, everyone, listen up," he yelled into the clubhouse. "Fifteen minutes, everyone in here, okay?"

A round of murmurs echoed around the locker room.

Hack took a few steps toward the lockers and smashed the bat into the metal mesh of the row of lockers in front of him, already dented by his handiwork on the first day of the job.

"Fifteen minutes, here. Got it?" Hack asked.

"Yes, Coach!" The team responded more wholeheartedly.

Hack wiped his face with his arm, "And somebody check the goddamned AC in here—I'm burnin' up."

It was a remark made all the more odd by the fact that several pitchers already had their jackets on.

3

Hack immediately picked up the glass on the table and brought it to the shelves next to the sofa. He had Sam Rappaport and Barry Wojciechowski rearrange the binders and other assorted baseball papers on the upper shelves, as the lower shelves now housed most of Hack's various living supplies.

Cases of Robitussin and chicken noodle soup littered the cabinets, and innocuous-looking cardboard boxes stacked three high between the shelves and the couch housed handle upon handle of Old Reliable.

Hack opened one of the cases of "chicken noodle soup," and removed a large ziplock bag of pills from one of the compartments.

He opened the baggie and grabbed a half-dozen vicodin, which he could easily swallow in one gulp even without a chaser. He unscrewed the top to a half-finished bottle of Robitussin and drained its contents before he stumbled over to his desk and swigged off the Old Reliable he had pulled out in front of Truck until his thirst was slaked.

He sat in his chair and, feeling spry, decided to spin around in it several times.

As he came to a stop, the room continued to twirl several times. His brain plummeted toward his feet momentarily; Hack shot up out of his chair, and regained his senses.

Closer… The gruff voice inside his head called to him once more. *Just a taste…*

Hack shivered, now in a cold sweat. His back ached, though it was more of a dull, aching thud as he reached to scratch his shoulder.

Satisfied he had given the team enough time to relax and let the Traynor "incident" calm down, Hack pushed the door to his office out and gimped with the aid of his bat toward the locker room.

Even though Hack's frame was slight, this time it appeared to fill the entire doorway. A low hush fell over the previously gregarious clubhouse; even Mitch Henry was solemn and quiet. Pete Moray spit his entire dip into the styrofoam cup in his hand.

Willie broke his meeting with the outfielders to stand next to the manager.

"Alright men," Hack's eyes lit up. "As you're probably aware, we've worked our way back inta' the playoff picture."

A round of cheers went up from the players.

"It's been a long, tough climb to get where we're at now. We still don't have too good'a shot. We're three-and-a-half out with seven to play. After that, fer' some'a you, the good ones, or lucky ones, doesn't matter, it's off ta' Cleveland fer' a September call-up."

All eyes turned toward Truck.

"What?" Truck said with false modesty.

At least one player lobbed a glove in his direction as everyone else groaned.

"Now, Westfield and Palooka," Hack let out a low, thin whistle, "boy howdy, they are *tough*. Normally, I'd talk about how we already showed both those teams that we can play with 'em, since we've swept *both* of 'em this season!"

The players gave Hack a chorus of "Yeah"s

"Normally, I'd say that because of gutsy, brass-balled plays like what Flash, Truck, and yes, even Sunday—"

"Hello!" the Korean smiled and nodded, which broke up the room into a series of "Hello"s and loud laughs.

Hack put his hands together under his chin and nodded his head right back, which left the room howling with laughter.

"All'a ya' showed *guts*. All'a ya showed *grit* and goddamned determination. But that's not all ya' showed. Men, when I took this job, all the way back in May, do ya remember what I asked yas? I asked you for *respect*. I asked ya' fer' more *goddamned* respect than you've ever given another one'a yer' coaches, wherever it may've been.

"Now, I know I ain't normally the sentimental type. Hell, sometimes I can be a downright S.O.B. ta' play for."

The players erupted with mock protests.

"No, no, it's true—" Hack struggled to keep from grinning. "—true to my word back then, I don't think any'a us are 'best friends.'"

He looked at Truck.

"And some'a yous, well, I've been pretty damned tough on ya' all season."

He looked first at Fynch, then at Patrón, though the entire room again offered mock protests.

"But men, I have'ta admit: over these last three months, on whole, you all've given me the respect I asked fer', the respect my actions *demanded*."

More cheers.

"And in so doing, in listenin' to what I had ta' say, in the way you've handled yer'selves day-in and day-out, the way you've all come together as a goddamned *team*, one goddamned *unit*, you've earned *my* respect.

"So from here on out, men, and I do mean men, since every one'a yas—even you, Mitch—" the players laughed, except for Mitch Henry, who smiled and shook his head, "—I'm gonna' pay you the highest possible compliment. From this day forward, feel free to call me just plain old 'Hack.'"

Truck started applauding before Hack even finished his impromptu pep talk, and the rest of the players followed suit. Even Juan Patrón, still miffed about the old buzzard's "hit or else" edict just minutes before, offered a half-hearted attempt at applause.

Hack basked in the attention and let it wash over him.

They're a good group, Hack thought. *This might be just the push they need…*

"Now, men, all that said, we *do* still control our own destiny. We get Westfield fer' four games, then we get Palooka fer' three to close the year, all at home. So let's not just stand around, pickin' our noses, let's get out there, and raise some *fuckin' HELL!*"

The players cheered as they jogged down the hallway to the field, the tell-tale "click-clack" of metal spikes against concrete somehow an exuberant percussion despite the grating screech that any one pair made.

Hack looked at Willie, who nodded and put a hand on Hack's shoulder.

"You did good, Coach."

"Thanks Willie," Hack said.

Willie may as well have been hit in the face with a shovel. He twisted his head to one side.

"The *hell* you just call me?"

"You heard me. You've earned it, too."

Willie couldn't believe it. Here he was, a grown man, seeking the approval of an 84-year-old degenerate, racist fool.

If that's the case, why can't I keep from smiling? Willie asked himself.

"How 'bout me, Coach?" Pete Moray put his arms around both mens' shoulders. "Can I call ya' 'Hack,' too?"

"Pete, I don't think ya' even called me 'Coach' back in the day when I told ya' to," Hack said.

"Ah, maybe. I don't remember gettin' the butt end'a the bat like Henry did."

Hack raised the bat and made a spearing motion toward Moray, stopping just short of the man's midsection.

"Now we're even," Hack said as Moray flinched.

"You guys ready?" Willie asked.

"Actually, fellas, there's somethin' I need ya' to take care of before we head out there. Why don't you come with me into my office?"

4

Hack turned right out of the tunnel from the field and made his way to the dungeon. Even though he hadn't worn his turtleneck, the sweat still poured off of him from the humid Hoplite evening.

Once inside the press room, Marc Blake approached him, as usual.

"Hey, Coach Hack, way to go! Only what? Two-and-a-half out now?"

"It's Coach O'Callahan to you, Blake," Hack replied.

"I thought you said everyone can call you Hack now?"

"The *team*, Blake. Not you front office-types."

Blake raised an eyebrow, "But Keith calls you Hack all the time!"

Hack didn't flinch, "You want me to treat ya' the same way I treat him?"

Blake blinked several times before he extended a cool hand toward the podium.

"Right this way."

Hack's legs dragged in the muggy summer air as he limped toward the podium. He arrived out of breath for the first time in a long while.

The gaggle of reporters was surprisingly thick; Channel 2 News even brought a camera crew to film the presser for the stretch run. Though Hoplite had always loved the Magpies, Hack reignited the passion of the fan base, if only because of his colorful theatrics and penchant for unconventional strategy.

Despite the evening's victory, Hack was his usual, stern self as he labored to get behind the short podium.

"Yeah?" Hack asked, already annoyed. "Go ahead?"

As was customary, Jim Taggert lobbed the first question.

"So what the hell did ya' feed Juan Patrón tonight?"

The press corps chuckled.

Hack smiled with his eyes, "Juan and I had a nice chat before the game, really got him set straight mentally. He's a good kid—I think he'll be just fine the rest of the way."

"Three-for four with two homers and a double is a little more than 'just fine,' isn't it?"

"I'm not gonna' lie, Jim, we all know he's been in a slump lately. Tonight's a good first step, but he has'ta string a few'a these together before we throw him a parade 'er whatever."

April Barker was next, "What about the rumors that given the injury to Armando Armiguez, the Indians are going to call up Truck Traynor on an emergency basis as of tomorrow?"

Hack bit his lip, "I ain't heard nothin' about that. Willie hasn't heard nothin' about that. I haven't heard nothin' from Keith or George Tavatelli, I don't know nothin'." Hack paused and leaned in toward the microphone, "Nothin'."

Liam Canard was next up, "Coach, even with the win tonight, the Magpies only have a 27.8% chance of making the playoffs. Is this just a case of too little, too late?"

Hack turned his head, "To little, too late? Son, I have no idea what kind'a computer or…uh…robot you get these numbers from. The way I see it, we're only 2 1/2 out. That seems like—"

"But you're playing the teams directly ahead of you in the standings, and," he snorted twice for good measure, "statistically speaking—"

"*Don't* interrupt me again, son." Hack glared at the nerdy hipster-wannabe for several seconds to let the sentiment sink in. "Now I know you've never been in a locker room before—most kids yer' age in yer' line'a work haven't.

"But ya' know who has?" he pointed at the door to the clubhouse, "The twenny'-five guys in *there*. Twenny'-*eight* if yer' includin' coaches, and even more if ya' count interns, batboys, the trainer, *all* the folks who have a stake in the day-ta'-day'a this operation."

Blake couldn't hide his scowl when Hack completely ignored the front office.

"We started a bit slow—I'm sure Willie'll be the first to tell ya' that he's a helluva lot better manager now than he was at the beginnin' of the year. Hell, the whole damned *team* was a mess when I got here.

"But ya' know what, son? We've *all* been bustin' our *asses* to turn this thing around. Every one'a us, *to a man*. And that's what I *love* about this group. Fer' as damned *dumb* and stupid as they were when I got here, well, they're givin' me their very best. Is it enough? I guess we'll see. But that doesn't change that I'm damned proud'a them...no bullshit, *damned* proud..."

Taggert raised his notepad again, "With the big lead, late in the game tonight, it seemed like a prime opportunity to rest Manny and get Tommy Stearns some work in mopup. Why go back to Poblado there in the ninth?"

"I tell ya' what, Jim, I have the utmost respect fer' Manny."

Is this the same guy who's been such a shithead to us all year? Taggert thought.

"He's done more than I ever asked him to as a closer. Damned fine one, too. Very coachable. Pete Moray and him've been inseparable workin' on that secondary pitch. We have an off-day or two down the stretch—we need him to get used ta' pitchin' every day fer' us here, every inning he can throw is a plus. Havin' Stearns down there in case he can't go, well..." Hack paused two beats too long, his eyes glazed over before he snapped back, "That's, a, uh...real luxury fer' us."

The Channel 2 guy was next—a former football player, he seemed stuffed into a suit about two sizes two small, "Talk a little bit about what Sun Dae Woo's meant to this team."

"Well," Another lengthy pause, "Sunday's great. No problem there."

Channel 2 chuckled, "Of course you don't have a problem with what he's doing, it's just we don't get access to the players here. Give us a little bit about what he's like, what he might say, that sort of thing."

Hack grinned, "You wanna' hear what he'd say?" He pressed his hands up against one another and bobbed his head with a big grin on his face, "Hello!"

Hack was the only one who got the joke.

He didn't care.

The conference dragged on for another fifteen to twenty minutes—Marc Blake refused to cut off the inane and repetitive questions, the media relations director's feeble attempt at payback for slighting him twice earlier.

To his credit, though Hack had to pull out his handkerchief several times to dab his forehead, he stuck around and answered every question, no matter how dumb.

"One more question, coach," it was Taggert again. "Any guarantees? About the rest of the year?"

Hack leveled his gaze at the veteran newspaperman, not with anger or spite, but rather with a profound matter-of-factness that sent a shiver down Taggert's spine.

"Nope. None at all."

With that, Hack slowly made his way out of the dungeon and walked right past the coaches' locker room.

I could use a drink, he thought.

Though to be fair, the sentiment was usually floating around somewhere in the manager's mind at any given moment.

He sniffed the air several times. Though he had been coughing intermittently the entire year, he hadn't had a full-on fit in quite some time. It made the pungent aroma of oranges and nail polish remover that seeped through his throat and into his nasal cavity.

But there was something else.

Something dark and sinister like…ashes? That wasn't quite it.

He turned and opened the door to his office, and nearly had a heart attack.

Seated in his chair, again, was Meadow Dressel.

5

*Truck's other girlfriend…*Hack thought.

Dressel was dressed as scandalously as ever. This time, she wore a sundress that had been taken in at the hem to show a little more tanned skin around her thighs. The bust line also looked to be modified to accentuate her pendulous breasts as she swayed from side-to-side in Hack's chair.

"Sulfur!" he exclaimed. "I knew I recognized the smell."

"Well, well, *Coach*," Meadow opened her legs ever so slightly, "Long time no see."

"How the *fuck* did you get in here?"

"Friends in high places, or *low* places, I guess, when it comes to this shithole."

"You've got some nerve, goddamn it!"

"Relax, *coach*," she laughed her flirty, lilting laugh, "I heard the rumors about Truck, movin' up to Cleveland. Bright lights, more fame, more *money*," she sucked in air after the last word, "I just came down here to surprise my little Trucky Wucky, get him ready to go."

"Yeah? So why're ya' in *here* then?"

"He's in the trainer's room," Meadow said. "And I didn't feel like being ogled by that Neanderthal Mitch Henry or his minions, or that Manny Poblado for that matter. Talk about the roving eyes in this clubhouse," she said, without a hint of irony.

Hack's eyes widened as he chuckled, "So you don't—" he stopped himself.

You don't KNOW about Manny? He thought.

"I don't *what?*"

"You don't see the irony?" Hack recovered. "You dress like *that*, then complain 'bout the attention ya' get?"

She feigned concern as she skipped out of the chair and put her arms around Hack, "Oh, Hack darlin', you don't understand, do ya'? Kind'a precious, really. No, I'm not interested in any old *loser* out there. I just want to be with the big stars, the guys who'll see eight figures one day. You only've got one'a those, and he's *mine*."

Hack pushed himself away from the seductress and pointed at the door, "Get the fuck outt'a my office."

She laughed again, "Oh, Hacky Wacky, why don't we just relax a lil' bit, and—"

"God *damn* it!" Hack slammed the flimsy desk. "I ain't fuckin' around. I'll call security if I have'ta. *Nobody* comes into my clubhouse and calls me or any'a my players a fuckin' loser!"

"You mean Al Wenner? Head of Security? I think you'll find that he and I are on relatively *close* terms."

"I'll call fer' Sam Rappaport then," his eyes narrowed.

Meadow paused for two beats before she affected another phony smile, "You're bluffin', muffin. You wouldn't *dare* do—"

Hack pushed the door open, "Sam! Pollack! Need ya' here, *now*!"

Sam and Barry rushed to the office.

"Yeah Hack?" Sam asked.

"*Brownnoser!*" Barry muffled his nasally voice with a sneeze.

"Excuse me?" Sam asked.

"Sorry…allergies," Barry said.

"Can you two escort this hussy off the premises, please?"

Sam smiled thinly, "With pleasure."

The two interns eagerly moved to take an arm each for wildly different reasons.

"Easy, *easy!*" Meadow said, pulling away. "I'm a big girl. I can do this myself." she turned to Hack, "Goodbye Hack. Guess we'll never know what could'a been."

"I have a pretty good idea…" Hack replied, unfazed.

Sam smiled at Hack's resolve.

"Gett'er outta' here!" Hack said. The two interns walked Meadow out of the office, though Hack noticed that Barry snuck a peek at Meadow's cleavage on the way as she smiled imperceptibly.

"Christ, I thought these crises were over!" Hack raised his hands at the sky before he brought them down to his head, removed his hat, and then covered his face.

He needed to relax, needed a drink, really could use a—

"A massage…" Hack said to no one in particular.

His scheduled massages had been decreasing in frequency as he continued to explore the boundaries of non-lethal dosages of pain medication. Though he had already seen Randy Edwardson three days before, he doubted that the trainer/masseuse would object to a little more work. He actually seemed to enjoy Hack's stories when the old timer was on the table.

Hack exited the office, still dressed in his uniform. The press conference had taken far longer than he had thought, as nearly all of the locker stalls sat empty. The final Magpie in the room, Manny Poblado, was zipping up his bag and offered a wave to the manager.

"Have a good night, jefé Hack!" Manny said with a broad smile.

Hack grinned with amusement, "Good work tonight, Manny. See ya' tomorrow."

Manny ambled down the hallway to the exit and pushed through the double doors to the outside world.

Hack sighed. He was still in uniform, but Edwardson had towels in the training room he could use. He scuttled down the hallway toward the training room, a fresh bounce in his step from tossing Meadow out of the clubhouse.

He didn't bother knocking as he pushed the training room door open.

It was a mistake that he immediately regretted.

"Well, Randy, sorry ta' keep ya' late, but the presser was a helluva mess—"

The tall, blond, Scandinavian-looking masseuse stood in front of Hack, with Truck Traynor on the table in front of him, face up, towel cast aside.

Unfortunately, Hack's eyes strayed toward the absent towel, and what he saw shocked him for entirely different reasons.

Edwardson was jerking off Truck Traynor.

Hack didn't even bother saying anything. His eyes glazed over in a zombie-like trance. He turned on his heels and walked slowly back down the hallway toward his office.

"Coach? Hack? Wait—it's not...it's not what you think!" the star catcher's words were barely an echo as Hack slowly, deliberately put one foot after the other, thinking only of one thing:

How many bottles of Old Reliable is this *gonna take*?

"Whoa, whoa, Coach? This really isn't what you think." Edwardson's surfer cadence was the next ethereal noise to break through the sudden ringing in Hack's ear. He pulled the door open, Truck and Edwardson hot on his heels.

He didn't sit, *couldn't* sit as he stretched out a shaking hand, grabbed the handle of whiskey on his desk, unscrewed the cap, and started guzzling it down.

"Coach—hey, hold on, there!" Truck said as he fastened a towel around his midsection.

"Fuck *you*!" Hack finished the bottle. "Whattid I tell ya' about turnin' this inta' a fuckin' *bathhouse*?"

"Whoa, Coach, hang on," Edwardson interjected. "This isn't, like, Truck and me..."

"That sure as shit is what it looked like ta' me!" Hack threw up his arms. "What am I missin'?"

"Look," Edwardson partially kneeled to bring himself to Hack's eye level. "Some of the dudes on the team need a little bit'a tension release after their massages."

"Lemme guess—Manny too?" Hack glared at Truck.

"What? No!" Edwardson was shocked. "Never Manny. Just a couple other guys, who obviously asked me to keep their names on the down low. It's not a gay thing or anything—I call it full service, *holistic* medicine."

Hack widened his eyes sarcastically, "O—oooohhhh!" he let out, his mouth tremulous, "I get it now! *Hole*-istic medicine. Riiight! Of course! How could I've thought *you were fuckin'* JERKIN' *him off*?!"

Truck shook his head, "It's not like *that* with Randy and me. You heard him—plenty of guys do it."

"A couple! Not *plen'ny*," Hack fought back the tears, "And right when poor Manny's out here packin' up his shit...and yer' other girlfriend too." Hack momentarily smiled to think how shattered that hussy Meadow Dressel might have been if she had only stuck around for five more minutes...

"I...I don't know what I can possibly say to make this seem okay," Truck said.

"I'll tell ya' what *I* can say," Hack said, grabbing for the phone. "I can tell George Tavatelli all *sorts'a* interestin' stuff!"

"No, Hack, please DON'T!" Truck reached across the desk for the receiver.

Hack ignored him, "Yes, operator? Cleveland, Ohio. Cleveland Indians baseball team, please..."

Truck had moved around to Hack's side of the desk. He wanted to physically restrain the man, bind his arms, reach out and cut off the line—

But his hands stayed by his sides.

"Please, don't! You promised me in the strictest confidence that you'd never—"

"Ah, fuck yer' promises," Hack said. "They aren't worth shit any—yes, hello? Hack O'Callahan fer' George Tavatelli, please." he paused for only a moment, "Yeah, George?"

"Hack! I was planning on calling you in a few minutes. What's up?"

"Well George, it's actually about Truck."

Hit him, you fool! Truck's brain screamed at his arms, willing them to smack the old man in the face.

They didn't move.

"Really? That's why I was going to call you, too."

"Well..." Hack looked Truck in the eye. The catcher's eyelids trembled, wide and wild, though not entirely fearful. There was something else behind those eyes. Could it be?

Hope? Hack thought.

"He...uh...I don't right know how ta' say this, so here goes..."

Truck's eyes pleaded once more.

For what, though, was unclear.

Hack paused another second. Two. Truck's heart thundered what seemed like a hundred times each lingering moment, ready to explode out of his chest.

For his part, the sweat poured off of Hack's face as it reddened. Was he ready to potentially end such a promising young player's career? He'd done it before, but Truck was...different. Promiscuity aside, Hack didn't think the kid deserved that harsh of a fate.

The manager struggled for air. The orange scent overpowered everything as he forced himself to stay steady.

Hack bit his lip, "He's...he's learned everything he can here. I, uh, think you guys could probably use him up in Cleveland fer' the rest of the season."

Truck exhaled like a banshee. Tears started to stream from his eyes as all of the mixed feelings he felt on that bus ride so long ago, the shame, the anger at his own weakness, all swirled in his head, with one notable exception:

Relief.

Or rather the lack thereof.

"Hack, we've already called him up on an emergency basis. He's to report to Cleveland for the game tomorrow. You might get him back after that, but—"

Hack smiled, a thin, dopey, smile. His eyes looked positively dewey to Truck, the first time that the manager's expression had taken on anything close to a happy lilt.

The illusion was fleeting, though, as Hack's head sunk, and sunk, and suddenly dropped to the floor, along with the receiver, not but a foot from the errant ball he had encouraged Manny to throw earlier that day. Blood leaked from his mouth and onto the ball, as Hack lay on the floor, dopey grin and all.

Seventh Inning

1

The darkness overcame Hack swiftly as his consciousness sank away from his eyes toward something deep below. It pulled at his mind with all of its might, twisting and sucking at his very being, trying to tear him away from the broken-down vessel he occupied.

Then the nightmares began. Every player he had ever berated or smacked on the bill of the cap (or worse) for failing to heed his instructions. Every time he had cursed out an umpire just to make a point. Perhaps most troubling of all, every time he had only made it out to his house once during a homestand, and offered only the most dispassionate kiss to little Lisa as he thought about the next day's game while she regaled him about what was going on in her life.

What had it all been for? All of the drinking and smoking and neglect? A game? Baseball?

Yer' damned right, *baseball!* Hack's mind thundered back.

I said...not...YET! The gruff voice from deep inside that had so tormented Hack for months now cracked the old manager's spirit like a whip.

Suddenly, as if rebounding off of a trampoline, Hack rocketed back toward the bright portholes of his eyes. His consciousness raced to refill the empty container of his head.

A thunderbolt of thought smacked the manager across the face. He felt a thin blanket across his lap, and though he wanted nothing more than to shoot out of whatever reclined seat he now found himself, all the salty old manager could do was blink his eyes weakly before he opened them.

"My God—I think...he's alive! He's waking up!" a female voice said.

He blinked several more times and the world came into a blurry focus through the hammering fluorescent bulbs.

A beautiful face hovered over his, in line with one of the bright, overhead lights of the room. Through his short, dry breathing, he thought he saw a halo around the shoulder-length red hair of the ethereal being.

"Hack!" Sam Rappaport cried. "Say something!"

Hack licked his spittle-caked lips several times to wet them before he spoke.

"Either the devil's playin' one helluva trick on me, or somehow I wormed my way inta' heaven," he punctuated the statement with a thin smile.

"Oh, thank God!" Sam hugged the ornery old manager. He managed to raise an arm around her.

"What the hell did I miss?" Hack asked.

"Oh, it was *horrible!*" Sam barely could stifle her tears. "You died for a minute there. They had to restart your heart, and even then you were out of it for a good twenty minutes or so."

She stood up and motioned to the corner of the room to reveal Truck Traynor dressed in a hospital gown of his own.

"Truck saved your life. If it wasn't for him, they said that you would've died in your office for sure."

Truck nodded slowly to confirm this seemingly heroic fact.

Hack grinned briefly before his eyes narrowed, "Well, 'guess that makes us even, then."

"What?" Samantha took a step backward.

"He knows what I mean—" Hack pointed a stubby, gnarled finger at Truck, "I didn't blab ta' Tavatelli 'bout—"

Truck hook his head, "Not with Sam here, Hack!"

Hack swallowed the revelation about Truck's sexuality as it was about to escape.

"—'bout, uh, where Truck was gonna' live in Cleveland. Had 'im in a real shithole of a hotel."

"Truck's been promoted?" Sam looked at the catcher for confirmation.

He nodded slowly in reply.

"Christ, can ya' blame 'em?" Hack's face slowly gained color. "He's been murderin' the ball all year!"

"It's just an emergency call-up, covering for Armiguez for a few days."

"I didn't even know Armiguez was hurt," Sam was genuinely shocked.

Truck took a deep breath, "Officially, he wrenched his back in B.P. Now, unofficially, I don't know how he was takin' B.P. on the fifteenth tee box, but…" Truck grinned.

Samantha smiled, "Well, congratulations, Truck! Wow, everyone at Baucomb'll be so jealous that I know a real live major league ballplayer! Although…" she bit her lip.

Hack rolled his eyes, "Whatta' *you* keepin' from us, missy? Go ahead—spit it out!"

"Well…George told me to keep it a secret, but…"

"Fuck George, and fuck Keith too while we're at it," Hack practically spat the words.

"I didn't mention Keith," Sam said.

"I know. I was just talkin' generally."

Sam inhaled deeply, "George offered me a job as special assistant to the GM for next season. I'm going to take classes in the fall, and then go part-time through the spring, summer, and fall online through Case Western to get enough credits to graduate!"

She could barely conceal her glee.

"Well, that's good, kid," Hack said, "Real good work. Ya' got what ya' always wanted. Certainly got a better future in the sport than that shithead Keith Myrick."

Several raps on the door broke Hack's tirade.

A nurse walked into the room with a small bouquet of what appeared to be discount flowers.

"Hello, Mr. O'Callahan!" the overweight black woman said as she handed the bouquet to the manager.

"What in the *fuck*?" Hack asked as he looked for the card. He found it and read it aloud: "Dear Hack, We all know you'll be leaving the hospital soon enough. Speedily yours, Keith Myrick and the Magpies."

"What a nice gesture," Sam nodded the last words at Hack to prove her point.

"What're ya' *talkin'* about?" Hack raised his voice, "He meant leavin' in a body bag!"

Truck shook his head.

"Well, I still think you're too hard on Keith sometimes, Hack. He tries, he really does."

"If ya' mean he's tryin' ta' kill me, he's gonna' have'ta try a little harder!"

Sam crossed her arms and frowned.

"I hope that was a joke."

Hack met her eyes with a sour glare.

Another several raps broke the silence. A tall, thin black man wearing a button-down shirt and slacks walked into the room.

"Mr. O'Callahan?"

"Thanks, but I got plen'ny'a pilla's. Could use another blanket 'er two, though…"

This time, it was Sam's turn to roll her eyes. She wordlessly took five dollars out of her purse and gave it to a smiling Truck Traynor, who had just won a bet about Hack "going racial."

The doctor shook his head, "Mr. O'Callahan, I'm Dr. Barker."

Hack's eyes went wide, "Oh…Ohhhhhh," he extended his hand to take the doctor's, "Nice ta' meetchya, Doc. What can ya' tell me?"

Dr. Barker looked at Sam and Truck, "Is it okay to talk in front of these two? Are they family?"

Hack looked at the two scared young people to his left.

"Yeah. Yeah, they're family. This is my daughter—*grand*daughter, Samantha—" he corrected himself.

*And this is my other granddaughter…*he wanted to say.

"And this is my grandson, uh…Truck. We all call him Truck."

Sam and Truck exchanged glances and slowly nodded.

"Mr. O'Callahan, I live in Hoplite. You don't think I know who Truck Traynor is?"

Hack frowned.

"I don't care. I'm tired—whatever ya' have ta' say in fron'na me, ya' can say in fron'na them, *too*."

His head began to swim from a decided lack of Old Reliable.

The doctor's eyes went wide, "You want to stay in here, guys?" he asked Sam and Truck.

Both nodded.

He sighed, "Okay then, Mr. O'Callahan. Let me first ask when did you get your cancer diagnosis?"

"May 13th," Hack said, without hesitation.

"Cancer?" Truck whispered.

Sam stood, mouth agape for several moments. She choked out several deep sobbing breaths.

Hack grabbed her hand and offered her a tight smile before he put a finger up to his lips.

"And when they diagnosed you, how far had the cancer progressed?"

"Stage three. Liver cancer," Hack replied in the same monotone, unaffected tone as before.

"Did he say anything about a tumor in your stomach?"

"Yeah. He said there was one'a those, too. Guy's a bit of'a crackpot, though—I don't know that I trust a word he—"

"We took an x-ray, and sure enough, the cancer has spread to your stomach. There was a small, sharp object that punctured the tumor, and hastened the cancer's spread to the rest of the stomach lining."

Hack's face reddened. Even pumped full of pain meds, he remembered his spiteful, tumultuous bout with the glass splinter back in Featherstone, Colorado, now months ago.

Hack nodded, "Go on," he said through clenched teeth.

"Quite frankly, it's a miracle that your cancer hasn't spread more quickly than it has, given the circumstances."

"Must not like Ol' Reliable," Hack mustered a smile as he patted Samantha's hand.

She chuckled through a sob.

Dr. Barker furrowed his brow, "The fiber supplement?"

Hack waved him away, "Fer'git' it. So what does this all mean, Doc?"

"You have to have surgery. The sooner the better."

Hack shook his head, "No way. I ain't gonna be cut up like—"

"Mr. O'Callahan, this is *not* an option…" The Doctor said firmly. "The stroke, or seizure, or 'episode' that you had may be a symptom that the cancer is already in the bloodstream, and spreading to the brain.

"We don't have the type of diagnostic equipment in Hoplite to confirm such a diagnosis. Fortunately, you're only a few short hours away from the Cleveland Clinic, one of the finest hospitals in the world. Thankfully your major league retirement benefits will cover it all. There, they will be able to tell you whether you should undergo surgery to try to remove the affected area of the stomach, or if you should enjoy your last few days in the comfort of family and friends."

Hack's eyes had involuntarily widened as the doctor leveled his death sentence upon him. Through it all, through the diagnosis, through the coughing fits, through every single step of the journey, he had tried to pretend that it wasn't real, that the cancer was somehow a figment of "that damned fool doctor" in Cleveland's imagination.

But now, confirmed by a second doctor, with few options left, Hack realized:

He was going to die soon.

I'm com-ing... the raspy voice in his head said ominously, almost sing-songy.

He allowed himself two deep, choking breaths of panic, two gasps of abject terror where he allowed the fear to consume him. *My life is going to end...forever...there's nothing I can do about it.* The weight of the helplessness fell squarely on his chest, as he heaved those two deep breaths to try to shrug it off.

Hack's eyes narrowed as he composed himself.

"If I get this surgery, how long is the recovery time?"

"Assuming you make it through?" The doctor asked, and immediately regretted it, "I mean, it's no sure thing, Mr. O'Callahan. Gives you a better chance than not doing anything though."

"How long?" Hack asked.

"If successful? A few days, probably, assuming all goes well."

"So I could be back fer' the playoffs?"

The doctor tilted his head in thought.

"I suppose so, yes."

Hack nodded, "Awright then, I'll do it. Call up whoever ya' gotta' at the Cleveland Clinic and let's set this up fer' tomorra' night."

Dr. Barker smiled, "Excellent. We'll keep you overnight for observation, in case anything else pops up, then sometime tomorrow morning, we'll release you to one of your," he cleared his throat, "grandchildren here."

"Great," Hack said. "I'll get in the Green Hornet and speed on off'ta—"

"The Green Hornet?" Dr. Barker asked.

"It's what I call my car. She's a beaut'—beautiful teal, '67 Chevy, in 'bout as good'a shape as the day I got'er."

"Oh, there's no *way* I'm going to let you drive," Dr. Barker frowned. "Someone else will have to take you to Cleveland. Do you know anyone who's on their way there?"

Before Hack could even look at Truck, the catcher piped up, "I am."

Dr. Barker smiled thinly, "Great. Now, Mr. O'Callahan, get your rest. You have a very big day ahead of you tomorrow."

"Aw, come on, Doc—can't the kids stay a little longer?" Hack's eyes pleaded with Sam and Truck.

"I'm afraid not. No exceptions. Say your goodbyes and then it's nighttime."

Sam didn't need any more encouragement; she leaned in and gave Hack another hearty hug.

"Good night, Hack," she said.

"Good night, sweetheart," Hack replied.

"I'll talk to Keith and see if he'll let me head over to Cleveland once I'm done at the stadium tomorrow. Shouldn't be too tough; we have an off-day."

Hack playfully smacked an invisible hat brim far in front of her face, "I know that, kid! I ain't gone totally loony yet!"

Sam smiled.

Truck stuck out his hand, "Good night, Coach."

"See ya' tomorra', bright an' early, Truck."

Truck smiled thinly as he took the old man's hand and shook it.

"And Truck?"

"Yeah?"

"I ain't too good at apologies 'er nothin', but thanks fer' savin' my bacon in the clubhouse."

"No problem."

Sam exited the room, followed closely behind by Truck.

"Oh, and Truck?"

"Yeah, Hack?"

"Thank Randy fer' me, too."

The words stopped Truck dead in his tracks. He looked over his shoulder briefly and nodded.

"Any other 'family members' you want me to tell about your trip to Cleveland?" Dr. Barker asked.

Hack thought for five full seconds.

"Mr. O'Callahan?"

"Yeah. Call Lisa Marsden, in Westfield, Indiana." He gave the doctor the number from memory; he had stared at it so many times through the years, contemplating whether to call to try to make amends, that it was burned into his brain.

"I'll make sure she knows. Good night, Mr. O'Callahan," Dr. Barker said.

"Doc," Hack nodded. The lights went out and Hack had no problem falling asleep.

Right before he drifted off, though, the Doctor's words resonated in his head.

What was it he said? "You have a very big day ahead of you tomorrow?" Hack thought.

He had no idea just how right the doctor would prove to be.

2

The next morning, Hack leaned on the window of Truck's Lexus RX350. The vehicle was a hand-me-down from Truck's mother, and it showed. Cans of Coke Zero littered the backseat, and the front right running panel was beginning to peel away from the door.

Hack felt right at home.

They were only five minutes outside of Hoplite on Highway 20 when Truck finally broke the silence.

"Why didn't you tell us you had cancer, coach?"

Hack affected a mocking tone, "Why didn't ya' tell us ya' were *queer*, Truck?"

"Fair point," Truck said, through gritted teeth, "But we could've helped you. Gotten you to Cleveland sooner so that you could've—"

"So they could'a hooked me ta' a bag'a *chem-o-therapy* drugs and I could'a spent my last few months on this earth miserable, leakin' piss and shit into a bag, watchin' highlights'a dumb shit managers makin' mistakes instead'a doin' things the right way myself?"

"So that you could spend more time with the people who care about you?"

Hack pointed over his shoulder, "The only people that care about me in this world are in that town back there, in the clubhouse'a the Murph. And Sam, a'course. But none'a yas would give half a blue shit about me if I'd done things 'the right way,' fightin' fer' a life not worth livin'."

"You don't have any real family?" Truck asked.

Hack sighed, "Did I ever tell ya' why they call me 'Hack,' Truck?"

"Uh, no. You didn't even let me call you 'Hack' until yesterday, remember?"

"Oh yeah..." Hack said. "Most guys just ignore that little edict, but you all had yer' heads and hearts in the right place. Showed me respect. Damned proud...damned proud..."

Hack stared off into space for a moment.

"Anyway, where was I?"

"Why everyone calls you——"

"Hack! Right, right. Well, I was comin' up through the Cardinals system, before I got traded to the Yankees. Long before I managed the Redbirds in the late nineties."

Hack took a deep breath, "I've never really been the popular sort, on any team I've been on, even as a player. You know Milt Ford? That fat-ass catcher we had I was talkin' 'bout on the bus?"

Truck managed to mostly hide his revulsion as he nodded.

"He shat up the bus, sure as shit. But it wasn't lil' Cap Harrow they were holdin' up to his asshole. It was me."

Truck covered his mouth with his right hand and coughed to keep from retching.

"So before the Green Hornet, I had a used Studebaker, first thing I bought after the war. I loved that goddamn car, washed and waxed it every week, good fer' the arm, ya' see——"

He looked at Truck and found the catcher's eyes glazing over.

"——So anyway, I would drive that car to the ballpark every day. Back in the day, it was odd fer' a minor leaguer ta' have his own car. And after every game, ta' endear myself ta' the rest'a the team, I would offer ta' drive Milt and Paw Greely and some'a the other popular guys on the team out so that they could get shithammered.

"I usually kept my mouth shut, and let them do most'a the talkin' when we were at a gin joint. And they'd just talk—mostly 'bout broads, but every now-and-then, they'd start talkin' 'bout the game that night and I'd light up, like a Christmas tree. If there's one thing we all shared, it was a *love* fer' goddamned baseball. I've always been able ta' chat about it fer' hours.

"So we get ta' be a bit friendly, and I think things is goin' famously. They start invitin' *me* out when we're on the road. I think this is about the greatest thing since rubbers."

"Condoms?" Truck interrupted.

Hack smacked the bill of his hat.

"Ow! Not while driving!" Truck yelled.

"Galoshes, ya' deviant. Though, come ta' think'a it, yeah, rubbers, too…"

Truck shook his head, half-scowling.

This man is dying, he reminded himself.

"Well, one day, ol' Paw Greely couldn't wait 'til the end'a the game ta' get bombed, so he's stumblin' around the clubhouse, and he yells at me, 'Hey, Hack! Need a fare?'

"Everyone thought it was the funniest goddamn thing they ever heard. Back then, a hack was a cabbie, usually a fat, smelly Greek fella' who was sick'a runnin' numbers.

"I was embarrassed as'a zebra without stripes. 'How could they do this ta' me?' So I went home and I opened a bottle'a some ha'rrible whiskey and drained half'a it.

"You know what? It made everything not so bad. Brightened up my world a bit. So then I started havin' more and more, and, well…you saw what I am now. A fuckin' addict."

"My God," Truck said. "That's awful. I'm so sorry that—"

"*Sorry?*" Hack narrowed his eyes. "Let me fuckin' finish! So I start drinkin', and the next day I come in'ta the clubhouse still a little shitty. An' I let Paw *have it*, boy. I never called a man so many names in my life outside'a *church* before."

Truck opened his mouth to interrupt, but thought the better of it.

"And at the end, I call him a fuckin' scumbag. You know where that word comes from, right? Scumbag? It's a used rubber."

Truck shook his head.

"Used'ta be one'a the worst things you could call someone. So I says ta' him, 'Yer' a *fuckin'* scumbag, Paw!' And he just looks at me, three full seconds, like he's gonna' 'BAM!' pop me one, right in the mug.

"He just stares, and stares, and stares, and then, you know what the sonofabitch does? He starts *laughin'*. He thinks it's hilarious.And whenever Paw laughed, that meant Milt laughed, and pretty soon, the rest'a the locker room joined in. I was on top'a the world. After that, everyone just called me 'Hack,' and I would give it right back to 'em."

Hack turned to face Truck, "Do ya' get the *point*'a the story, son?"

"That your teammates poking fun at you forced you into alcoholism?"

"First'a all, nobody forced me ta' nothin'," Hack shook his head, "Secondly, instead'a worryin' about bein' embarrassed about what yer' teammates might, 'er might *not* think about ya' based on what they say, just give 'em shit right back, and put 'em in their place."

Truck shook his head, "God damn it, Hack, it's not that *easy*. This is different!"

"Ain't no different than what I went through!"

"*You* weren't gonna' get shot by Mitch Henry's crossbow!"

"Aw, come on, now—Henry wouldn't do that. He's not a killer."

"He kills deer all the time!" Truck raised his right hand in the air, "I think he actually has more respect for the deer than 'fags,' as he so wonderfully calls us."

Hack shook his head, "Can ya' git' *over* yer' fuckin' self already? Nobody cares about this shit near as much as you do!"

"Oh really? Then tell me why there are so many of us hiding in plain sight in the minors alone?"

"'Cause yer' *scared*'a somethin'?"

Hack meant it as a joke, but Truck nodded, "You're fuckin' *right* we're scared. Scared of the Mitch Henrys of the world." He thought for a moment, "You remember Pedro Ascención, the—"

"The second baseman fer' Palooka—I remember. Manny beaned the piss outta' him. Second batter he ever faced. I was proud...damned proud."

Truck nodded, "Well down in winter ball, he stole Manny's old boyfriend. They were out at a bar one night, and—"

"Okay! I get the picture," Hack said.

"My point is, yeah, there *are* a lot of us. You said it yourself—your old double-play partner, Frank Falstaff—"

"*Fancy* Frank," Hack corrected him.

"—He was probably scared, too."

"He was *not!* Back then, no one cared. No one wanted ta' hear about it. Frank was just one'a the guys."

Truck raised his right hand off the wheel, "Exactly—no one wanted to hear about it. You said it yourself—most of the guys on your team, all they talked about is girls. How do you think that made Frank feel?"

"Well if they were talkin' about purses matchin' shoes, prob'ly pretty good!"

Hack smiled through the silence.

"He was a cross-dresser, too?" Truck asked.

"Fuck, how should I know?" Hack asked.

"But that's the thing! See, look at all of the *shit* we have to put up with! I have no interest in women's clothing—none. But that's a stereotype that—"

Hack's eyes narrowed, "It was a tailor-made openin' ta' bust some balls about bein' an ignorant old cuss, that's what it was. And ya' passed it right on by on the way ta' yer' 'woe is me' soapbox."

Truck opened his mouth but stopped and rubbed his chin.

He shook off the moment of contemplation, "Frank Falstaff didn't have to deal with ESPN, with mean-spirited blogs waiting to pounce on every defect, every personal flaw. He didn't have Liam Canard at that dumbass site begging him every day for an exclusive interview just so he could smile and yell '*gotcha!*' if I mess up."

"Fuck 'em," Hack said. "That's what I think about the press. A tool ta' be used as I see fit. No more, no less."

"*Oh*, so you're telling me that I should just tell everyone, 'I'm here, I'm queer, deal with it!'? Maybe have a big old press conference on the field at the Murph?"

Hack hit the bill of Truck's hat again, "Did I say that? All I'm sayin' is that first'a all, it's up ta' *you* ta' decide whether ta' tell folks er' good or ill. If ya' can't stand livin' with the demons that keepin' it bottled up leaves ya' with, then by all means, tell everyone what Fancy Frank couldn't or didn't wanna' tell 'em.

"But more important, I don't think near as many'a yer' teammates would give a shit. Christ, ya' heard what Randy said, half'a 'em are gettin' handjobs from him anyway."

"He said a couple," Truck said.

"Overly defensive, are we?" Hack asked.

Truck shook his head.

"This all coming from a guy who thought it best not to disclose his *terminal illness* to the team he was managing—"

"*Is* managin'," Hack interrupted.

"—because he was afraid to tell anyone?"

Hack leaned over in Truck's ear, "Don't you tell me about keepin' secrets, son. I've chosen ta' wrestle with my demons."

"Wrestle? Or run from?" Truck asked.

A long pause filled the ride. Each man knew what he had to do, each one knew what the other was pushing him toward, the inevitability that awaited.

And each man was scared.

Hack shook his head, "Not a gay thing…" he said.

Truck shook his head and grinned, "I guess now that I think about it, it *is* kind'a gay…"

Hack chuckled.

"Eh. Who gives a fuck?" he asked as he lowered the brim of his ballcap to cover his eyes.

And before Hack could think anything else, the answer came to him. Not in his own thoughts, but rather that deep, dark voice that rattled his innards.

Everyone…

3

"The results aren't good, Mr. O'Callahan," the doctor deadpanned.

Truck covered his mouth with his fist. That he had to quietly take a nurse aside and explain that it would likely be for the best if they could find a "non-ethnic" oncologist to examine Hack had already caused the young catcher sufficient consternation and embarrassment.

Fortunately, Dr. Fishbaum was on duty, a stout, bald, middle aged man with a similar no-nonsense disposition to the ailing manager. Though they had to drive to his office on the edge of the campus, it was a small price for Truck to pay to ensure that the ornery old cuss didn't make a further scene.

Sadly, it appeared Fishbaum's bedside manner also mimicked the manager's temperment.

Hack's eyes narrowed, "How bad, Doc? Surgery?"

The doctor nodded, "First thing tomorrow morning. And I mean *first* thing—one a.m. I'm amazed they let you go this long without it."

"Are ya' *sure*? Can't I just make it another couple'a weeks, finish up the season and croak in peace?"

"My main concern is that you won't even make it to surgery." He pulled up a colorful chart on the monitor next to the bed in the exam room and pointed at a hazy patch of red and grey, with a large white spot in the middle.

"Do you know what this is?" The doctor asked.

"Yeah. The worst goddamned storm ta' ever rip through Kansas since *The Wizard'a Oz*," Hack smiled.

Truck chuckled—the PET scan *did* look a bit like a doppler radar map.

"It's your cancer. Your *stage four* cancer." The doctor pointed to a dozen or so small, white dots on the left of the scan, "This here is the cancer in your liver. You have lymph nodes the size of golf balls. And this," he pointed to an area immediately below the white blob, "Is the opening that leads from your stomach to your intestine. Now, lucky for you, the cancer hasn't spread to the blood yet, but as soon as this opening is shut off by the cancer, like a valve, you're in big trouble. Maybe one day, two days, tops."

Hack's smile faded.

"So it's pretty bad, Mr. O'Callahan. I recommend immediate surgery. Unfortunately, I'm all booked up for the afternoon. My first opening is at one a.m., and I'll cut you open and see what we can do about it."

Hack nodded, "The doctor in Hoplite said this ain't no routine operation or nothin'."

The doctor's eyes widened with condescension, as if he hadn't realized he had been speaking with an idiot until this question.

"It most *certainly* is not. I'm good, but if there's any sort of external stress—" the doctor brought a finger to his mouth, almost as if to pick out the proper words, "You're eighty-four years old, Mr. O'Callahan. Your veins are fragile. Your heart, though beating strong, has had eighty-four years of wear-and-tear on it. And judging by your blood pressure, you're either a hopeless alcoholic," Truck and Hack stole a glance at one another, "Or that heart has seen its share of work, as well.

"So no, surgery is never a sure thing at your age. But it's better than the certainty of death you'd expect otherwise. *Especially* if you want to have any hope of finishing out the season."

Truck's cellphone rang. He looked at the caller I.D. and glanced at his watch.

"Oh, *shit*. It's probably the Indians wondering where I am." He put a hand on Hack's shoulder, "You gonna' be okay, Hack?"

Hack patted Truck's hand, "Yeah, I'll be fine. I won't spoil my decision when ya' get back, neither."

Truck nodded. He walked briskly out of the room as the door shut behind him with a "ca-LUNK."

The doctor pushed his glasses up on the bridge of his nose, not even bothering to hide his annoyance at the interruption, "Ultimately, Mr. O'Callahan, the decision is yours and yours alone. Die in a day or two, potentially fine until an agonizing few last hours, or undergo the surgery and risk death, but potentially live long enough to finish the season."

Hack didn't even hesitate. He knew deep in his bones what he had to do—there wasn't any other option.

He just hoped that Dr. Barker back in Hoplite would respect his wishes.

"Pencil me in fer' one a.m., Doc," Hack said.

Dr. Fishbaum nodded, "Okay then. I've got to go do some paperwork to get you checked in. *Don't* go *anywhere*," he extended a dead fish hand for Hack to shake.

This *is the hand that's gonna' be cuttin' on me later?* Hack thought.

"And I think it goes without saying, no food or drink until the surgery. Wouldn't want you to have any problems with the anesthesia."

Hack nodded. He still fully intended to chug down a Mean S.O.B. or two, but the old man considered that "medicine" more than anything else.

As Dr. Fishbaum left, Truck re-entered the room. He held his phone toward his slouching manager.

"Hack, it's George Tavatelli. He wants to talk with you."

"With *me*?" Hack couldn't believe it. "Awright, give it here—hello? George?"

"Hack!" The GM's voice was overly high-pitched and eager, "George Tavatelli, how the hell are ya'?"

"Just fine, Georgie," Hack said. "How'd ya' know I was with Truck?"

"Well, Hack, I guess that's part of the reason I called. First of all, I'm so, *so* sorry to hear about your illness."

Hack's eyes narrowed. He hadn't bothered telling anyone other than Sam or Truck about his health, and while Randy Edwardson and Keith likely knew that *something* was wrong, they didn't know quite how bad the diagnosis was.

"Illness?" Hack ground the answer out through gritted teeth.

"Yeah, we…uh…someone called me and told me. Cancer…boy, that's nasty business, just horrible."

Hack took a deep breath and sighed. He wanted to deny, wanted to thrash and throw a fit and let George Tavatelli know he was *wrong*, the old man wasn't sick and there wasn't a damned thing he could do about it.

But Hack was tired. Tired of all of the lies, the layers upon layers of deceit and trickery. Tired of keeping this latest secret of his in a long and memorable line of deceptions and half-truths.

"Yeah, it ain't great, George. Goin' under the knife later tonight. I was gonna' call Willie this afternoon and let him know—I prob'ly won't be back fer' the game tomorra' night, but—"

"Hack, Hack! No need to apologize! We already informed Willie, and he called the team in and let them know, too."

Hack wound up and nearly threw Truck's phone against the wall. At the last minute, he decided to hang onto it and instead pounded the exam table several times before he brought the phone back to his ear.

"Oh?" Hack evened his tone.

"Yeah. Look, Hack, the Indians are very grateful for everything you've done over in Hoplite this year. You've really whipped that team into something special, and, well, now we're just damned happy to have Truck with the big club for the next few games until Armiguez gets his back right."

"Don't mention it," Hack hoped Tavatelli could hear his scowl.

"So, to honor all of your accomplishments, Hall of Fame manager who obviously never lost your touch, we'd like to invite you to be our guest of honor before we play the Twins tonight."

"What?" Hack's mouth hung agape.

"We're thinking of calling it 'Hack O'Callahan Night.' You'd get to make a speech before the game and everything, just our little way of showing our appreciation for everything you've done for the organization back in the eighties and again this year."

What Tavatelli didn't add was that with it being a late August matchup against a fellow cellar-dweller, the team also hoped to sell a few thousand last minute seats to the game.

Hack was shocked. Normally he would've mocked protest, but he was genuinely concerned that Tavetelli would rescind the offer at any minute.

"Uh, well, I...sure. Sure, that sounds just fine, George." His vanity got the better of his obstinance.

"Great! I'll get on the phone with the folks in Bristol and work on getting you all of the attention you deserve. It'll be a hero's send-off, one—"

"I ain't plannin' on goin' anywhere, George," Hack hoped the lie was convincing.

"No—no of *course* not. But we'll make sure there'll be *plenty* there to honor your career, and maybe a surprise or two, as well."

"Right." Hack looked at Truck; the catcher and Tavatelli didn't need to know that he had his own surprise in mind.

"Now just head on over with Truck whenever you're done and we'll make sure that you're nice and comfortable until game time."

"Sounds good, George. Thanks."

"Thank *you*, Hack. See you soon." The phone made a clicking noise, though Hack continued to hold it up to his ear. After almost a full minute of silence, Hack reasoned that the call was over. He held the phone out to Truck.

"What'd he say?" Truck asked.

"You've got some *fuckin'* nerve!" Hack thundered at him. The manager rose from the exam table.

"What?! Where're we going?" Truck asked.

Hack muttered curses under his breath as he shuffled out the door, Truck following close behind.

4

Hack scowled quietly all the way from the exam room into Truck's car, and continued to stew for several minutes in the passenger's seat before Truck broke the nervous silence.

"So…am I taking you home now, or—?"

"Ya' know goddamn well where yer' takin' me!" Hack shot back. "Same place's yer' goin'. The Jake."

"What? Why?"

"I can't believe ya' told him."

"Told who? What?"

"You of all people! I never *once* spilled the beans about you or Manny or anyone. Not *one* goddamned time. And *this* is how ya' repay me?"

"Hey, relax, Hack! I didn't tell nothin' to nobody!"

"The *fuck* you didn't! How the hell did George *fuckin'* Tavatelli know I had cancer then?"

"I dunno. Maybe Keith told him. Or what's-her-name? Sam? The intern girl."

"She would *never*," Hack shook his head, "She wouldn't. Nope, I can't believe it. I knew y'all were a bunch'a nancy-gossips!"

"What?"

"You heard me. Fancy Frank was the same way."

237

Truck's nails dug into the steering wheel, "How *dare* you. If you were anyone else, I'd leave you on the side of the road right now!"

"Bah!" Hack waved away the threat and folded his arms. He looked out of the window, deep in thought.

I guess he might *have a point*, Hack thought. It could have very well been Sam Rappaport who called Tavatelli. And would that have been so bad? If not, why was he so angry at Truck? Was it because he knew the struggle that constantly raged inside of him, wrestling constantly with the distinct possibility that any day he might mess up, blurt something out, and then nothing would be the same? That Truck may have somehow betrayed that confidence?

He let Truck simmer down for the next five minutes or so until the SUV pulled into the gated driveway with a big "Authorized Personnel Only" sign and Chief Wahoo logo next to the guard shack.

"I, uh, sorry about that crack earlier about the nancyin' and whatnot."

Truck didn't even turn his head, "Forget about it."

"No, no, that was wrong. I'm sorry, Truck. So what if ya' told George—"

"I didn't tell George!"

"I don't even care!" Hack yelled as Truck lowered his window.

"Hey," Truck said to the guard. "Robert Traynor."

For a brief moment, Hack wondered if his senility had worsened—who was this "Robert" that Truck was speaking of? Did he somehow get in the wrong car back at the hospital?

It was only several seconds later that it dawned on him that Robert was Truck's real name.

The guard checked her list, "Here you go—welcome up Robert! First time in the show?"

"Yeah," Truck gave a curt smile.

"That's great. And ya' brought your grandpa with you. I can call the front office and get him a—"

"He's not my—"

Truck didn't even finish before Hack leaned over, "Hack O'Callahan. Guess they're havin' a big ta'-doo fer' me here tonight."

The guard chuckled.

Hack's face remained stony.

"Call George Tavatelli if you need to."

The mention of Tavatelli's name was enough. The guard waved them on through.

"Look, all's I'm *tryin'* to say is that I'm sorry. I know ya' ain't one'a them swooshy—"

Truck turned and gave Hack a cautionary glare.

Hack shook his head, "What I meant ta' say was Truck, yer' one'a the toughest sonsabitches I've ever seen in the game. Jackie, Mantle, ya' name it—yer' right up there. Tough enough ta' handle bein' the first one'a...you know..." Hack nodded, "One'a the first ones who's open about it. One way or another."

Truck's eyes went wide. *One way or another? What does that mean?* He thought.

He shook off the comment and attributed it to the stress Hack was under.

"No problem." Truck pulled into a spot, got out, and helped Hack down from the seat. "Now what's all this about a big 'ta-do' for you?"

Before Hack could answer, he felt a meaty hand on his shoulder.

"How's it going, old friend?"

George Tavatelli's faker-than-cubic zirconia grin lit up the parking lot. His hair was unnaturally brown and coiffed into a near pompadour. His sunglasses, polo shirt, and khaki shorts completed the stock major league general manager uniform.

"George," Hack nodded. He grabbed Tavatelli's outstretched hand and shook it.

"And you must be Truck. We've really liked what we've seen so far, kid. You have a big future in this town."

"Hi Mr. Tavatelli," Truck shook the GM's hand. "Thanks for the opportunity."

"No problem, no problem. We might not be in a pennant race like the Magpies are right now, but hopefully you and some of your friends down there'll change that soon enough."

D.J. Gelner

"Just happy to have the chance to prove what I can do," Truck said.

"Now, you realize this is probably just for a few days until Armiguez's back gets right. I still don't understand how these guys have the energy to golf on top of all those games," Tavatelli shook his head. "We'll get ya' back to Hoplite for the playoff push, and then we're thinking of bringing you back up for September. How'd you like that?"

"Sounds great to me!" Truck couldn't hide his enthusiasm. With the extra cash he'd make from being on the major league roster for the last month of the season, maybe he'd be able to afford a new car, one that his parents hadn't given him. One that he had *earned*.

"Fantastic. Now go on and get dressed—they've got you set up with a locker and everything. I'll get Hack here all settled in—if you have any questions, feel free to ask any of my staff or even just pick up the phone and give me a call, okay?"

"Yes sir," Truck said with a short, non-ironic salute that he immediately regretted. He cringed, then quickly gathered his duffel bag and nearly jogged into the clubhouse.

Tavatelli shook his head, "Great kid, isn't he?"

Hack nodded, "Damned fine. One'a the best."

The over-broad smile vanished quickly from Tavatelli's face, "So, *so* sorry to hear about your illness, Hack. If I had any idea, I wouldn't have made you jump through so many hoops for the job in Hoplite."

Sure, ya' wouldn't've... Hack thought.

"No prob," he waved the remark away. "We all gotta' die sometime, don't we?"

"I suppose," Tavatelli shrugged. Hack got the feeling that George Tavatelli thought himself immortal. "You feeling okay? Need anything?"

"I could use some Robitussin if ya' got it. This damned cough won't go away."

"Sure. Sure, no problem! I have some in my executive washroom."

Leave it to Tavatelli to mention he's got his own crapper, Hack thought. *Who even calls a john a washroom anyway?*

"That'll do," Hack nodded. The two walked through the glass doors into the stadium. "I'll tell ya' what, George, I could use a nap. Aside from the Robitussin, I could use somewhere ta' get a little bit'a shuteye before the game."

"Right, right—we need you to absolutely get your rest before your big surgery tonight."

Hack half-expected the GM to tousle his hair and offer to get him some ice cream.

They walked down a long hallway and made several turns past cubicles deep into the bowels of the stadium. Whenever the duo came across a team employee, Tavatelli would plaster that fake grin on his mug and wave at the staffer, making sure to call the person by name.

What a kiss ass... Hack thought.

"What was that?" Tavatelli asked. Maybe he had accidentally said it...

"Uh, I said 'nice staff.' Looks like you've got capable folks here, George."

Hack said the phrase as they came across an overweight mouth-breather of an analyst.

"Hi Mr. Tavatelli," the man said through his dingy, too-thick glasses.

"Hi Fred," Tavatelli said. "Yes, they *are* mighty impressive, I suppose." He opened a door and flicked on a light. Inside was a cot opposite a desk and a mini fridge. An older flat-panel TV sat on the wall. Another door was ajar on the wall opposite the hallway.

"This is the relaxation room. It's usually where we put visiting dignitaries and whatnot before a game, let them get comfortable. You have your own washroom with a shower, snacks, soft drinks, you name it."

Hack didn't mention that he wasn't supposed to enjoy any food or drink, and merely nodded.

"This'll be just fine, Georgie. Just fine…" Hack waddled over to the cot and threw himself down upon it.

George acted as if something had startled him, "Oh, I almost forgot! The Robitussin!"

"Yeah, go get that," Hack dismissed the GM with a wave of his hand. Immediately after the door shut, Hack dug in his pocket for the bottle of vicodin and flask of whiskey he had smuggled into Truck's car. He fumbled with the cap to the pill bottle for a few moments before it yielded and he swallowed a handful of pills. He expertly unscrewed the flask and took several deep pulls of Old Reliable. He hid both containers under the cot, and no sooner had he wiped his mouth with his shirtsleeve than the door opened again.

Tavatelli held out a bottle of Robitussin that looked to be about as old as Hack.

"Here ya' go, sport," Tavatelli said. "One bottle of Robitussin, as requested."

Hack motioned for the bottle and Tavatelli tossed it to him. Hack received it with the soft hands of a former second baseman.

"Anything else I can get our guest of honor for the evening?"

"Naw, naw, I'm fine now, George. Thanks."

"Great. Oh—one more thing. We'd be *honored* if you would wear an Indians jersey tonight. Absolutely tickled, with your old number and whatnot."

"I—uh, I'm not sure if that's such a good idea, George," Hack thought about what he was planning on telling the world during his speech. He didn't know if the Indians would want their uniform associated with the potentially bombastic piece of news he was prepared to give.

Not ta' mention those cheap-ass jerseys were the most uncomfortable shit ever, Hack thought, oblivious to the fact that the team had most certainly improved their uniforms since he had last coached there.

Tavatelli's eyes went wide.

"The coughin' gets pretty bad sometimes—don't wanna' spit up all over yer' nice home whites like a goddamn infant."

Tavatelli gave Hack a thin smile and a nod.

"No problem. I understand completely."

"But I would like ta' wear a Magpies hat, if ya' don't mind, George."

Again a grin, "Of course! Of course! I'll get an intern on it right away!"

"Thanks George. Oh, and Georgie?"

"Yeah Hack?" Now the GM was as earnest as Hack had seen him since he was a fresh-faced rookie playing for the ornery manager over twenty years before.

"Shut off the lights, will ya'?"

Without another word, the room plunged into darkness. Hack swigged off the Robitussin, and was asleep before the door even shut.

5

Hack awoke to a knock at the door.

"Eh?" He half-blurted out.

The door cracked and flooded the room with the greenish fluorescent light of the hallway.

"Hack? It's George. Half-hour 'til showtime. Might wanna' get up and ready."

"Yeah, yeah, I got it." Any politeness that the previous altercation with Truck had instilled in the curmudgeon had vanished in his sleep.

"*And* I got you this—" Tavatelli threw a black Magpies hat with its distinctive purple brim on the cot. "Should fit like a charm."

"Great. Thanks."

The old man got up and showered. All the while, what he was going to say, what he *had* to say to the masses rattled around in his head.

You MUST *tell them!* The cancer growled into his ear as he soaped up his underarms.

"Ah, fer' Chrissakes, I don't need *you* actin' up now, too!" Hack yelled at the voice.

He toweled off and dressed in the same plaid shirt and blue slacks that he had worn to Cleveland. Now that he thought about it, it was the same outfit he had worn that fateful May morning when he blew into Keith Myrick's office and demanded to become the Magpies manager.

Hack chuckled at how things might have been different if Keith Myrick would have been perceptive enough to pick up on the full extent of the old man's illness.

I'm glad he wasn't, Hack thought.

Otherwise, I wouldn't get ta' make history tonight.

He proudly put the Magpies' black-and-purple hat on, and as he looked in the mirror, a chill ran down his spine as his vision went blurry with tears.

"Damn proud'a you boys," Hack said, staring at the cartoonish, mean-looking Magpie wrapped around the "H" on the front of the hat. "Damn proud."

He cooked up another Mean S.O.B., downed it, and teetered into the hallway.

Surprisingly, George was already waiting to take him down to the field.

"Right on schedule! I'll tell ya' what, Hack, you really look great in that hat. You wear it well, like it was made for you."

Hack nodded without a thank you; he already knew.

They navigated the maze of hallways and rooms under the stadium, and eventually came to the double doors that signified the field entrance to the clubhouse. From there, the men made a quick right turn and walked as briskly as Hack's barking knee would allow to the dugout.

The Indians were already in the dugout, and a sandy-haired, middle-aged man rushed over to greet them.

"Hack? I'll be damned…I had to see it myself to believe it."

"Hack, you know Eddie Martell, the manager of the Indians," *for now*…the GM didn't have to add.

"Sure. Eddie was my hittin' coach in Pittsburgh fer' a couple'a years there. How the hell are ya', Ed?" Hack shook his hand.

"Ah, I've been better. Guess I shouldn't complain to you, though. Sorry to hear about—"

Hack cut him off, "It is what it is, Ed. We all get dealt cards in life, until the dealer stops."

Martell cocked his head, trying to understand the phrase as Tavatelli ushered Hack onto the steps and held him at the railing. The GM pointed at Country Engle, who was at a microphone set up behind home plate.

Engle nodded with a sneer before he forced a smile.

"Ladies and Gentlemen, your attention, please."

He waited for the unusually large crowd to die down before he continued.

"Indian nation received the shocking news today that one of our own, the great Hack O'Callahan, the manager of the Indians' double-A affiliate, the Hoplite Magpies, is fighting a brave battle against the scourge of cancer."

The building went silent.

"Hack has given so much to the city of Cleveland and the game of baseball, though, that we thought we'd invite him on up here so that you can show him exactly how y'all feel about him. So without further adieu, please welcome, the legendary, Hall of Fame manager, number sixteen in your program but number one in your hearts, the great Hack Ohhhhh'Callahan!"

The crowd erupted with cheers as George guided Hack to the top of the dugout steps. Hack shrugged off the GM's help as he practically jogged along the first base line toward home plate, all of the searing pain in his knees and back subsumed beneath the joy and adulation directed at *him*, of all people.

Hack waved to the crowd and couldn't hold back the broad smile as he made his way briskly toward home plate. Engle's over-broad grin couldn't hide the pure hatred in his eyes as he extended a hand to Hack.

"Guess you *really* got 'em fooled, eh Hack?" Engle said through gritted teeth off-mike.

"Go fuck yer'self, John," Hack hid his own sentiments through a forced smile.

The thunderous applause washed over Hack as he removed his Magpie hat and waved it at the crowd. Everyone in the crowd got on their feet and cheered for this brave old man who had the courage to get in front of a crowd and lay his illness bare.

As the ovation finally calmed, Engle stepped back up to the microphone, "The Indians have prepared a short video to honor all of Hack's on and off-field accomplishments. Please direct your attention to the video screen in center field."

The crowd went quiet and anxious again as the house lights dimmed in the twilight.

Engle's pre-recorded voice boomed from the loudspeakers, "Hack O'Callahan. Baseball great. American hero."

Engle covered his mouth and whispered into Hack's ear, "I asked 'em for a bucket when they made me record this—nearly retched half-a-dozen times."

Hack didn't skip a beat, "I didn't know yer' wife was cookin' again."

Engle fumed through gritted teeth.

Hack smiled and pointed at the video screen.

"As a young boy growing up in Springfield, Illinois, Hack always dreamed of becoming a major league ballplayer," the video board flashed a black-and-white picture of a dour-faced young Hack.

"And of gettin' a date with the starting quarterback," Engle whispered.

Hack caught himself. Normally he would've been right back at Engle with a pithy comeback, some sort of affront to his own sexuality.

But Hack's tongue was slack and lifeless. He thought about Truck, and their exchange in the car earlier that day. And Hack did something he hadn't done in over fifty years.

He just took the insult.

That's *why I'm doin' this*, he thought. *It's fer' the best...fer' Truck...*

The voiceover continued, "After several years of minor league ball, Hack put his career on hold to bravely serve his country in the Korean conflict."

The video screen showed stock newsreel footage of an old-school aircraft carrier.

Hack's eyes narrowed. *Yep...fer' Truck...*

"After he returned, he spent time in the St. Louis Cardinals organization before he was finally called up to the majors with the New York Yankees in the early sixties. After several years in the majors, Hack hung up his spikes and turned to his true calling: managing."

"Perhaps the most successful manager ever," Hack noticed that Engle couldn't hide his condescension through the reading, "Hack's teams were known for their tenacity and grit."

Hack smiled at the sentiment.

"Hack won four World Series with the Pittsburgh Pirates, St. Louis Cardinals, Cincinnati Reds, and Florida Marlins. In all, Hack managed nine teams in his career, leaving nine cities that much better for having him as an influence on their ballclubs."

The music took a stirring, patriotic turn, "And now, at the end of his career, Hack has done the impossible again, turning around your double-A Hoplite Magpies—" the crowd cheered; apparently Cleveland loved their Magpies as much as Hoplite did, "—and leading them to the precipice of a playoff berth."

Something caught the corner of Hack's eye, a bright light from the right field stands. He looked for the source and was bathed in the beam as he held his hand up to the brim of his hat.

He lowered his gaze to field level and chuckled through a sob:

The Magpies had made the trip.

All of them.

Led by Willie, the men all grinned as they stormed Hack and patted him on the back, one at a time.

Hack couldn't hold back the tears any longer; he started to cry openly as the players came up to him one-by-one, shook his hand, and thanked him. Even Sid Fynch and Juan Patrón gave hearty thanks to the man who had treated them fairly roughly.

Mitch Henry was one of the last in line, "Sorry ta' hear about all this cancer, coach. Fuckin' *sucks*."

"Thanks Henry," Hack patted the monstrous pitcher on the small of the back. "You teach Manny well, ya' hear?"

Henry blew out a mouthful of air, "Whatta'ya' *mean* teach Manny well? You'll be back in no time ta' teach him yourself."

Hack smiled at the southerner and patted him a couple more times.

Manny was next. The gangly reliever took Hack's hand in both of his, "Thank you for everything, señor jefe." He didn't even have to say it: *thanks for keeping my secret.*

"No problem, Manny. Yer' gonna' be one helluva pitcher."

Willie circled back around and nearly brought up the rear.

"You sonofa*bitch*!" Willie's face was stern and cold. "Why didn't you tell me?"

"Ah, sorry Willie. They would'a never let me manage if they knew—"

"Well if *I* would've known, I would'a *begged* 'em to bring you on board, ya' ornery ol' *cuss*!"

Hack furrowed his brow, "That ain't quite how I remember ya' felt when I first got ta' Hoplite, Willie."

"Maybe not at first," Willie grinned, "But you had me from that story about Jackie."

Willie beamed, but Hack's smile wavered, ever so slightly. The men half-hugged as Willie whispered in Hack's ear.

"You better make it through this tomorrow," Willie said.

"Yer' ready, Willie," Hack said. "You've been ready since I got kicked outta' that fourth game I was in Hoplite."

Willie rubbed something off of his glasses and patted the old man on the shoulder.

Truck brought up the rear in his Indians uniform, but he wore the proud purple-and-black Magpie hat along with it.

"Thank you, Hack, sincerely, like Manny says, for everything."

Hack pulled Truck close and whispered in his ear, "Fer'give me, Truck. Fer' what I'm about to say," his eyes went wide "...for everything."

Truck's chest tightened as his jaw went slack. Sweat almost immediately poured off of his brow and soaked his uniform. His stomach churned as he felt sick—he wanted desperately to grab the man, to stop him from going forward, from *telling*.

But he couldn't.

His body refused to obey.

Before Truck could question the sentiment, Country Engle was back on the mike.

"Now, please welcome Hack's daughter, Lisa, and his granddaughter, Amy!"

Hack perked up. His head swiveled toward the dugout steps. Sure enough, Lisa was there, dressed in a flattering business suit and holding Amy's hand as she skipped across the field.

"I'll be damned!" Hack couldn't hide his excitement.

"Soon enough," Engle muttered under his breath.

Lisa smiled thinly, neither happy nor proud to be there. If anything, there was a resigned sense of calm in her demeanor, a feeling she had been fighting far too long.

Amy was somewhat more jubilant. Her gap-toothed smile out-shined the spotlight as she waved to the cheers and "aw"s of the crowd.

Hack opened his arms wide, and Lisa embraced him.

"Hi'ya, sweetheart!"

"Hi Hack," Lisa responded coolly in his ear so that Amy couldn't hear. She sighed, "Sorry to hear about your cancer. Was that what you wanted to tell me back when you visited us in Westfield?"

Hack's eyes went wide as he paused in contemplation, "…Sort'a…"

Lisa frowned, "Why didn't you just *tell* me, Hack?"

He nodded the question away, "It's complicated." He kneeled down, the pain in his screaming joints subsumed beneath the blissful warmth and cover of the whiskey and pain meds, dopey smile affixed to his face, "And you must be little Amy!"

"Amy, this is…this is Hack," Lisa said.

"Hi Whack!" Amy said as she threw her arms around the short manager.

"Hi'ya baby doll!" Hack fought back the tears as he clutched her tightly to him, so close that he hoped she might never get away.

After an extra couple of seconds, though, his muscles inexplicably relaxed and let her go back to her mother's side.

Engle retook the microphone, "Before Hack imparts some," Engle narrowed his eyes at his adversary, "*very* brief wisdom onto us, please cheer him on as he throws out tonight's ceremonial first pitch to the newest Indian, Robert...'Trrrrruck'....TRAYYYY-NORRR!"

Truck waved to the crowd with a dazed smile as he still pondered Hack's words.

Forgive me, Truck, for what I'm about to say...

The catcher took his spot behind the plate as Hack hid his limp as best as he could and took the mound. It was odd to see the little man walk without the aid of his bat. Even odder to see him on the field in anything but his uniform.

Engle flipped Hack a ball as the manager strode toward the mound. Though the broadcaster had a "This ought'ta be *good*" grin on his face, Truck shook his head—he knew far better than to underestimate Hack O'Callahan on the baseball field.

Hack toed the pitching rubber. Much to the crowd's delight, he faked taking a couple of signs from Truck before he launched into a long, windmill-like windup and delivery.

The ball traveled in a firm arc, the entire sixty feet, six inches. Though Truck had half-expected his manager—his *minor league* manager, he reminded himself—to either dribble one over the plate on several hops or launch a ninety mile-per-hour fastball, the actual result was somewhere in-between.

Truck caught the delivery with barely a "pop." Hack waved as he forced himself forward off of the mound. Truck jogged to meet his...ex-manager? Hopefully not. Confidant? That wasn't quite right, either—Hack had stumbled upon Truck's secret quite by accident.

As much as it pained Truck to admit it, the word he searched for was "mentor." This crusty, foul-mouthed, if not outright "racist," then certainly xenophobic old man had become his *mentor*, not only as far as baseball was concerned, but also life as well.

And yet...

Why did he get the sinking suspicion that this man was about to out him to the entire world?

Truck stuck out his hand and bent down to talk to Hack.

"Thanks again, Hack," he leveled a serious gaze on the man, "You aren't planning on—?"

Hack patted Truck on the shoulder, his eyes wide, his lips pulled taut into his mouth, nodding slowly.

"I'm sorry, Truck," he fixed his gaze on the star catcher, "I have to."

Truck wanted to reach out for the old man's hand, wanted to lift him up with one hand and cover his mouth with the other, wanted desperately to force the man's silence so that he could divulge his secret on his terms.

Instead, he nodded.

Then he took his place behind the microphone with the rest of his teammates.

He needs it, Hack thought. *Truck needs a lesson in courage, in humility. It's for the best...*

Hack waved at the cheering crowd one more time as he settled behind the mike, adjusted it, and readied himself to make headlines.

Eighth Inning

1

"Good evenin', folks," Hack flashed a close-lipped smile. "Believe it 'er not, I ain't usually one fer' makin' big speeches in front'a people, but I have somethin' important'ta tell ya' all ta'night.

"Fer' almost seventy years now, baseball's been everything to me. And I mean everything. It started out 'cause, well, guess I don't rightly know. I always was good at it, and I always did what I was told, and I liked *winnin'*. *Loved* it. More than anything in the world. I wasn't ever the most popular guy on a team. But God da—uh, gosh *darn* it, I would run through a brick wall ta' help my team win.

"And people respect that. They do. S'pose they like ta' see someone put themselves at risk fer' the group. 'Er at least disregard their own safety, their own well-bein' fer' the collective whole.

"Now, sure as shhhh—" he caught himself, "—shhh-I-nola, I did plen'ny'a disregardin' through the years," he looked over at Lisa and offered a thin smile and a nod, one that Lisa's own heavy, sad eyes returned. "I ain't proud'a everything I've done, not by a wide measure. At times, I've acted like..." he paused to collect his thoughts, "...like a *fool*. Sometimes on purpose, sometimes not.

"But through it all, I still had that fire, that sense that the good'a the whole is better than my own good, my own *health*, as you all see me tonight."

"WE LOVE YOU HACK!" a group of fans yelled from behind home plate. A short cheer followed.

Hack waved, but remained stone-faced.

"I guess that's why I sort'a forced myself on the Magpies this year. I was startin' ta' get the sense that this new generation ain't got the *grit* and *determination* that we had back in the day. They were self-absorbed and *soft*, with their video hoo-dads and tele-whatzits. So I thought I'd drive on up ta' Hoplite and teach some kids a few lessons.

"Good Lord willing," at this statement by Hack, half of the team rolled their eyes, though Mitch Henry only nodded, "I've been able to do so."

"But somethin' strange happened ta' me on the way through this year. Maybe I'm gettin' soft in my old age, or maybe the Reaper's breathin' down my neck, but I realized somethin' that I never knew before. Somethin' that would'a helped me in all'a my years and years'a managin' before.

"*That*, ladies and gentlemen, is the value of honesty."

Truck's throat tightened. Sweat poured off his brow and coated the collar of his uniform. He felt chained to his spot, unable to breathe, let alone speak out, and stop this lunatic.

"It don't mean a hill'a beans ta' run through fifty brick walls fer' yer' teammates if ya' ain't honest with 'em. The whole suffers fer' the sins'a the cowardly few, even with the support of so many strong individuals."

Hack looked down the line at Truck and nodded.

Truck nearly swallowed his tongue.

"True courage is the ability ta' embrace yer' inner demons, yer' deepest darkest secrets and fears, lay 'em bare, and let the world decide what ta' do with 'em."

Hack paused and took a deep gulp. Though the booze and pills still coursed through his veins, his mind was clear as a bell.

Yessss....that deep, bass voice inside him thundered through his head, *Tell them*...

"Some...someone on this field—" he pointed abruptly at the ground, "—right here, tonight, has a secret. A shameful, terrible secret that he's lived with fer' far too long, that's caused the team to be not nearly as great as it could'a been. Someone who's a coward, who hasn't taken the help offered by others."

Hack looked down the line again at Truck.

Truck's heart sank. Was *this* what Hack really thought of him? That he was a bad teammate? Truck choked back sobs as Hack's sad, lonely, old eyes locked with his.

I'm sorry, they said.

"And that person—" Hack took a deep breath, "—Is me."

Truck nearly fainted before the words were even out, then quickly shot a glance toward the microphone.

The crowd murmured audible confusion.

Hack removed his Magpies hat, ashamed to sully the logo, certainly not wanting to forever taint the Magpie team name by what he was about to say.

"I never served my country in Korea. I'm a fraud."

Hack maintained an even glare as the flashbulbs descended on him, each one a stone to the face, exposing the awful truth that he had hid for so many years.

Truck wanted nothing more than to run up and seize the mike. *No! Don't crucify* him! *It's* me *you all want to know about! I have a secret too!*

Instead, his mouth hung agape, along with roughly forty thousand others in the stadium.

After several moments, Hack continued, "Fer' sixty years now I've been livin' a lie. Like most lies, it started out little, just a fib ta' get some player or another fired up, or Christ, I don't know."

Goooooooodddd…the voice fed off of the admission. It was gaining strength.

"I was in the Navy. And I was on the *U.S.S. Antietam* during the Korean conflict. But we weren't like Teddy Williams over there in dubya dubya *two,* flyin' fighter jets. We were playin' baseball. We were 'ambassadors' fer' America, puttin' inta' port and puttin' on exhibitions against each other in places like Japan and Taiwan.

"I never even saw a rifle. We never saw combat other than one time when the North *Ko*-reans saw it fit ta' attack us. And even though I shot at those bastards with the damned biggest gun on deck, when they fired back—" he choked on the words, "—I dove away. I hid. Like the damned coward I am."

Other than the momentary surge of emotion, Hack delivered the speech confidently, efficiently, like he had gone over it thousands of times in his mind, words that haunted him so much that he drowned them in whiskey until they faded first into whispers, then echoes, in his head.

"I sincerely apologize ta' any'a my players, past or present, that I've misled. I'm ashamed'a my actions, of—" he looked at Amy, who looked back blankly. Hack smiled even as the tears started to pour forth, "—of the example I've set fer' generations'a this nation's youth. It ain't okay, lyin' ain't never okay, no matter if it's fer' a good cause or to protect someone from the truth, 'er whatever.

"I fully understand if the Indians organization or any of the other teams I managed for want nothin' to do with me anymore. I stand before ya', finally an honest man, offerin' yas' my sincerest apologies, but not expectin' any mercy.

"I just hope—" he looked down the line at Truck once more, "That this can be a lesson ta' the rest'a yas, be honest, not only to your teammates, not only to your families and those close ta' ya', but with *yer'selves*. 'Cause if you aren't, ya' might end up like me, old, friendless, and confessin' yer' sins ta' all'a Cleveland, and beyond. Thank you, and good night."

2

Feedback resonated through the stadium speakers as Hack turned too abruptly and brought his head too close to the microphone.

Feedback of another sort entirely quickly followed from the stands.

Initially, Hack was shocked. A groundswell of applause and cheers washed over the field.

It was mildly repulsive to him. Here he was, explaining what a horrible person he had been, and yet, there were more than a few people ready to sweep it all under the rug, ready to forgive him almost immediately.

But then the boos started, first a smattering, then a loud chorus as fans let him know how they felt.

"Bum!" Someone yelled.

"You *suck*!"

Hack reveled in the abuse. Though he couldn't even look his teammates—*former* teammates?—in the eye, he didn't even try to hide his limp as he left the mound.

As he stepped onto the infield grass, though, a funny thing happened.

The cheers swelled again and overpowered the boos.

Over half the stadium rose to their feet and fought against the negativity, they cheered Hack on with encouragement, that he had finally done the right thing.

The cheers and boos rose and fell for a while as Hack stumbled step after step toward the dugout. Some Magpies and Indians front office types followed him, desperately trying to get some clarification, some idea as to what the old man had just said.

But Hack only heard one voice, throbbing with regularity like a horrible metronome inside his head.

I'm commmmminnnnnggg... the deep baritone voice said, mocking and sing-songy.

I'm commmmminnnnnggg...

Hack slapped himself in the face as he picked up steam into the dugout and down the tunnel. Eddie Martel tried to stop Hack and say something to him, but Hack shoved him aside and continued on toward the clubhouse.

At the entrance to the clubhouse, Hack was met by Jerry, ever-gregarious.

"Good for you, Mr. O'Callahan!" Jerry beamed.

"Fuck off, Jerry," Hack said. He was in no mood for positivity.

Jerry ignored him, "Aw, who cares if ya' didn't fight *in* Korea, you were around there, right? Representin' your country? And like you said, you *did* see combat, right?"

Hack shook his head.

Jerry didn't get it.

Nobody got it, save for the ones who booed him. *They* understood.

Everyone else, he thought, *is fuckin'* nuts.

He pushed through the double doors into the clubhouse, and grabbed the nearest bat he could find to help him hobble the rest of the way.

"Hey? Mr. O'Callahan? You're not supposed to go in th—"

The door slammed shut before Jerry could finish.

Hack moved quickly through the clubhouse, then left through the players' entrance and out to the street. It only took him a couple of minutes to hail a cab.

"Where to, my friend?" The cabbie asked with a thick Eastern European accent.

"The hospital. The, uh, Cleveland Clinic."

259

"Hospital? Are you sick?" The cabbie asked, seemingly concerned.

Hack answered the question the only way he knew how once he felt the sickly-sweet acetone taste in the back of his throat:

He reared back and launched into a coughing fit.

This time, the aroma became stronger as the fit wore on. It was a tempest of deep whoops; it was all Hack could do to force down big lungfuls of air to keep from choking.

He fumbled for the handkerchief in his back pocket, but it was like trying to stop a hurricane with an umbrella. The fabric was quickly coated with mucous and blood, to the point where Hack cupped his hands and caught most of the phlegmmy mess in a pool.

"Cleveland Clinic, you got it." the cabbie said as he threw the car into gear and took off.

As the car pulled away, Willie and Pete Moray tore out of the players' entrance.

"Where'd he go?" Pete asked.

"He didn't drive here, so thank God he's not behind the wheel," Willie said. "Where'd they say he was in the hospital again?"

Pete shook his head, "Christ, I dunno'. I kind'a thought that you knew."

"Shit!" Willie slammed the fence around the players' lot. "Who would know where the hell—?"

The answer hit Willie like a thunderbolt.

"Truck!" Willie rushed inside to find his young star.

In the cab, Hack stared at the mess in his hands, mostly red, and far more expectorant than he had ever produced before.

He's lear-ning! the ominous voice in his head sang again.

"Shut UP, *damn* you!" Hack yelled as he hit the window with his palm. The handkerchief fell to one side as the mess landed in Hack's lap, covering his shirt and pants in a pool of red.

"Hang on, hang on!" the cabbie yelled. "Almost there."

Hack didn't, or more accurately couldn't, appreciate that the cabbie was less concerned with the interior of his cab than the well-being of his customer.

After a quick right turn and a left, the cab pulled into the hospital.

"Whatta' I owe ya'?" Hack reached for his wallet.

"No charge, no charge, sir, just get help. Please."

Hack grinned. *One more good deal*, he thought.

"Thanks hack," Hack said.

The cabbie squinted, searching for the meaning of the word.

Hack patted the man's seat a couple of times, "It's a nickname fer' cabbies, good ones. Sort'a a term of endearment."

The cabbie's face remained blank.

"An honor," Hack tried again.

This time the cabbie smiled.

"Ah, well thank you, sir," the cabbie produced his own handkerchief and wiped the stain Hack had left on his faux-leather seat cover.

Hack picked up his bat, opened the door, and exited the car. He wobbled toward the emergency room entrance and stood in the hospital's lobby.

A line five deep waited to see the frazzled E.R. nurse, whose baggy eyes and unkempt hair gave her the appearance of a woman on a double-shift.

A dozen more sat in the cozy chairs provided by the tony hospital, watching the Indians game on the large, flatscreen TVs.

And just like that, Hack had an idea.

"Excuse me," Hack said. "I'm Hack O'Callahan, and I'm here fer' surgery!"

A mix of cheers and looks of disgust met Hack's bemused gaze.

The E.R. nurse barely turned to look at him.

But at least he had gained a sliver of her attention.

"This is E building—Emergency," she said with just a tad too much condescension. "The surgery center is P building. Jeez—Steve!" she yelled to the other side of the nurse's bay.

Hack couldn't make out the reply.

"Can you take *Mr. O'Callahan* here to P building...now?"

Hack couldn't tell if the E.R. nurse was a fan or not. The terse, semi-smart alecky smile she gave him left him more confused.

261

A burly man with hairy arms wearing scrubs pushed through the double doors with a wheelchair.

"Mister O'Callahan?" The man asked.

"Right here," Hack raised his hand.

"Have a seat, please."

Hack did as he was told. Before they even exited the building, a wave of fatigue washed over him.

"So, big night for you, I see," Steve said.

Hack yawned. He wanted to talk to the man, he really did, wanted desperately for someone to call him on the carpet, to berate him for what he had done.

"Yeah, somethin' like that."

The orderly paused for several seconds.

"How're you holding up?"

Hack bristled and looked over his shoulder, "I'm great. Just fuckin' *dandy*. I just became a laughin' stock on national TV, and now I'm about'ta get cut on fer' bad cancer. How the hell do ya' *think* I'm doin'?"

The orderly smiled, "Look, I know you've been through a lot tonight, but I have to say, what you did took a lot of guts."

"*Guts?*" Hack's eyes went wide with incredulity. "I lie my ass off fer' sixty years and everyone thinks it takes *guts* ta' come clean?"

The orderly shook his head, "It does. Believe it or not, damn it, it does! You said it yourself—you were attacked by the Koreans. You fought in the war."

They arrived at the door to "P" Building as a middle aged man attached to an IV drip shuffled out of the automatic doors.

"Asshole," the man said under his breath.

"*Thank* you!" Hack snorted before he turned his attention to the orderly, "Ya' see? *That* guy gets it! I lied!"

"Look, you may've lied about what exactly you did in Korea. And I have no way of knowing what you told your players about what you did or didn't do over there, but you could've easily tipped your cap and waved and basked in the cheers and applause, and died in a couple of months or whatever, but you didn't. You came clean. Very few people would've done that. And I respect it."

"Bah!" Hack waved the sentiment away, "Take me back'ta the 'asshole' guy. At least he doesn't sugar-coat it like a goddamned gumdrop."

Steve pushed the old man in front of the elevator and pushed a button. Hack's eyes went wide.

"Jesus Christ!"

"What?" The orderly was genuinely concerned.

"You just pushed that button right through this guy's head!" Hack thumbed the air to the right of his chair.

Steve furrowed his brow, "What guy?" He realized what Hack was seeing, and shook his head with a knowing frown.

Hack chuckled at the empty space in front of the elevator buttons, "We may be old, but we ain't crazy, right fella?" Hack waited several moments and broke out in a gut-busting laugh, "Yeah, you tell 'im." The doors to the elevator opened, "You want this one or—oh, okay." Hack frowned, "He'll catch the next one."

"Of course he will, Mr. O'Callahan," Steve shook his head and raised his eyebrows, "Of course he will…"

3

The Magpie players exchanged confused glances as Indians personnel ushered them into a vacant party room on the second level.

The usher was a kindly elderly man with coke-bottle glasses and teeth that were varying shades of amber. He waited at the door for all of the players to enter, and once Juan Patrón and Sid Fynch had filed in, tipped his faded, flimsy Indians hat at them.

"You boys enjoy the game now!" he cackled as the door shut behind him.

The game was underway. John Stevenson appeared to be feeding off of the mixed feelings in the building; he already had struck out the side once and was now churning through Twins like Hugh Hefner in the top of the second.

As usual, Mitch Henry broke the silence as he pointed toward the field.

"Okay, what in the *fuck* was that out there?"

"I know, Stevenson really is poppin' 'em tonight. If he keeps it up, you'll be in Hoplite for another year," Sid Fynch retorted.

"Don't make me do it, Sid."

"Do what?"

Henry sighed and rolled his eyes, "Whatever you say, *Linus*."

Fynch's head reeled as if Henry just connected with a right cross.

"The *fuck* you just say?"

"It *is* your name," Zeke Bailey nodded.

Sid/Linus formed his right hand into a fist and took a step toward Henry.

The towering righthander's scowl ensured that he retraced that step almost immediately.

"Let's cut the shit," Henry continued. "Hack? Korea? Was I the only one paying attention out there?"

"You *seriously* have to ask that?" Flash Gamble asked.

"Fuck off, Flash!" Henry nodded at the shortstop.

The room descended into a rabble. Even the soft-spoken Zeke Bailey and Nev Friedmann reengaged one another over their long-simmering theological debate.

Manny Poblado shivered. The band of fabric around the brim of his hat went cool with sweat. This was normally where Truck stepped in, or, in his absence, Willie or Pete Moray would pipe up to placate the mob.

Unfortunately, all three were nowhere to be found.

His stomach dropped. His lungs tensed. He knew exactly what he had to do, yet despite pitching in front of thousands without a problem, speaking in front of a group of twenty some-odd teammates, some of whom were friends, caused his mouth to go dry and his tongue to seize.

Henry put a meaty finger squarely on Fynch's chest. Sid swiped it away. Nev Friedmann pointed toward the door as Zeke Bailey folded his arms across his chest.

It was too much for Manny to handle.

He removed his hat and wiped his forearm across his brow.

"Hey!" Manny said.

The arguments continued.

"Hey!" He yelled more loudly.

Some of the players stopped their feuds, but the two big fights raged on.

Manny put a finger in each corner of his mouth and let out a sharp, loud, two-tiered whistle.

"Feeeew—FWWEEET!"

Henry and Sid stopped, as Bailey cringed and Friedmann turned to see who or what had caused the high-pitched noise.

"Everybody quiet!" Manny shouted. His voice was surprisingly deep and firm.

Henry pointed at the closer, "That's the first fuckin' word he's said to me all year, swear to *God.*"

"Shut up, Mitch." Manny said, matter-of-factly.

Henry may as well have been hit in the face with a shovel, "F...fine. See who gets the remote tonight. Hope you like *Duck Dynasty.*"

"Is all we've been watching for months now, Mitch. One more night don't make a difference," Manny said. He cleared his throat, "Señor jefe, perdón, señor Hack did something very brafe out there," Manny nodded, "*Very* brafe."

Sid shook his head, "Fuck that, he *lied.*"

Juan Patrón nodded sternly.

"Oh, and jou were *so* hurt by that, Sid?"

Sid nodded, "It's *fraud*. Out-and-out *fraud!*"

Henry cleared his throat, "Did he even mention that he was in Korea to any of us?"

Eldrake nodded, "Yeah, a few times. I never really thought much of it, though. And, I mean, still, he was in 'the conflict.' He did fight."

"He dove away from the gun! Like a coward!" Sid's face reddened.

"Shit, I'm sure you would've taken out every one'a those zeros by yer'self, right Sid?" Henry condescended.

Fynch bit his lip.

Manny held out both hands, "Look, I think it was incredibly brafe, to keep something secret like that, all those years—" he paused for a half-beat, "—then tell everyone, an' I mean *er'ryone*, about it. I know he' done great by me, an'—"

"Because he *gave* you my job!" Tommy Stearns barked.

"Is true. I won't deny it. All I' sayin' is that most of us, a lot of us, owe a lot to that man. And he's going into surgery tonight. I think we owe it to him to let him do so with a clear mind."

"Whattaya mean…?" Fynch narrowed his eyes.

"What I mean is that we vote, right here, right now, on whether we want señor Hack back as manager."

A few players exchanged confused glances as a low rumble ripped through the room.

"I know tha' Clevelan' don' have to listen to us, but I think it would do a lot for him, one way or'a the other, if he knew where he stood with his team."

Stearns nodded, "So how do we do this? Speeches for and against?"

"Fuck, Tommy," Henry huffed under his breath.

"I'm just saying, everyone remember what a miserable old cuss Coach could be sometimes. Those of you who aren't his pet projects," Stearns glared at Manny with those words, "may not have thought he was so great. Now, I think it's clear that he is what he is: a dying, crusty, miserable, oh yeah, *lying* old man. Nothing more, nothing less!"

A few nods cascaded through the party room.

Manny narrowed his eyes, "I did'in want this to turn into speech time, but every one'a you think about how we were, as a team, before señor Hack got here, and how we are as a team *now*. Most of us never talked to anyone differen' than ourselves," he looked at Patrón, Fynch, and Henry in turn. "An', true, he moved some'a us aroun' a bit, but it was for the best'a the *team*. Ask yourselves honestly, not even 'am I a better player now than at the beginnin'a tha' year?', even though it may be true. But ask yourselves, 'Are we a better *team* for having señor Hack as our manager? An' don' we owe it to him to let him still be the manager for the rest of the year?"

Manny looked around the room, but didn't see much reaction one way or another. All he saw were Patrón, Fynch, and Stearns's scowling faces, set off against the rest of the crowd.

"Just vote 'jour hearts. That's all I can ask." Manny took two steps back and faded into the crowd.

Sid pointed toward the field, "But Truck's not even here now!"

"Camión will be the tie-breaker," Manny didn't allow his grin to escape; he had some idea how his battery-mate would vote.

"And *who's* counting?" Stearns spat the words at his successor, "you, Manny?"

Manny shook his head again, "No—Eldrake will. He's the smartest and fairest outta' all'a us."

"I don't know about 'fairest,'" Mitch said. "What with...you know...the skin and whatnot..?"

Blank faces greeted his broad smile.

"He's *black*," Henry blurted out. "The opposite'a 'fair-skinned?'"

A chorus of groans went up from around the suite.

Curiously, Eldrake Gamble laughed.

"Christ, Henry, why do you always have to make shit *racial*?" Nev Friedmann asked.

"'Cause it's *fahkin'* wicked *pissah*, that's why!" Murph Murphy said.

"Guys, I don't really have a problem with it," Eldrake said.

"Huh. A rare miss, I guess..." Henry mused, ignoring the target of his initial, cringe-worthy jest.

Manny let out another shrill whistle, "Okay, okay. Everybody cover your eyes and wait until'a Flash says calls out what you wan' to vote for, then rise' your hand. Got it?"

Everyone nodded.

"Good. Okay, then heads down, cover 'jour eyes, and Flash, is all 'jours."

Manny tried to conceal his sigh of relief at having gotten through the awful situation unscathed. As he covered his eyes, the thin smile on his face faded away at the realization that he had no idea how the vote would go.

Everything he had told his teammates was true; Manny owed so much to Hack, more than his teammates would ever realize. He wanted nothing more than for Hack to go into that operating room without further care or worry.

And yet this was the way it had to be. Democratic. Everyone gets a vote. Hack's fate didn't rest in the hands of a single person.

It would be up to the team.

"All in favor of censuring Hack O'Callahan, raise—"

"*Sen*-what now?" Henry asked, over-earnestly.

Eldrake sighed, "If you want Hack to be kicked out as Magpie team manager, raise your hand."

Manny didn't so much as peak, though his free hand remained by his side. He waited several tense moments as his heartbeat thundered through his skull, waiting for Flash to tally the votes.

"All in favor of retain—*keeping*—Hack O'Callahan as manager, raise your hands."

This time, Manny lifted his free arm into the air. He worried that he didn't hear enough swooshing of fabric-on-fabric to mean that enough arms had been raised, and thus that there weren't enough "yes" votes to retain the manager.

"Okay, heads up," Eldrake said.

The room sat in rapt silence as Eldrake delivered the results.

"I guess someone needs to tell him, then," Eldrake said, stone-faced.

"Hey!" Mitch Henry boomed.

"Where the hell is Sunday?!"

4

Hack found himself in a gown in a spacious, well-appointed private hospital room. The tile was fresh to the point that the grout was still a pristine white, and the walls were recently painted.

Why is it that all I can smell is oranges then? Hack thought.

He had Steve turn on the TV before he left.

"Any requests?" Steve asked. He dreaded the answer but already knew it.

"Put it on ESPN," Hack said.

Steve grimaced, "Are you sure?"

"Yes, yes, goddamn it, *yes!*" Hack thundered, though the outburst was followed by a short (but deep) coughing fit.

Steve shrugged and clicked the button on the remote and several characters in costumes screamed in Spanish at one another.

"Just a second," Steve punched in three buttons and the image switched to the familiar *Baseball Tonight* set. Karl Paulus's overly-tanned face was framed by thick, blonde hair.

More surprising to Hack was the image of his own face on the monitors around the set. Chin up, defiant, with a thin smirk. Hack reveled in the devil-may-care attitude his jaw exuded.

But then he looked into his eyes on the picture, those same dull, lonely, old man eyes he had seen in the reflection of the broken glass from his TV set all those months ago.

They had left during his months with the Magpies—at least, he hadn't seen them in the coaches' locker room.

Now, though, the dull eyes returned to haunt him, and the rest of the country, for that matter, once more.

"Well guys, the big story tonight is obviously Hall of Fame manager Roger 'Hack' O'Callahan's shocking admission that after years of claiming, or at least not denying, that he served bravely in the Korean War—"

Conflict, God damn it! Hack thought. He recognized the irony and smiled.

"—That he was never actually in Korea. Gentlemen, your thoughts?"

"Big" Bill Marsh chimed in, "Well, it's all the more bizarre because he was in the Navy. He was in Asia. But he was on an aircraft carrier barnstorming around, playing baseball the whole time."

"Now, Big Bill, you played for Hack O'Callahan in Pittsburgh. Did he ever use the War as a motivational tool?" Karl asked.

Bill squinted and shook his head, "You know, I don't really remember it. If he did, it wasn't really a huge deal for us."

Hack raised an outstretched hand at the set, "What're you *talkin'* about, Big Bill?! I told ya' that you were uglier than a Korean whore so many times, I—"

"I think I'll be going now," Steve said. He politely bowed and excused himself as Hack waved toward the door without looking.

"Neil, your thoughts?"

The image cut to a thin, middle-aged man with glasses that Hack had only seen on the show a couple of times. His nasally, whiny voice perked Hack up in his chair.

"Well, Karl, in my book, a lie's a lie. He said he was in Korea, but he wasn't," he shook his head with a shit-eating grin, "That's just unforgivable to me."

Hack struggled to reconcile his appreciation of the sentiment with his general dislike of the rat-like man delivering it.

"Unforgivable is a strong word, Neil," Big Bill piped up, "You were never in a locker room with the man, never—"

Neil interrupted, "I *was* in a locker room with Hack O'Callahan *several* times getting interviews, or I should say trying to get interviews, and every time he—"

Big Bill smiled, "Pfft—don't bring personal grudges into this, Neil."

"How's that bringing a grudge into this?" Neil's voice was light and flighty.

Karl tried to play referee, "This situation is made all the odder by the revelation that O'Callahan is waiting to undergo surgery in Cleveland right now."

Big Bill puffed out his chest and stared into the camera, "Yeah, and if I know Hack O'Callahan, he's watching us right now from his hospital bed. Hang in there, Hack—know that there are lots of us out there rootin' for ya'."

Karl stiffened and cleared his throat, "A strange situation, indeed. Back with more, after this."

"Bah! *Fuckers!*" Hack reached for a bottle of Old Reliable to chuck at the screen, but frowned when he came up empty and had to settle for a box of Kleenex. The box connected with the screen with an impotent "poof," and dropped gently to the floor.

It made the knock on the door all the more jarring.

"Well, come to yer' senses, have ya'?"

Hack expected to see Steve the orderly in the doorway.

Instead, the diminutive form of Sun Dae Woo was there, for once, the smile wiped off his face.

"Hello, Mr. Hack," he said in barely accented English.

"Sunday? Oh boy, look, I know when we first met is gonna' be a bit confusin' now, but I'll let you have at it, lay it on me."

Hack folded his arms and waited.

"I did not come here to berate you, Mr. Hack."

"Then why in the sam *fuck* did ya'—"

It hit Hack like Eldrake Gamble had plowed into Shane Marcos, Westfield's catcher, those many weeks before.

"Yer'…yer'…speakin' *English!?*"

Woo's frown dragged his head down into a bow as he nodded.

"I, too, have carried this secret with a heavy heart since long before the day I met you. It has brought me deep shame and intense discomfort."

"Ya've spoken English *the entire time?*"

"Forgive me—you were not exactly the most accommodating person in the world when we first met."

Hack scowled, "Can ya' blame me? That wasn't a goddamned act—that was a fuckin' *flashback.*"

"I now realize that, and I apologize for any thoughts that you might have been a racist or somehow fabricating it."

"*You* apologize? *I*—" Hack swallowed his growing confusion, "—I should…uh… 'pologize ta' *you.*"

Woo shook his head, "It is not necessary. I came over here to play at the highest level of competition in the world. My entire baseball life, I have been an outcast in the locker room. The players I played with in Japan often mocked me, insulted me, and called me horrible names, like—"

Hack waved the man off, "I don't need'ta hear the specifics, Sunday."

He nodded, "I was ashamed. So I made it a habit of keeping to myself, not engaging with the other players. And I carried that over to America. Here, it was much easier to pretend that I didn't know the language, so I nod, and I always say—"

"Hello!" Hack put his hands together and bowed his head.

Sun Dae smiled thinly, "Yes, exactly. I thought this would be enough, especially given your," he took a deep breath, "history with my people.

"But then Coach Williams engineered it so that Juan and I roomed together, and I finally was with someone who was even surlier and more withdrawn than me every day on the road."

Hack allowed himself a half-smile.

Sun Dae lit up, "And I noticed that even Juan could let loose and play cards every now and then, and get in a fight with Manny and everything was still okay. And I thought about this very carefully, that maybe it was *me* who was the problem in Japan. Maybe those players were, how do you say? 'Kidding' me, to make me feel like one of the group. And I never kidded them back.

"So I made an effort with the Latin players here, to learn Spanish, to play in their games, and yes, to kid them more. And they accepted me. And Juan, who I thought was a very mean man when I first met him, I now count him among my closest friends."

Willie and Pete Moray appeared in the doorway, both huffing breaths like they had just run a marathon. Willie's eyes went wide at the sight of Woo and Hack in the same room.

"We, uh, got here as soon as we could," Willie said.

"How big is this fuckin' hospital, anyway?" Moray asked. He punctuated the question with a large wad of dip spit into a styrofoam cup he carried.

Willie reached his thumb over his shoulder, "If you want, we can come back later."

Sun Dae took two steps toward Willie and reached up to put his hand on the coach's shoulder.

"Thank you, Willie," Sun Dae said. He turned to the bedridden manager, "And thank you, Coach Hack. I bear you no animus. You both have made my profession—my *life* more fulfilling than you can possibly know." He walked out of the room in his short, choppy steps.

Pete pointed at the door, "Has he *always* been able to speak English?"

Willie's eyes narrowed, trying to process what he had just seen. He opened his mouth, but no words came out.

Hack shrugged, "Fer' git it. Ya' were seein' things. Well, guess the gig's up, huh?"

Willie furrowed his brow, "I, uh, don't know what to say, Coach. I—"

"Well, fer' one thing, ya' can still call me 'Hack.' 'Less ya' think I don't rightly deserve it any more, which I understand 'pletely."

"Oh, for Chrissake, Hack!" Pete Moray spit his entire dip into the cup.

Hack and Willie's mouths hung open.

"So ya' weren't *in* Korea. So what? I don't care *how* many times you used that when I played for ya', Hack, but we didn't remember it, damn it. Nobody gave half a *shit* if you told us you were 'knee deep in the muck fightin' commies.' You know *why*? 'Cause even then we knew they were old war stories, probably exaggerated by some old cuss lookin' to inspire us. And god *damn* if that wasn't the case. So stop feelin' sorry for yourself and recognize that you were the best fuckin' manager to ever live, and leave it at that!"

The words hit Hack in the face like a car without brakes. He regained his composure and glared at the pitching coach.

Pete remained resolute.

"Pete, you listen *real* close now. That wasn't the first time I' been told off by a former player. And it sure as *shit* ain't the first time a coach'a mine's told me I'm a damned *fool*. But son, comin' from you?" He paused and shook his finger at Pete Moray, "That's about the damned *dumbest* thing I ever heard outta' ya'."

"What?" Pete's glare faded into a crestfallen stare.

"How *dare* you tell me what ya' did and didn't get outta' some'a my speeches. You might think I'm just a fuckin' *fool* fer' lyin' ta' all'a yas', but each one'a those speeches had a point, each one had a *reason* behind it. And fer' you, of *all* people, Pete, ta' say that you all fer'*got* about them? They might as well kill me now."

Pete struggled to close his mouth and clench his jaw without his usual dip in place.

"Get over yourself, Hack!"

"Fuck *you*, Pete!"

A silence hung over the room.

"Are you two *through*?"

Willie's voice broke through the quiet like a hammer through glass.

"God damn it, Pete, have a little respect for the man. He's about to go through surgery, God *damn* it!"

Hack smiled at Pete. He may as well have stuck out his tongue.

"And as for *you!*" Willie bent over toward the manager in the bed. Hack stiffened. "You're tellin' me that *all* of those stories you told were made up?"

Hack rubbed his chin, "Well...not *all* of 'em. I *did* go hunting with Mick, though things may've gone a bit different' than I said."

Willie sighed. It pained him to ask the next question, but he knew he had to do it.

He took a deep breath and steeled himself.

"What about Jackie?"

Hack blinked twice, "What about him?"

"The Jackie story, Hack. Was *that* bullshit, too? 'Cause I did the math—when he was in the minors, with Montreal, you were only sixteen."

"I lied!" Hack shot up out of the bed.

Willie turned his head and nearly retched.

"I lied to play the game I *loved.*"

Willie's eyes widened as he turned his head back toward the bed, "The *fuck* you just say?"

"A scout fer' the Cardinals came by the family farm in Illinois. Guess it wasn't too far away fer' him to look. He saw me play in a semi-pro game on a Thursday night. We didn't really have high school games then, ya' see, it was all sort'a on our own time.

"Well, this guy says, 'Son, you wanna' play pro ball fer' the St. Louis Cardinals?' Shit, I was overjoyed! 'Where do I sign?' I asked. he pulled out a piece of paper and handed me a pen.

"But then, right before he was set to give it to me, he pulled it back. 'Son, you sure you're eighteen now?'

"Of course I wasn't—I was only sixteen. I looked at Pa, an' he nodded at me with his awful, intense stare. I couldn't tell if he was sayin' 'ya' better not, er' else I won't have no one ta' work the farm,' or 'you better, so yer' Ma' an' I don't have'ta support ya' no more.

"So I looked that scout in the eye, and I said, 'Yes'sir. Eighteen last week.' And I signed that paper and I've been two years older ever since."

"You're eighty-*two?*" Pete Moray asked.

Hack rolled his eyes, "Add it ta' the list'a lies!"

Willie looked the manager up and down for several seconds as the sweat beaded on his brow. He stuck out a lean finger at the man in the bed.

"The Jackie story—*was it a lie!?*"

Hack raised his nose, nostrils flared, and jabbed a tiny finger right back at his coach, "Willie, I'm gonna' tell ya' this, and I'm gonna' tell ya' this only once." He paused and met Willie's measured gaze with his own. "It ain't a lie. *That* was true. It's the only goddamn one I didn't embellish, even a bit. Jackie was the toughest S.O.B. I ever saw play."

Willie looked deep past Hack's eyes, into the depths of his soul Gone were the tired, dull orbs, replaced by the fire Willie only noticed when the old man was managing his Magpies.

Willie nodded, "Okay. Okay."

"Shit, that can't be true, since you saw me play too, Hack!" A deep, Southern drawl filled the room, almost as much as Mitch Henry's large frame completely occupied the doorway.

"Oh boy," Hack folded his arms.

He was shocked to find that trailing Henry were the rest of the Magpies, every single one of them with one notable absence.

"Where's Truck?" Hack asked.

"Great ta' see you, too, Hack, you old cuss," Henry said.

Manny flashed a smile, "Camión is finishing up with the game. He will be here shortly."

Hack stared past the last three players in the door, Juan Patrón, Linus "Sid" Fynch, and Woo, who had returned after his ever-so-brief absence.

"I, uh, thanks fer' comin' by, fellas, I s'pose," Hack said. "Wouldn't blame none'yas if ya' never wanted ta' see me ever again."

"What? Why?" Eldrake Gamble asked.

Hack soured, "You know damned well why! I'm a fraud!"

"Fraud? Most successful fuckin' fraud I' ever seen!" Henry reached over and rubbed the old timer's bald spot.

I'm still yer' manager! Hack wanted to thunder at the overgrown pitcher, but he caught himself; he didn't know if he could honestly say as much.

"Liar then. Better, Mitch?"

"Most successful liar I' ever seen, too."

Patrón and Fynch made their way through the chuckling crowd of purple-and-black hats to their manager's bed.

The room went silent.

"Coach Hack, you're probably the meanest, most conniving, lyingest, no good human being I've ever had the misfortune of meeting. You're dispicable," Fynch said. He leveled an intense stare on his coach.

Hack stifled a grin. *Go on, Sid…* he thought.

Patrón nodded, "Un cabrón," he added. "But before you get here, Magpies no good. Even though Patrón no hit well until yesterday, we better *team* for it. I better team*mate*."

Fynch raised a finger, "And you made me realize I still have a lot of growing up to do. A man fights his own battles. I may not be a man yet, but I'm on my way. And I have to thank you for that."

Hack smiled, "Well, that's just great. Just *fuckin'* grand!" He swatted Fynch on the hat bill, "Were none'a yas' *listenin'* out there tonight? It ain't just *you* that I lied to, but everyone! Shit, sometimes I believed my own bullshit myself."

"Who cares?" Eldrake Gamble asked.

"Un mentrejilla," Ozzie Cabrera pinched his fingers together.

Manny nodded, "A little lie, jefe. Do you know what other men 'jour age lie about? Far worse. Or they lost their minds long ago."

"Hell yeah!" Henry chimed in. "There's this bum back in Darrensbourg that takes down his pants around his ankles and dances on a streetcorner all day long, and he's probably twenn'y years younger than you. Crazier than a junebug in Joo-ly."

"How *is* your father doing, Mitch?" Fynch couldn't resist.

Henry grabbed the diminutive centerfielder by the shirt collar and pulled him up to eye level. He bore his teeth as spittle caked Fynch's face, "Don't you *ever* make fun'a my daddy, fer' *anything*, Sid. Understand?"

"God damn it, *put him down!*" Willie wedged himself between the two men and scowled at Henry.

Mitch glared right back.

"So nobody here has a problem with what I said tonight?" Hack screamed over the erupting din.

Henry lowered Sid to the ground as everyone else exchanged confused looks.

"No. No, jefe," Manny said. "The team, we put to a vote. Keep jefe in charge, or throw jefe out. We made'a speeches," he eyed Stearns, whose eyes still burned red with frustration, "An' we let Eldrake tally them."

Hack looked to the tall, rangy shortstop, eyes wide with anticipation.

Flash nodded, "We voted *overwhelmingly* to retain you as manager of the Magpies. We'd be honored to have you back."

The room erupted in applause, catcalls, and whistles as Hack breathed a sigh of relief. The sound waves washed over him and shook him ever-so-slightly, to the point where he felt a lump form first in his throat, and work its way to his face, where it leaked out of his eyes in two tiny, almost imperceptible tears.

Hack brought his hands to his face and fake-rubbed his eyes to hide his outburst of emotion from his players.

"We're happy to have you as manager, Coach," Gamble bent over the bed to pat Hack on the shoulder.

"Aw, thanks Flash," Hack reached up and rubbed the shortstop's head over his hat. "You've done a damned fine job, just *damned* fi—"

"Hold on!" someone shouted from the elevators. The tell-tale click-clack of baseball spikes on the tile floor reverberated down the hallway.

Moments later, Truck Traynor stood in the doorway.

"Not everyone got the chance to vote yet."

5

"It's about time!" Hack cackled.

Truck still wore his Indians uniform, caked only with a thin layer of dirt from catching various bullpen sessions on the side for pitchers not pitching that day, as well as a forgettable, pinch-hit pop out.

"I got here as quickly as I could, Hack," Truck said.

"Well, well, well, if it isn't the golden *shit* of King Mountain!" Henry said.

"Mitch I...don't have time to tell you how wrong that is right now," Truck said.

Henry stroked his heavily-stubbled chin.

Truck turned to Eldrake, "Did I hear right? Hack stays?"

Eldrake nodded, "Yep. Overwhelmingly passed."

Truck allowed the smile to take over his face momentarily before he narrowed his eyes and steeled his jaw, "Fine. That's just fine."

The glow faded from Hack's eyes.

Manny stopped himself from placing a hand on Truck's shoulder before he continued.

"Anyway, jefe, we just wanted to say that we suppor' you, and we know you'll be back on the bench managin' us in no time. You are a Magpie for life!"

Manny looked around the room for the Magpie hat that Hack had held in his hands as he delivered his stunning admission to the rest of the world. Not finding it, he instead removed his own cap and forced the too-small hat on Hack's surprisingly bulbous head.

The players clapped and cheered. Occasionally, one would dart a hand up to an eye ever-so-briefly, hoping to play the gesture off as "dirt in the eye," even though they had been on a baseball field for all of five minutes earlier that day.

Each one then took his turn shaking Hack's hand and giving him a hearty pat on the shoulder.

"You'll beat this, Coach."

"Hang in there, Hack—we'll be waiting."

Even Sid shook the manager's hand and said a brief, "Thanks."

Stearns offered a dead-fish hand, which Hack took overly vigorously.

"Give 'er hell, Hack," Mitch Henry said. "Beat the *fuck* outt'a that cancer. We need ya', bud."

"Better watch out Mitch—seems like these guys are gettin' ya' ta' be halfway presentable."

"Shit, compared ta' you, anyone looks downright respectable-like."

The two men shared a laugh.

Finally, only Patrón stood in front of the manager, hands on his hips for several moments before he snorted and the corners of his mouth curled upward.

"Thank you for helping Patrón find his swing. Patrón swing *enojado*—angry—for rest of year."

He extended a dark, rippling forearm toward the manager.

"Thanks fer' hangin' in there, Johnny," Hack allowed his hand to be swallowed by its much larger counterpart. Both men met eyes and nodded.

"Buena suerte, Hack," Patrón said.

It was only several seconds after Patrón turned around that he squinted.

"Qué significa, 'Johnny?'"

Manny put his arm around the burly slugger, "Es como estó," he began to explain the translations of names from Spanish to English.

They followed the other players out of the door, but before they exited, Manny stopped to look over his shoulder.

"Good luck, Hack," he said.

"See'ya, Manny," Hack waved him off.

Only Willie, Pete Moray, and Truck remained.

"You gonna' be all right?" Willie asked.

"Yeah Willie. Much better now," he met Truck's eyes. "You all get back to the hotel—you've got ta' get all the way ta' Hoplite tomorra'. It ain't exactly an exit 'er two down the highway."

Willie put a hand on Hack's shoulder, "You pull through this, now, ya' hear?"

"*Nooo*, I ain't been listenin' ta' the *last* twen'ny guys in line."

"Prick 'til the bitter end," Willie said with a smile and a chuckle. He patted Hack's shoulder three times for good luck.

"It ain't the end yet," Pete Moray said as he packed a fresh dip. The omnijovial assistant coach relaxed his genuine smile for several moments as he extended a tobacco-stained hand, "You'll be fine, Hack. Just fine."

"So will you, Pete," Hack said. He forced a grin, "So will you…"

The three coaches nodded at one another for several seconds before Willie put his hands in his pockets and turned to Truck.

"Congrats on the call-up, kid."

"Ah, just a pop out tonight. They say Armiguez is doing better, so they might just send me back down a couple days from now, but we'll see."

"Shit, we'll be ready whenever they wanna' send you back," Willie said. "I'll give ya' a call in the morning."

"Sounds good, Willie. Pete." Truck nodded at the men. "I'm gonna' talk with Hack for a little while here—keep him company 'til surgery."

"Get your rest now," Willie said.

"I will," Truck nodded.

"Give 'em hell, Hack," Willie said.

"You too, Willie."

Willie still smiled at hearing Hack call him by his nickname. Pete exited the room first, with Willie close behind.

"Oh, and Willie?" Truck asked.

"Yeah?"

"Close the door, please?" He looked at the manager, "Hack and I have some things to discuss."

"Sure thing, Truck. 'Night, fellas."

The door shut behind the men with a satisfying "ca-CHUNK."

Truck's thin smile faded into a scowl, "You son of a bitch!"

"Great ta' see you, too, Truck," Hack's eyes narrowed, half in shock, half craving someone to chew him out.

"I almost had a damned *heart attack* out on the field. I thought—!" Truck looked back to make sure the door was closed before he leaned in toward the manager and whispered, "—I thought you were gonna' out me."

Hack recoiled in his bed like someone was coming after him with a knife.

"Out *you*? How fuckin' self-centered can'ya get?"

"What?"

"Shit, I'd *never* think'a doin' that ta' one'a my players. *Especially* someone like you, Truck, and *especially* if George's gonna have ya' back in Hoplite before the end'a the year."

Truck furrowed his brow, "So then what the *hell* was all of that about 'sorry about what I'm about to say,' B.S.?"

"Did it ever occur ta' ya' that I thought ya' might've actually respected me?" Hack shot back.

The room went deathly silent for several moments.

"I was ashamed—*am* ashamed—of what I had'ta do."

"Ashamed? It's a white lie, Hack! No one cares! Hell, I don't know how many of the guys on the team are juicin' one way or another, and they all lie their *asses* off about—"

"Don't they, though? Care, I mean? I just watched some pinhead on *Baseball Tonight* read me the fuckin' riot act. Met me all'a three 'er four times. *He* seems ta' think it's a big deal."

Truck shook his head, "Fuck *him*."

Hack snorted, "Bet ya' won't be sayin' that when he asks ya' fer' an exclusive."

"You're totally in your own head on this one. *No one*, and I mean no one, watching that TV truly cares. Sure, it might be a big deal for a couple of days, until this all blows over, 'cause that's the way news works nowadays. But soon enough, there'll be fresh meat in the water, and the goddamn press will move on to something else."

Hack pursed his lips, "Oh. So yer' tellin' me that no matter how bad *I* think it is now that my secret's out, it really ain't that bad after all?"

He arched an eyebrow to punctuate the statement. He stared into Truck's eyes for one second…two seconds…desperately hoping that the connection had been made.

Fortunately, for Hack, the connection went in both directions.

"You *didn't!*"

Hack shrugged.

"It was all to teach me a *lesson?*"

Hack waved his catcher off, "In part, in part." The manager cocked his head, "I wanted ta' show ya' what bottlin' all this up inside'a ya' through the years got ya'. Keepin' folks at arms length 'cause yer' always deathly afraid someone's gonna' find out—it all just makes it so ya' end up a lonely old man in'a hospital room, waitin' ta' die like everyone else."

Truck's eyes went wide.

Hack shook his head before the catcher could open his mouth, "But *damn it*, Truck, don'tchya *see*? What Manny did there—what *all'a* yas' did there—I gotta' family now. Even if my real family—" he looked at the door, "don't want nothin' to do with me."

He pointed at the door, "When those twen'ny-five, twen'ny-seven guys if ya' count Pete and Willie came in here and said they didn't give a damn, except pro'lly Stearns and Sid, but fuck 'em anyway— when that *happened*, I couldn't give less'a a shit what everyone else thought. 'Cause you guys," the tears welled up from deep in Hack's chest. He didn't try to fight them this time; instead, he reached for the bloody handkerchief on the nightstand and brought it to his face,

"Yer' all I got. Fer'git' the *money* and all'a the cash—ya' can't take it with ya' son. What matters," he sniffed, "is *people*. The people that care fer' ya', no matter how much'a a fuckin' *prick* ya' been to 'em. Because without them, life ain't nothin'." He dabbed his face several more times as faint red outlines slicked the skin under his eyes, "It's just a goddamned *shame* I had ta' wait eighty-two *years* ta' figure that out."

Hack sobbed into the handkerchief, and Truck couldn't hold back any longer. He bent over and hugged his mentor, tears streaming down his cheeks in torrents.

"I'm scared," Truck said. "I want to tell them, but I'm scared."

Hack's eyes widened, "Don't be. Ya' got a whole team behind ya'. Err...in front'a ya. Whichever type you are."

Truck laughed through the sobs, "Christ, another gay joke?"

Hack smiled thinly over Truck's shoulder, "An opportunity, ta' put an old man in his place."

"I...I love ya' Hack."

Hack released the catcher from his embrace and raised his eyebrows, "Whoa, good thing Manny 'er that hussy Meadow ain't here ta' hear that."

This time it was Truck who hit the brim of Manny's hat, still perched precariously atop Hack's head.

"You know what I mean, ya' old jackass."

"Yeah, yeah..." Hack waited several beats. He sighed and looked at the catcher, "Guess I...kind'a..." he trailed off.

"What was that?" Truck grinned.

"I said I guess I love ya' too, Truck," Hack said.

Ahhhhhhh...the voice bellowed deep in Hack's gut.

Truck came in for another embrace, but Hack shrugged him off.

"Aw, come on with the mushy shit. I ain't mean that in—like Manny would, ya' hear. I love all'a yas'. Just don't tell the other guys, ya' know?"

Truck winked at him, "Your secret's safe with me."

Hack smiled at the irony, "Ya' see? I knew ya' had it in ya'!"

Both men turned to face the door as they heard a commotion out in the hallway. Hack thought he heard a muffled "daughter" through the thick wooden door before it abruptly unlatched and swung open.

Hack's visage brightened.

Could it be? he thought. He saw the flash of strawberry hair, the worried smile.

It wasn't Lisa or Amy, but the old codger still couldn't help but grin as Sam Rappaport entered the room in a huff.

"Grandpa!" Sam proclaimed, with two nurses following close behind.

"Hiya' sweetie!" Hack said. He swung his arms out wide and accepted her warm embrace, with the added bonus of a peck on the cheek.

Even Hack couldn't help but blush.

"These nice women weren't going to let me in to wish you good luck before the surgery," Sam said.

Hack didn't even need the wink she offered, "It's okay, she's my granddaughter."

"Oh?" one of the nurses raised a skeptical eyebrow. "It's just that the doctor's scheduled to come in to get you any minute now, and visiting hours are—"

"Well, then every minute with my family is precious, now isn't it?" Hack squeezed the words out through gritted teeth.

The nurse shrugged, "Okay. Maybe a minute or two, tops, but I can't stop you. Do save your strength, Mr. O'Callahan." The nurse nodded to her counterpart and both women left the room.

Sam re-embraced her "grandfather."

"I'm *so* sorry. I got caught up at the Jake, and then—"

Hack patted her on the back several times, "It's okay, it's okay, sweetheart—I fer'give ya'," he cupped his hand around her ear, "though I'd fer'give ya' a lot more iffin' ya' had some'a yer' famous Old Reliable on ya'."

Now Sam was crying and she stifled a laugh through the tears.

"You're five minutes away from major surgery!" Sam exclaimed with a smile.

"It ain't a joke," Hack said, stone-faced. "I'm gettin' the jitters, 'er somethin' here."

"I just, I wanted to make sure that if something happens during surgery or whatever, not that it will, but if it does——"

"Fer' Chrissake, spit it out already!"

"Thank you, Hack, for everything. For getting me a head start in this business, for believing in me when no one else did, everything."

"What about the Pollack kid? He didn't make the trip."

Sam's eyes went wide, "Barry? He, uh, Keith needed him——"

"Well, give him my best," Hack nodded.

She hit him playfully on the shoulder, "You tell him yourself, you big drama queen!"

Hack raised an eyebrow at Truck.

The catcher shook his head.

Sam didn't notice.

Hack cleared his throat, "Thank *you*, sweetheart, fer' all'a yer' help. I couldn't've done it without ya'. You make sure that cheap fuck Keith gets you a ring when these guys," he nodded at Truck, "win the Northern League."

She rolled her eyes, "Jeez, we were *just* over this. Tell him yourself."

"I know, I know, just in case I 'see the light' 'er anything like that and come back a big old *softie*."

Sam smiled and bobbed her head, "Well, I——"

Two quick raps on the door jolted her away from the old man in the bed.

Dr. Fishbaum stood in the doorway, chest puffed up, confident as he could possibly be for someone of his otherwise diminutive size. He affected the hint of a bothered frown in his otherwise "down to business" glare.

"Wow, they weren't kiddin'," Hack muttered to Sam.

Dr. Fishbaum's scowl deepened as he walked in the room and extended a hand toward his patient.

"My, somebody's been in the news, Mr. O'Callahan!"

The condescension sent the hairs on Hack's neck on end.

"Ya' ain't gonna' get ta' me that easily, Doc!" Hack winked at Truck.

"Trust me, Mr. O'Callahan, I have no intention of 'getting you.' I simply want you to be as relaxed as possible going into surgery," he huffed out a deep sigh, "even if you directly disobeyed me this afternoon."

Hack's face reddened. Much like how his impending mortality hadn't struck him until earlier in the day in Fishbaum's exam room, the surgery had seemed something distant, an item on the "to do" list far down the road.

Now, though, it was far too real. Worse still, the man who prided himself of anticipating every nuance, forseeing every wrinkle to every game he had been a part of, realized that there was nothing he could do to stop it.

He checked the clock.

"12:59"

Two orderlies strode into the room. Hack was shocked; they seemed unperturbed by the late-night surgery. Both remained steady and even. More than anything else, the fatigue hung heavy on their eyelids as they took their spots next to the bed and grabbed it.

"Hack!" Sam cried out.

The manager reached out for her hand, but her lithe fingers slipped through his stubby, sausage-like digits.

"Come with me!" Hack pleaded. He turned toward Dr. Fishbaum in the doorway, "*Let 'em come with me,* God *damn* it!"

Dr. Fishbaum nodded gravely, "They can follow you down the hall a bit, but we have strict protocols that—"

"Fuck yer' protocols!" Hack yelled.

Truck put his arm around Sam as both followed Hack out of the room into the hallway. The orderlies made a left turn out of the door, but only carted the bed twenty feet or so before a shrill cry buzzed through the hallway.

"HAAAAAAACK!" the female voice cried.

Hack tilted his head. She sounded familiar, but he couldn't exactly put his finger on—

"HAAAAAAACK!" the voice yelled again. This time, it was followed by the pitter-patter of two sets of feet on the tile of the hallway.

"Hold it, *hold* it!" Hack put his hand up to the orderlies. "Can'tchya *hear?*"

Dr. Fishbaum rolled his eyes, "Please, Mr. O'Callahan, this is a very delicate surgery and time is certainly of the essence," He pointed down the hallway and nodded to the orderlies, who continued to push the manager down the hall.

Truck and Sam reflexively stopped and rushed back around the corner.

Lisa flew toward them, practically dragging Amy along next to her as a male nurse pursued both of them.

"It's *well* after visiting hours, ma'am!" The nurse yelled.

"Hack!" Lisa yelled as she passed Truck and Sam. She met each of their eyes briefly and nodded at the nurse behind her as she gained on the still-moving bed.

The male nurse was large and lumpy, like a linebacker who put on a few extra pounds after his playing days.

Fortunately for Lisa, Truck Traynor was no string bean. He bent his knees and put up his hands, anything to slow the rapidly-approaching nurse down.

The nurse gritted his teeth, but only for a second before he could process Truck's powerful frame, and pulled up, trying to squeeze past the catcher down the hallway.

Truck shuffled from side-to-side, frustrating the nurse at every turn as Lisa and Amy finally caught up with the bed.

"Dad!" Lisa threw herself over the bed and grabbed her father's shoulder.

Hack was too stunned for words. He placed his hand on top of hers, not ever wanting to let go.

"Grampa!" Amy yelled. Lisa broke away and hoisted the youngster up to her chest.

"Move it!" Dr. Fishbaum implored the orderlies.

Hack looked at his granddaughter, smiling and gap-toothed and angelic all rolled into one. She reached a tiny finger out toward the old man, who shot a hand up and shook it for one second…two…before the orderlies picked up their pace and pulled away.

"I love you!" Hack looked over his shoulder. "I love ya' both!"

"We love you!" Lisa cried. "We love you!"

"I love you, Whack!" Amy half-screamed.

As they pulled away from the cadre of visitors, Hack exhaled deeply and sunk into the bed. A broad smile worked across his face and stayed firmly planted there even as they wheeled him into the operating room.

Even as the technician prattled on about counting backward from one hundred, and plugged the anesthetic into him.

Even as everything faded to black.

Ninth Inning

1

An overcast sky hung low over the open field, freshly lush and green from the driving rainstorm of the previous evening. Though the slate-grey clouds did their best to darken an already ominous occasion, an odd ray of sunlight poked through the foggy phalanx, and kissed the dew that still lay fresh on the grass.

Somewhere in the distance, a church bell clanged rhythmically, each "gong" a soft reminder of the day's grim activity.

Orderly rows of stones pocked what should've been a relatively flat, verdant oasis from the rolling hills and thick foliage surrounding Hoplite.

A large crowd gathered around one such stone, dark attire concealing darker thoughts even amid the bright TV lights, which seemed oddly in place.

In front of the assembled mass stood an easel, and upon it sat a blown up picture of an impossibly young Hack O'Callahan, proudly wearing his Yankee ballcap and smiling kindly, his eyes alight with a lifetime full of possibilities ahead of him.

Next to that easel sat his coffin.

A row of ten or so chairs was slightly skewed toward and facing the crowd next to a podium that had been set up at the gravesite.

Lisa O'Callahan Marsden stood behind the podium, dressed in a modest black dress with frayed threads peeking out from worn seams.

Her glossy eyes strained against the halogen bulbs that forced their way through the veil she was thankful she had thrown on at the last minute.

"Good morning," she began. She swallowed as more flash bulbs went off, complimenting the metallic, cricket-like chirping of camera shutters firing rapidly. "Roger O'Callahan was a man whom the world never knew. Maybe that's because most people knew him as just 'Hack,' the successful, opinionated baseball manager who knew how to get his way, no matter what. Come hell or high water.

"And even though we had the high water last night, with that terrible storm, I'm sure that whatever kind of God is up there will see it fit to skip over the 'hell' part."

A few thin chuckles darted through the crowd.

Lisa cleared her throat.

"I'll be honest; my father and I weren't the closest people in the world, for a variety of reasons. Maybe I should've reached out to him—" she choked on the phrase as she brought a tissue to her face to catch the stray tear running down her cheek, "—a little sooner. I should've tried to talk to him about the secret that so pained him for so many years without all of the judgment and nonsense."

She gathered herself, "But all of that changed some five nights ago, when he stood at a similar microphone to this one, and admitted to the world that he had been living a lie.

"No matter how innocuous it may have been to most, it was deeply troubling to Hack, who was set to carry the secret to his grave so ashamed was he of the consequences of letting it loose. And as I stood there, and listened to the boos, and the cheers, wanting nothing more than to get out of the stadium and back home to Indiana, I listened.

"I was shocked. For the first time ever," her voice broke as a sob rippled through her, "I could say I was *proud* of my father. Of his courage to say something in the face of awful, baseless judging by others."

She paused and waited for the shutters to die down before continuing.

"Per the terms of my father's recently-written will, he asked that one of his players, Robert Traynor, deliver the eulogy at his funeral. Robert?"

She looked past Amy in the row of chairs to Truck, dressed in a dark blue suit that was perhaps a half-size too small, leftover from his high school days. He nodded gravely as he rose from his chair, embraced Lisa and gave her a peck on the cheek as he passed.

"Sorry for your loss," Truck said.

"Thank you," Lisa sniffled, "Sorry for you, too. I know you meant a lot to him—"

—*More than I ever could*, she didn't finish the thought. Instead, a couple more tears steamed down her cheeks as Truck patted her on the back gently several times, holding her, willing the tears away.

She choked down several more breaths and composed herself enough to walk over to the empty chair next to Amy and force herself to sit.

Amy leaned her head on her mother's shoulder as she wrapped her tiny arms around her mom's midsection.

Lisa patted her head and smiled.

Truck took his short, powerful, strutting steps to the microphone and grabbed the sides of the podium with his iron grip. Though he had never sought out public speaking, or even been involved in so much as a press conference, he felt comfortable, and at home in front of the crowd. He didn't even consider the millions of viewers watching from their couches, likely cursing that *Sportscenter* was being pre-empted for some old codger's funeral.

He reached in his coat pocket and unfolded a typed-up speech, a page-and-a-half of the best material he could come up with given the circumstances.

Truck turned toward the row of chairs next to the casket, "Thank you, Lisa," he said. He faced the crowd brought his lips thin and taut.

"I, uh, apologize if I'm a bit nervous, but our last game of the year's tonight, and the playoffs are on the line. I know if Hack was here he'd hit me on the hat and tell me to 'suck it up, dummy.'"

The Magpies all snickered, even through the rest of the crowd's nervous laughter.

Willie shook his head and grinned.

Truck took a deep breath, "I only knew Hack O'Callahan for the last year of his life. Actually, it was more like a few months, but those of you who knew Hack know that his personality is certainly large enough to make it *seem* like a year or two."

A small swell of laughter rose through the audience.

"Hack was certainly a character, and to be fair, that's probably how a lot of you remember him, yelling at reporters, or yelling at an ump after a blown call, or…some other kind of yelling."

More laughs.

"But very few of you got to see the *real* Hack O'Callahan, behind closed doors. Got to witness the man's passion for all things baseball. He loved the game. *Loved* it. Sometimes, he loved the game so much, it was to his detriment."

He looked over at Lisa who locked eyes with the catcher and nodded with an appreciative, thin smile.

"Despite his flaws—and he was certainly flawed, but who among us isn't?" Truck waited a half-beat for people to consider the sentiment, "—Hack had something that so many folks nowadays just flat-out lack:

"He cared."

"Whether it was one of us acting like an idiot," Truck searched for Mitch Henry in the crowd, though if the hulking pitcher thought the catcher spoke of him, the blank look on his face hid it well, "or about one of his players getting buzzed by the other team, Hack always possessed a sense of fairness and justice about him equal to the sum of his years and years of experience."

Truck chuckled, "It's funny, he would always play these mind games on us, try to find a psychological edge—" he paused for a second.

He wouldn't… Truck thought.

From beyond the grave, *even?*

Truck felt the knot form in his stomach.

Here? Now? he thought. *Really?* His eyes drifted upward toward the dark sky involuntarily.

"—psychological edge that I still don't think most of us even got a lot of times."

More chuckles from the crowd.

Truck cocked his head and bit his lip. He wasn't even controlling what his hands were doing as he carefully folded up the speech and slipped it in his pants pocket.

"You know, I've heard a lot about what happened about a week ago, back in Cleveland. I don't mean to recount what Hack said, but in the wake of it, a lot of folks were outraged about what all he said. 'How dare he,' this and 'he should be ashamed,' that.

"It's a weird concept, shame. Why do we even feel it? So often we think we feel shame deep in our gut because we've done something *wrong*, something so inherently *bad* that we should be embarrassed about it.

"I spent a lot of time with Hack during his last day on this planet. A whole lot of time. I think it's safe to say that he felt ashamed of the secret that dogged him for so many years.

"It *was* wrong of him to stretch the truth. I won't argue that. But there was truth to stretch. He *did* serve his country in the Korean conflict, and did so ably and, for the most part, valiantly.

"It was *wrong*, but he certainly did his time. He served his sentence, silently pondering his secret for so many years, allowing the doubt and the fear to envelop him and nearly swallow him whole."

The first droplets of sweat beaded on Truck's forehead.

He ignored them.

"It took courage to face that shame that he rightly or wrongly leveled on himself for so long, to look it in the eye and say, 'Yer' not gonna' control me anymore!'" Truck's impression of the manager, though barely passable, was met with guffaws by the Magpies.

Truck sighed deeply. The knot was working its way up his chest, trying to catch itself in his lungs, struggling to cut off the air he so desperately needed to continue.

Truck shrugged it off, "And that shame had some basis, however shaky, in fact. Millions of people suffer similar shame every day, quietly burying their feelings because their friends, family, and even total strangers have told them: this is wrong, *you* are wrong."

A hint of a murmur rippled through the array of onlookers in front of him.

"And yet, these people have done *nothing* wrong. Nothing other than trying to live their lives the ways others have told them to out of fear of mocking or exile or God Almighty Himself!" Truck's eyes shot upward.

The rabble grew louder.

Mitch Henry may have even let out a "What the *fuck?*"

Truck bobbed his head and smiled, "You may wonder what all this has to do with Hack. Like I said, he used to play these mind games with us, anticipating three, four moves ahead, trying to get us to realize truths about ourselves that we hadn't even begun to scratch the surface of."

The knot panicked. It made one last shrieking gasp, one final pained effort to lodge itself in Truck's throat, to stop the madness he was about to level on the entire country.

Truck's eyes darted through the crowd, looking for the one thing that could anchor him through the shitstorm he was about to create.

Second row, third chair to from the right, he found him.

Manny.

The closer's eyes were wide with fear. He wanted to shake his head, to stand up and yell "Stop!," but instead found himself nodding along with Truck, tears welling in his eyes.

"I've ignored one such truth about myself for far too long. And I think Hack asking me to speak today was his way of gently nudging me along, getting me to save myself before I allowed this shame to consume me, and drain me from the inside. So here goes."

He inhaled deep lungfuls of thick, August, Hoplite air. Somewhere in the cemetery, a bird sang as Truck's powerful hands dug into the chipped wood of the podium.

"I'm Truck Traynor," he said, though it was almost as if he witnessed the entire scene from somewhere far above the ground, as if it was happening to someone else.

"And I'm gay."

2

The door to the manager's office slammed shut behind Truck, to the point that it caused the catcher to jump.

He attributed it to the fact that he felt lighter, more unburdened than he ever had in his life.

Willie put his hands on his hips, "What the *fuck*'re you smilin' about?"

Truck tried to wipe the grin off of his face, but was only able to turn it into a thin smile.

Willie removed his hat and rubbed his thinning hair, "Shit, right before the last game'a the *year*, Truck?"

"Willie, I can explain—"

"Ya' couldn't have waited another god damned *day* to tell everyone? Just gotten us through this game before you had ta' deposit this whirlwind'a…a'…a' *shit* at my feet, without Hack here, to boot?!"

Willie put a hand on the desk to steady himself, "We were so *close*, Truck. So damned close. Now I have'ta manage this last game with a goddamned circus with everyone from ESPN and Fox and Mars, and who the fuck else all knows—?"

"Technically, I doubt there'll be any Martians in attendance."

Willie raised his hand to swat the catcher's hat brim, but caught himself.

"Wise ass little shit," Willie huffed, unamused. "May as well hand Palooka the goddamned league title on a silver platter."

Truck shook his head, "I'm going to go ahead and ignore that you didn't ask how I was holding up, not even a 'you doin' okay?'"

"Right, since I'm *sure* that's what Hack would've done if you would'a pulled this stunt," Willie rolled his eyes.

Truck cocked his head and bit his lip before he continued, "Did you ever think that Palooka has to put up with this too, now? It's going to be on every Palooka player's mind. And guess who they have to talk to every time they're up?"

Truck planted a thumb squarely on his own chest.

Willie raised an eyebrow. His eyes softened as a mischievous glint returned.

"You cagey little—" the grin faded as Willie's expression darkened, "What the *hell* am I sayin'? Mitch is pitchin' tonight!"

"I can handle Mitch, Willie," Truck steeled his jaw.

"Really? Remember what happened when he met Sun Dae?"

"That was..." Truck half-swallowed the words before they escaped, "...a while ago."

"What, a month? Maybe two? You think Mitch Henry's suddenly become some 'enlightened' do-gooder over the course of a month, singin' the goddamned 'Rainbow Connection' with Kermit the *fuckin'* Frog?"

"He's *not?*" Truck grinned ever-so-slightly.

"I liked the old Truck a helluva' lot better," Willie shook his head. "Should'a never signed that will with Pete right before Hack's last game. S.O.B. lied about bein' *broke*, too."

"I'm not tryin' to be a smart-ass, Willie. Shit, do you know how much I agonized over telling people? About how many nights I've worried that a guy like Mitch Henry would find out and beat the shit out of me—or *worse?*"

"So why'd you pick *now* to tell everyone?" Willie's upper lip quivered with the question, "Especially with Slappy and this business'a not bein' able to play tonight."

The Magpies' backup catcher, Guillermo "Slappy" Arias had been sent down to high-A Chesterfield earlier that day to be eligible to play for them during the playoffs. It was a common occurrence at the end of the minor league season as the organization tried to get its prospects as much playing time as possible before winter ball.

Truck thought for a moment. He shrugged, "It seemed like the right time."

Willie didn't say anything. He calmly marched through the door to the coaches' locker room and re-emerged with his tablet. He swiped a few quick commands on it and turned it to face Truck.

Sportscenter played on the screen. Truck's media guide picture showed on the monitor on the upper right side of the frame, with "Traynor" printed neatly underneath, and an overly-stylized rainbow-themed logo imposed behind it.

"—Ending years of speculation over who the first major league baseball player to come out would be. Who would've thought it would be a top prospect out of Cleveland, who has a grand total of one major league at bat? Shelley Jensen has more from Hoplite, Ohio."

The picture changed to show an overly-made up (if attractive) woman in a business blouse in front of the players entrance to the Murph. A dozen other satellite trucks and vans set up shop in the small parking lot. In the back of the frame, Keith Myrick opened the trunk of his SUV and grabbed his golf clubs before he turned, saw the camera, did a double-take, and put them back down in the trunk. He fumbled for a piece of paper and stared at it for several minutes in faux contemplation before he sheepishly closed the rear door.

"Thanks Tom. Well the day began on a somber note, as legendary manager and recent lightning rod for criticism Hack O'Callahan was laid to rest in a local cemetery.

"A will executed by O'Callahan the day before he died stipulated that one of his favorite Magpies players, up-and-coming star Robert 'Truck' Traynor, was to deliver the manager's eulogy. But none of the mourners in attendance could have possibly anticipated what followed soon thereafter."

"I'm Truck Traynor. And I'm gay." Truck was on the screen, looking at the crowd.

"On a day when the often cantankerous manager's life was to be celebrated, recent admissions of fabricating his involvement in the Korean War notwithstanding, the tone of the day changed rapidly with Traynor's own admission. The reaction has been swift and overwhelming."

The screen flashed to an elderly gentleman with mangled teeth and a week's worth of stubble shaded by the Magpie hat atop his head.

"I don't curr' what'in the *hell* Truck Traynor does in his spare time. I got the chance ta' meet him once, good kid, *nice* kid. If he's one'a the gays, so be it."

A college-aged girl was next, "I mean, it's a shame 'cause he's so *hot*. All the good ones are taken or gay, am I right?" she giggled an annoying, high-pitched whine. "But seriously, it's up to him. Whatever he wants to do," she turned to the camera, "Baucomb supports you, Truck!"

An enormous, ruddy bald man was next, "'Long as he can still crush the ball, bro, it's fine. Good fer' him, man!"

The reporter's voice came in again over the segment, "His teammates have offered similar support."

Flash Gamble wore his thick-rimmed glasses, "I, uh, think we all support Truck here on this. He's the heart and soul of this team, he's our leader, our field general. We'll be just fine."

Zeke Bailey was next, "Well, I'm a Christian, now, but that means having compassion for all of us as God's creatures—"

The editor cut off the rest of Bailey's spiel. Instead, he was replaced by a trembling, wide-eyed Manny Poblado.

"I, uh, I mean sure, we're all on Camión's side here. No, uh, har' feeleens."

Truck reflexively swallowed.

He nearly gagged when the tablet cut to a hulking, surly-looking Mitch Henry slamming the door of his pickup truck.

"But not all of his teammates were so forthcoming," the reporter said.

"Get that [BLEEP] the [BLEEP] outta' my [BLEEP]in' face. [BLEEP]in' disgusting." Henry's hand extended toward the lens and the frame shook.

Willie tapped the home button.

"So slugger, still think you're ready for tonight?"

Truck clenched his teeth.

"I'll be just fi—"

He was interrupted by a knock on the door.

Willie and Truck eyed each other, brows alert. Truck nodded at his new manager.

"Yeah?" Willie asked.

The door opened without a reply.

Fortunately, for Truck, Keith Myrick's overbroad smile greeted the men.

Willie heaved a sigh of relief, "Heya' Keith."

"Willie," the G.M. nodded, "And there he is!" Myrick spread his arms and nearly hopped slowly from leg to leg toward the catcher. Truck didn't quite know how to respond, so he just stood motionless as Myrick enveloped him in a hearty, too-long embrace.

"Hi, Mr. Myrick," Truck said.

Myrick pulled away and put both hands on Truck's shoulders, "I am *so* proud of you. So, so proud. We have big plans for tonight, Truck, *big* plans! I have Marc Blake and Sam Rappaport on the preparations right now. We're thinking a pre-game address, followed by local gay leaders taking a couple minutes each, and then—"

Truck shook his head and interrupted, "Gee, I don't know what to say, Mr. Myrick. I just, I don't think tonight's the right time for all of this, you know? What with the division title on the line and everything."

Willie's nostrils flared, "So *now* it's too much of a distraction!"

"I want it to distract Palooka, not us!" Truck shot back. "I never said I wanted a circus."

Keith tilted his head, "You sure? I think we've really hit on something with this whole 'gay thing.' The game's already absolutely sold out. I had to bribe the fire marshall to let us sell a thousand more SRO tickets."

Truck nodded, "I get it—it's your job to make money for the team, and I respect that. But with all due respect, Mr. Myrick, aren't you making enough money off of this already? I'm just happy to not have to pretend to be someone I'm not anymore. It's a new feeling—a *great* feeling—but I'm still kinda' getting used to it."

Myrick stroked his chin in feigned contemplation, "Yeah, I get that, but then there's *Sportscenter* and all of the talking head shows, and—"

Willie snorted, "Honestly, Keith, you don't think we'll be the lead story on all'a those already? Wearin' Magpie purple-and-black, broadcast all across the damned country?"

This fact hadn't occurred to the GM, and he paused to think.

"Tell you what, Truck, how 'bout an interview after the game?"

Truck furrowed his brow, "But Hack never—" he didn't even bother to finish.

Keith smiled and shook his head, "Hack's *gone* now, and I say it's fine for you to have a press conference."

"You really think that's the best idea, Keith?" Willie asked.

"What's the worst that could happen?" Keith said. "Look, kid, you better get real' used to talking in front'a cameras for a while here. That's the choice you made. Besides, I'll be there to help you through it."

Truck could've sworn that the GM's chin tilted upward, almost as if already posing for the audience of millions tuning in.

The catcher nodded, "Okay. Press conference tonight, after the game."

"Great!" Keith clapped his hands.

Willie jumped.

"I'll see you after the game. Oh, and kid?"

"Yes, Mr. Myrick?" Truck asked.

"You might wanna' check your e-mail. Something tells me you're bound to have a lot of folks wishing you well."

This time, it was Willie who had to cover his mouth with his sleeve to prevent from having a coughing fit.

"You *sure* that's a good idea, Keith?" Willie asked.

"You know, as much of a pain in my ass as Hack could be at times, I don't remember him questioning me on organizational matters like this."

"Oh, so this is an *organizational* matter now, I see…" Willie sold the sarcasm well.

"It is as long as I *say* it is, Willie," Keith said. He turned to Truck and flashed his phony smile, "Go ahead, kid, answer 'em."

Truck nodded as Keith continued to stare at him.

"Right now?"

"Sure, why not?"

Truck pulled out his phone. He had put it on airplane mode because of the torrent of calls, texts, and e-mails earlier that day, but quickly swiped it back on and waited for the e-mail app to connect to the network.

What he saw was shocking.

There were messages of support, plenty of well-wishes from folks around the country.

But only the message at the top of the screen stood out.

The subject line?

"I'L KILL U FAGOT."

3

"Oh…oh my…" Keith said blankly.

"God *damn* it, Keith, I *told* you to let him wait until later!" Willie thundered.

Truck fought the sinking feeling in his stomach. He clicked on the e-mail involuntarily, and had to keep from throwing up as he saw the rest, in all caps:

"DEAR FAGOT,

IF YOU CAN GET THE COCK OUTTA UR MOUTH LONG ENUF TOO READ THIS, NO THAT UR MY NEXT TARGET.

ANONEMUS

P.S. I'LL SAVE A BULLET FOR UR NIGUR MANAGER, TO"

"What does it say, Truck?" Willie asked.

Truck nodded, lips drawn taut as the manager looked over his shoulder. Willie's eyes narrowed as he read through the entire message.

"I knew it."

Truck's eyes went wide.

"What?"

"Yeah, back when I played for the Pirates in the early 90s, we had that epic NLCS against the Braves. I made a diving catch off of Dave Justice late in Game 4 to keep the game tied, sent it to extras. A couple days later, you wouldn't believe some'a the shit I got. Telegrams—God damned *telegrams*—sayin', 'N-bomb' this, and 'kill you' that. I upset more crackers than a jittery forklift driver at the saltines factory."

Willie waited for a hint of a smile.

None was forthcoming.

"But...no one *really* ever tried to kill you, right Willie?" Truck asked.

"Nope. Not to my knowledge. And that kind'a shit happened off-and-on through my career. But goddamn if it didn't fuck with my mind the first few times, put me 'on edge.'"

Keith picked up the phone.

"What're you doing?" Truck asked.

"Calling security. Getting some cops for tonight's game."

Truck shook his head, "No."

Willie nearly smacked the catcher upside the head.

"The *hell* you say?"

"You said it yourself, Willie, it's probably an empty threat. The last thing I wanna' do is the *day* I come out, seem like a coward. I'm gonna' play, no extra cops on the field, no nothing."

Willie turned to Keith phone still in hand and stared at him.

"*Now* you decide to say nothing?" Willie asked him.

Keith held up a finger, "Yeah, Hoplite police? Keith Myrick, G.M. of the Magpies. Good, good. Hey, listen, I'm sure you've heard we're dealing with a lot over here today, and I was wondering—oh? Oh, okay. Is there any way we can...? Good...I see...*I* see...good. Okay then, thank you so much. Uh huh. Buh bye." He hung up the phone with a grin.

"So?" Willie asked.

"They're gonna' send over a coupla' plainclothes guys to sit near the dugouts, just in case."

Willie breathed a sigh of relief.

Truck's face went flush, his head nearly boiling with anger.

"I'll be fine," he managed through gritted teeth.

Keith waved the comment away with an overbroad grin, "Nonsense, nonsense. No need to risk it. I know, it's the 2010s, but still, better safe than sorry."

Truck looked to Willie for confirmation. The manager nodded his head slowly.

"Fine," he filled his lungs with air and puffed out a long, shaky sigh, "If you think that's best, that's fine."

Willie shook his head.

Keith nodded.

Willie patted Truck on the shoulder a couple of times, "Now you better go get ready, Truck."

Truck nodded, "I gotta' meet up with Mitch, go through the scouting report."

Keith raised an eyebrow.

Willie merely nodded.

"Thanks Mr. Myrick. I appreciate it."

Keith smiled, "Think nothing of it, Truck. Anything I can do to help, just let me know," Keith said, even as he was leaving the manager's office.

Truck got up to follow him. More than anything else, Willie wanted to take the kid by his shoulders and shake some sense into him, tell him that he didn't realize that even though attitudes had mellowed, he was going to have to go through some of the same awful stuff Jackie had put up with, that it only took one asshole to shit in the punchbowl.

Instead, he stayed quiet. As uneasy as it made him, Truck was leaving the room angry, an animal barely contained.

Willie's gut told him that might not be such a bad thing.

Truck left the office and shut the door behind him. He took a couple of short strides into the hallway, then turned to enter the locker room.

Nervous laughter percolated the room.

Mitch Henry pointed at Sid Fynch.

"I'll say it—I think it's fuckin' *disgusting*. How all'a you assholes can say otherwise, I got *no* idea. None."

"Hey, don't look at me, I told ya' already, it's fahkin' *gross*." Murph said.

Flash Gamble looked at the doorway and cleared his throat.

"What's the matter, Flash? Cat got yer' tongue?" Henry asked.

Flash nodded toward the doorway and cleared his throat four or five more times.

"Shit, you might wanna' get that checked out. Don't wanna' end up croakin' like Hack did."

"You got somethin' to say to me, Mitch?"

Truck's voice silenced the room like the crack of a whip. He stared the hulking pitcher down, both sets of eyes locking with boiling anger as both men strode toward one another.

"I, uh, gotta' go get'a son' treatment," Ozzie Cabrera said.

A cacophony of muttered agreements and half-phrases about "extra swings" enveloped the room as all of the Magpies filed down the tunnel to the field.

Manny was one of the last to leave, and though Truck thought he saw the closer's eyes widen momentarily, Manny forced them blank and forward as he continued out onto the field.

Truck only mulled the slight momentarily as he went face-to-neck with the towering Alabama starting pitcher.

"Go on," Truck dared him, "you were saying?"

Henry towered over the catcher and remained silent.

"Shit, Mitch, say *something*!" Truck screamed in the pitcher's face.

Henry remained stone-faced.

"It's the biggest game of the season, and you aren't even gonna' put aside your personal bullshit to go over the Palooka scouting reports?"

Henry continued to stare. Truck thought he saw the pitcher's lip quiver once or twice, a brief hint that he was getting ready to speak, Mitch remained resolute.

"Fine! Be that way, ignorant hick fuck!" Truck yelled. He walked over to his locker and began to dress. The death threat was one thing, but he thought for sure Henry would be man enough to insult him to his face, at least offer some kind of a jumping off point to discuss the night's game.

Instead, the pitcher offered a half-snort, half-harumph before he launched a huge dip spit right on the concrete drain and followed his teammates out to the field.

Truck was left.

Utterly alone.

4

The atmosphere at the Murph was lively as the over-capacity crowd started to make noise long before the game started. The scent of cheap beer and peanut shells hung low in the hazy late summer air.

"THWACK"

Truck caught another Mitch Henry warmup pitch in the bullpen. Though Henry still hadn't said a word to him, he appeared to be taking his frustration out on Truck's mitt, which was just fine by the catcher.

Before Truck could fire the ball back to Henry, a swell of cheers descended on the field.

"Batting third for the Magpies and warming up the pitcher in the bullpen, *number* fif-teen, Trrrrrruccck Trayyyyyy-norrrrrrrr!"

The applause rose in a swell, though Truck felt the sharp chorus of boos underneath cut through the wave like a ship's bow, needling him, feeding his anger as he reached back and whipped the ball back to Henry without so much as a nod to the crowd.

Amid the rainbow banners that waved through the crowd (which Truck honestly didn't know exactly what to make of quite yet), he also noticed an usher ripping a sign that read, "Truck Sucks Willie—RIP Hack!" from a drunken townie's hands.

Eventually, Henry finished his warmups, and made it a point to trail Truck by at least four or five steps as they made their way back to the dugout. Normally Truck would've stopped and started a few times just to mess with Henry, but the way the starter was locked in in warmups, Truck didn't want to alter a thing.

Let him hate me, Truck thought. *Not like we were friends before.*

Henry's intensity carried over through the anthem to the first pitch of the game, a called strike. The crowd erupted in cheers, a cry only surpassed when, two pitches later, Henry dropped a hammer-like curveball practically on top of the plate, and got the Princehens' leadoff batter, speedy little Moises Montero, to flail at the pitch for strike three.

Henry stabbed at the ball each time he received it back from Truck. Each time he pulled off his hat and wiped his brow with his sleeve, the dark circles around his eyes perfectly framing his stormy disposition.

He wouldn't so much as nod to confirm Truck's signs. The two settled into a rhythm where Truck would put the signal down, and Henry would rock and fire.

After his fifteenth pitch, a particularly nasty, heavy fastball that kissed the inside corner, Henry had struck out the side.

As the enormous righthander strode off the mound to wild cheers, Truck pulled his hockey-style mask off and trotted back to the dugout. As he arrived on the steps, Willie was waiting for him. The manager gave Truck a hearty pat on the behind.

"I don't know what the hell kind'a fight you two had before the game, but keep that shit *up*," Willie said. He pushed his thick, plastic glasses up onto the bridge of his nose.

Truck nodded.

He put on his helmet and gripped his bat without batting gloves. He enjoyed the coarse feel of the wood chafing his palms, especially on this evening; even pain was better than the hatred that he felt focused on him from throughout the stands.

After Oiler Derrick and Flash Gamble rolled over on weak grounders and were thrown out easily, it was time.

"Catcher…Trrrrruck…Trayyyyyyy-norrrr!"

Truck walked to the plate, head held high. If someone was going to try to kill him, then he'd give them as big of a target as they'd need.

He rubbed the back line of the right handed batter's box out with his spike.

"Well, if it ain't the Princess'a Hoplite," Scooter Herman said as he hit his mitt.

"Fuck off, Scooter."

"Whoa, whoa, easy there, fella," Scooter said. "Didn't ever know'ya to be such a delicate little flower."

"BANG!"

Truck shot up with a jolt, startled, head on a swivel.

Palooka's manager held a bat that still rung from being hit against the metal helmet rack.

In his haste to find the source of the noise, Truck had forgotten to call time. The Princehens' pitcher, Dane Calhoun, didn't waste any time in throwing an easy, get-over strike past Traynor.

"Steee-*rike!*" The ump stuck out a fist.

Truck glared at the Princehens' manager.

The old man shrugged, shit-eating grin ever-present.

Scooter Herman chuckled, at least until Truck's icy scowl washed over him, and caused the Princehens' catcher to gulp loudly.

Truck dug in again, determined to hit the next ball a mile. Calhoun got his sign, wound up, and fired.

Truck picked up his front foot and put it down, but was way ahead of the change-up, and lunged for the pitch.

"Steee-*rike!*" The ump bellowed again.

"I mean, I got nothin' against you people," Scooter said, "But right now, you're makin' it so damned *easy*, Truck."

Truck knocked his bat against his cleats, as clumps of dirt fell into the batter's box. He gripped the bat in his hands and worked them around the handle until he could feel a blister forming underneath one of the callouses on his hand. He pointed the bat squarely at Calhoun once…twice…three times before he brought it above his shoulder.

Calhoun stifled a laugh.

Truck drowned out the crowd and focused on those big, goofy, goober teeth of his, taunting him, almost daring him to knock them out.

Calhoun brought his hands over his head, broke them over his knee, rocked back, and fired.

The ball rotated tightly in a circle.

Another curve, Truck thought.

It started about belt high, which meant it was headed harmlessly for the dirt—

Until it maintained its height and "slid" on by, right on the outside corner.

Truck hadn't even swung.

"Steee-*rike!*" the ump cried, as he punched Truck out.

Truck grunted at himself as he prepared to slam his bat on the ground in rage.

Instead, he casually tapped it on the plate and flipped it to himself before he handed it, along with his helmet, to the bat boy, who nervously approached the slugger.

Truck could only shake his head.

5

Truck's second time at bat resulted in an impotent pop out to a laughing Scooter Herman in foul territory.

If even possible, the foul out made Truck even more enraged than his strikeout the first time up. At least when you struck out, there was a sense that the pitcher had beaten you, the idea that you could tip your cap to the other guy and go about your business.

A foul out, though, was clearly a mistake by the hitter, one that is equal parts unhelpful to your team and harmless to the opponent.

Fortunately, Mitch Henry tore through Princehens hitters through six innings, only allowing an infield single on a bunt base hit by the Palooka leadoff hitter, Moises Montero, his second time up.

Dane Calhoun matched Henry pitch-for-pitch. As Truck took his swings in the on-deck circle in the bottom of the sixth, it was undeniable that the teams were locked in an old-fashioned pitcher's duel.

"Hey Truck, ya' gonna' hit a *homo*-run heeya!?"

Truck looked for the source of the insult and found it in the form of a fat fellow with a wart on the tip of his nose, and equally hideous long, grey hair and beard to match. The fan smiled broadly, to reveal a couple of rotten gaps and a gold tooth where his right front central tooth should have been, as he raised a nearly-empty beer toward the on-deck circle.

The catcher immediately looked downward and swung again.

"Get it? *Homo*-run!" The man punctuated the statement with a deep, whooping laugh amidst the eye-rolls and sighs of the fans around him, one of whom was dressed in a conspicuously inconspicuous, tan windbreaker, that almost certainly pegged him as one of the undercover cops.

Truck caught his head from snapping back toward the rowdy patron. Instead, he redoubled the force of his practice swings, each one focused on smashing an imaginary version of the fan's diseased, troll-like grin.

"Huahhhhhhh!" The home plate ump yelled as he punched Flash Gamble out on a called third strike.

Truck slammed the knob of his bat on the ground to work the weighted donut off of it and walked calmly toward the plate. The ugly fan yelled something else, but the catcher was already thinking about the upcoming at bat.

"Back already, sweetheart?" Scooter Herman asked.

Truck didn't so much as look at the vile catcher.

"Aw, what's the matter, boyfriend throw you out on the couch last night?"

Truck pointed at Calhoun once…twice…three times as he rubbed out the back of the batter's box with his spikes.

He knew Calhoun liked to get ahead in the count with a fastball from his first at bat, and this time, he was going to be ready.

Calhoun nodded at the first sign Herman gave him.

This is it… Truck thought. He ground his teeth in a rhythm as the lanky righthander went into his windup, reached back, and delivered.

"CRACK"

Truck's bat connected with the ball and sent the white sphere high and deep into the outfield. It towered above the stadium's lights at one point as it reached its apex.

Truck trotted out of the box and watched as Palooka's huge left fielder, Terry Simon, lumbered back toward the wall, and tracked it as it fell back to earth.

The Magpie catcher craned his neck as Simon stopped maybe five feet short of the warning track, hit his chest a couple of times, reached into the sky, and clutched the ball in his glove for the third out of the inning.

Truck stopped his trot and grimaced. He grabbed his helmet and tore it off. He walked slowly, deliberately back to the dugout, doing his best to drown out the obnoxious fan, but failing to do so when he yelled, "*That* what ya' call a *homo* run!? Figures…"

It took every ounce of strength Truck had not to charge into the stands and beat him to a bloody pulp.

Mitch Henry continued to dominate Princehen hitters. Though he wasn't quite as sharp as he had been his first couple of times through the lineup, the determined scowl never left his face as he continued to light up the radar gun, and scattered four more Princehen hits through the eighth inning.

After going to a full count with two outs in the top of the eighth with a runner on second, Henry looked in for the sign. The hot, humid air dripped off his face as Truck flashed three fingers.

Change-up.

Henry finally acknowledged the catcher.

He shook his head.

Truck sat in his crouch, shocked. He narrowed his eyes as he put down three fingers again.

Again, Henry shook him off.

Truck wanted to shrug, wanted to go out to the mound and dress down the laboring starter, call him out on his juvenile behavior and let the world see what an ignorant hick he was.

Instead, the catcher looked into the pitcher's eyes.

Still hungry.

Still angry.

He may have lost a little zip over the course of the game, but the look said it all:

One more.

Truck knew what it meant. He flashed a single digit toward the ground.

The edge of Henry's lips quivered upward.

For the first time all evening, Mitch Henry nodded.

He brought his hands together briefly before his meaty left arm extended backward until it pointed squarely at centerfield. He brought his hand forward with first inning-like power as he released the ball toward the plate.

It started about belt high, but Truck saw the backspin on it and elevated his glove two inches...three inches...four. The ball seemed to defy physics as it rose through the air to reach its target.

Devon Fulcrum, the Princehens' batter was overmatched. he checked his swing, desperately trying to foul the pitch off.

It was too late.

"Huahhhhhh!" The home plate ump bellowed.

Henry had struck him out to end the inning.

Truck pointed at Henry as he jogged off the field, and the hulking pitcher locked eyes with the catcher and nodded almost imperceptibly.

They arrived at the dugout steps at the same time, and though Truck wanted to confront the starting pitcher, both about the "silent treatment" he had levied upon the catcher and on a game well-pitched, Willie was waiting with Truck's helmet in hand.

"You're up, slugger," Willie said, with only a hint of irony. "You put a good swing on it last time, but we could use one here," Willie said.

Truck looked at the grinning idiot with the long, grey beard in the stands as he put on his helmet.

Willie snapped his fingers in front of the catcher's face, "Don't pay any attention to that hick. I've talked to ushers twice about him, but they say he's not violating any team policies. Christ, I wish Hack were here—he'd kick the guy's ass himself and wriggle his way outta' it."

Truck grinned at the thought—in his mind, he envisioned the crusty old manager muttering a swear, then vaulting into the stands and beating the hell out of the heckler with his omnipresent bat.

At this point, he didn't even care if the bearded guy was the one who had made the death threat; Truck just wanted him to—

He rubbed his eyes. Was he going crazy, or was the vision of Hack turning and making its way down the steps toward the field?

Truck looked around and saw Dane Calhoun about midway through his warmup pitches.

When he turned back, the apparition of Hack was staring him in the face.

"Hack?" Truck whispered.

The ghostly figure swatted him on the brim of the helmet, though it neither connected nor made a noise.

"Hack, I could really use your help, buddy," Truck chewed the words out of the side of his mouth.

His former manager stared at him and put a phantasmic hand on the catcher's shoulder. Truck looked at it and blinked, but when he opened his eyes, the ghost was gone.

"Comin' down!" Scooter Herman yelled from behind the plate. Truck was almost up.

As he took his first step toward the plate, though, he heard a voice in his head, clear as a bell.

It was a tailor-made openin' ta' bust some balls about bein' an ignorant old cuss, that's what it was! And ya' passed it right on by on the way ta' yer' 'woe is me' soapbox.

"Hack?" Truck muttered under his breath.

"Hey Truck, ya' gonna' hit another *ho-mo* run this time!?" The heckler yelled again before he launched into his deep, booming laugh.

Then it clicked.

All this time, Truck had let his anger get the better of him, since that was the only way he knew how to deal with his secret.

Hack had been right all along; the words he heard in his head were those the former manager spoke to the catcher in the car on the way to Cleveland.

Bust some balls…

That was it! He didn't have to give in to his anger, yield to every insult hurled at him by some asinine hick. The glint in his eye returned as he realized exactly how to deal with the heckler, Scooter Herman, and all of the other ill-wishers.

Bust some balls…

Truck cocked his head. He turned back toward the grinning heckler behind the dugout. Instead of the death glare and profanity-laced tirade or angry battery he had so fantasized about before the game, Truck did the last thing he would've expected at the start of the night:

He smiled mischievously as he winked at the bearded man and offered him a coy wave.

"Hey!" The bearded man got out of his seat. "Hey, what the *fuck* was that!?" He yelled.

The ushers were upon him even before he finished the thought.

"Sorry, sir, team policy, no loud swearing in the stands."

"What? I bought a ticket, same as these *assholes*, an'—"

"Come with us, sir," the ushers, who also happened to be lacrosse players at Baucomb who decided to stick around Hoplite to party and picked up ushering for a little extra cash, each grabbed the man under an arm and hauled his considerable girth into the archway, where he proceeded to berate the men rather loudly.

A hearty cheer went up from his former section-mates.

Truck grinned and nodded.

He strode to the plate, calm and purposeful.

"Hey there, Lady Traynor," Scooter Herman said. "Anderson Cooper says hi."

Truck's eyes went wide, "Oh? So *you're* the hot little number with the small dick he bailed out on dinner for last night?"

Scooter was stunned.

"I—uh...*no!*" he patted his mitt twice. "Whattaya' say now, Dane-o!"

Truck could've sworn he heard the ump chuckle under his breath.

Truck settled in, the bat barely held in place in his soft grip. It was just him and Calhoun now, in that unique tunnel that the great batters use to block out everything else, every thought, every smell, every sound, that might distract them from making contact with the ball.

Calhoun's uniform was soaked. His skin was pallid and damp, his eyes sunken to the point where Truck thought he looked almost like a cholera patient.

The thin righty nodded and entered his windup. Truck noticed that his release point was almost three-quarters, which meant that he was looking to get more side-to-side movement on—

His slider, Truck thought.

He tensed his hands as the ball sailed toward him.

Outside, Truck thought.

"Ball one!" The ump yelled as the ball hit Herman's mitt.

Herman glanced back at the ump, who stared down the overweight catcher in kind.

Calhoun received the ball and removed his cap. He took a thick handful of his long, brown, wet hair in his hand and slicked it back over his head before he jammed his hat back over his eyes.

Truck reset his stance. Calhoun looked in for his sign and shook his head.

Scooter wants him to throw a fastball to get a strike, Truck thought. *That must mean...*

Slider. Or curve.

The pitcher licked his lips and nodded.

Truck waved the bat over his shoulder as Calhoun came set. The laboring righty brought his hands over his head, broke them over his leg, reached back, and fired.

Right over his shoulder.

Curveball, Truck thought.

The ball rotated in a circle out of Calhoun's hand. Truck waited for the snapping motion on it to take effect, and drag the ball down, but it never came.

And it's hanging, Truck thought.

He flexed his forearms as his iron grip brought the bat down toward the flight of the ball, simultaneously easy and powerful as the barrel shot toward its intended target.

"CRACK!"

For the briefest of moments, Truck thought he had missed, since he didn't feel the ball off the bat.

Then his ears caught up, then his eyes as he saw the ball absolutely crushed to left field.

He hit it as hard as the line drive he hit earlier in the year in Westfield, but this ball was much higher off the bat as it sailed through the night sky.

As it flew over Terry Simon, the left fielder took off his hat and threw it on the ground.

Truck threw the bat aside and started to run out of the box, more not wanting to jinx the ball's flight more than anything else.

Only an errant aircraft could hope to do so.

The ball fell, well past the outfield stands, utterly outside of the Murph.

Truck had just hit a monster homerun.

He pumped his fist wildly in the air as he slowed into his trot around first. The crowd roared its approval as Truck circled the bases, head held high and proud.

It was only when he got around third that he worried whether or not the ignorant hick that had sent in the death threat was anywhere in the stadium.

He eyed the crowd suspiciously for several steps before he broke into a broad smile.

He didn't care.

He raised his fist again as the crowd continued to thunder on. As he reached home plate, he jumped on it with both feet and winked at Scooter Herman.

"Asshole," Herman said.

"Then eat my shit?" Truck asked him enthusiastically.

Scooter kicked the dirt behind the plate.

Truck noticed his bearded heckler still arguing his case in the archway before he turned toward the field, mouth agape.

"Good one, mang," Juan Patrón said as he offered a fist to the catcher.

Truck hit it, "Thanks Juan!" he yelled. Before he reached the dugout, he locked eyes with the heckler in the stands and blew him a kiss.

This inspired a loud cheer from the crowd, and fresh gesticulating by the bearded man as the plain-clothes cops in the tan windbreakers both whispered into their jackets and made their way over to the disruptive patron to escort him out of the stadium.

The Magpies stood in stunned silence as Truck smiled broadly and approached the dugout steps.

"Not bad for a fairy, eh fellas?" he said.

The players looked at each other for one second...two...

Then they laughed.

Every one of them, from Sun Dae to Murph Murphy hooted and grabbed his sides, with one notable exception.

At the end of the bench, jacket on, Mitch Henry merely tipped his cap at the catcher and nodded.

Truck did the same with his helmet, then waited several more seconds before he ascended the dugout steps one more time and tipped his helmet to the entire crowd. Truck felt the concrete steps under his feet vibrate as the roar threatened to tear the Murph apart.

Though Truck still heard a few scattered boos, they no longer bothered him. The piercing arrowheads of their previous insults had been replaced by paintballs. Hurtful, yes. But any injury from them was sharp, short-lived, and utterly rebuttable in kind.

6

The Magpies failed to put any more runs across, and entered the ninth up 1-0. Willie trotted Mitch Henry out for another inning of work, despite his bag-heavy eyes and bucket-damp skin.

The manager reasoned that Manny needed his warmups, and if Henry could get an out or two, then maybe he could go the distance.

Instead, Henry walked the first two hitters on eight straight.

Willie stroked his chin. Truck was all but begging him to pull the moose of a pitcher with regular looks over toward the dugout.

Or so Willie thought; while it was true that Truck wanted Willie to pull the righty already, he was more vexed that the plainclothes cops that had escorted the bearded heckler out of the stadium hadn't yet returned.

After walk number two, Willie had enough. He jogged to the top of the dugout steps before he slowly, methodically made his way out to the mound, hoping to give Manny time to sneak in a couple more warmups in the bullpen.

Willie held his right arm in front of him and tapped it twice with two fingers, signaling for Manny even before he reached the mound.

Truck jogged out to meet both the manager and Henry.

"Aw, shit, skip, I got these morons," Henry said.

Willie shook his head, "Naw, ya' did a helluva a job, Mitch, helluva job. Got us all the way here—let Manny finish the job now."

Mitch nodded and took two steps off the mound.

"Hey Mitch," Truck said.

The giant righty turned to look over his shoulder.

"You did great tonight," Truck said.

"Thanks, Truck," Henry said matter-of-factly.

Truck didn't know what to say. He stood on the mound, mask in hand, mouth agape.

Manny jogged in from the bullpen, his usual exuberant energy subsumed beneath a steely, impenetrable façade.

He reached the mound and Willie dropped the ball in his hand.

"It's all yours now, kid. Just relax and do your thing." Willie patted Manny on the behind before he walked back to the dugout.

Manny rubbed the ball in his hands.

"Manny, I'm sorry I didn't get a chance to—"

The closer shook his head, "Now is not the time, Camión. First, we beat the Princehens. Otherwise, we have *all* winter to talk."

"They have me talking to the media after the game, so—"

Manny shook the sentiment off, "No problem. Just us now, Camión. Let's get us to the playoffs."

Truck met Manny's eyes, which were dark and focused. He steeled his own resolve and nodded.

"You got nobody, men on first and second with the two hitter coming up, he'll probably be looking to bunt 'em over."

"I know," Manny nodded with a thin smile. "I'll be ready."

Truck met his nod as he pulled his mask down over his face and caught Manny's warmups. The catcher was shocked at how loose and easy Manny was throwing, all in spite of not only the events of the day, but also the most high-leverage situation of his young pitching career.

Truck fired the ball back one final time as the umpire took his place behind the catcher.

"Batter up!" The ump boomed as he pointed a thick finger at Manny.

Pablo Estrada, the Princehens' number two hitter, strode into the batter's box like a bullfighter, even though everyone in the stadium knew he was about to sacrifice himself.

He knocked the dirt off of his spikes casually and made no pretensions about feigning a swing as he gripped the barrel of the bat with his right thumb and index finger, and pivoted to face the hard-throwing Magpie closer.

Truck put down one finger.

Fastball.

Manny nodded. Both he and Truck knew that if the other team was offering up an out when you only needed three more to close out the game, you take it, especially with Manny's ability to get a strikeout or two.

Manny came set in the stretch. The thick August air already beaded on his forehead. His arm reached back in that easy, fluid arc that had first clued Hack in that the young Dominican had a future as a pitcher all those months ago.

He delivered the ball, a perfect strike, right down the middle.

Estrada deadened it perfectly. The ball came to rest seven or so feet to the left and in front of the plate.

Truck flung off his mask. He barehanded the ball and looked toward third—the Princehens' runner was already within twenty feet. It would've been a close play, but Truck was in no position to look a gift horse in the mouth.

He turned toward first, "Inside! Inside!" Truck yelled at Juan Patrón.

The first baseman stuck out his bare right hand with the outside of his left foot up against the bag. Truck had made the throw thousands of times before, but for whatever reason, this time the ball slipped out of his hand early and flew toward first on one bounce.

Patrón's eyes went wide, if only for a moment. He deftly switched his feet and stuck out his first baseman's mitt to backhand the shorthop. As the ball connected with the conditioned leather mitt, Truck watched as Patrón closed the pocket around it with a satisfying "THWACK."

"Ouuuuuuuut!" The first base ump yelled.

The crowd erupted in a cheer as Patrón held the ball in his glove in the air in a rare display of showmanship.

Truck's eyes went wide as he ground his teeth. He pointed at the first baseman and then hit his chest protector three times.

Thanks for picking me up, Truck's gestures said.

Patrón pointed right back.

No problem.

"Alright, one down, now!" Truck held up his index finger. He mustered as much bravado as possible as he casually lowered his mask over his face and dropped into his squat.

Terry Simon strode into the box, bat on his shoulder like a woodsman carrying his axe to fell trees.

"Sorry, Truck," Terry said as he dug into the box.

"About what?" Truck asked, innocently enough.

"About stealin' your thunder by bein' the hero tonight."

Truck chuckled and shook his head. He put down one finger and Manny nodded. The righthander came set, rocked, and fired.

Terry swung, but missed the offering by a good inch or two.

"Heeeeiiiii!" The ump boomed.

Truck patted his mitt and threw the ball back to Manny; Terry Simon never could handle Manny's heat. Now Truck was about to exploit that little advantage.

He flashed the fastball sign again, and Manny nodded, eyes narrowed. He came set, rocked, and fired.

This time, the pitch was high and outside.

"Ball!"

Truck fired it back.

"Looks like wonderboy's a little jumpy tonight," Simon said.

Truck just hocked a loogie into the other side of the batter's box.

He flashed the single digit again, and Manny dutifully nodded. The closer went into his abbreviated windup and delivered.

This time it was low.

"Ball two!"

Truck double-clutched before he threw the ball back.

Come on, Manny. Hit the zone! Truck thought.

He patted his mitt several times.

Truck gave Manny the fastball sign once more. Manny nodded again. He came set and pitched.

This time, it was well inside, causing Simon to spin away.

"Ball three!"

Truck shook his head.

What the hell is he doing? the catcher thought. He jammed out one finger, hoping to convey the gravity of the situation to Manny.

This time, Manny paused before he nodded. His eyes flashed wide for a moment before he brought his hands together, pulled them apart, and shot the ball toward the plate.

It was a perfect pitch, right on the outside corner.

But Terry Simon swung.

And he connected.

The ball rocketed away from the plate with inhuman force down the right field line. Simon leaned back from the left-handed batter's box, willing the ball fair as Truck whipped off his mask and stood.

Both men watched as the ball sailed…and sailed…and sailed…*just* to the right of the right field foul pole.

"Foul ball!" the home plate ump bellowed.

Simon let out a low whistle, "Didn't miss it by much."

"It's just a *looonnng* strike, Terry," Truck said. The slugger glanced over his shoulder at the catcher, and Truck shrugged.

He put down two fingers.

Slider.

Manny nodded and came set, resolute. He rocked and fired a nasty slider, starting belt-high before it done down and in on the left-handed Palooka left fielder, into the dirt.

Truck's reflexes kicked in. He fell to his knees and blocked the ball on the shorthop, throwing his torso at it, anything to keep it from becoming a wild pitch that would almost certainly allow the run to score from third and tie the game.

It connected with his chest with a muted "BOOM," and fell harmlessly to the dirt in front of Truck before the cather quickly gloved it.

"Ball four, take your base," the ump said.

"Well, guess Pedro gets all the glory tonight," Simon said as he undid the small shinguard he wore and tossed it toward the Princehens' bench. "Oh yeah, Truck?"

"Yeah Terry?"

"Good on ya' for doin' what you did. Shows a lotta' guts."

"Thanks man," Truck was shocked. Terry Simon was just about the last person he expected to say something, though in hindsight, he couldn't quite put his finger on why. The catcher just shrugged as the hulking batter trotted to first.

He had bigger problems at the moment, namely Pedro Ascencíon, the Princehens prodigious second baseman and target of Manny Poblado's ire.

As Manny picked up the rosin bag and squeezed it like he was trying to kill it, Truck realized why he may have walked Terry.

Truck stood up to call time so that he could conference with Manny and settle him down, but as he did so, Manny glared back at him with dark intensity, a look that froze Truck in his tracks and caused him to squat back down behind the plate.

The catcher looked at Willie in the dugout, who ran a quick hand over his balding head before he replaced his cap. The manager looked down toward the end of the bench at Tommy Stearns, who, Truck noticed, kept his intense stare focused on the field, perhaps to compensate for his jittery legs.

Willie turned back toward Truck and nodded.

"Look alive now!" the manager said. He clapped his hands five times.

Ascencíon dug in and blew a large bubble of chewing gum as he held the bat over his head.

Truck went right back to the fastball, but made a special point to flash his pinky after the sign, to keep the ball away from Ascencíon.

Manny nodded his assent.

This time his motion was lethal, like a ninja stalking his prey. Without a sound, Manny cruised through the stretch and delivered a fastball that snuck up on everyone, including Truck. It was all the catcher could do to stick out his glove as the pitch nicked the outside corner.

"Heeeerike!"

Truck bobbed his head as he flung the ball back to Manny. Manny swiped at it with his glove hand, nearly flinging it into the mound before he recovered and brought the ball into his throwing hand.

Manny didn't waste any time. He looked in for the sign. Truck went through the situation quickly in his head. He had been going fastball too much; Simon had nearly made them pay for the oversight.

He flashed two fingers for a slider.

Manny nodded. He came set, then stealthily delivered the ball, a howling missile that initially headed toward Ascensíon's belly button before it dove over the plate.

"Stiiiiiii!"

Truck nodded and threw the ball back to Manny, who looked the ball all the way into his glove. He took the rubber once more, his hat dark and heavy with sweat.

There was only one pitch that Truck knew would cross-up Ascensíon:

The change-up that Pete Moray had been working on with Manny all season long.

The closer had only used the pitch sparingly up to that point, largely because he lacked command of it; it was just as likely to end up in the batter's ear as it was to cross the plate.

Truck didn't need it to be terribly accurate, though; he just needed to fool Ascensíon one more time.

The three fingers descended swiftly, and Manny could barely conceal his grin. He forced a scowl and nodded as he came set. His limbs moved effortlessly through the thick air as he pulled his arm back, brought it over the top, and whipped it through the air, full speed.

The three-fingered, circle-change grip had the intended effect of slowing the ball down.

Before the ball was ten feet out of Manny's hand, Truck knew what would happen.

Ascencíon licked his lips as the ball floated through the air. The second baseman lowered his hands toward the ball, which was a bit inside, but belt high. The barrel of the bat shot out toward the advancing projectile.

"THWACK."

Ascencíon reeled with the force of connecting with nothing but air as the ball dropped harmlessly into Truck's mit.

"He's ouuuut!"

Truck could barely contain his laughter. He pointed at Manny before he raised his thumb and pinky.

"Two down!" he bellowed at his teammates. "Any base, infield."

"Gracias, Truck."

The catcher turned toward the retreating Ascencíon, who already was halfway back to the dugout, but who had unmistakably uttered the phrase under his breath.

"No problem," Truck mimicked the second baseman's tone.

As Truck stared at Ascencíon with his furrowed brow hidden by his mask, he caught himself looking for the plainclothes cop, who still hadn't returned to his position along the third base line.

He instinctively turned toward the first base stands, only to see another of the many sights he had been dreading that evening: Meadow Dressel climbing over the railing and onto the field.

While her brashness didn't necessarily surprise Truck, he was shocked about one thing:

The revolver she held, outstretched, pointed straight at him.

7

"Gun! Gun!" The cries rang out from the stands as the formerly beautiful seductress took long, measured steps toward Truck.

Her normally playful curls were a sopping mess. Her heavily-applied makeup ran down from her red eyes in tears all the way to her heaving breasts, barely constrained by her thin sundress.

Truck instinctively pulled off his helmet to get a better look.

"Meadow?"

He could hardly believe the word even as he uttered it.

The crazed woman's gun trembled as she sobbed uncontrollably.

"You couldn't leave well enough alone, *could you*!?" she shouted. "You were supposed to take me to *Cleveland*, to make me your *wife*. And you had to fuck it up because you *had* to tell *everyone* you're a fucking *faggot*?"

In the stands behind the plate, Sam Rappaport furiously scrambled for her cell phone.

Meadow turned the gun on the intern and released the safety.

"Not so fast, you little goodie-two-shoes *bitch*!" She yelled.

Sam froze. She dropped her purse, and her face along with it.

Truck took the opportunity to take two inconspicuous steps toward Meadow. Juan Patrón and Sun Dae crept ever-so-slowly toward the deranged woman.

She leveled the gun at all three men, then turned to face Manny.

The pitcher was gone.

In the chaos, he had rushed to Truck's side.

Truck hit his chest protector several times, "On me, Meadow. Don't worry about anyone else. It's *me* you're mad at, remember?"

"Fuck all of you!" She aimed the gun skyward and pulled the trigger. The resulting boom shook the stadium and caused fans to scramble over one another through the overcrowded aisles for the exits. Other than Woo, Patrón, Manny, and Truck, the players on the field ran for the stands.

"Meadow, I can explain—"

She leveled the gun back at Truck, "No, *I* can explain. You're a coward. You're too...too *chickenshit* to be a real man, to handle *this*," she motioned to her cleavage with her free hand. "I bet it's all you can think about when you're sucking some other guy's—"

Manny stepped forward, "Thass' *enough!*" he yelled.

"Manny, stay out of this," Truck said through clenched teeth.

"I don't give a fuck—I'll shoot him, too. I've still got enough for all've y'all. Even Jackie Chan and Tonto over here."

Sun Dae and Patrón eyed each other, eyebrows arched.

"Truck is a *brave* man. Bery, *bery* brave. Braver than you can imagine, you ugly *bitch*." Manny punctuated the statement by launching a loogie toward the crazed lunatic.

"Why would you...unless..." Meadow's eyes gained an evil glint, "Oh my *God*! *You're* the one! *You're* a faggot, too—*his* faggot!"

Manny held his chin up, but didn't say a word.

Meadow shook her head, "I should've seen it! Damn it, I should've!"

Sun Dae took a step forward and Meadow leveled the gun on him without looking, stopping him in his tracks.

"All those nights 'with the guys.' Always helpin' Manny with his English or some other damned fool excuse. I should've seen it. But I didn't."

A full, evil grin overtook her face as she pointed the gun back at Truck.

"Yes. Yes, is all *my* fault," Manny said.

"Well, then that's a goddamned shame, now isn't it?" She pointed the gun at the closer as Truck took two steps toward his side. "You would've made a hell of a closer for the Indians, Manny." Her finger started to squeeze the trigger.

"Meadow, don't!" Truck yelled.

The next few seconds happened in slow motion. Truck hurled himself in front of Manny.

"BANG!"

Truck reeled from the force of the bullet. He felt nothing for a moment, followed by the odd sensation of water running over his right shoulder, underneath his chest protector. He tumbled to the ground in a heap as Manny knelt over and yelled toward the dugout in both Spanish and English for help.

His eyes turned to Meadow, who was being wrestled to the ground by Woo and Patrón. Her own shoulder was red with blood, and though the whole scene was a blur, Truck could've sworn that he saw an arrow sticking out of her fresh wound.

Even more oddly, Mitch Henry stood at the top of the dugout, crossbow in hand, still pointed at Meadow Dressel, restrained on the ground.

Truck rose to a knee as Henry rushed over toward the injured catcher.

"God *damn* it, ain't anybody gonna' call an ambulance!?" the pitcher screamed, ice still on his throwing shoulder. "My teammate's injured here!"

The hulking pitcher ran right in front of Truck and knelt.

"Mitch...Mitch you saved my life, Manny's life. Both of—"

Henry's eyes went slick with tears. He sniffled even as he interrupted Truck, "My daddy's a homo—a gay. Whatever. My daddy's a gay, too."

Truck locked eyes with the starting pitcher. *That's* why he had been so aloof all game. *That's* why the pitcher always was so critical of anything homosexual.

Even Mitch Henry has his secrets, Truck thought.

Truck smiled wanly and reached his good arm up, wincing through the pain as he patted Henry on the shoulder.

It was too much for Mitch; he started to bawl uncontrollably as the situation overtook him.

"It's okay, Mitch," Truck said. "Everything's going to be okay."

8

Paramedics arrived within ten minutes, and quickly attended to Truck's bullet wound.

When the plainclothes cops finally showed up, Willie was livid. He hurled just about every expletive he could think of at the officers, who hung their heads and took it before they finally had their say.

"It turns out this Meadow Dressel arranged for the e-mail, the guy with the sign, the heckler, all of it as a distraction to clear the plainclothes out of the way so that she could get a clear shot at Truck."

"So you're telling me there wasn't a death threat, then?" Willie asked.

Truck shook his head. He didn't have the heart to tell Willie about the five other, similar e-mails from different addresses he had received before the game.

Sam Rappaport rushed onto the field and hugged Truck on the gurney. He was shocked, but patted the redhead on the back in kind.

"I'm so sorry, Truck," she said.

Truck's eyes went wide, "What're *you* sorry about?"

"About not seeing this coming. About letting an armed lunatic storm the field on your big night!"

Truck shook his head, "Don't worry about it. It's my own fault for getting involved with her," he paused and thought for a moment, "for lying. To her and myself. For trying to convince myself I was something I wasn't, and picking the wrong lunatic to do it with."

Sam smiled thinly as she bobbed her head once or twice before she sighed.

"What?" Truck asked, genuinely concerned.

"Eh, it's just now I have to talk to Willie and the Palooka manager about rescheduling, and—"

"Qué?" Manny's ears perked up.

"Rescheduling. You know, the game will have to start again."

"No, no, no!" Manny shook his head. "We aren' gonna' let a crazy person intimidate us!"

"Manny, now's not the—" Truck was tired. Tired of everything.

"No. I say we keep playing. Two outs, bases loaded." He turned his gaze to Willie, "Willie, we can do this. Le's finish it *now*. Show we won' be bullied around."

"I, uh, well…" Willie removed his hat and wiped his forehead. He turned to face Truck, "Is this okay with you?"

Truck nodded gravely, "Beat these sons-of-bitches *tonight*, and get us to the playoffs," he spat the words through gritted teeth.

"I'll have to talk with the other manager, and I don't know where he's—"

"Right here, Willie," the middle-aged manager of the Princehens took two steps through the crowd surrounding the ambulance at the right field gate. "Hey, if your kid wants to play, I'm all for it." A sly grin wormed its way onto the manager's face.

Willie turned to Manny, "You sure you wanna' do this?" Willie asked.

Manny nodded his head, his eyes dark and ominous.

"Absolutely," he said, without a hint of an accent.

The Palooka manager had already gotten the home plate ump, and explained the situation to him. The mustached official walked over to Willie and discussed the situation.

"You, uh, really wanna' *play*?" the umpire asked.

"Why not? Both teams are okay with it." Willie nodded.

"Well…okay then. Let's clear the field and finish the game."

The other umpires looked at each other and shrugged. The ambulance door shut, and its sirens blared as it rolled off toward Hoplite General. As Sam Rappaport and Barry Wojciechowski began to clear the field, the Palooka manager let out a cackle.

"What the *hell* is so goddamned funny?" Willie asked.

"Nothin'. Might wanna' check your lineup card, though…"

Willie's heart sunk.

In the heat of the moment, in his haste to listen to Manny, he had forgotten one crucial piece of information:

Slappy Arias wasn't on the bench.

The Magpies were without a backup catcher.

Willie's walk slowly became a trot, then a jog as he raced to the dugout, desperate for a solution. He was just about to swallow his pride and plead with the umpire, Manny, and the opposing manager for an extension, but it would do no good; Truck would still be injured and thus unavailable.

He was about ready to ask if there was anyone among the sparse remaining crowd who could conduct a seance so that he could get Hack's opinion on what to do when the answer presented itself:

In the dugout, Sun Dae Woo was already strapping on Truck's much-too-large spare set of catcher's equipment.

"Sun Dae? What the hell are you doing?" Willie asked.

Woo finished strapping up his second shinguard and rose to his feet.

"When I was with Seibu, they made me be the emergency catcher, since it was far from a desired position, and I was, sadly, the least-liked player on the team. It would be my honor to put on Truck Traynor's equipment and finish out this game for him."

The second baseman's eyes were set and intense. He stared at Willie, trying to will the manager to allow him to finish the game behind the plate.

Not that Willie needed much convincing; it was the best of his rather limited options. Aside from that, though, his intuition took over, and led him to believe that maybe, just maybe, it wasn't such a crazy idea after all.

Feedin' the gut... Willie thought.

He nodded, "Okay. Sun Dae's catching. Friedmann!"

The deposed second baseman rushed to the manager.

"Yeah, coach?"

"You're in at second. Everyone in, gather 'round, gather 'round!" Willie yelled at the dugout, which was finally full once more.

"Our leader, our *teammate* was just attacked by a lunatic. A crazy woman who wanted nothing more than to kill him for having the *courage* to be who he was.

"Now I know Hack'd have something profane and poetic to say right about now. I also know that not all'a you agree with Truck's decision to talk about his stuff today, with this game on the line," Willie glanced at Henry, who hung his head, "But God *damn* it, Hack's not here anymore, and Truck's still the same guy he's always been. What he does in his free time doesn't *matter*. I think he proved that today by being the goddamned *difference* in this game!"

The Magpies let out a few low "whoop"s.

"So let's go out there and win it for Truck! Win it for Hack! And send those Princehens, whatever the *fuck* that is, back to podunkville Palooka where they belong!"

The players cheered and clapped as Willie raised his arm toward the field. The team rushed out to take their places on the field and found the Palooka runners already limbering up on the basepaths.

Palooka's manager laughed as little Sun Dae Woo jogged behind the plate, equipment flapping all over the place as he chugged along.

Sun Dae merely smiled and offered a terse bow toward the Princehen dugout before he snorted and spouted a line of Korean swear words under his breath.

Manny took a few warm-ups, and though Woo initially had some trouble corralling the powerful offerings, his superior hand-eye coordination soon kicked in, and he was able to catch the pellets Manny threw with relative ease.

Scooter Herman waddled across the plate and settled into the first base side of the batters box.

"Jesus Christ, doesn't this team have anything but pussies at catcher?" he asked as he crouched into his toady stance.

Sun Dae smiled. He flashed Manny a single finger and the pitcher nodded. He waited until Manny started his windup, then looked at the catcher, "Mr. Herman, might I kindly suggest that you go take a flying fuck?"

The startled Palooka catcher barely had time to wave at the hundred-plus mile-per-hour pitch as it whizzed by.

"Steeeeeiiiiii!"

"Little fucker," Herman muttered under his breath.

The ump arched an eyebrow under his mask.

"Not you—this little *pissant* behind the plate."

The ump snorted.

Woo smiled as he threw the ball back to Manny, who was all business. Woo settled back into his crouch and flashed one finger again.

Manny nodded, came set, and fired.

"THWACK."

"Steeeeeeeiiiiii...TWO!"

Herman slammed the bat on the ground before he raised the bat over his shoulder once more.

Manny's mind raced back to the first series against the Princehens, the first night he had ever pitched. He remembered the look on the pudgy Palooka catcher's face as Truck set him up for the first changeup of his young career.

Maybe I can use it to my advantage, Manny thought.

Unfortunately, bright as Sun Dae was, he knew nothing about calling games from behind the plate. He flashed a single finger again.

Manny shook him off.

He flashed two fingers.

Manny shook him off, with the hint of a grin, as Sun Dae was clearly just going through the numbers in order.

Maybe I can use that to my advantage, too, he thought.

Sun Dae showed three fingers. This time, Manny nodded and brought his glove from his knee out in front of him. He gripped the ball with four fingers, in the circle change grip, and allowed himself a small sigh as the few remaining die-hard fans cheered for their electric young closer.

Manny brought his hand back, the bottom of a perfect circle in motion. He reached back, giving the illusion of looking for a little extra velocity, and brought his hand forward, whip-fast, and released the ball.

"CRACK!"

Apparently, Scooter Herman remembered the earlier at bat, too.

The ball shot to Manny's right, toward the hole up the middle. The closer cursed as he dove for the ball, even though it was already well past him, well on its way toward center field.

As it neared the end of the dirt infield, all Manny could do is watch as it kept rolling…and rolling…and rolling…

…And stopped.

Flash Gamble, all 6'4" of him, lunged out for the ball. He stretched his arm up, willing it longer than it already was, creeping forward millimeter by millimeter until the very end of his glove collected the ball.

Without time to transfer it, he flipped the ball directly from his glove toward Nev Friedmann, already standing, shaking, on second base.

The ball soared through the air, higher and higher, past where Sun Dae would have been, and over Friedmann's head.

The shaky-fielding second baseman rose to his tip-toes, stretching much like Flash had to corral the errant flip.

He felt something hit the pocket of his glove and squeezed.

A half-beat later, his foot left the bag.

A half-beat after that, Terry Simon slid into second base.

The ump bent over, replaying the scene in his head as Nev landed back on the bag, both men staring at the official, pleading with their eyes for the call to go their way.

The ump squinted and raised a fist in the air.

"OUT! HE'S OUT!"

Friedmann and the other Magpies nearly lost it. Flash Gamble raised his arms over his head as he rolled in the dirt. Terry Simon was livid; he got in the umpire's face and followed the official past the mound, toward the Magpies' tunnel. His manager joined him, jawing at the ump, pleading their case.

It didn't matter.

He had gotten the call right.

Friedmann jumped on Flash, followed by Juan Patrón and Manny as Pete Moray and Willie embraced and ran out to join the celebration.

"We did it!"

"Playoffs! Playyyyyoffffffs!" Gamble repeated over and over, giddy as a schoolboy.

Manny relished in the celebration and jumped around with and hollered with his teammates as the tiny crowd went nuts in the stands for their Magpies.

He hugged Willie, then Pete Moray, and put his arm around Sun Dae. Even amid the commotion, he made a point to approach Juan Patrón and shake his hand.

He didn't have to make any such effort with Mitch Henry; the large pitcher picked up his skinny Dominican counterpart.

"Playoffs, baby! We did it!"

"Yeah, we did it!" Manny echoed the starter.

"You and me, Manny—we're one *hell* of a team."

Even as Manny nodded, he couldn't help but think of *Camión*, likely in a hospital room somewhere, taken out of what should've been *his* day, *his* moment by his lunatic ex-girlfriend. Truck wouldn't even get to enjoy the press conference to celebrate the—

The press conference! Manny thought. He patted another teammate or two on the back as he strode purposefully, confidently toward the dugout, down the steps, and into the tunnel.

"Great game, Manny!" Sam Rappaport yelled over the bannister.

"Gracias rojita!" he said with a smile. His spikes scraped along the worn concrete, leaving sparks in their wake down the tunnel and into the absolutely packed dungeon, filled with local and national media alike.

The reporters had obviously been busy through the attempted murder, as many haggard and weary faces greeted the Magpies closer. Jim Taggert launched into an impromptu round of applause, journalistic impartiality be damned, and the local press followed suit, though their national counterparts thought themselves "above" any such display of emotion.

Manny raised an appreciative fist and shook it as he smiled and approached the podium.

Marc Blake attempted to intercept him, "Manny! My man! Look, we're waiting for Willie, and maybe Truck—"

Manny pushed his way past the media relations director, "Is okay, Marc," he said, placing a spindly hand on the man's shoulder. "Is time."

Blake's eyebrows rose well above his thick plastic frames as he furrowed his brow and the closer approached the podium.

Manny had no introductory statement, no initial thoughts. He had something to say, just three little words that would, nonetheless, reverberate around the concrete room.

He adjusted the mike and opened his mouth to speak.

"I'm gay too."

With that, Manny walked away from the podium, even as the din of reporters fighting for questions swelled in the media room.

He ambled over toward the entrance to the clubhouse and ignored all of the requests. As the door shut behind him, Manny couldn't contain his broad, genuine smile.

Extra Innings

The rays of sunlight shot through the dry Arizona air, hindered neither by cloud nor humidity as they shined on the lonely patches of emerald green below.

On the main field of Goodyear Park, a few fringe prospects threw in the outfield, either seeking to impress the various coaches that milled about, or hoping to escape the grim winters of their off-season homes.

Even more likely still, they perhaps hoped to be caught in the corner of an errant picture taken by the throng of media that gathered in the seats behind home plate next to the Indians' dugout.

Though the players weren't so naive as to think that the pack was there to cover their early spring training workouts, there was a noticeable buzz in the air to go along with the opening of Indians camp.

Two players wearing Indians batting practice jerseys strode down the tunnel toward the field. As they approached the dugout, the familiar hulking form of Mitch Henry strode into the tunnel.

"Well, if it ain't the kings of cocksucking," Henry said.

Truck Traynor and Manny Poblado grinned.

"Shit, at least I'm gettin' laid, Mitch. When's the last time you got any?" Truck shot back.

"Fucked your mom last night," Henry said with a low chuckle.

"That's right—I was busy fuckin' your dad," Truck laughed.

"Hey, if it means I end up inheritin' any of that endorsement money you've been gettin', he can fuck you 'til his dick falls off for all

I care. Nike, BMW, whoever's payin' you—I'd like a piece'a that action," Henry said.

"I said *I* fucked *him*," Traynor said.

"Whatever. Same difference." The three men chuckled and half-embraced.

"Mitch, I never had a chance to say—" Truck grew serious.

"Aw, shit, don't mention it," Mitch waved off the comment. "We're teammates, ain't it? More than brothers. Not, *you know*, like you two are, but—"

"Gracias," Manny said. He hugged Henry, whose eyes bulged with surprise momentarily.

When Manny released Henry, the pitcher couldn't help himself, "Uh oh—I think this motherfucker's sportin' wood. You might have some competition, Truck."

"No sabes a qué de hacerlo," Manny said.

"What the fuck did this'un say?" Henry asked Truck.

"I said, 'you wouldn't know what to do with it.'" Manny's eyes narrowed with mock contempt.

"Whoa, Manny Mute-a finally hits back!" Henry took a step back. "Next thing you know, he'll be tellin' me to fuck off."

"Fuck off!" Manny didn't skip a beat. The three laughed.

"Speaking'a which, did you guys see what that chickenshit linebacker for Denver was sayin' about you fuckers on ESPN the other night?"

Truck and Manny looked at each other and shook their heads.

Henry pulled out his phone, and after several swipes held the screen toward them.

"Look, man, I ain't cool with that [BLEEP]. If'a teammate'a *mine* brought that gay [BLEEP] in the locker room? We ain't gonna' be on good terms now. Nothin' against those type'a people, just think that shit is gross. It ain't fer' *me*, what with all the fly honeys I bring around!"

Truck drew his lips taut. He had half a mind to tell Manny and Mitch about the evening he enjoyed with the linebacker that winter at a prominent New York-area gay bar, but decided against it.

A man's entitled to his secrets, he thought.

He shook his head and sighed, eager to change the subject, "Seriously, though—thank you. From the bottom of my heart." He hugged Henry, and Henry threw a meaty arm around Truck's shoulder.

Truck winced in pain.

"Shit, man, I'm sorry. I forgot about that bitch—"

Truck held up a hand, "Don't worry about it. It's a lot better now."

Willie Williams sidled into the conversation and cleared his throat.

"Jesus, Willie, you 'bout scared the shit outta me!" Henry said. "Can't you wear some spikes or somethin'?"

"It'd only make it hurt more next time I have to boot you in the ass, Henry." He turned toward Truck and Manny. "You guys ready?"

They looked at each other

"Have fun with yer' little 'Pride Parade,' or whatever the fuck it is," Henry waved his glove toward the backstop.

"Say hi to your pop for me," Traynor replied with a wink. Both men chuckled as Willie put an arm around each of the two men of honors' shoulders and escorted them out of the dugout.

As soon as they set foot on the field, the familiar sound of thousands of camera shutters filled the air. The assembled media stood and applauded as Truck and Manny offered polite waves. They walked over to the cloth-draped table where Josh Stein and Marc Blake already stood.

George Tavatelli was already seated at the table. Keith Myrick had even driven in from the Cubs' complex, where he had recently been appointed Assistant General Manager to the big league club. The usual forced grins were replaced by broad, beaming smiles as the two men took their seats, microphones in front of both.

The applause continued long after it should have naturally calmed down, to the point that Tavatelli had to raise his arms to shoulder level and signal for the media to stop the thunderous torrent of approval that filled the cavernous, mostly-empty stadium.

Samantha Rappaport, dressed smartly in a button-up blouse and business skirt, as her new position as special assistant to George Tavatelli required, bent over and spoke into the mike.

"Now, I know there are plenty of questions for Manny and Truck, so let's try to keep this orderly, okay?" she paused for a second as the media quieted down. "Good. First question goes to Jim."

Jim Taggert stood up and cleared his throat, "So, how's the shoulder, Truck?"

The media laughed at the anticlimactic question.

Truck exhaled and grinned, happy that the first question was comfortably ordinary.

"It's good—coming along. The doctors say I won't be able to catch this year, but I've been rehabbing it every day over the winter, and I should be full go as far as swingin' goes. I'm just happy for an opportunity to compete for a spot as a DH wherever the Indians see fit to put me. Thank God for the American League, right?"

This inspired a round of overeager chuckles from the throng as Truck shrugged.

Tavatelli grabbed the mike in front of him and brought it to his face, "I think it's safe to say that, barring a horrendous slump, fans in Cleveland will be happy to see what the mythical Truck Traynor can do with the bat."

"Like I said, I'm happy to have the chance to earn that opportunity this spring," Truck said with a nod.

Tavatelli blinked the dollar signs out of his eyes.

Karl Paulus, the lead anchor on *Baseball Tonight*, raised a hand.

"Truck, obviously we don't want to get too into your private life here, but how was the offseason for you? Especially after the vicious attack by your ex-girlfriend that led to the career-threatening shoulder injury you sustained?"

Truck smiled, "It was good. Tough, with the rehab, like I said. For the most part, folks have been really supportive of me, of *us*—" Truck glanced at Manny, who nodded, "You know?" He pointed at Manny, "I mean, *this* is the guy you should be asking. He showed more courage finishing that game, refusing to be intimidated, than anyone I've ever seen."

"Manny, your thoughts on that game?"

"I wanted...I thought it's what Señor Hack would've done, you know? Is what he would've wanted. Is the pro move, the right thin' to do. I wanted to honor his memory."

"I think that goes for both of us," Truck said. "And Flash, and Juan, and Sun Dae, and everyone else on the Magpies at the end of that game. What Coach Hack meant to us, what he taught all of us, I think Willie included, but he can tell you himself, I think his impact can't be underestimated."

"I will speak for myself," Willie deadpanned. More laughs from the crowd, "But I have to say, in my twenty-three years in baseball altogether, I learned more in one season under Hack O'Callahan than I did in any of the other twenty-two. A lot about what to do, what not to do, everything. That's why I'm sittin' here, manager of the Indians now.

"He had his own demons, to be sure. Just like we all do. Every one of us, you, me, Truck and Manny here, we all have secrets that we'd prefer to keep quiet, prefer that other folks not talk about for fear that we'll be ostracized and laughed at. That for some reason we won't fit in.

"But then a funny thing happens: look around," Willie waved a hand at the assembled media, "at this outpouring of support. A lotta' times, the blowback isn't nearly as bad as we think it'll be."

"But Truck got shot!" one of the reporters shouted out.

"To be fair, I think she would've shot me if I would've left her for another woman. She had problems. But you know what? I forgive her. As tough as it is, I forgive Meadow for what she did. I think we'll be fine going forward, as long as she stays 500 yards away from me as mandated by Hoplite County district court, which, let's be honest, she'll have to do for the next three to five years anyway."

A smattering of chuckles from the crowd.

"If you don't mind, Truck, I wasn't finished," Willie asked his player. Truck nodded his approval. "That's why I think what you folks did to Hack when he had the courage to step forward and admit that he was wrong was *shameful*."

Willie lowered his eyes at the reporters, who immediately went silent.

"Absolutely *shameful* with the mock outrage and terrible things you called him right before he died."

"But he lied to us!" A reporter shouted out.

"He lied to *everyone*!" Another reporter.

"He *was* in the Army, wasn't he? Sorry—Navy, right? Serving his country in the Far East. It wasn't his fault that he was blessed with enough God-given talent at a game that he loved—*loved*—more than anything in the world so as to avoid having to go out on the front lines.

"He could've kept his mouth shut and taken his secret with him to the grave, and you all would've been none the wiser.

"Instead, he made a *choice*, and showed us what true bravery is. He came clean. Even though he didn't have to, God *damn* it, he came clean. And his reward? For the last four or five hours of his life, he gets to hear about what a horrible person, what a phony he is.

"Well folks, even if it makes me unpopular with you all for a while, I have to say, Hack O'Callahan was the most real person I had the great fortune of meeting. Love him or hate him, you always knew where you stood with him. And to the extent that you people didn't do your jobs and find this out sooner, and the extent that he used you because of your own preoccupation with your self-congratulatory *bullshit*, well…can you blame him?"

This caused a row among the reporters, who shouted out pointed questions toward the new Indians manager.

"Simmer down, everyone," Sam Rappaport bent over toward the microphone. "Yes, Liam."

Liam Canard smiled smugly, "Truck, what about the reports that you and Manny are romantically involved off the field?"

"What about 'em?" Truck shot back.

"I mean, are they true? What do your teammates think?"

"First of all, would you ask that question of a straight athlete? Isn't that crossing the line into a man's personal life?"

Canard shrugged, "Depends on who his girlfriend was. If she was a celebrity or athlete—"

Truck glanced at Manny. The closer bit his trembling lip.

"No. Absolutely not. Look, just because we both happen to be gay doesn't mean that we go around, sneaking out sex encounters whenever our teammates' heads are turned. That's just not how a clubhouse operates."

Truck sold the lie well enough that a number of the reporters laughed in reply.

Neil Aubuchon, the antagonistic, nerdy little analyst from Baseball Tonight stood up and raised a pencil.

"Can you please speak to—"

Before he could finish the question, though, the sprinklers behind the plate activated, pointed directly at the stands for some reason. The press ran and scattered, searching for cover from the odd little deluge.

Truck chuckled. He stole a wistful glance at the sky, sure that Hack had gotten the final word, after all.

Then he reconsidered, and found his eyes widening and drifting toward the ground.

He cocked his head in thought, and finally lifted them skyward once more.

"Gonna' need your help, Hack," he whispered.

He could've sworn he felt something hit the bill of his hat, and he smiled.

"I think we're done here," Tavatelli said. He walked between Truck and Manny and made a point to practically drape himself over both mens' shoulders. "Thanks fellas."

"No problem, Mr. Tavatelli," Truck said.

"Thank *you*, Geor'," Manny echoed.

Tavatelli lingered a second or two too long before he gave a hearty sigh, "Sam?!" he yelled.

"Yes, Mr. Tavatelli," she was immediately next to him, taking down notes. A hint of a smile crept across her face.

Willie walked over, looked each man in the eye and nodded. The three men made their way back down the steps, through the dugout, and into the tunnel.

"I'll see you guys later—bullpen at eleven *sharp*."

"Sure thing, Willie. Thanks," Truck nodded as the manager walked down the hallway, past the indoor batting cage, and into the clubhouse.

Manny and Truck stood next to the cage, finally away from the prying eyes of the media.

Truck didn't quite know what to do. Hack had taught them a hard lesson, a valuable lesson, about discretion and disclosure. Manny stuck out his hand and moved to bring it toward Truck's face.

Instead, Truck caught it halfway and held it, first with his right hand as he winced through the pain in his shoulder, then with his left. He shook his head ever so slightly, his eyes glossy.

Manny shuddered, then nodded. He blinked several times, eyes slicked as he brought his other hand up to Truck's, and left them both linger for a second.

Unbeknownst to the two men, four Indians passed by the entrance to the tunnel in the dugout.

One of them was the old knuckleballer, Andy Dinkins.

"Gross," he muttered under his breath as he ascended the stairs toward the field.

Two of the other Indians looked at their new teammates, looked at each other, and shrugged. They followed Dinkins onto the field.

Only John Stevenson, the subject of Hack's ire the day before he headed down to Hoplite, lingered, eyes wide at the scene that unfolded in front of him.

Even as the two players released each other's hands and walked into the clubhouse, the words he whispered were unmistakable.

"Thank you."

THANKS FOR READING!

Hope you enjoyed the thrilling conclusion to the *Hack* saga. It was certainly a difficult project in the sense that I stepped way outside of my comfort zone in certain regards, but somehow the characters were always so real to me that it was easy to throw myself right back into it after a break. I hope you all enjoyed reading it as much as I did writing it.

If you did enjoy it, please feel free to leave a review wherever you bought it and/or Goodreads. Every positive review you leave makes it so that other folks can find these books easier and helps me to pay the bills—I read every one multiple times, and I truly am grateful for them.

Feel free to peruse some of my other works below, e-mail me at djgelbooks@gmail.com (I try to answer every one of them), or follow me on twitter @djgelner. Thanks again for making it all the way through, and I hope you enjoyed!

D.J.'s Other Works

Jesus Was a Time Traveler

Time travel. Every sober scientist thinks it's utterly impossible.

Of course, Phineas Templeton is no sober scientist in any sense of the word. A quirky English chap with a taste for fine scotch, Dr. Templeton builds a time machine at the behest of his mysterious Benefactor. His mission? To meet Jesus Christ Himself, and garner all of the fame, recognition, and accolades that writing an epic time travelogue would bring.

Unfortunately for Finny, Jesus is actually a fellow time traveler, a hippie named Trent from Colorado. While He explains that the past is fixed and immutable ("What happened, like, HAPPENED, man…), Dr. Templeton realizes that he's made a horrible oversight in his calculations, and can't return to his own time period.

The only way home is to follow a list of very specific instructions his Benefactor has hidden on the time machine, which sends him on a madcap, at times hilarious voyage from watching his hero, Sir Isaac Newton, be berated by a high school physics teacher, to hunting dinosaurs, to rescuing two colorful American soldiers and fighting Nazis hellbent on his destruction.

All the while, Phineas is left to question his Benefactor's true intentions. Just who is the shadowy person pulling the strings of a conspiracy thousands of years in the making? And why is Finny so key to their machinations?

A novel that's been called "equal parts *The Da Vinci Code* and *Back to the Future*," *Jesus Was a Time Traveler* is a book that will please fans of Dan Brown and Douglas Adams alike with quirky humor, thought-provoking puzzles, cryptic clues, and a finicky universe that would like nothing more than to keep things as they are.

HERE'S WHAT REVIEWERS ARE SAYING:

"A thoroughly enjoyable novel: equal parts *Da Vinci Code* & *Back to the Future* make it a novel you don't want to put down! I thoroughly enjoyed this philosophical--and funny--adventure through the centuries!" –A Merchant Site

"I found the book engrossing. The trip through history and our future was fun to take with the Doc!!" -A Merchant Site

"It made me want to keep turning the page to see what would happen next. It was engaging and I thought the plot was creative and interesting." -Goodreads

Rogue

Men and women huddled hundreds deep, hoping to will their way into the secretive facility. Struggle or interfere on the long desert trek and they're shot. Getting in is tough; thousands will be turned away. Once inside, hard labor and years of servitude await.

Far fewer still will accomplish their ultimate goal, a whisper of a shadow of a dream in the face of soul-crushing hopelessness.

So why do those who make it inside consider themselves the lucky ones?

COMING SOON

Corcoran's Log—A JWATT *Companion*

Corcoran Was a Time Traveler

Debt of Souls

Stay Tuned for Updates:

Follow D.J. on twitter @djgelner

E-mail D.J. @ djgelbooks@gmail.com

Check in at www.djgelner.com and add your name to D.J.'s quarterly newsletter e-mail list for more details and special offers

ACKNOWLEDGEMENTS

This book (these books? Is it one novel in three parts, or three short novels in an anthology? I think the stories stand up alone, but having the full text always helps, too…) was an amazing experience.

I have to admit right up front—I'm not gay. To write a book about a cantankerous old cuss of a manager, balanced against Truck and Manny's relationship, required more empathy than any project I've ever undertaken. Nonetheless, as I got further into the book, the characters took on lives of their own, and it became an absolute joy to take them all the way through to the ending. I hope the final result affects you as much as it did me to write.

I have so many people to thank. Mom and Dad, as always, thank you so much for everything. I love you both very much, and truly wouldn't be where I'm at without your support and encouragement.

Grant, thanks for being a great brother and sounding board whenever I'm stuck. You never fail to make me laugh, man. Much appreciated.

Thanks to my fantastic beta readers—Sara Eagan, Chris Burke, Lauren Clasen, and for Innings 7-9, Jessica—you guys are the best, and I appreciate all of your hard work and attention to detail.

Thanks to Dr. Dave Johnson, my good buddy, who was kind enough to lend his medical expertise to some of the medical scenes throughout the book. Though I didn't always adhere strictly to your input for story reasons, I do appreciate the help.

In a similar vein, thanks to my friend Josh Hartshorn and his cadre of Spanish experts. Josh is a fluent Spanish speaker living in Mexico, and he enlisted the aid of a Dominican buddy down there to help with translating one particularly difficult passage in *Innings 4-6*. Thanks guys—*Innings 4-6* would be subpar without your help.

Thanks to all of my baseball coaches through the years who taught me so much about the game. There are a lot of you, but the ones who especially stand out are Randy Lynn, Brian Statler, Lee Kiefer, Jim Lemen, Andy Katzman, and of course, the legendary Lee Engert. Without your guys' help, my knowledge of the game wouldn't be anywhere near what it is now, so I do appreciate it.

Also, thanks to my teammates throughout my baseball playing days. There are too many of you to mention by name, but the countless hours of B.S.ing on the bench helped color a lot of the dialogue between the players—again, my sincerest thanks.

I'll thank Adam Carolla again in this book. Ace man, something in your podcast while I was on a long walk one day triggered my subconscious to start whirring toward this ultimate goal, so for that, I thank you.

Thank you to Jenga and Sully for being fantastic co-workers.

And finally, last but not least, thanks to you, the reader. Without your help and support, I'd just be shouting into the wind like a lunatic. Well, I suppose I do that anyway regardless...no matter! Thank you so very much for reading (and getting this far). I do sincerely hope you enjoyed the journey. And who knows? If enough folks like the book, maybe we can come back and visit Truck, Manny, and the rest of the gang during their first year in Cleveland.

Thank you so very much from the bottom of my heart.

-D.J. Gelner
May 21st, 2013

ABOUT THE AUTHOR

D.J. Gelner is a lifelong Cardinal fan from St. Louis, Missouri. An attorney, sportswriter, sports talk radio host, and novelist, D.J. lives in Clayton, Missouri with his dog, Sully.

www.ingramcontent.com/pod-product-compliance
Lightning Source LLC
Chambersburg PA
CBHW020822180626
46814CB00001B/66